RISE OF
THE LAST
DRAGON RIDER

RISE OF
THE LAST
DRAGON RIDER

Shawn Wilson

Podium

Published in 2024 by Podium Publishing
www.podiumaudio.com

Podium

RISE OF
THE LAST
DRAGON RIDER

Prologue

"You are lucky he beat me here, boy!" shouted Stioks over the wind.

Each of the three dragons hovered in place, beating the wings to stay aloft as they all faced each other. Kaen and Pammon were off to the side of Elies and Tharnok, staring at the massive black dragon that seemed happy to display his huge mouth full of teeth.

"I would have offered you the world, yet it appears you have chosen the losing side! Worse, it seems I have found my missing dragon egg. You have no idea how angry that really makes me!"

Kaen noticed how the black dragon glared at them. Blood fury raged in its red eyes. It was slightly smaller than Tharnok, but it was just as powerful. He could tell it was different. Like a crazed beast barely controlled by its master.

"We are at an impasse," Elies yelled back. "He will not go with you, and I will not leave him undefended. If we fight today, you might not like the odds!"

Stioks began to laugh, his head lifting to the skies as he mocked them.

"You and I both know you cannot do anything. I can smell the rot taking you over. Those words do more to lift your own spirit and that boy."

Kaen was flustered. The way he talked about how he and Pammon were nothing more than an insect he could squash at any moment.

"Who was Hoste Marshell to you?!" Kaen cried out. "What did you do to him?!"

Stioks's head slowly turned as he gazed at Kaen; a frown formed on his face.

"I won't bother responding to that question. He was nothing, and I made sure he suffered for a long time before I snuffed out his life."

The block that had been preventing Kaen from activating his lifestone was gone. In a moment, it went from as cold as ice to hotter than a volcano.

"HE WAS MY FATHER!" Kaen shouted as he drew his bow back, loading an arrow into it. "YOU WILL PAY FOR THOSE WORDS!"

Stioks laughed again, waving his hands and dismissing Kaen's threats.

"Take your best shot, boy! I will give you one free attack before I cut you down like I did your father."

Power filled the arrow in a way it never had before. Every ounce of power and mana in his body flowed into the tip of the arrow. It went from red to white to black-blue in an instant. Kaen felt power, and something else, coming from Pammon. Hate.

A hate that burned for some reason neither of them understood.

The arrow blasted from his bow, flying faster than he had ever seen an arrow go.

As it streaked across the sky, like a star at night, Stioks smiled, never flinching, and somehow snatched the arrow in his gauntleted hand, snapping the arrow between his fingers.

He laid his head back and laughed, shaking from how hard he seemed to be enjoying himself.

"A fair attempt but a feeble one," Stioks shouted. "Now die!"

Juthom raced forward, his mouth opening as a cloud of blackness started to spill out.

Panting, Kaen woke up, sweat pouring off his body.

The same dream?

Wiping his face with his hand, Kaen sat up, wrestling with his blanket before tossing it off of him. It had wrapped itself around him while he slept.

Yes . . . it's been six months since the last time I had that dream. Why now?

Kaen heard Pammon moving toward him. The massive room he and Pammon shared in the elven king's castle had a place for both of them.

Those claws and talons of his scraped across the stone floor as he moved. The double doors that let them fly in and out were open slightly, and light spilled into the side of the room where Pammon often slept.

That will never happen. We have gotten much stronger since that day.

Reaching for the cup of water on the nightstand next to his bed, Kaen nodded as he gulped down the water.

We can still train harder. I need to train harder.

You are making great time! Keep going!

A grunt escaped Kaen as he acknowledged what Pammon was saying. He didn't have time to worry about responding right now. He needed to hurry up.

The forest zoomed by in a blur. The weights Kaen carried on his body barely affected him right now. His lifestone was slowly burning, his mind consumed with thoughts of the dream and needing to get stronger and faster so he could protect people.

His people.

Leaves flew up as he ran through them, and branches crumbled and crunched as he sprinted down a trail he had run hundreds of times. He dodged around trees, leaped over logs.

He had chains and weights wrapped around him, a backpack and chest pack filled with metal that the elvish blacksmiths had helped create for him. He had gained strength, speed, and constitution running this course at least once a day since he had made it. Sometimes, he ran it four or five times. Today would be one of those days.

Here comes the wall; don't misjudge it!

Pammon was overhead, flying his own path through the trees. Both of them were working together, each getting stronger and encouraging the other. Kaen's pants and shirts no longer fit him. His leg muscles had grown, and his upper body reminded him of what Hess must have looked like as a young man. He was no longer willing to wait on gains. He would make them happen.

The *wall* Pammon had mentioned came into view as he darted around a massive tree. It was twenty feet high, made from solid logs stacked on each other and braced. He sprinted toward it, feeling the power in his legs. One might consider the four hundred pounds on his body a bad idea, but that wall had grown. Once it had only been ten feet.

Slowing just a step, he planted his foot and leaped up toward the wall. His left hand and right foot found purchase on the wall past the halfway point, and he drove off a small gap in the logs, letting him grab the top easily with his right hand. Flinging himself over, Kaen grabbed the rope on the other side and slid down without losing speed.

The second he hit the ground, he rolled, springing to his feet and taking off again.

Glancing up in the air, he saw Pammon overhead, working on his own course. *Don't miss that arrow!*

Resisting the urge to groan, Pammon ignored the laughter that was coming from Kaen as he ran below. This arrow was the bane of his life. Each time, Kaen buried it more and more into the tree limb and put it into harder places.

Swooping between the limbs and branches, Pammon dodged a trunk and whirled his body, corkscrewing between a tight set of branches. He had grown a lot over the last six months, and it was becoming a tighter fit now.

Once through the branches, he rolled till upright and saw the arrow waiting on him.

A flick of his wing broke it off just a few inches from the branch it had been shot into, and a small trumpet of victory rose from his throat as he raced toward the next target.

He would not let Kaen win this time!

* * *

Both of them lay on the grass field, huffing and puffing from the exertion. Kaen had won but only by a few seconds because Pammon had to turn around and get an arrow he had missed.

Maybe next time you won't whine like an eggling when you lose.

Rolling over from his back, Pammon put his head next to Kaen and cleaned his sinus cavity, depositing a mountain of mucus on Kaen's topless half.

"UGGHHH!" groaned Kaen as he stood up, snot and chunks dripping from his body. "Some got in my mouth!"

Pammon began to thrum as he laughed, quite content to remind Kaen that just because he won, he didn't need to rub it in.

There is a stream only a mile away. Perhaps you can beat me to it.

Kaen nodded as he shook his hands, and then his eyes slanted as he pointed across the field.

"What's that?"

Pammon turned his head, looking to see what Kaen might be talking about.

A moment later, laughter erupted from Kaen, and Pammon groaned as he felt his rider rubbing his mucus covered body along his neck and chest.

Oh, I will make you pay for that one!

Kaen took off running as Pammon rolled over to his side and prepared to chase him.

No fair! No fair! You win! I surrender! Kaen shouted in his mind as Pammon raced across the ground after him.

In a foot race, Kaen would most likely win, but he knew Pammon wouldn't stay on the ground forever before taking to the air and snatching him from the ground with his talons.

As they ran along the field of grass and weeds, a shadow moved across them, and Kaen stopped running, letting Pammon nearly bowl him over.

I can give you other tasks if you two have this much time to play and not work.

Groaning, Kaen glanced up at Tharnok, who had swooped down from the sky to give him another earful.

Time is of the essence, and you two keep wanting to play games. Now stop acting like an eggling and get back to the training area.

Grunting, Kaen ran back to where his pack was and began slipping things on over his mucus-covered chest.

You should have told me he was watching, lamented Kaen. *I would not have played around like that had I known.*

Perhaps I should have said something, but neither of us worked as hard when Hess wasn't watching. Why change now?

Maybe the thought of a two-hundred-year-old dragon breathing fire down on me motivates me a little more than Hess ever did.

Thrumming, Pammon enjoyed that thought until he groaned as Kaen climbed onto his back with the extra four hundred pounds.

It's almost like flying with Hess now.

Kaen started to laugh and stopped as their teacher's shadow flew over them again.

Let's go before we get in trouble.

Springing into the air, Pammon thrummed as he flew. That dragon was much stricter than Hess had ever been.

Wooden swords, spears, shields, and other weapons littered the sandy arena as men and women limped away.

Kaen stood smiling as he tossed the spear and shield down and quickly flung a quarterstaff with his foot into his hands.

A pair of elves holding wooden training swords circled around him. They had just seen two of their training partners get destroyed by Kaen with his spear and shield.

None of them had managed to get any hits in today, and the masters were still watching. They had only trained him once and, after making Kaen look like a fool, told him he had much to learn.

"Stop watching and make a move already," he taunted as the two warriors took up positions on either side of him. Both of them had skills in the twenties, and Kaen had been working hard on the spear and quarterstaff lately.

He was already above a twenty-three on the spear and was close to getting a twenty with the staff. All he wore was the blood ring. Elies had told him it was better to train with as little magical assistance as possible. Occasionally, it would help, but if one only learned to fight when wearing them and something happened, and they did not have them, they would be worse off.

Both warriors attacked. The female to his right came in faster than the man on his left, but neither of them was close to his natural agility. He spun the staff, knocking away her attack with the sword before pivoting on his foot, bringing his staff around to crash into the man who had charged him with the sword held low.

The elf had tried to bring it up in time, but the speed of it took the sword from his hand, sending it bouncing across the floor.

Continuing his spin, Kaen snatched a handful of sand as he stood up, tossing it into the woman's face, who was coming in for a second attack.

Blinded, she held her hands to her face, taking the butt of the quarterstaff to her gut.

"Cheater!" cried the man he had just disarmed as his partner dropped to the ground, trying to get air back into her lungs as she fell to her knees.

"Enough!" shouted Elies, as he slowly applauded Kaen and walked over. "Some might say that is cheating, but there are no rules or honor in battle. This is why you fail to improve. You attack in unison, allowing her to close first and hoping to strike right after. If you attacked at the same time, your odds would be better."

Using his forearm to wipe the sweat from his brow, Kaen grinned until he saw the look Elies gave him.

"They are right. Honor is important here, but you are smart to realize there is a time when honor does not matter. Remember this lesson. Against the wrong opponent, if you allow them to trick you into thinking they will fight with honor, you might find a dagger in your back."

Nodding, Kaen understood. A Dragon Rider was expected to fight differently, but the truth was that more people would fight dirty when faced against him.

"Thinking of checking your stats?" Elies asked as he watched Kaen's face.

"Uh . . . no," Kaen said, lying, and gave a slight shrug of his shoulders. "You told me not to waste my time doing that. Something Pammon never lets me forget."

A rare chuckle escaped Elies's lips as he smiled.

"I'll remind you, I went fifty years once without worrying about my stats," he informed Kaen. "Trust the process. It will reward you if you put in the work."

Grunting, Kaen bobbed his head. Another eighteen months of this seemed so far away.

As Kaen began to move toward his equipment, Elies returned to his chair. Kaen saw the wince Elies had tried to hide. The rot was spreading.

He prayed he had eighteen months to train.

1

Roccnari

Dive!

Pammon immediately dropped altitude as the horde of teratas converged on them.

Fourteen left. I'm rolling soon.

Clenching his stomach, Kaen prepared for the spin move they had practiced more times than he wanted to remember.

As Pammon spiraled through the air, he leaned backward and let an arrow go. Drawing another arrow, he watched as the closest teratas took the arrow through its long, leathery neck and flopped wildly.

Thirteen.

Ten seconds till I have to get back to climbing. Hurry up.

Chuckling, Kaen pulled two arrows and lined both of them up without having to think about speed, wind, direction, or anything. His lifestone barely smoldered as he was so used to this by now. Twinshot activated, and two more teratas took arrows to their bodies, sending them on a death spiral to the ground.

Five seconds.

One more arrow leaped from his bow a second before Pammon flared his wings and pulled out of the downward spiral he was in. The force held Kaen flat on the back of his dragon and those massive scales. His saddle provided a little more padding, and the leather straps stretched from the pressure they were under.

Ten left, and they are still following us.

Those mindless birds give new meaning to one-track minds.

The thrum of Pammon's amusement did nothing compared to the wind buffeting him as Kaen spun around in his saddle, facing the backside of his dragon and the ten winged creatures trying to catch them.

Multishot took out three more, and two single shots brought their total down to five.

How many did you want to handle this time? Two?

You say that like it's not that big of a deal. Each of those is as big as a horse, and some of us must be careful of our wings.

Pammon knew he was joking, and their bond betrayed his inability to be sarcastic.

Just let me know when you are done playing around. None of this is difficult for you, and we are wasting time. Elies and Tharnok are waiting for us.

Grunting, Kaen sent arrow after arrow at the mindless creatures. They had been bothering an area in Roccnari for a while, and he was fulfilling a request by the king, Havannath. He had not asked for much the last two years, but when he did, Kaen felt obligated to respond. No task yet had been deemed worthy of Elies's or Tharnok's time.

Two are left, both in a standard flight pattern. They are about one hundred yards away.

Without warning, Pammon banked sharply and stopped his speed, spinning quickly to face the two creatures that were out of their league.

Pammon caught them as they got close, one in his mouth, biting off its head and everything else down to its chest. The other he snatched in his front talons, carefully ensuring the teratas's claws and teeth were far from his wings. Both were dead in seconds, hanging limply from Pammon's mouth and talons.

Let me know when you are done eating those. I cannot stand the way it looks when you chew on them.

Pammon thrummed as the sound of bones cracking and flesh tearing drifted to Kaen's ears as he looked behind Pammon.

The fields beneath them were massive, with rows of crops growing in perfect lines. Water canals ran up and down the fields, crisscrossing with small dams and levees that helped control where the water ended up.

Trees were everywhere around the farms, and some reached two hundred yards into the air. It was a different land than where Kaen had grown up, but it was beautiful and clean. The elves here had been kind hosts, gracious to him and honoring him, even though he felt he deserved none of it. Ridding the kingdom of this pack of beasts that had moved in recently would earn Kaen and Pammon more renown. Something he cared very little about.

The sounds of a swallowing and a burp made Kaen chuckle.

All done?

I really could use a drink of water. Let's visit one of the canals, and you can report that we are finished.

Turning around in the saddle Elies had designed for him, Kaen smiled. He was safely harnessed in yet able to move with ease. For the last two years, he had impressed the man with his dedication to everything they were taught, and now he knew it was time he went back home.

"All forty-seven of the teratas are gone," Kaen informed the elder. "I wish I could have gotten all of them out of your fields. I know they caused damage as they fell to the earth."

The older elf smiled and bowed. His hair was silver, and even though Kaen knew he was over one hundred years old, no wrinkles showed on the man's face. His blue eyes seemed like water, flowing with wisdom and knowledge.

"My people thank you, Dragon Rider," elder Thalion declared. "The earth will take the nutrients from the beasts. I fault you none for the damage their deaths have caused the fields. Your actions have saved our flocks and my people from their ravenous appetite. I only wish I had something I could give you as thanks for accomplishing this."

"No reward is needed," Kaen answered as he waved off the elder's statement. "The king himself asked me to take on this task, and your people have been gracious in providing us a place to stay and train. I am happy to give back to you and the land."

The elder smiled and bowed.

Kaen noticed the few children in the village who were all staring and watching from a distance. Pammon was at least twice as large as he had been when they arrived. He stood taller than their house, and his appetite was often alarming.

A cow . . . or two would be a good reward. You could ask him for at least one.

I will not, though. They need each of their cows, and the king has provided you with plenty. Besides, we need to move quickly, not take forever because you stuffed yourself.

Blowing air out of his snout, Pammon shook his body, giving Kaen the perfect opportunity to end the small talk.

"It appears we are needed somewhere else, Elder Thalion. I wish you and your people a blessed day."

Kaen smiled, giving a small bow and putting both hands on his chest, palms together. The elder returned the gesture, allowing Kaen to return to Pammon.

Man, they sure like to talk.

Thrumming, Pammon bobbed his head and stuck out his tongue in the direction of the elven children, sending them laughing and running away.

Yes, they do. Almost as much as you enjoy not talking. I guess it is good you have learned to stand there and smile.

Patting Pammon's neck, Kaen waved with his other hand as they left the ground, sending up dust clouds with the movement of Pammon's wings.

Has Tharnok told you anything about what Elies wants today?

Pammon paused, and Kaen could tell he knew something but was unsure how to explain it.

He isn't doing well. You don't have to say it.

Tharnok is nervous. Once Elies does pass, it will be bad. The elves have offered to give him a place to stay, but Tharnok knows he will die soon after. He says if the heartbreak does not strike first, the madness will.

Kaen felt the pain from Pammon. Learning from Elies and Tharnok about why they itched so much had answered so many questions. If they were separated for more than a month, death or madness was a possibility for both.

We will have to trust them both to make the best decision. I am not sure what I would ask if we were in their place. They have been together for over two hundred years.

Neither one wanted to talk much after discussing the truth that Elies would soon be gone.

I'm going to miss this view. Don't get me wrong, I can't wait to see Ebonmount again, but this is a whole different level of amazing.

He felt Pammon's agreement as they flew over the capital of Roccnari.

Round white walls surrounded the city in different layers. Each wall was easily forty feet tall and had spires armed with massive siege weapons with which to fight dragons. Elies had done his best to help them prepare for the day Stioks came.

Perfectly straight streets ran from each gate in all four directions, and the circle of the city stretched on for miles. Eventually, it was cut off as it ran into the massive river they had used as a barrier, which ran from the east side, around the south, and then back up to the west. Farms dotted the landscape outside the river.

In the middle of it all was a massive castle that spanned a large chunk of the inner third part of the city. Two huge openings were there, high up in the sky, one for him and Pammon and the other for Elies and Tharnok.

He is inside the castle. They are waiting for us.

Nodding, even though Pammon couldn't see it, Kaen had no doubt where Elies was. His flying had been reduced to one or two days a week in the last two months. The elves had done everything they could to try and slow the rot that was eating him alive. All they could do now was help with the pain.

Take us in. We need to get this finished so that we can return.

Do you still believe that decision is the best one? The king and the nation have been gracious to us. Staying here might be better for us long term.

And when Stioks attacks Ebonmount, and we are too far away, then what? We have heard the reports. We know what is coming. We can help hold off the potential threats and attacks if we are there. Losing that kingdom would hurt us in the long run. The dwarves have dug themselves in. Supposedly, they have learned how to grow crops underground and are stockpiling food. War is coming at some point, and I do not want to run.

Be honest. You just want to be close to Hess and their daughter, Callie. Oh, wait, you want to convince Ava to return to you. It seems that you did hit your head the other day when sparring if you think she will easily forgive you.

Slapping Pammon's scale did nothing but cause Pammon to chuckle.

He was right. Ava was not happy with him, and no letter or the occasional visit had done much to calm her down.

Don't forget my academy. I need to be there next week. We are having a ceremony where Phillip and Frederick get their lifestones. Things are changing, and we are needed.

Pammon grumbled.

I think you are confused. We are wanted and needed everywhere. Do not forget the third option Elies gave us. It is the most dangerous, but it also has the highest potential for helping with what is coming.

Kaen said nothing as Pammon approached the spot where they would land. The open-air den for Pammon. Doors could be shut if needed, yet they had been left open since he was out and expected to return. The guards on the innermost wall waved flags moments ago, announcing they saw and expected them.

Forget it for now. We need to focus. A meeting with the king and Elies means trouble, and we both know it.

Slowing as he swooped into the large room, Pammon touched down with grace on the stone floor. He remembered the first time he tried this and slid a few feet before almost falling on his side. Now, it was second nature.

Don't look now, but someone else is here for you.

Glancing at the door leading into this area, Kaen saw who Pammon had noticed and groaned.

Some things were worse than meetings with the king and Elies.

2

A Costly Mistake

Pammon thrummed as Kaen watched Huethea approach him. She had no problem tossing her rank and position around at him. Where other elves had been reserved in demanding things because he was a Dragon Rider, she felt it was okay to play the *my-dad-is-the-king* card every time she saw him.

"Rider Kaen, you are late," she informed him with a look of frustration, obvious to anyone who saw her. "We have been waiting for well over an hour in the throne room. Do you enjoy making us wait?"

"I'm sorry, Princess, but I was actually finishing up a quest your father personally asked me to complete," replied Kaen as he gave his best smile, hoping to placate her. "I had not imagined forty-seven teratas would pester your people's farmland. It does take time to fly there, defeat them, and fly back."

She tapped her finger against her arm as she stood there with them crossed. Her silver hair was in a braid that hung down to the middle of her back. She was attractive, but her personality reminded him too much of Fiola's.

"That would have taken Tharnok half the time it took you two," Huethea informed him as she rolled her eyes. "Perhaps you are not as skilled as Elies, as my father believes you are."

A gust of air blew his hair forward. Kaen felt Pammon's frustration with this girl. It was hard to call someone who was sixty-something years old a *girl*, yet the elves who had confided in him during his stay often referred to her as one.

Do you think I would get in trouble if I blew a small stream of fire near her? Not enough to actually hurt her, but perhaps just to take her down a notch or two.

Oh, I have no doubt you would be fine. I would get in trouble, but when has that stopped you from doing something?

His thrum echoed in the chamber, and Huethea glared at Pammon before turning her gaze back to Kaen.

"It is not considered polite to have conversations with your dragon in the presence of nobility. Why do you continue to be such a brute?"

Her voice was like ice running down his back every time she spoke.

"I will have another talk with my dragon," Kaen replied as he began to undo his bow-riding gear and moved to set it on the hooks. "It is not my fault if he chooses to ask for permission to breathe fire in your direction, and I have to inform him not to. I guess next time, I will just let him do as he pleases so that I don't offend you."

"He what?!" snapped Huethea, pointing a finger at Pammon. "Do you forget who I am?!"

"No, princess," Kaen declared with a shrug. "Every time we see you, barely any time passes before you remind us of your position in the kingdom. I have often wondered if I should inform your father, the *King*, that you are one of the main reasons we will not make this our home."

Nostrils flared, eyes bulged, and Pammon took notes of how her face looked. Her pale skin turned red like a cherry. Kaen felt a storm of electricity gathering around them as she pulled mana into her.

"Why . . . I never . . ." she stammered, fuming with anger. "Just wait till my father hears about this!"

She turned and began to stomp toward the door, making sure each step sounded as loud as possible.

"When you do, make sure to tell him what I just told you," Kaen called out as he winked at Pammon.

I don't want to get in trouble for what you just did. There are cows with my name on them, and if I lose them because of you, I will not be happy.

Welcome to the club . . .

Kaen chuckled as he walked toward the door she had just slammed.

He could not wait to be back in Ebonmount.

"Forgive me, your Highness, for being tardy," Kaen declared as he bowed slightly toward him. "I was not expecting almost fifty teratas, but I wiped out the nest and destroyed all their eggs."

The king nodded. His face never changed as he watched Kaen standing before him. He was well over two hundred years old, and his hair was solid white. Whiter than the string on Kaen's bow. His skin had hardly any wrinkles, and his blue eyes still sparkled with wisdom and power as he leaned back in his chair.

"Thank you for doing that for me. Elies and I felt it would be better if you took on that quest instead of him."

Kaen nodded and glanced at Elies, struggling to sit still on his cushioned chair. The smell of rot and decay wafted across the room, even with magical devices designed to replace the smell of death with something more natural.

"How are you today, Elies?" Kaen asked as he sat on a chair near him.

The man winced as he shifted. The pain he felt was evident.

"I am managing, but I am not sure how much longer I can. You and the King both know I do not have much time left," he answered with a wheeze.

He looked nothing like the man he had met two years ago. His hair was gone, and most of his body was covered in bandages and wraps. Part of his face was covered from where the rot had moved past his neck. All the muscle and strength he once had quickly vanished in the last three months. The only thing keeping him going was Tharnok and his strength. Every day, the dragon shared more of his power with him.

"Can I do anything?" Kaen asked as he watched his mentor fight back a cough.

He shook his head, careful not to move too fast.

"I am glad you were late," Elies stated as he lost the fight against a cough. "I have informed Havannath there is nothing more I can teach you. Tharnok and I have often spoken about how you have done the impossible. Knowing you two were completely bonded when we found you had surprised us immensely. Seeing the two of you together doing what you do has made this next stage easier."

"Elies is right," Havannath interrupted. "I wish you would consider staying here, but I also understand your reasoning for returning to Ebonmount. I want you to know that we will always have a place for you and your family if you ever need to return here."

Kaen gave a slight bow with his head as he watched the two of them.

They were both old and had spent over a hundred years together. They were a team unlike any Kaen had seen before. Neither cared that one was human and the other was an elf. They were like brothers the way they acted sometimes, and he knew it pained Havannath more than he let on that Elies was soon to depart this world.

"I appreciate the door that will always be open to Pammon and myself," he replied. "You both know how badly things have progressed in the last year for the other kingdoms. My hope is that my presence will slow down their advance."

Havannath motioned to a servant across the room. It was really more of an open-air courtyard, with sunlight and a slight breeze coming through the open roof. A tree grew in one section of the massive room, and walls with weapons, pictures, tapestries, and more lined the circular room under their protective stone ceilings.

The male servant came forward, and Kaen heard the two of them speaking in elvish.

"Go and get my daughter and tell her to bring the gift I have. Make sure she knows I expect her to behave."

Taking a drink from the cup that was provided for him, Kaen did his best to hide his smile. He had spent months learning the language from one of his sparring partners. No one knew he had mastered the language. It had served him well in a place where people would chide him for conversing with his dragon yet chose to speak in a language they thought he didn't know.

"When do you plan to leave again?" Elies asked as he watched Kaen play with his drink.

"Three days. I need to finish a few last things and ensure everything is in place. I owe a few people for the training they have given me, and I want to make sure they are shown gratitude."

A raspy chuckle escaped Elies, and his head bobbed slowly. Kaen had learned the way in which the elves showed gratitude. Words were nice, but small personal gifts were best to show one's favor. The larger the gift, the more they meant to them.

Ten minutes had passed as they made small talk when Huethea came into the room with a long package wrapped in fine silk and tied with a black ribbon. She wore an outfit that revealed her curves, yet the way she glared at him almost made him want to shift in his seat.

"My father would like me to give you this parting gift," she proclaimed, though the words felt like a dagger was held against her neck to make her say them. "Your sacrifice and dedication in helping keep our people and kingdom safe must be acknowledged."

Kaen glanced at Elies and saw that his eyes betrayed him as he watched the gift she held. Something was off.

"I am honored," Kaen replied as he stood and came forward. "I have done all this, though without expectation of a gift. Your roof and food have been a gift worthy of more than I could hope for."

Needles seemed to leap from her eyes as she narrowed her brows and held back a frown that would have cracked her perfect skin.

"Yet we must. Honor demands it," she answered as she held out the nine-foot-long gift, dropping to her knee and holding it above her head.

Embarrassed to see her like this, Kaen quickly took the object from her and felt the shaft of it beneath the silk.

A spear.

"I am honored and will never forget this gift."

Huethea nodded and slowly rose up and backed toward her father.

Havannath moved to replace his daughter's spot and extended his hand to Kaen.

As he and Kaen clasped forearms, as was their custom, Kaen was alerted of a notification.

[Charm Resisted]
[Charm Resistance Skill Increased x4]
[Charm Resist Skill Evolved]

He saw the King's eyes widen in shock, and Kaen gave a slight nod of his head.

When Kaen spoke, his voice had lost all of the warmth he usually displayed. Now his tone was low and had an edge.

"Perhaps you wanted to add something to receiving this gift?"

"How?" Havannath demanded as he squeezed Kaen's forearm tighter, shaking his head.

[Charm Resisted]

"It won't work," Kaen declared as he frowned.

He shook the King's hand off his arm and glanced at Elies to see if he had been part of this plan. When he noticed the confused look on his mentor's face, Kaen realized that Havannath had not discussed this at all with Elies.

Leaning the wrapped spear against his chair, Kaen glared as he shook his head.

"I won't ask what you just tried to bind me to, but I am afraid it was a poor decision to attempt such a thing," he informed the king and his daughter as they stared at him. "I was content to keep my promise and come here regularly and help. Now, I must weigh if that is the proper decision."

"Havannath, what have you done?!" demanded Elies as he tried to stand but fell back into his chair. "Tell me you didn't attempt to do what he is saying!"

The king's head lowered, his chin dropping toward the floor, his eyes nearly closed. The look of shame washed over him, and he shook his head, muttering in elvish.

"We will die, and this boy is a fool to think he can save us all."

"Am I a fool for making a promise, or am I more of a fool for believing the king of the elves would act in a way that dishonors his entire kingdom by trying to bind the last Dragon Rider to him?"

His head snapped up so fast that Kaen wondered if his neck would snap. When Huethea realized that Kaen understood her father's words, a gasp escaped her. That he had to have understood what she had said all those times.

"You know our language!" she shouted, oblivious to what her father had done.

"Only a fool would not learn a language in a land he has lived for two years," Kaen replied as he moved to Elies's side. "I will not be party to this right now. I have been dishonored more than words can attest, and no gift, regardless of how pretty the bow on it may be, will make me forget this wound."

Bending to his knee, Kaen looked up at Elies, who was still struggling to rise.

"It appears I must leave earlier than I had expected," Kaen said as he put his hand on the man who had poured everything he could into him for the last two years. "I cannot thank you enough for what you and Tharnok have done for us. I owe a debt I cannot pay."

Ignoring the look he was getting from Huethea and the fact that Havannath had fallen to the ground and was shaking, Kaen turned and began to walk toward the exit.

"Wait!" Elies rasped as he willed himself to stand.

Turning around, he saw the Dragon Rider shaking as his legs struggled to support him. His arm trembled from the effort required to stabilize himself with the chair.

"Forgive them! Forgive them as payment for what you owe me!"

Growling, Kaen shook his head in disgust and spat on the ground.

"You would ask that?!" he shouted, pointing to the two of them now looking at Elies. "After what he just attempted to do?! Surely you must be upset that he attempted to . . ."

Kaen paused. His lifestone did what it had so many times before as he worked out problems and found solutions. It made him think. It helped him see their facial expressions and understand what he had not noticed before.

"He bound you to him," Kaen whispered as he squinted at the pained look on Elies's face. "Even now, he is forcing you to ask, not because you want to but because he is making you."

Elies said nothing as he stood there shaking. He tried to open his mouth, but words would not form.

Turning his wrath on Havannath, Kaen moved so fast that he was almost instantly standing over him, glaring at him as he shook with rage.

"Free him now from that bond, or I swear to you I will fly to Stioks and tell him this kingdom is his. I will tell him I will not defend it at all. Anything he does here will be free game."

Havannath's eyes flashed with rage, anger filled his face, and a sword was heard being drawn in the room.

As things looked to take a bloody turn, two distinct sounds echoed through the building. Two different dragons roared in rage.

"I suggest you put that sword away before Stioks does not need to come here for that to happen," Kaen stated as he pointed to a servant across the room. His eyes never left Havannath. "Now release him or suffer consequences far worse than you can imagine."

Gulping, the anger and rage were gone, replaced by fear, knowing he had made a mistake he might never recover from.

"You do not under—"

"I will not ask again," interrupted Kaen. "If you fail to do so in the next moment, I will leave, and you will be alone for what comes next."

He opened his mouth once more and then closed it. He was defeated, and he knew it. An almost twenty-year-old Dragon Rider had done what a one-hundred-year-old one couldn't. Standing, the king walked to where Elies struggled to stand and put his hand on him.

"You have fulfilled your debt," he whispered.

Jerking from something that happened in his soul, Elies fell backward into the chair. A breath left him, and he groaned as he hit the padded pillows.

Dashing to his teacher's side, Kaen saw the look on Elies's face, the tears that were beginning to well in his eyes.

"Thank you," he whispered as he smiled. "Now go. Leave him to me."

Kaen gazed at the man, who looked like a weight had been lifted from his shoulders. He was still tired and dying, but he seemed different. Freer.

Sighing, Kaen nodded and bent over and kissed the bald, splotchy head of Elies.

"Be safe, my friend."

As he left the room, Kaen was shocked by the sound he heard coming through the walls. They seemed to vibrate, and then it hit him.

Tharnok was laughing.

3

Parting Gifts

Elies stood there, looking different yet still barely a shadow of his former self. Kaen could not believe how much the man had changed in just a few hours.

"I know I should tell you thank you, but I am still at a loss for what I should say," Elies said after having stood quiet for so long. "It happened so many years ago. I allowed my friendship with him to weaken me, and once he bound me, both Tharnok and myself were collared like dogs."

A growl sprung up from Tharnok, which echoed through the landing room in his tower. The dragon looked ready to spring and catch Elies if he faltered or fell; it was apparent he was very protective of him now.

"He was hamstrung just as much as I was. If he retaliated and Havannath kept us separated or chose to command me to some faraway place, Tharnok would suffer as well."

Shaking his head slightly, a sigh escaped his tired lips.

"I still cannot believe you resisted a binding by the king. I know you have not shared all your secrets but to manage that is—"

Tharnok interrupted.

Why are you two so strong? I have told both of you that your rapid growth is unheard of. In all my life, I have never heard of such a thing. No dragon or Dragon Rider has matured as fast as either of you.

Pammon's thrum reverberated around the room, and Kaen saw Elies smile, even though Tharnok snorted. He still considered Pammon young, and he had never shied away from telling both of them their need for maturity.

"Do you two want to come with us? I know King Aldric would most likely welcome you both."

Glancing around the room, Elies spotted and moved toward the chair he was looking for.

"I would not put him in that position," he stated as he slowly made his way to his chair. "It would create conflict these two kingdoms do not need in the coming times. You still need to find a way to unite each king. A task worthy of one of your stations."

Plopping into the chair, he gasped from the pain, and Tharnok began to move toward him until Elies shook his head.

"I still need to decide how this will play out," he groaned as he shifted on his seat. "We have discussed the possibility of attacking Stioks one last time and dying there in the process."

"Let me know when, and I will join you!" exclaimed Kaen as he glanced between the two of them. "Together, we could defeat him!"

We have gone over this many times. He is not alone. His three females would assist, and four dragons against two, even with your skill with a bow, the odds are not good. You are not ready for that conflict.

"If that is the case, then why has he not attacked with them yet?"

As I have told you before, those females are wild dragons. They have their own goals and desires. They will defend if you attack the one they have chosen to follow. Stioks will have a hard time convincing any of them to assist in an attack. They gain nothing from petty human battles.

"Go to the chest by my armor and fetch the blue pack inside it," ordered Elies. "We need to discuss a few things before you go. Havannath is not happy, and while I doubt he will attack the two of you, leaving today is the best decision."

Glancing along the wall, Kaen saw the man's armor on the stand. It was an amazing set of chain mail and one that, if it could be altered, would be a blessing for anyone wearing it. Sadly, the man was smaller than he was, and it did not appear the elves would be willing to fix it for Kaen after his outburst at the king.

The chest he was talking about was just a normal wooden one. A few straps and a latch that were easily unhooked. Digging inside, he found the blue pack near the bottom and held it up for Elies to see. When he nodded, Kaen shut the lid and brought it over to him.

Elies unhooked the leather buckle and reached inside. There in it was a rolled-up parchment.

"Lay this on the ground and use something to keep it from rolling up. Tharnok has one last thing to share."

Pulling small knives from each of his boots, Kaen put them on the edges of the small map. It was a good two feet long by four feet wide, and as soon as he saw it, a shiver ran through him.

What is it? Pammon asked as Kaen heard his dragon moving behind him to look at it.

"A map of the sea and what lies beyond," he murmured as he tried to follow the lines and squares on the map.

"Correct," answered Elies as he laid his head back against the chair and closed his eyes. "Tharnok will tell you what you need to know. Listen carefully, as it will be important."

Clearing his throat, the elder dragon moved his head till it lay on the ground next to his rider and gazed at Kaen and Pammon. It looked like someone had moved a massive shack next to Elies, as that snout could easily have fit either one of their heads in a single nostril.

That map is worth more than most people could ever imagine. It shows exactly where my homeland is, and with it is a chance you might undertake when no other options are available.

Tapping a land mass on the west section of the map across a large amount of water, Kaen glanced up at Tharnok.

"Here?"

Yes. Over a hundred years ago, since last we had gone, that land was ruled by dragons. Humans, elves, and dwarves keep clear of it, for intruding without a dragon will often end in death. If you and Pammon attempt to go, you will be allowed access to the land and an audience with the council.

Pammon and Kaen both felt a wave of wonder from each other.

A council? How many dragons make up this council?

A brief thrum emanated from Tharnok before he quickly cut it off, not wanting to show his amusement at that question.

Long ago, seven elder dragons sat on it. Now I have no idea. It has been generations, and I cannot begin to tell you what it looks like today. If you travel there, remember they are wary of Dragon Riders. The bond is powerful and gives both the dragon and rider many gifts. A dragon loses some of the rage that can consume them. Petty things like wealth, land, and mates can cause dragons to kill each other and rampage. Power is everything. A Dragon Rider curbs that as their passion is for their rider.

Turning his head, Tharnok gently tapped Elies's chair with a talon.

The dragon I would be if it were not for this man would be a monster. I am temperamental and easily angered. He has calmed me a lot. The other dragons I knew before the council cut off the alliance between those who had riders. They all spoke about when riders kept dragons and men in check. I doubt you can convince them to consider those days again, but you might be able to request a short alliance to help with Stioks. If he gets a dragon egg and bonds, terrible things will take place for all of us.

A shudder seized Kaen as he thought about it. Stioks was already one of the strongest adventurers the guild once had. There were no others like him now. Two hundred or more years with him only getting stronger would destroy the world.

Take the map and some of Elies's gear in the cabinets behind you. Visit your people and stay with them. Prepare the defense and seek out those you can defeat. We both know that the orcs and goblins have not given up, and the reports state they are three times larger than they were two years ago. War is coming, and you must be prepared.

"I just . . ." Kaen started and stopped. "How much can I really do against these creatures? While Pammon and I have gotten stronger, we are not able to take them on by ourselves."

Who said by yourselves? Aldric informed you of the army he was building. You told me that the adventurer guild in Ebonmount had grown. Do not try to win this war by yourself. You are a hundred years from being ready for that moment.

Groaning, Kaen felt Pammon's laughter at that comment, and soon, his front side was feeling it when Tharnok joined in.

Opening his eyes, Elies smiled and gave a slight chuckle.

"Kaen, we both know you are still growing. I told Tharnok the moment I saw you that you were our last chance to win against what was coming. You and Pammon will be the rise of everyone's hope for a future. Be smart and use the brain you have inside your head."

Pulling his daggers up, Kaen began to roll up the map as he thought about what Tharnok and Elies had just told the two of them.

"You remind me so much of him," stated Elies as he gazed at Kaen. "From your hair, eyes, and how you hold yourself. The one time I met your father, I knew right away he was a different breed of a man. You are just like him."

His face twinged as those words cut just a little. He was like Hoste, but he was also different. Hess had taught and raised him to be the man he is today.

As if sensing what Kaen was thinking, a grin appeared on Elies's face.

"Yes, you are just like Hess was too. He was a stubborn man when pressed but also one who would risk anything for his friend or others. You have been fortunate to have two men give you so much."

Chuckling, Kaen nodded and reached for the pack that Elies was holding out to him.

"Now go. Hurry up and take the things you can use. All my weapons are better than most you will find. Take them and use them, or give them away to someone who will, but you must leave. Havannath will be foolish, and his daughter will make him act in a way he shouldn't. Leave now before you have to fight your way out."

Nodding, Kaen stood up, held out his hand, and gently shook Elies's. That strong grip was gone, but there was still some strength left in this old man.

"Thank you for not taking it easy on me," Kaen said as he tossed the pouch over his shoulder. "I seem to learn better when I am getting my tail kicked."

Laughing, and then coughing, Elies choked before he spat out some phlegm and nodded.

"As with most Dragon Riders, we are all hard-headed. Just ask Tharnok anytime you need his opinion on that matter."

Kaen smiled and moved to Tharnok, watching him intently.

"Thank you for all your help as well, Tharnok. We could not be the dragon and rider we are today without you."

Nodding his head slowly, he put his snout where Kaen could touch it, letting Kaen scratch the underside of his jaw.

You give me hope for tomorrow and the coming years, Kaen Marshell. May you and Pammon show this world what they are missing by not having more like you.

4

Two Years of Hard Work

Tharnok said you have more honor than most dragons and owes you.

Kaen could feel the immense pride Pammon felt to hear Tharnok speak of him like that. Both had learned a lot by flying and talking with the older dragon. Two hundred-plus years of experience was drilled into them daily by a dragon that didn't take crap and ignored excuses.

I cannot believe he allowed the king to hold his rider hostage like that. Tell me you would not have done something to make him end it.

Pammon grunted as he flew over the trees, putting distance between the capital and eating away the miles till Ebonmount.

It wasn't that simple. Remember what you told me about your mother and the bond her father had over her? Tharnok could have ended Elies's life with one command if the king had wanted it. Had his dragon killed the king, both of them would have died. Only the healing that the elves continually gave Elies after being injured by Stioks kept Tharnock from acting on the anger he felt for Havannath and the chain he had bound his rider with.

Without thinking, he touched the spot where his lifestone was located. All the things Hoste had told him in his letters started to make sense.

I think I was able to resist the binding of the King and the Hurems because of the type of stone I have. It would be like one king trying to make another subservient.

Do not allow yourself to get angry. I can feel it still smoldering inside you. You and I know you could never have gone to Stioks and offered him that deal. Thankfully, the king was not able to tell.

Kaen started laughing as Pammon climbed higher into the sky and was soon going to be in the clouds.

I guess that storytelling skill was worth it, after all.

I know I'm going to regret asking, but when was the last time you checked all of your stats and skills?

It's been a few months, but I'll check since you asked.

Kaen felt the groan from Pammon. He laughed as both of them knew he had been dying to check before he let the thought run through his mind.

Full Status and Skill Check
Kaen Marshell - Adolescent
Age - 19
HP - 1225/1225 (25%)
MP - 400/400 (25%)
STR - 40 (25%)
CON - 41 (25%)
DEX - 44 (25%)
INT - 31 (25%)
WIS - 26 (25%)
Blessings:
Dragonbound Complete - 25% current bonus to all stats
Hunters Tunic - +3 to Str / Con / Dex
Blessed Vambrace - +1 to Dex / Int
Blessed Vambrace - +1 to Dex / Wis
Bonded Bow of Archer - +5 to Dex +3 to Archery *Locked*
Blood Ring - +5 to Con
King's Belt - +2 Dex
Eagle Pendant - +2 to Dex
Skills
Archery 36 (40)
Brawling 26
1H Sword 31
1H Mace 30
1H Axe 28
1H Club 30
Shield 32
Spear 30
2H Sword 28
2H Polearm 24
Staff 22
Magic 27
Charm Resist 30
Dragon Riding 28
Story Telling 34

Haggle 26
Dancing 29
Sneak 21
Tracking 22
Cooking 27
Mining 21

It seems all that hard work has paid off. Are you going to share those with Hess so you can finally prove to him yours is bigger?

Scratching the scale near his hands, Kaen smiled as the wind rushed over him.

I'm not that petty, am I?

Spraying mucus when he huffed, Pammon thrummed, knowing Kaen had dodged his attempt.

Ugh, you got it over the supplies. No one wants to clean that mess up.

Still thrumming, Pammon nodded his head as he flew. He was thankful he never had to worry about cleaning that up.

What is your plan? We are still almost a day out from Ebonmount, and unless you want to use my flight skill, getting there late at night has no real value, does it?

I'm fine with a night in the woods somewhere. Besides, we have almost a week until we need to actually be in Ebonmount for the ceremony. You and I both know Frederick and Phillip were excited the last time we were there.

An acknowledgment and sense of pride came from Pammon as Kaen brought those two boys up. Even though he would never admit it, Pammon enjoyed it when they visited for a few days, and especially when those boys came up to him.

Each of them had grown and put on some solid weight, becoming leaders of the academy that Kaen had started. No other boys were given rides except those two, keeping them working hard and setting an example for every other boy and girl there.

Yes, I do not think they would be happy at all if we did not arrive on time. After all, you did promise and sign a quest sheet for the two of them.

Besides, I need to go and see my sister. Callie turned a year not that long ago, and that last letter from Hess said she was already saying Pammon.

Lies! You need to do better if you are going to lie to me.

Laughing, Kaen smiled as the wind rushed against his face and through his hair.

All the frustration and anger he felt earlier today was gone. All he could think of was the things to come.

They had flown to the west side of the bowl of mountains surrounding Ebonmount and searched some of the sparser land areas for game and food. Southeast of Roccnari was a place that turned into a desert. Farther south was a range of mountains that boiled with lava and had little life.

Elies had taught him about the geography of the kingdoms and what one could find in each of them. They were searching for a plant to bring back to Sulenda. There was a cactus fruit that, when fermented, made an exceptional alcohol, and he knew she would love getting some for the inn.

Pammon grumbled.

I knew I should have eaten a cow or three before we left. That deer barely did anything this afternoon, and nothing out here is worth killing.

Perhaps if we find a chicken, you can eat it and finally get revenge for your honor.

Pammon huffed but kept his eyes on the ground. The sooner they found what Kaen was looking for, the sooner they could find a place with real food.

It had taken an hour to find a cluster of cacti with fruit on them and cost a few small injuries by their sharp needles, but Kaen had filled a bag of fruit for Sulenda.

They had flown to the base of the mountains, and Pammon had managed to locate two deer quickly and consumed both. He offered to share, but Kaen was content to eat some of the jerky he had brought with them, knowing they would be back in town and enjoy some real food tomorrow.

"Seems like a peaceful night," Kaen stated as he glanced up at the night sky, the moon three quarters full. "The sounds of the forest at night and your heart beating."

Leaning into Pammon's scales, Kaen smiled as he mindlessly scratched a few of them with his hand.

You better not go soft on me once we get back to Ebonmount. We have a lot of stuff to prepare for and do, and I don't want to have to worry about you turning into a fool over Ava.

Spitting on the ground, Kaen groaned.

"Really? Why bring her up? You and I both know how she acted after my last visit."

While your words say one thing, I know how your heart feels. Let's solve the problem at hand, and you can worry about her in ten or twenty years. By then, maybe I'll let you consider making an eggling of your own.

Chuckling, Kaen closed his eyes and just nodded. It wasn't worth getting into that discussion, and Pammon was right. He had other things to worry about right now than a woman whose feelings got hurt just because *he acted like a man.* Whatever that meant . . .

Grumbling, Kaen adjusted himself against Pammon's side and closed his eyes. He could worry about whatever problems arose tomorrow.

* * *

I think we need to go and scout south of the bowl. Your advice proves again you are smarter than me.

Pammon laughed as he finished eating his breakfast in the woods.

Kaen poked the fire with a stick while he waited for his dragon to return. His breakfast of dried meat and fruit was good enough for now.

I'm glad you can admit what we already know, but if you plan on meeting with Aldric, you should be informed about what is really down there. We have not looked in a year.

They had pulled back to their swamps, but do we believe they will stay there? Those caves had massive structures built outside them, and the piles of rocks could have built a town. They were digging deep into the mountains.

Yet no letter has come saying any of them have ventured into the caves that are watched.

Ripping a piece of meat off with his teeth, Kaen chewed as he considered what all this might mean. There was no way that army would give up so easily, and after learning Stioks had been behind the attack, it was only a matter of time before they struck again.

Half a day to fly down there and see, right?

If that. You and I know I am much faster now than last year.

That's because you eat all the wildlife and animals wherever we live. I cannot believe how many animals you have eaten in the past two years. It's no wonder kingdoms fear dragons.

Even though Pammon was not present to enjoy his attempt at a joke, Kaen felt a slight laugh coming from Pammon.

It makes me wish I had eaten more now, knowing what that elf has done.

I would agree, but let's not focus on that right now. Hurry up and get back here. I want to scout and reach Ebonmount by tonight. If we don't stop to hunt, you can probably get back in time for a cow from Aldric.

Satisfaction . . . no, anticipation came through their bond as Kaen sensed Pammon beginning to move in his direction.

Food was definitely the way to Pammon's heart.

The flight along the mountainside was a reminder of how barren this section of land was. No rain seemed to make it over these peaks, as the majority of it fell inside the bowl of mountains. The scorched land below and to the west was a harsh place.

They had learned from Elies and Tharnok about the few places in the desert. Some groups who lived out there were often a tougher breed than in most other kingdoms. The landscape required it.

The trade from these places was rare, but prices were not cheap for their exotic goods. Kaen had hoped to visit the cities, but Elies had warned him to stay away for another fifty years or so. Until Pammon was much bigger and presented a threat, none of them would want to attempt it.

That place is so nasty, those mountains and the smoke clouds.

It is still too far for me to see, and I know you can barely make them out. Volcanos are out there. I don't believe anything lives in that area anymore.

Tharnok says some beasts do. Usually, ones resistant to disease, but most are often very poisonous.

Grunting, Kaen squinted but couldn't make out what Pammon saw. As they flew south, way off to the west were the harsher parts of the land. Soon, they would be entering the area where the orcs, goblins, and other creatures called home.

How deep do you want to go into their territory? You are the one that has to fly us home tonight.

Kaen laughed as Pammon growled. They were miles into the air, and the cold wind did nothing to him now. Kaen had overcome that a year ago. Even with the air being a little thinner, he felt fine.

I am not worried about flying over their swamp. I am more worried about what may come out of it.

A shudder escaped Kaen as he remembered the last time they had come here. Being cocky had almost cost them their lives.

5

Old Promises

I hate those trees and how their branches and foliage cover so much of the murky water.

From up here, Kaen could not see anything but a mass of browns, greens, yellows, and black parts that made up land and trees when not surrounded by dirty, nasty water.

The water from the east side of the bowl flowed down here and ended up in this place. It was lower than all the other ground around them and sat there, unable to absorb it all, turning stagnant and deadly.

This was the home of so many things the adventurer guild had quests for. He knew there were other pockets of these creatures all over the different kingdoms, but here they were gathered in larger numbers.

Stories told of how they would grow for generations and then attempt to take over parts of kingdoms. Only the adventurers and the Dragon Riders in the past had held them back.

Tharnok had mentioned it had been at least five generations since an army had come. If they were moving now, it would not be a good thing for any kingdom, especially if Stioks was at the head of it.

Anything yet? I know you hate when I ask, but usually you see something by now.

Frustration floated through their bond, and Kaen knew the answer that was coming.

I cannot see much at all. There are a few creatures, small animals, and even something large in a lake down there, yet the armies I would expect to see still need to be included. We would have to fly deeper into their land, meaning we might be at risk of an attack.

No, I don't want to risk that. I only have about fifty arrows, and I don't want a fight like that again for a long time.

You act like you were the one they attacked. Those damn birds attacked me. Me! With their black beaks that tore at me. It took months for my wings to heal.

Absently, Kaen glanced at Pammon's wings as they flew. There were a few small scars from where the birds had attacked. They were not large, but a pack of at least eighty of them had come after them, shredding Pammon's wings before they realized how dangerous they were.

It had taken Pammon's breath and some dangerous flying for them to get all of them. The trip home had been long and painful for Pammon.

Let's turn back. I'll report what we didn't see to Aldric and find out what he might know.

As Pammon turned, he glanced across the land below him. Death was in that area, and he doubted one could ever eradicate it all.

There were still a good four hours before the sun would be down all the way when Kaen realized Pammon was not taking the usual trip back to Ebonmount.

Are we going where I think we are headed?

Thrumming, Pammon nodded his head.

You had promised, and I know you had forgotten. It is a good thing I always remember everything.

Which means you choose to do what you know is wrong.

Which means I choose to do what I want.

Both of them laughed as Kaen watched the town of Minoosh get bigger. Pammon remembered the promise Kaen had made so long ago.

The panic that had arisen at first as Kaen had Pammon land on the road north of town quickly faded when everyone realized who it was. Soon, the town was pouring out of the streets, and people were running to see the boy who left their town to become the famous Dragon Rider.

Welcoming cheers and shouts rang out from the crowd as people stayed a good distance from Pammon, biding Kaen welcome as he still sat in his saddle.

Not going to get down?

Only when the people we are actually here for show up. I don't want to have to deal with the crowd like last time.

The collective of people backed up as Pammon thrummed, his chest flexing from having not forgotten how Kaen was mobbed last time.

"Kaen!"

There he is.

Kaen saw Cale coming, waving both arms at him and smiling.

Hess had kept his promise, and seeing Cale with both arms working took some of the pressure he felt off for a bit.

"Cale!" shouted Kaen as he climbed out of the saddle. "Where is Patrick?"

"At the quarry," he called out as he pushed through the crowd that was still blocking his path. "By a dragon's beard, get out of my way!"

Hearing Cale call for them to move, the crowd created a path, and soon both men were sharing a brotherly embrace, laughing and smiling.

"Good gosh, what happened to you?" Cale asked as he stood back and looked Kaen up and down. "You been sucking on Hess's teat? You are thick like he was and have almost a beard!"

Scratching his chin, Kaen felt the stubble on his face. It was by no means something a dwarf could call a beard, but he had not worried about shaving and probably would not till tonight or tomorrow.

"Nothing but working out and eating," he answered as he motioned to Cale's shoulder. "It looks like it works perfectly."

Grinning, Cale rotated his arm a little and showed how his shoulder did indeed work.

"I won't say it was fun . . . Actually, it was awful. Worse than that potion you gave me, but those men and women Hess sent did what you promised," he stated, a few drops of moisture forming in his eyes. "I can't thank you enough for saving my backside and for everything else."

Leaning in close, Cale lowered his voice as he smiled.

"You have been gone too long, and I know you won't believe me when I say this, but I'm married and have a kid on the way!"

Ignoring the shock, Kaen grabbed Cale, threw him in a headlock, and started wrestling with him as the crowd laughed and watched the two of them act like fools.

"Which of these poor women in town gave in to your begging?" he asked as he let Cale escape.

"You remember Ella? Storven's maid?"

Cocking his head and furling his brow a little, Kaen glanced at his friend and bobbed his head.

"How did you manage that one?"

Grinning how he always did whenever they did something stupid, Cale just stood there, puffing out his chest.

"While some of us were becoming an adventurer and getting a dragon, I was being consoled by a young woman who was impressed with how I acquired my injury. Once she got past my personality, she said I wasn't that bad to look at and liked that I made her laugh."

Extending his hand, Kaen shook Cale and thumped him on the shoulder.

"Congratulations! I wish I could have attended the wedding!"

"It wasn't that big of a deal," Cale said. "Just the entire village and some of Storven's special brew."

Rolling his eyes, Kaen took off a pack he had been carrying and pulled out two pieces of rolled-up paper.

"I wish I could stay and chat more, but I need to return to Ebonmount and *see the king*," he stated, emphasizing the last part. "I wanted to give you this personally and make sure Storven lets the town know."

"Stop," Cale replied as he held up his hand and shook his head. "I don't want to hear about the king. It's hard enough knowing you have a dragon."

Shrugging, Kaen just handed him the papers.

"They are for the academy I started. Four kids from Minoosh will be admitted at my request. Tell Storven I said I trust him to pick the right four."

"You know what this will mean to everyone here," he replied as he took the papers from Kaen.

"I do, which is why I personally dropped them off. I mean to give kids here a chance to be what we all dreamed of being. When yours is old enough, I'll make sure there is a spot for that hell spawn."

Both chuckled and shuffled their feet. Knowing life was moving on quickly, the thought of children seemed impossible.

"I take it this means you will miss Patrick?"

"It does. I had actually planned on doing this later, but Pammon," Kaen said as he motioned to his dragon with his head, "reminded me I made a promise. That and I think he knew I needed to see you again."

Cale moved slightly to the side and gave Pammon a small bow.

"Thank you, Pammon, for keeping this sorry excuse for an adventurer safe."

Pammon thrummed and inclined his head slightly.

"On that note," Kaen said as he grabbed Cale and gave him a hug once more, "I need to go. Send a letter when your child is born. I will try to come when I can and warn your *wife* of all the mischief you got me into."

"Got you into?" stammered Cale as he shook his head. "I am pretty sure I was the one who got roped into most of that."

Laughing, Kaen nodded and waved at the crowd of people. They let out some frustrated moans, seeing that he was leaving.

"Stay safe. You are the closest to a brother I have had, and I'm glad to see life is going well for you."

"Likewise," Cale replied. "Be the adventurer you always told us you would be."

Choking down a ball of spit, Kaen smiled and turned, feeling like he had just been punched in the gut.

That comment hurt. Why?

Kaen wiped a small tear that had formed and began climbing into his saddle.

I told him why I wanted to be an adventurer a long time ago, and he told me how great I would be as one. Hearing him say that reminded me of how long I have wanted this but how hard it is. I guess I understand Hoste more and more.

Pammon grunted and began to turn around, preparing to leap from the ground.

Oh, you aren't . . .

Roaring, Pammon breathed a spout of fire up into the air, and the crowd behind him erupted in chaos, a few cheers and a few soiled clothes.

Pammon thrummed and leaped into the air, sending dust and wind back at those who had not panicked at his fun.

One day, you'll stop doing that.

It isn't today, though. Pammon was glad to have gotten Kaen's mind off of what had been bothering him.

Kaen found himself relaxed as they approached the city with still an hour of sunlight left.

He had missed this place; so much had changed in the last two years.

They were not flying as high as usual, wanting to be low so people could see them and know he had returned.

Still, from a half mile into the sky, they could see the walls that had been built along the farms before the forest. They were only ten feet high and about five feet deep but stretched for miles in both directions. The road had a new gate, which provided a choke point for all incoming southbound traffic on this road.

He could see the workers digging a trench on the south side of the wall, and there were a few soldiers manned every so often along it.

They have taken your advice and made great progress. It won't stop an army, but it will slow them down.

They started the second wall as well, which is good.

A mile away was the next line of defenses Kaen had recommended, with some sections complete and others marked off, matching the design of the outer one.

It has given many of the people in the city work to do, coins in their pockets, and the knowledge they are helping protect their homes. Elies was kind to let me pitch his idea as mine.

He knew your name would get more people invested in this project.

Elies had been right. They built upon his academy's success and the excitement of the people in having him as their Dragon Rider. Aldric had been able to begin forming an army, and even with a slightly higher tax to help provide for this, many did not complain after hearing what had taken place a few years ago.

It is hard to imagine what this place will look like if war does come. Against a dragon, this will do nothing to stop it.

Frustration and agreement flowed through the bond as Pammon flew quietly for a moment.

That is what we are for. To fight that which they cannot.

He was right, and Kaen knew it. If only he believed they could stop Stioks.

6

Returning Home

Organized chaos would be the only words that could describe what the gathering inside the training grounds at the academy looked like as Kaen and Pammon waited at the east end of the one they always landed in.

Every time they visited, more work had been done, and it looked like there were now three dorm rooms for students and countless other buildings for learning and for the staff who managed the facility.

How do they keep growing like this? Soon, the entire town will be here, it looks like.

Snorting, Pammon thrummed as he watched kids stream toward them in lines, quickly organizing in rows and columns. None of them wore their uniforms, but it was late, and even a few of the younger ones appeared to be in their night clothes.

Here are the two people we are waiting on.

Following Pammon's gaze, Kaen saw the headmaster and headmistress walking as quickly as they could. Both seemed a bit frazzled at his appearance this late and without warning. It had not been the nicest thing for him to do, but for now, they just needed a place to stay without all the fuss if they went into town. Tomorrow would come soon enough.

"Master Kaen!" shouted Finn, the headmaster, as he moved his dwarven legs as quickly as he could. "We were not expecting you!"

Nodding, he waved them off as both were red-faced and obviously embarrassed at no fault of their own.

"We were bathing some of the younger ones," Racha informed him as they drew close. "Forgive them for being in their night clothes, if you would!"

"You two, please stop," Kaen ordered them as he shook his head. "I did not send any notice I was coming, and the hour is late. These children are going to be sweaty because they have raced to pay me a respect I don't feel I am due. You two have done well, and this is evidenced by how quickly they all responded to the bell."

Motioning to the rows and lines of students behind them, Kaen sighed as he saw each group and class now neatly organized and waiting for him to inspect them.

"But still . . ."

"You are fine, Mistress Racha," he interrupted with a grin. "I have told Sulenda countless times how fortunate we are to have you both at this place. Now let me get this formality over with so that they can return to their dorms, get cleaned up, and tucked in for a night that I doubt will bring much sleep."

Chuckling, both of them nodded and laughed. Every time Pammon came for a visit, the kids were excited for days.

Finn turned around and held up his hand, ending all the noise of murmurs and laughter from the children watching them.

"Students prepare for inspection!"

Feet shuffled, and kids stood straighter after Finn shouted those words. Even the few staff members and a couple of the trainers he recognized had moved to attention.

Walking toward the children, Kaen smiled, unable to hold back the joy he felt, watching these students and children living the dream.

They stood, chest out, arms to their side, and gazing ahead. He noticed the younger ones struggling to keep their eyes in front of them and often were watching him until they realized he noticed before snapping them back into place.

Occasionally, he stopped and looked around at students as if inspecting them before smiling and nodding. As he walked past them, the breath they exhaled could be heard.

In one of the older lines, he noticed Frederick but said nothing, walking by as he had with all the others. After a solid five minutes of looking them all up and down, he turned and moved to where Finn and Racha were standing.

"Do you mind if I speak?" Kaen asked, knowing already what the answer would be.

"They would be honored," Finn quickly replied.

Willing to help me as I talk?

If that is all you want, I'm not a horse to show off.

You can know what I am thinking, so you know that isn't the point of having you by me.

Grumbling through the bond, Pammon moved forward, scaring Racha and Finn as he moved close to Kaen.

Yes, but it still feels like a pony show.

Well, if any other ponies show up, you can eat them.

A low thrum from Pammon caused a few of the newer children to take a step back, messing the lines up slightly as Kaen turned and held his hand up.

"Students, I must say you have impressed me by how well you responded to my unannounced visit! Even Master Finn and Mistress Racha did not know I was coming, which is why some of you were snatched right out of your baths."

A few chuckles, and some giggles broke out, and Kaen smiled at the group of a hundred-plus kids gazing at him.

"I made a promise two years ago to a pair of amazing boys, who I have watched work hard and train with everything they have. I will be presenting them each with a lifestone as promised."

Kaen paused. He heard murmurs and saw the kids giving looks to Phillip and Frederick.

"Both boys have no doubt shared with you their stories of flying on the back of my friend and dragon, Pammon."

A younger girl with red hair at the front of the line for the youngest group of kids clapped her hands in excitement.

"I want you to know that I will be offering a few other lifestones to those who achieve success in this place!"

Cheers rang out across the courtyard, and Kaen let them whisper and talk among each other for a moment.

When he held up his hands, they got quiet again.

"So tonight, when you try to sleep, remember you need rest to grow stronger. Work hard and rise up in the ranks. Perhaps in time, I may one day give you a lifestone of your own!"

When Kaen finished talking, he motioned to Finn.

"Three claps for Master Kaen!" Finn proclaimed.

Three sharp claps all echoed at the same time as the students did what they had practiced, no doubt, every day.

"Good! Now, head to bed and clean up for the night," Finn said. "Tomorrow will have something special if there are no problems at bedtime!"

Kids quickly bowed and turned, moving back toward their dorms without hesitation.

"What's the special treat?" Kaen whispered as the children departed.

"I'm not sure yet," Finn answered as he shrugged. "I have all night to figure that part out, though."

Kaen laughed, and Pammon joined in with him.

"If you don't mind, I am going to turn in while Pammon goes and finds himself something to eat."

"There are a few cows in the field," Racha said. "We were preparing for your arrival in a few days."

Pammon trilled and gave a small snort and smiled.

Tell her I appreciate her preparedness!

"Pammon would like me to thank you, and he appreciates your planning," Kaen declared as he bowed slightly to Racha.

Smiling, she turned and bowed at Pammon.

"Anything I can do to help keep him happy," she replied.

"I'll be busy tomorrow but perhaps in the next day or two, we can go over details for the lifestone event," Kaen said as he walked away, waving.

Finn and Racha nodded and took a few steps back as they watched Kaen climb onto his saddle.

"He has grown," whispered Racha as the two turned and moved toward their offices.

"They both have," replied Finn as he shook his head. "More than I can believe."

The bath felt amazing as Kaen sat there, letting the steaming water wash away the dirt and stress.

You look like you are going to explode. I mean, two whole cows?

Pammon started to trill until a burp rose, and he let it out, creating a deafening echo in their shared room.

"Oh my gosh!" exclaimed Kaen. "That smells worse than a dwarf's ball sack!"

Tell me again how you and Hess know what one of those smells like, joked Pammon as he laid his head back on the smooth brick floor.

Taking a deep breath, Kaen lowered himself under the water, hating the fact that he could taste the burp Pammon had just let out.

Lying in his bed, Kaen looked at Pammon, who was *sleeping* and yet still awake. The last few days had been a break from the constant demands and training for the last two years. No running, carrying weights, flying weird maneuvers and patterns; just time together and seeing old friends. Under these soft blankets and feeling the breeze that came through the open grates at the top of the building, Kaen sighed.

Tomorrow would have enough problems of its own.

It's like an army of people down there, all waiting to kiss your and my backside, joked Pammon as they prepared to land in the castle courtyard. **They should offer me many more things to eat if we are this important.**

I'm not sure you appreciate just how much food you are consuming. I talked to Elies, and he told me you should focus on pigs for a while. Cows take too long to reproduce.

Grumbling, Pammon said nothing. After almost a month straight of pigs in Roccnari, he had sworn them off for a bit, even when Tharnok had given him a hard time for it.

It could be worse. You could have to go fishing like Tharnok said some of the other dragons had to do.

I would prefer not to have to do that again.

Snickering, Kaen rubbed Pammon's scales the way he always did when his friend was being this way. Watching him learn to swim in the lake at Roccnari had been humorous, to put it mildly.

Turning his attention to the courtyard, he saw Aldric and some of his advisors waiting near a table and some chairs. There were a lot of people in the courtyard, more than usual.

I wonder if they have heard about Havannath and that fiasco yet.

I doubt it. Unless they sent a Dragon Rider, it would have only just arrived in the last day, and what King wants to admit they did something like that?

His gut told him that Pammon was right, but it didn't mean Kaen wasn't still worried about the fallout of that incident. Lives were at stake, and everyone would need to be united if they hoped to fight off Stioks.

Once Kaen dismounted and left everything but his bow and the sword he had taken from Elies, servants came out and brought fresh meat in a cart to Pammon, who was more than happy to accept their gifts.

Pammon quickly began devouring the treats brought to him.

Mutton, that is a different flavor.

Chuckling, Kaen ignored the waves of delight Pammon was giving off and walked to where Aldric was, smiling at him.

"Dragon Rider Kaen, it is good to have you back! For good, I hope?"

Shaking his head, Kaen reached out and shook Aldric's hand.

"You don't beat around the bush, do you, your Highness?"

"There is not enough time for that, and we both know it," he replied as he motioned to one of the cushioned chairs at the table. "Sit and let me get you something to drink. Wine or something stronger, perhaps?"

"Ahh . . ."

Laughing, Aldric waved him off and motioned to a servant who came out with a pitcher and a plain-looking cup.

"I jest. I heard you prefer milk, so I have some of the finest milk from my own cows for you."

Grinning, Kaen moved to his seat and sat down, releasing a small sigh of relief. He still managed to keep from drinking alcohol in the last two years.

After he was seated, the servant poured him a cup, and Kaen could see small flecks of ice on the surface of the milk.

Without waiting, he picked up the cup and took a long drink from it, feeling the cold, rich, and creamy milk hit his tongue. It was the best milk he could remember drinking.

Putting his cup down, he used his finger to make sure nothing was left on his lip as he smiled.

"You are correct, your Highness. That is the best milk I have tasted."

Waving his hand, Aldric grabbed a chair and moved it closer to Kaen so they would not be at opposite ends of the table. Servants started to come forward but stopped when he shot them a look. Even though the chair looked heavy, he lifted it with ease.

Once it was in place, he sat down and leaned back in his chair.

"I know we have much to discuss, but I must first say you look nothing like the boy who stood before me, telling stories two years ago," Aldric stated as he looked Kaen up and down. "You are every bit of your father and more."

"That's actually something I want to talk to you about," he replied as he motioned to the servants around him. "Questions perhaps asked where others cannot hear."

7

Catching Up with Aldric

Once the courtyard had been cleared of anyone within listening distance, Kaen motioned for Pammon, who had been waiting to come closer.

"He has grown as well. In fact, if I am right, he has grown a lot in the last three or four months."

Picking up his wine cup, Aldric took a small drink and motioned to Kaen.

"The floor is yours. Ask whatever it is you want."

Ignoring his fear, Kaen closed his eyes, took a deep breath, and willed his lifestone into burning just a little bit. Over the last two years, he had almost mastered it and found he could call upon it if his need were great enough in his mind.

"Tell me about my lifestone."

Aldric chuckled and then began to laugh harder and harder until he had to set down his cup lest it spill.

When he finally stopped, he grinned and bobbed his head.

"Kaen, out of all the questions I had anticipated, that one was not at the top of the list, yet I know it is an important one," he finally replied as he settled down. "Tell me what you know first so I don't repeat things or waste time."

"I know it's one meant for children of kings. One my father felt was important enough to risk his life for. What is so special about it?"

The facade Aldric normally wore disappeared, and a different expression of acceptance and authenticity came over him.

"You are just like him," he stated with a slight grin. "Your father specifically asked for the lifestone you have because I have no children. My wife died, and I found no one else I wished to sire with. There is still time, but it is hard to find a woman who likes me for who I am and not what I command."

He picked up his cup and took another drink, never letting his gaze leave Kaen's.

"That lifestone costs more than simply gold. It requires things I cannot share due to secrets only known to kings and a few crafters. They are rare, rarer than you can imagine. There is a reason for that," he explained. "A *king's* lifestone will allow you to live longer, draw men and women to your cause, and protect you against a variety of charms and other acts of magic meant to affect your mind."

He paused and extended his wine cup toward Kaen.

"That does not mean it will protect you against things like poison or alcohol."

Bobbing his head, Kaen smirked.

"I have found that out the hard way twice."

"A good lesson to learn early in life," Aldric informed him. "You will grow stronger than those with a regular lifestone and advance slightly faster but nothing too far out of the ordinary. Its biggest impact is in one like yourself."

"My family bloodline?"

"Correct!" he exclaimed as he held up all ten fingers. "These fingers represent the number of generations your father told me about regarding your bloodline. He and your mother both come from something very rare, and it is not spoken of for a lot of reasons."

"The speed of growth," Kaen interrupted.

"Exactly," Aldric said as he continued, unphased by the interruption. "Once long ago, it was normal for bloodlines to be like yours. Kingdoms were filled with them thousands of years ago. That was until the danger of them outweighed the blessing they offered. Wars were waged, and families were hunted down. Dragon Riders were called in to help."

"Dragon Riders? Why would they help?"

Aldric closed his eyes and winced as he sighed.

"The records we keep mention how a few Dragon Riders grew from lines like these. Some became evil and saw it as a chance to seize power for them. It was a messy war, and hundreds of thousands died. It opened the way for the orcs, goblins, and some of the other creatures you hear about to reclaim lands they once had been driven from. Slowly, the world ate itself, dragons resisting men because of the power they desired. Men were killing dragons for that slight or because they wanted the power the dragons' bodies offered."

Pausing, Aldric looked at Pammon and pointed his finger at him.

"They would butcher Pammon like one of those animals we gave him today, taking his organs, scales, bones, and more, all for the magical powers they possess."

A low growl came from Pammon as he listened.

I would never allow anyone to harm you.

There is no doubt about that. I did not mean to growl. It was just something inside me that reacted to that thought and imagery.

"I mean no disrespect," Aldric said as he shrugged and brought his focus back to Kaen. "I was simply stating the truth, what was taking place in those times."

"Pammon said it was nothing personal, just a response to the imagery."

Glancing at the two of them, Aldric smiled and chuckled.

"What I wouldn't have given for a friend like you, Pammon. I won't lie, as a boy, I often wished we still had relationships with dragons, but none of that has worked out in hundreds of years."

Taking another drink, Aldric returned to his story.

"Imagine men and dragons fighting each other. From what the records say, the magic it takes to bring down an adult dragon is mindboggling. How they managed to cleave the mountains in Ebonmount is a testament to the power that men once wielded."

"All so they could come after the dragons. They did that so they could come here and hunt them."

"My kingdom is built on a graveyard," he admitted. "I don't know how many, but I do know it was once a safe place for dragons. The mountains protected us. Knowing that the goblins and orcs have tunneled through them tells me that they have been doing this for a while. With no dragons patrolling the mountains, the barrier is not what it once was."

"We scouted them yesterday, and there were no signs of any orcs or goblins. We did not go far into the swamps as there are things we would rather not fight if we could avoid it."

He nodded as he rubbed his chin and looked away for a moment.

"That information seems bad to hear. We both know they have not abandoned this area. Any idea which direction they may have gone?"

"We flew in from the west, and none were in the desert area that we saw. East would be the only thing I could imagine unless they have traveled further south into the swamps. I have no idea how far they extend."

"Those go just as far south as our kingdom does," he answered, watching for Kaen's reaction. "Hiding in their homes is something they can do, gathering far out of sight until they move. Without someone watching that side all the time, there is no telling how quickly they could attack again."

Rubbing his eyes with his fingers, Kaen moaned as he considered that truth. If an army surged like that again at all seven points, or perhaps more if they had built other tunnels, how could they hope to stop them?

"Enough about that for now," Aldric said, waving his hand as if dismissing the last few minutes completely. "Your lifestone. What does it mean for you?"

Aldric pulled out a necklace from underneath his shirt.

"I won't begin to bore you with details, but know that this necklace gives me more stats than almost any other items in the kingdom. It is over a thousand years old and was crafted during a time when this was not as legendary as it would be now."

Putting it back, he pointed at Kaen and winked.

"Something tells me from what I know about your father and how you look now that I would struggle in a fight against you. Don't get me wrong, I have some tricks and trump cards I keep very close, but with a dragon and what your father gave you, there will be a day when you become a legend in storybooks, if you live long enough."

"I don't care about being a legend," Kaen declared, frowning. "I want to prevent a child ever having to live how I did. From losing their parent. I want to protect families."

"A noble task, but difficult," replied Aldric. "Hess told me of your desire. He mentioned how you risked yourself and Pammon to save him from the belly of an orc. This is why I will never try to sway you or bind you to me."

When Kaen's eyebrows rose and he sat back in his chair, Aldric chuckled.

"So he tried, that stupid fool tried, didn't he?"

"I assume you are talking about Havannath?"

"I know what he did to Elies. I was afraid he might try the same on you," Aldric admitted. "I hoped the lifestone would prevent that, and it seems it did. I only wish I had been there to see that smug elf's face when it failed."

Kaen started laughing, and even Pammon began to thrum.

"He tried, and I told him he either breaks the bond with Elies or I would fly to Stioks and tell him that Roccnari was fair game for him, and I would not interfere."

Bewilderment and glee fought for a place on Aldric's face. He smiled and shook his head, and then he began to laugh, and caught himself and abruptly stopped.

"Forgive me. I should not take joy in how you turned the tables on him."

"You do not need to apologize to me for what you said or how you acted. He was a pompous arse, and his daughter was much worse. If it was not for Elies's and Tharnok's teaching, I doubt I would have stayed there long at all."

Chuckling, he picked up his wine cup and realized it was empty. As he poured him some more, Kaen asked a question.

"If I didn't have the lifestone I have, would you have tried binding me?"

The pitcher flinched, spilling wine on the table before Aldric regained control and finished filling his cup.

He let out a small breath of air as he gazed at Kaen.

"Honestly, yes. My back is against the wall, and I would prefer to say I would not have, but I cannot promise that. Knowing who you are, knowing what you have inside you, and knowing what you will become is a scary thought. You would be a powerful weapon if wielded by someone."

Rubbing his thumb against his palm, Kaen mulled over what Aldric had just shared.

"I appreciate your honesty," he finally replied. "I know that was probably not easy."

"You're wrong," Adric stated. "Lying is harder because I know the road it would take me down. I have lived a long life and will be here for a while to come. If I want my kingdom to be what I tell people it means, I must be honest first. Lying would go against what I say drives me."

Mulling that over, Kaen saw the truth in that. If he went against what he believed, then his lifestone would not work as he needed it to. Only when he focused on what his goal was did it respond accordingly.

"Finish your milk," joked Aldric as he saw Kaen thinking about what he said. "We have a while to spend together today, and I don't want it going bad on you."

8

The Dragon Rider Inn

Three years ago, Kaen would never have even dreamed of sitting with a king, discussing troop movements and military plans, let alone being alone with him in a courtyard.

Yet now he was sitting here, his mind aching from everything they were discussing. Elies had given him some training about these things already, and he had to understand troop movements and supply chains, all while also understanding their weaknesses against one like himself.

Flying creatures, especially dragons, could take out the weaker supports of an army without a problem. Knowing when to protect one's allies or considering how to attack an enemy was useful.

"In the last few months, trade has come to a halt almost into the eastern sections," Aldric informed him while running his finger along roads on the map they were studying. "There are now patrols of adventurers who manage this section, along with the normal guards up to this point. After that point, it is a perilous journey for anyone else."

"And information on Stioks has changed?"

Aldric shook his head as he took a drink.

"Our assets there have relayed information each week. He has been traveling a lot between his kingdom and Pensworth. Rumor has it he has worn them down to the point where they are going to surrender or join him."

His voice sounded weaker as he relayed the information to Kaen.

"Two kingdoms will have a lot of resources and manpower to use against us. Havannath will be a pain for a few months after what he did, and don't get me started on the dwarves."

Returning to his chair, Kaen watched Pammon as he dozed a few yards away. His steady breathing might fool some into thinking he was deeply asleep.

You have been quiet. Usually, you have an opinion when Elies and Havannath talk about battle things.

This all smells like that goblin cave I found. We know something bad is inside, and our options aren't really ones we can ignore. Would you prefer to wait and see what they do first, or go after them when they won't expect us?

Grunting, Kaen knew neither of those options were good.

Moving into Stioks's kingdom would bring four dragons against us, and I have no doubt that would not bode well for us. We need to figure out our next move. Fortify here, scout the areas around us, and train.

Focusing back on Aldric, Kaen saw him smiling as he waited.

"Sorry, bad habits," he sputtered, realizing Aldric had been waiting for him.

"It's not the first time I've waited on a Dragon Rider who was communicating with their dragon," he said with a chuckle. "I am not one to get upset, and your attitude and personality make it much easier for me to look past the things you do not know. Besides, I have one last thing to give you before today ends."

Moving past the table, he walked to a small wooden box that was sitting at the base of one of the stone pillars in the courtyard. Pammon and Kaen wondered what he had inside it as Aldric carried it back to the table and sat it down.

"Here are three possible locations for what you requested last year. My personal scouts and Herb's have been scouring the kingdom and the lands beyond for the things you asked for. Some of what we have found are rumors and nothing more. One is a large area, but we believe the creature you are still looking for is there. None of this will be easy, so please be careful when approaching it."

As Aldric slid the box toward Kaen, he felt his fingers trembling a little bit. Had it really been a year, and they finally had some actual intel to go off of?

Opening the wooden box, he saw three different rolled-up sections of paper, all bound with a leather cord.

"Thank you," Kaen said, his voice cracking from excitement.

"I wish you luck in your hunt," Aldric replied with a chuckle. "There is also a sheet for each creature with a list of items the guild or my own alchemist would like if you manage to locate and dispatch it."

Are those the creatures I need to eat? Pammon asked, excited by what he was hearing.

Yes! I'll look over them later today, and we can figure out which one we might want to look at finding first!

Drool dripped from Pammon's mouth as he thought about getting to hunt and consume the creatures on the list.

Elies had mentioned that consuming some creatures helped dragons grow stronger or faster due to the magical power stored within them. It was one of the reasons dragons ate other dragons they defeated.

Standing up and picking up the box, Kaen gave a slight bow to Aldric and smiled.

"You have given us a few other things to put on our list of things to accomplish. For now, I need to go and terrorize the citizens outside the walls of Ebonmount as I go and visit Hess and Sulenda."

Roaring with laughter, Aldric shook his head and smiled.

"Those two are not who you are actually planning on seeing. I have met their little girl once, and I am afraid she already has her dad wrapped around her tiny fingers."

A grin appeared, and Kaen shrugged.

"Perhaps her older brother as well."

Pammon was his usual self and flew low across the outer cities, stirring up dust and dirt, as well as announcing himself to the local population. News had already reached the people that they were in town, and some children were outside on the streets waiting and hoping to see them.

I would roar, but I promised not to after last time, Pammon stated with a bit of frustration in his tone.

You caused a massive accident with those horses bolting and running through town. Sulenda told me how much it cost, and yes, inside town is not a place to show off.

As he slowly flapped his wings, Pammon snorted, not wanting to dwell on that moment. It had caused more destruction than he had imagined it might. The buildings they soared over were being outfitted with new roofs. Only one out of four were completed, but the city was preparing for Stioks's possible attack.

New tiles had been developed that were resistant to dragon flame. It would not hold off prolonged exposure to a steady stream but would not break from a passing breath. The magicians' guild had a few samples for Pammon and Tharnok to test over the last year and finally found one they felt worked. All magical enchantment gear had been suspended, and every available enchanter had been set to the task of preparing the long tiles for homes and buildings. The downside is that the tiles were white, creating a sea of black, brown, and white roofs that dotted the cityscape.

I will probably just drop you off, if that is ok. I feel the need to fly and look for some food.

Are you ok? That doesn't sound like what you wanted to do this morning.

Listening to Aldric talk about what is happening just reminded me that I need to keep training and getting stronger. When all of this goes down, we both know most of it will fall upon us.

Kaen could feel the frustration and concern from Pammon. He was trying to hide it, but their bond had grown to the point where hiding things was almost impossible now.

We will do this together but do not forget we are not alone. We are buying time and building an army of our own. Every day that goes by, you and I get stronger. The longer this takes, the weaker and more desperate Stioks will become.

That is exactly it. If he gets desperate, how bad can things become? Do not forget he is far stronger than either of us can imagine.

The dream Kaen had off and on for the last few years echoed in his mind. He had no idea how powerful Stioks really was. There would be no second chances once they engaged him. Every second could be their last.

Stop worrying about it for now. Go and enjoy time with your family. Tell them I said hello. I just need a few moments to myself to fly and hunt instead of sitting in a courtyard inside the city.

Kaen scratched that scale that got all the love and put on a happy face.

I will. Just make sure to stay away from the cows.

Thrumming echoed across the roofs as they sped past them. Kaen knew exactly what Pammon had intended to eat.

"Kaen!"

Cheerful voices shouted out his name as he walked into the inn he had called home so long ago.

New wooden floors had been laid, stained with a vibrant and warm dark brown color that made it feel welcoming just to walk on them. The new tables and chairs he had seen half a year ago still looked newish, and the tavern had been completely remodeled. Copper and bronze adornments, molding, columns, and more all accented the inside, reflecting the new name it had received when the remodel was finished.

He had ignored the sign outside. It was bad enough the first time he saw it.

Somehow, Hess and Sulenda had found someone to make a sign that looked *somewhat* like him and Pammon, with fire occasionally coming out of Pammon's mouth. Neither had commented on the cost, but both had said it was worth it.

"Welcome to the Dragon Rider Inn!" Eltina shouted from the bar. "Would you care for a Kaen Special? They are stout because they are named after our patron!"

He saw the smile on her face and the wink she gave. Business was good, and with the birth of Callie taking up Sulenda's time, Eltina was running this place. She loved business, and if Kaen could make this place make money, she loved Kaen.

"Maybe two," he shouted, winking back at her as he waved at the myriad of people at the inn, hoping to catch a glimpse of him.

"Welcome home, Kaen!"

"Glad to have you back!"

"Have you eaten a bear? You are huge!"

Bobbing his head as he shook the occasional hand, Kaen made it to the new bar. Wood and polished brass were worked together on it. On the side facing the guests was a mural displaying Kaen and Pammon fighting against the orcs and goblins at the south end of the kingdom.

Behind the bar was a copy of his bow and an empty quiver.

Trophies of the battle, he thought as he sighed a little while glancing at them.

A pitcher of milk slammed onto the bar, and Kaen turned his attention back to Eltina.

"You're looking pretty happy today. Things going well, I take it?"

"If business were doing any better, I would open a bank next door to hold all the money we are making," she replied as she motioned to two of the servers standing around, staring at him. "Are you done growing yet? You seem a lot bigger than last time."

Taking a big drink, Kaen swallowed the milk. It was good. Cold and fresh but nowhere near as nice as the king's milk had been.

"I eat, workout, eat some more, and workout about five more times," he answered as he plopped down on one of the new stools, dropping a sack he had over his back next to him. "I don't think I have taken more than two weeks off in the last two years. Every day was something that Elies or Tharnok wanted us to learn."

When he mentioned Elies's name, his voice stumbled for a second, and Eltina raised her eyebrow.

"Something you need to share?"

"Maybe later in private," he stated quietly. "Now, where is my beautiful sister who takes after her ugly father?"

Letting out a loud laugh, Eltina pointed toward the office.

"They are in there. I think she might be asleep, so don't go barging in, or I'll never hear the end of it from Sulenda."

Lifting his drink to his mouth, Kaen gulped down the rest of his milk as he nodded.

"You going to see your girl?" asked Eltina when he was almost finished with his drink.

Coughing, he sputtered and choked on the milk, eyes running and holding his hand out for a towel that Eltina handed to him.

"That was wrong," he gasped as he got air back into his lungs. "Wrong on two different levels."

Smiling and talking in a much perkier voice than usual, she leaned on the counter toward him.

"I know! I have missed you and the money you bring. Now hurry up and go see those three. They have been wondering when you would stop by since word reached us that you had arrived last night."

Wiping his face and chest off with the towel, he tossed it at her face, watching as she easily caught it.

"I got something you will enjoy later," he said as he picked up the sack from the floor. "A little treat from the cactus in the desert."

Her eyes sparkled, and Kaen saw her lips curl in anticipation.

"Are those what I think they are?"

"Yes, and a whole sack full."

Laughing, she walked across the solid stone block that ran the entire length of the back of the bar and stopped when she got to the copper bell, flashing Kaen a grin.

As she rang the bell a few times, the entire bar cheered and smiled. They knew what was coming.

"A free round of drinks!" she shouted, followed by cheers, whistles, and hollering.

"Drinks are on me!" she shouted, causing the patrons to cheer even louder.

Chuckling, Kaen waved as he walked to the office door, looking forward to seeing who he knew was behind it.

9

The Enemy You Don't See

"My gosh, son, which of you is eating more?" Hess whispered as Kaen withdrew from the embrace.

"Pammon, definitely Pammon," he answered as he moved to hug Sulenda, who was waiting her turn. "Is she really asleep?"

Nodding, Sulenda gripped him tight, and he knew she was trying to show off a little bit.

"She has been worked up all morning since we told her you and Pammon were back. She could not stop babbling. I'm still a little upset that Pammon was her second word."

Chuckling, Kaen shrugged as she let go, and he looked around her at the little girl, fast asleep on the bench in the office.

It had changed a lot. Now there were padded chairs, lots of light globes, the dust and the paperwork were mostly gone, and a large padded bench that served as her *sleeping* area had a wooden rail all the way around it. He was amazed that the side facing him could be lowered.

He gazed down at his little sister. She was sleeping soundly, and though she was only a little over a year old, she was massive. Her red hair was in curls, and he knew some blue eyes were behind those closed lids. She was bigger than many three-year-olds, and Kaen had been on the receiving end of her playfulness before. She had a temper, one Hess said came from her momma. At this moment, she looked peaceful, but he knew the truth. Once she woke up, she would be like a ferret, moving everywhere, in everything, and never slowing down.

"You sure Hess is the father?" he teased as he moved to the chairs they were sitting in.

"Every time you are here, you ask that. When will you give this crippled man a little joy?"

His voice sounded like he was hurt, but they all knew he expected the question.

"How long do we have before she wakes up?"

"Maybe thirty minutes," Sulenda answered as leaned back in her chair. "You going to steal Hess from me?"

"Just for thirty minutes!"

She snorted and nodded.

"That's fine, but make sure you don't go anywhere, or I'll make you wipe the tears she sheds when she finds out you left her."

Nodding, Kaen stood up and pushed Hess toward the door.

"We both know she only likes me because of Pammon."

"Hairy dwarf balls," muttered Hess as he looked across the table at Kaen. "You look more like your father than you know. The only difference is he was attractive, and you aren't."

Chuckling, Kaen just grinned as Hess spun his glass on the table. His one hand rotated it around at the base, and his stump was lazily hanging on the back of the booth.

"Stop staring at it. I have learned to live with it and wouldn't trade it for anything, knowing I am still here because of you and Pammon."

His voice was a little rough, and Kaen knew he was frustrated with the attention his stump brought. Pity was not something he wanted.

"Besides, I managed to do fine training those students at your academy. Even Bren would tell you I'm a match for most of them still."

"You just look old," Kaen finally blurted out. "You have gray in your hair!"

"Almost dying does that to ya!" he exclaimed before lifting his drink to his lips and downing it. "You saw what happened to Selmah. Her hair is completely white because she was willing to burn her entire life force in order to stop that Magus. She managed to stop before it killed her, and your smart thinking with that potion is the only thing that kept her from dying."

Sighing, Kaen nodded as he stared at the man who had raised him. He had aged a lot in the last six months. Maybe it had been in the last year. He seemed . . . smaller. More . . . vulnerable.

"I'm glad the two of you, as well as the others, are managing. It still hurts a little bit knowing how many have died and that we have yet to fight. Pammon and I scouted the swamps' outer edges a few days ago, and we couldn't see a single orc or goblin. It was as if they had moved completely."

Grunting, Hess cleared his throat, went to spit on the ground, and stopped. He swallowed it and took another drink.

"She would have hurt me for that," he stated as he chuckled. "We have heard rumors, but Herb will not tell me much. I understand why, but it hurts knowing the man acts like he can't trust me."

"I haven't spoken to him in a while either. Someone else took me the last time I went to the vault."

Tapping all his fingers against the table in a rhythm, Kaen recognized the act as one Hess had done whenever he was perplexed. His face scowled at no one, but it was obvious Hess was struggling to figure out what had changed.

"I'll pay him a visit. I know he can't deny me as a Dragon Rider."

"You would do that for me?" he asked as he cleared his throat once more.

"I would do a lot of things for you, even drag your gimpy, old, smelly arse back to town, missing half an arm."

Both grinned and started chuckling. Kaen always took the opportunity to bring up the fact he had saved Hess. Glad to be able to rib him about it.

"Tell me about Ava," Hess said as he wasted no time digging right back at Kaen's weak spot. "How have things been between you?"

Kaen's voice became gruff as he crossed his arms and leaned against the back of the booth.

"It hasn't. She got upset the last time I was here because I was always gone. Like she wanted or expected me to take her with me or something. What was worse was the fit she threw because I only had two days, and all I could offer was a few hours before Aldric and Elies needed me."

Groaning, Kaen watched as Hess flashed a grin.

"Women aren't easy to understand, are they?"

"Son, you have no idea," Hess whispered as he looked around the room to make sure no one was close. "There are days I think we are from different places. Men think one way, and women believe we are wrong. Beyond that, I often just do the opposite of what I think I should do, and Sulenda seems happier that way."

"Pammon!" Callie cried as she tapped Kaen's chest. "Pammon!"

Sighing, Kaen playfully tickled his sister's neck and heard her giggle and squirm.

"We will go find Pammon, you silly troll, but first, I need some love!"

Laughing, Callie gave him a huge hug and squeezed him tight.

"Pammon?"

"For the love of all, can we go see him?" Sulenda pleaded, her voice cracking as she shook her head. "Ever since she has woken up, it is all she has asked for."

Hess laughed and stood up from his chair.

"He is close and said we can come now. Apparently, he was eating."

Jumping up and down, Callie laughed, her red hair bobbing as she moved around the room.

"Well, let's not keep Pammon waiting then, shall we?"

* * *

All his concerns and worries seemed to be gone as Kaen watched Callie rubbing her hands and face against Pammon's scales. They were rough and tough, yet somehow she never seemed to care, as each time she did it, Pammon trilled, sending her into a fit of laughter.

She would run and hide under a wing, listening to Hess stomp around outside, trying to find her. When Pammon lifted his wing, and her dad found her, chasing after her, Pammon would then use his head to block him.

"She is in heaven," Sulenda declared. She was holding Kaen's arm in hers and smiling. "You know, if you keep growing, you might one day be as tall as Hess."

Snorting, Kaen shook his head.

"You and I both know that will never happen. I am glad to see both of them enjoying each other. I know she needs this just as much as you two do."

He felt her shaking, and he turned, seeing a few wet spots on her cheek, but a smile never left her face.

"I owe you and Pammon so much, and I cannot ever repay you for that," she said, a tremor in her voice as she stared at her family. "I will always treat you like a son if you want it."

Pausing, she turned and winked at him, sending a tear down her face.

"A pain in the arse for a son, but one I would gladly call my own."

Nodding, he stood there, grateful for what family life should be like. This was what Pammon and he were fighting for. So families could laugh and play and live together. Without thought, his heart burned a little as he watched the three of them play in Bren's school training area. It had become the primary landing place for Pammon anytime they came back.

The four of them played for a good thirty minutes before one of the men brought out a tray with some drinks.

Laughing, Kaen left the three of them with Pammon as he met the servant to collect the tray. As he took the tray, he saw a flash of metal and reacted without thought.

The man attacked with a dagger, sliding it toward his ribs and chest as he gripped the tray.

All those moments of practice caused him to react and not think, his lifestone igniting before his heart could beat. The man's attack was pushed up as he pressed against Kaen, the tray sliding his arm upward and away from his chest.

The dagger barely sliced through his sleeve, nicking his arm as Kaen brought his other hand and tray along the man's jaw, knocking him so hard it snapped his head around, facing his backside.

Dropping to the ground, the body fell, the dagger landing in the dirt.

Pammon roared, causing Callie to start crying as Hess and Sulenda grabbed her, wondering what was causing him to act like this.

You're hurt!

Wincing, Kaen nodded and tore his shirt the rest of the way. He saw a cut on his arm, no longer than an inch and barely deep at all, yet it burned like someone was putting a lump of coal against his skin.

"Kaen!" Hess shouted as he handed Callie to Sulenda and sprinted toward him.

Holding his head, Kaen felt dizzy.

"Poison," he muttered as his voice slurred. The cut was close to his artery, meaning it was flowing fast through his body.

I got you! Shouted Pammon in his head, pouring his life force into him.

Blinking his eyes rapidly, Kaen felt the strength of Pammon flowing into him. The courtyard stopped spinning, and he saw people rushing out into the training area to see what had happened.

"The blade, it's poisoned!" Kaen said as he pointed at the dagger.

Sliding to a stop in the dirt, Hess grabbed the torn sleeve that was hanging on Kaen's arm and took it the rest of the way off.

"Let me see!" he demanded as he held up Kaen's arm, ignoring his wincing.

Small black lines had formed quickly, but it was not spreading at the moment.

"We need to get you a healer!"

"Pammon, can you fly him to the guild hall? They will have someone there first!"

You know I can't help him get on. I am giving him my strength, but it is taking more than I had originally expected. We will need to hurry.

"I can hear both of you," Kaen said as he groaned. His arm felt worse than anything he had felt in a long time. "Get me on Pammon. I can do the rest."

Glancing across the courtyard, Kaen saw Callie crying, her face hidden in Sulenda's chest.

We must go before I draw any more danger to those I love.

This isn't your fault, Pammon informed him as Hess helped him climb onto the saddle. **You and I both remember what Hess said when you left Minoosh. People will try to strike at you and people near you to weaken you. This isn't a fight you can win alone, though. We need them, and they need you.**

Straining, Kaen just focused on getting clipped in.

"I'll race that way!" Hess shouted before Pammon took off. "A HORSE! I need a horse!"

Men in the courtyard started running and scrambling. A dead man lay in the dirt. An injured Dragon Rider was being flown out on his dragon, causing chaos and fear in the courtyard.

Worst was the one-armed man they knew could kill them all shouting for a horse.

Not the way they had expected their day to go.

10

On Death's Bed

The trip there was a struggle for Kaen and Pammon as he collapsed against his dragon's neck.

I will be there in just another minute. Just hold on! Pammon cried in a panic.

Kaen felt the fear and worry through their bond, telling him all he needed to know.

Pammon was getting weaker, which told him whatever this poison was, it was stronger than he had first imagined.

I'm sorry, I didn't notice the man. I should have . . .

Nonsense! You could not know he would do that, and we both know Bren will be beside himself knowing someone from his school did this to you. Focus on holding on!

The multiple training grounds were in sight, and Pammon picked the one with the most people, hoping someone there was a healer. As he landed, people scattered, most running away.

Unlatching the straps that held him on the saddle, Kaen fell to the ground.

A whine rose from Pammon as he watched the others.

Two older healers, a male and a female, ran toward them and held up their hands as they came closer to Kaen, who was trying to stand up.

"Poisoned . . . arm," he managed to get out, his voice struggling to work at all.

Pammon whined again and nudged Kaen with his snout.

Both of the healers bent over Kaen and rolled him onto his back, the male healer letting out a gasp and covering his mouth the moment he saw Kaen's arm through the cut fabric.

"We need help!" he shouted as he dropped his hand and turned to face those around them. "Summon the guild master and tell him the Dragon Rider has been poisoned!"

Multiple adventurers took off running in different directions toward entrances to the hall. Someone would make sure he was summoned quickly.

"How is he alive?" the woman asked as she put her hands over his arm, which was now covered in black lines running up and down his veins.

"The dragon," the man whispered, joining her in healing.

Both of them closed their eyes, light radiating from their hands as they tried everything they could to keep Kaen alive.

"You'll never win," Stioks informed him as he pressed the sword into his arm.

Kaen was lying on dirt, somewhere with large rocks all around him. Perhaps in the mountains, but he wasn't sure.

He tried crying out in pain, yet nothing seemed to work. Kaen glanced around, looking for Pammon, yet he couldn't find him no matter where he looked. Pain lanced through his arm and body. It burned as he looked at the man who had killed his father and was now killing him.

"A sorry excuse for a Dragon Rider and a Marshell," he sneered, leaning forward as he grinned.

Hatred filled his eyes, and Kaen felt the weight of him pressing down. He couldn't fight.

"There is no way you will defeat me. I will kill you and all that you love, leaving everyone fatherless and alone."

He tried to cry out, but his voice never came. No matter how wide he opened his mouth, silence was the only thing it brought.

Laughter from the man he sought to defeat echoed all around him.

The world went dark as he felt his life slipping away.

Kaen, I'm here!

"He's awake."

His eyes fluttered open slowly, and light seemed to almost blind him, even though he knew it was not that bright.

"Stay still, and do not try to sit up!"

The voice sounded familiar. He knew it.

"Sulenda?"

"You were expecting someone else?" she teased as he felt a cool, wet cloth against his forehead. "Now, stay still, and let me give you something to drink. You are still burning up."

Relax and rest. Hess will be back in a moment. I told him you were awake, and he took off running.

Pammon's voice brought him comfort after that dream.

Where am I?

The bed didn't feel like his bed, and the smell of it was different, too. It was clean and yet something else. Lavender. Why would anyone use lavender in a room?

Keeping one eye closed, he groaned as he looked out the other.

Sulenda was smiling. Her hair was going in every direction. She looked worn out, and he could not imagine how late it must be.

"Where am I?" he asked, choking down a tiny bit of water she poured into his mouth. It had felt amazingly cool and refreshing.

"You are in the guild hall infirmary, Kaen. You were poisoned, do you remember?"

Nodding, Kaen flexed his left arm, and a jolt of pain shot up to his shoulder.

"Hold still, you fool!" she snapped when she noticed him jerking in pain. "You are still recovering and will need a few more days before you can get up."

"How long have I been out?"

No reply came for a moment, and Kaen opened both eyes, looking at Sulenda and seeing the pain on her face.

"Nine days."

Her voice was pained, and it seemed to take everything she had to tell him.

Nine days? That wasn't possible. It was just a small scratch. Had it been that bad? What about the lifestone ceremony?

"Phillip and Frederick?"

A mix between a cough and a laugh, Sulenda sounded as if she might choke. She held a cup to his lips and poured more water into his mouth.

"The ceremony went fine. It was smaller than originally planned, but only a few know what happened to you."

Frustration and anger filled Kaen's mind. Who had done this and why?

Pammon, what can you tell me? Who was the man that tried to kill me?

We do not know. He had moved to the city over a year ago. He had trained with Bren and his staff for more than a year. It is obvious they learned and planned, waiting for their time. I am sorry I did not protect you as I promised.

Sorrow and hurt washed over him like a river. Pammon was blaming himself for this.

I don't think I would be alive if it weren't for you. I didn't see it until it was almost too late. The only saving grace in all this was how fast I was.

He had a lifestone, Hess told me. There is no telling who he was or how long he had trained, but they say the poison he used was from a wyvern.

A shudder like flame ants running up one's leg sent his body reeling from the thought.

A wyvern? We were considering hunting one of those . . .

We were. Perhaps we were fortunate that we had not. Neither of us really knew how deadly that poison was.

Pammon was right. Had they gone and attacked the wyvern and been poisoned while alone in the wild, both of them might have died.

Perhaps we should research a little more before we go after one.

Kaen was relieved when he felt Pammon laugh at his poor excuse for a joke.

I have never thought of you as being smart until now. It seems like staying far away from them would be the right move for a while. Hess informed me that wyvern poison is very rare. It often requires multiple people to die to kill one and harvest the sack. Any group that attempts to attack one knows that people will die.

Except for you and me, it seems. We are too foolish to think that far ahead.

Perhaps, but for now, rest. Hess will be back in a few minutes, and you should rest. It has been a long week.

Focusing on his room again, he saw Sulenda watching him.

"Talking with your bow?"

Chuckling, he grimaced as his body shook.

"I was. Perhaps we are not as smart as I once thought."

"Perhaps," she answered with a grin. "For now, take another drink and relax. You will need your strength."

"Hairy dwarf balls, Kaen," Hess muttered as he sat next to him. "The fact you are alive is a miracle. No one survives wyvern's poison."

"I owe it all to Pammon and, I'm guessing, the guild."

Herb shrugged.

"You actually owe a lot of people, but I doubt you want to pay the person you owe the most," Herb responded as he gave Kaen a weak smile. "The truth is Lord Hurem and Ava are the ones you owe. They used a wide variety of poison potions and were able to find a cure for you. I have no idea how much they spent in gold or resources to make that happen."

Closing his eyes for a moment, Kaen thought about what that might mean.

"When did they find a *cure?*"

"Two days ago. They gave it to you yesterday. I hate to tell you, but Pammon has been giving you the needed strength to stay alive while healers kept pouring everything they could into you and him. He has also eaten a herd of animals to stay well fed so that he could focus on keeping you on this side of the ground."

Kaen winced and closed his eyes. Letting out his breath slowly, he opened them again and gazed at Hess, who was watching him. The concern he had was written all over his face.

"I'm sorry this happened, and you all had to fuss over me like this. I promise it won't happen again."

Herb and Hess both started laughing at his empty promise.

"You cannot control who will strike or when. There is a world of espionage and things like this on both sides. Your problem is you are not prepared like your enemy is. The good news is they decided to try a poison like wyvern's poison. Had they used something in the drink they gave, everyone but you may have died."

His pupils dilated as he realized what that meant.

"Everyone but me? Like Hess, Sulenda, and Callie?"

Herb nodded, and a grunt could be heard from Hess as he shifted in his chair.

"Most would not expect a poison you eat to kill you. Pammon has already proven his ability to keep you alive. It had to be something deadly most would fear, including Stioks."

A knock came from the door as he lay in the bed, thinking about what Herb had just said.

"Come in," Hess roared, louder than he'd intended.

Kaen's heart thudded in his chest as the door swung open and he saw Ava. Her hair was pulled back in a simple ponytail, and her eyes were blue seas along an angry red landscape. It was apparent she had been crying.

"You're alive," she said with a soft sigh. "I am so glad you didn't die, or I would have killed you."

All of them laughed.

"If you will excuse us, Hess and I have a few things we need to attend to," Herb said as he bowed slightly. "Be nice to him, Ava. He still can't defend himself."

She glared at Herb as she slowly nodded her head.

"I cannot make any promises, but I will do my best to help him continue to heal. We both know the need for Kaen Marshell in this kingdom."

He nodded, and Kaen felt a squeeze on his leg, seeing Hess give his goodbye as they left him alone with her.

"Thank you," Kaen blurted out the second the door was closed. "Thank you for saving me."

Standing at the end of his cot, she watched him, her eyes taking all of him in.

"You are welcome, Kaen Marshell. I am happy that our family could be of service to the kingdom, and to you. Perhaps this will pay my family's debt for saving my life years ago."

"I never asked for that to be a debt!" he shouted, wincing as his shoulder ached from the exertion. "I did that because I cared about you. Because I still care about you."

"Words spoken from a death bed are sometimes things people believe others want to hear."

Taking a deep breath, he let it out slowly.

"Ava, I have never lied to you. I have always been truthful."

"You never told me you were a Dragon Rider!" she shouted. "How can you claim to be truthful when you did not share that with me?"

"I told that to no one. It was a secret that I could not share with anyone, not even Sulenda. The world could not know about him until the moment came to reveal the two of us. You know that and are just using that as an excuse to keep this chasm between us."

She clenched her fist and her face reddened. He saw the anger she still had toward him.

"You could have taken me with you," she growled. "Instead, you left me here, rejected and left to spend my days wondering if you would ever return. The last time you came, you did not show me the affection you once told me you had for me."

He began to respond but kept silent. His lifestone had started burning a little, and he knew it was not the time to speak.

"I love you, Kaen Marshell. Enough to give up my family name, enough to give up my title, and enough to follow you anywhere you go. Do you love me just as much? Say it now or know this moment will never come again!"

She stood there. Her lip quivered as her voice spiked. The hurt, core-wrenching pain she felt as she bared her soul was fully displayed for him.

As Kaen prepared to share his heart and soul, he felt something coming from through their bond—Pammon.

You cannot promise that. I sense what you are about to say, but we both know that is impossible.

But—

Would you curse her with the pain of your death if we fail? What if she is used against you? Then what?

Kaen sighed. He knew Pammon was right.

"Ava . . ."

11

Hard Choices to Make

Kaen swallowed as he lay there, unable even to move as he wanted to speak. His throat was immensely dry and he felt the pain of that simple movement.

"I would make a promise and let you bind me, but we both know that would not work. I can only tell you the truth. That I wish I could promise you right now that I would court you and marry you, but I cannot at this time."

Ava started to speak, and he held up his trembling right hand to stop her.

"Wait, please," Kaen asked as he struggled to speak. Clearing his throat, he continued.

"Pammon is right, and he knows what I would say and what I would promise. What took place last week proves how dangerous it is for anyone to be close to me right now. I barely survived. What might I have done in anger and pain if it was you who had been poisoned and died because of me?"

Her face contorted, and she grimaced. He could hear her foot tapping rapidly on the floor. Her hands were wringing themselves behind her back.

"If that were to happen, I would try to make Pammon fly me to Luthaelia, and I would rush head-first into a battle against Stioks. We both know I am not ready for that."

Her lip quivered as a few tears started falling down her cheeks.

"You would deny us both what we feel for each other because of what might happen?" she asked, her voice gruff. "I could die choking on food or a hundred other things. You expect me to accept some foolish notion that you must put duty before your love for me?!"

Closing his eyes, Kaen broke her gaze, unable to withstand the piercing effect of his heart.

"I do love you," he whispered. "More than I have ever admitted to myself or you. Those letters you wrote are still in my pack, and I have often worn them out reading them. The touch of your lips against mine is something I can recall when I close my eyes and think about you. Leaving you and everyone else was not easy, but I had to. I had to learn how to be what I am."

Opening his eyes, he felt the wetness on his cheeks. Even with a dry throat, his next words were steady and true.

"I would promise you that if you wait for me, once this threat is over, I will marry you without delay. I will not ask you to wait, though, as I may not return from this threat, and it pains me more to know you might waste your life waiting for me. Look at what you and your father have accomplished in the last two years! The progression of—"

She cut him off as she moved to the right side of the bed and grabbed his hand on top of the covers.

"I will wait," she whispered. "You do not have to promise me, but I will promise you I will wait."

Kaen stared at her, watching her as she lifted his hand to her lips and kissed the back of his fingers.

"Why? Look at me now. You see what I will face! Why would you wait for me?"

She opened his hand and placed it on her chest where her lifestone was.

"Can you feel it?"

Flustered, as he realized his hand was on her chest, Kaen realized what she'd said.

"Your lifestone?" he whispered.

Nodding, she bit her lip.

"The first time I met you, it acted in a way it never had before. It scared me then. Now, as I sit here with your hand over it, I feel it pulsing in my chest. No one else has ever caused it to do this before."

Her voice was trembling, and Kaen felt the way her hands quivered as they held his.

"I was never one to believe in *soulmates,* but here I find myself questioning that. Does yours do the same thing when I am around?"

Hope and fear were written all over her face. She had bared her soul, and Pammon was a surge of emotions in the background.

Taking a slightly labored breath, he nodded and squeezed her hand.

"That night we first danced, my lifestone did something similar. Every day, my thoughts drifted to you. I will promise you that if you wait for this threat to pass, that if you will still have whatever I am when I get done, it will be yours."

Pausing momentarily, he freed his hand from hers and touched his temple.

"Yours and Pammon's. I cannot promise he and I won't share something you can never have. Not because I don't want to share it with you, but because it's different. He is a part of me. A part of my soul. When he hurts, I hurt. I can only imagine how he has been since I was poisoned."

Laughing suddenly, Ava bobbed her head fervently.

"He never left the side of the building. We had to bring food to him and," she paused as the face she made caused Kaen to laugh, ignoring the pain that still lanced through his shoulder, "the smell of what he did in the courtyard."

"Yes . . . that smell is something special."

Taking her hand in his, they both sat there smiling in silence for a few moments.

"Will you forgive me for not taking you with me to Roccnari? I doubt you would have enjoyed it with the nonstop training."

"Oh, I know a few things about that," she replied as she rolled her eyes. "Selmah has been teaching me a lot since that day. She is not as strong as she once was, but that is not my place to speak about."

Closing his eyes, Kaen let out a sigh.

"Do you mind just sitting here for a few? I am worn out and want to sleep, if I can, and I know it would come faster if you were here."

She moved to the floor and laid her head on his arm as she leaned against the cot.

"Sleep, Kaen. I'll be right here."

Closing his eyes, he felt peace and relief. Something he had not felt in a long time.

I'm sorry, Pammon. I made a promise, but it will be a while before I can make good on it.

I am aware, he replied with a distinct sense of acceptance. **I know you will yearn for her. Tharnok shared with me a story of Elies and a woman he loved. It pains me to know you will one day experience what he did.**

Loss . . . He had mentioned it to me also, cautioning me about it, but also told me that living without love isn't really living. Just like I cannot imagine life without you.

Sleep, you are tired. It has been a long week. I will cut the strength as you sleep and see how you do.

Nodding to no one, Kaen drifted to sleep, praying that nightmares would not come again.

When he woke up the next morning, Kaen found a few notifications waiting for him.

[Poison Resist Skill Acquired]

[Poison Resist Skill Increased x16]

He rotated his left shoulder a little as he opened his eyes, and other than a little soreness, it felt amazing.

There, in a soft chair on the other side of the room, was Ava, fast asleep.

He started to sit up in the cot, and the wooden frame creaked as he moved, causing her eyes to open.

"Kaen! You shouldn't be moving!" she exclaimed as she bolted out of the chair and approached him.

"I'm fine. Really," he answered as he waved her off with his hand. "Look, my arm moves fine, and other than being sore, I can move it without any issues."

She stood there with her eyebrow cocked and crossed her arms over her chest.

"You sure you are fine? No lasting issues?"

As he started to rise up from the bed, he realized that besides not having a shirt on, he also had nothing on underneath the covers.

"Uh . . ." he muttered, his face red as he grabbed the blanket over him and tucked it around his waist. "It appears I am missing some clothing."

Laughing, Ava's face turned a shade of crimson as well, and she nodded while pointing to a cabinet on the other side of the room.

"They put all your stuff in there. I'll go and let everyone know you are ok while you get a few things on. Would you like some water to wash with, or should I contact the guild nurse to help with that again?"

Kaen tried to resist the embarrassment he felt, knowing someone had been washing him for over a week.

"I should be good," he groaned, his voice betraying his confidence. "Some water and towels would be appreciated."

She nodded and moved to his side, taking his head in her hand and kissing him on the forehead.

"Good because you and this room stink!" she teased. "I'll return in a while, but I expect you to be overwhelmed with visitors in the coming hours."

As she began to walk away, Kaen reached out and grabbed her arm.

"Ava," he said as she turned, looking at him as he smiled at her. "I meant what I said. I'll keep fighting for everyone here so I can return to you."

Swallowing, she nodded and sniffed.

"I'll hold you to that, Kaen Marshell," she squeaked as she patted his hand.

"Now relax and I'll get some water sent in. No point changing and then having to undress again just to clean up."

Nodding, he let her go and watched as she left.

"Gosh, she makes my brain mush . . ." he muttered aloud.

Pammon, what are you doing?

Besides wondering why your heart flutters like a bird in the forest, I am relaxing in this courtyard. You feel better this morning, I can tell.

I am, and I owe it all to you. Thank you.

Pammon was overwhelmed by the flood of gratitude and love that came through their bond.

I . . . I have never felt such a strong reaction from you before. You owe me nothing. I know you would do the same for me.

A weird emotion hit Kaen, and it seemed different yet familiar.

What are you trying to convey? I can feel you, but it's different than usual.

It is what I feel from you. Dragons don't think like you do. Love is a weird concept for us. Not that we do not love our child or our mate, but it is a different kind of emotion for us. What we have goes beyond that simple word. I would kill for you, and I would die for you. Both without hesitation if it meant you would live. I would scorch kingdoms to bring about revenge.

Pammon paused, and Kaen felt the words he was about to say.

Tharnok . . .

Havannath has yet to learn what is coming for him if Elies cannot convince him to let it go. Stioks will be the least of their worries. He will ravage the elven kingdom like they have not seen in millenniums.

And if that happens, what are we supposed to do?

Kaen knew the answer even before he asked it. He didn't like it at all.

We would have to stop him. Just like someone would have to stop me if I was overcome with that same rage.

Lost in his thoughts and the conversation, Kaen heard the knock on the door. "Come in."

An older man and woman came in, carrying a large copper tub. Behind them were others, all with pitchers of steaming water.

"Guild Master Herb said you might need a bath before you would feel like meeting with others," the older woman said as they set the tub down.

"That would be appreciated!" Kaen exclaimed. "Tell him thank you! If it is possible, I find myself wanting food."

The older man chuckled and nodded.

"We have some food prepared, but bathe first. Welcome back to the land of the living, Dragon Rider Kaen."

They moved back, letting the servants come in, pouring buckets of warm water into the tub, and letting the steam rise up into the room.

"When you are ready, we will be outside the hall to take you to those waiting to see you."

Laughing, Kaen nodded his head.

"It may be a few," he snorted as his eyes ate in the steam rising from the water.

"Take your time," the woman replied.

Once the door shut, Kaen leaped from the bed and moved quickly to the tub. Putting a hand in the water, he let out a slight moan.

"I need to get me one of these," he muttered as he swung a leg over the edge and climbed in.

12

The Ones Responsible

It was harder than Kaen had imagined as he tried slowly eating the porridge and sipping the bone broth they brought him. Over and over, they reminded him to slow down, but he had not realized how hungry he was until the smell of the food hit his nostrils.

"I'm starving!" he exclaimed as he finished the porridge and glanced around the table.

"And you will throw it all up if you gorge yourself," Herb informed him, watching him fidget and scrape his bowl with a spoon for every last speck of food. "Give it thirty minutes, and we can give you more, but you must wait. Your body will recover fast, but trust the process."

Kaen saw Hess was nodding as he sat in his chair, his arms folded across his chest. It was weird how it looked, seeing him with one arm holding a stump at his elbow. He could see that Hess's left arm had gotten smaller. His right arm looked just as strong as always, but the difference was now very noticeable.

"Herb is right, son. Just relax. We aren't going anywhere; you will have plenty of time to eat. If you overdo it, that day you recovered from *goblin's piss* will seem like a walk through a field."

Groaning, Kaen set the bowl down and pushed it away.

He saw Herb glancing at the both of them.

"That's a story for another day," Hess declared with a snort. "Let's talk about the specifics we need to deal with now."

Herb produced a stack of papers from nowhere as Hess spoke and slid a few toward each of them.

"If you look at the top sheet, you will see what I have learned from the one who attempted to assassinate you," he said as he looked at the sheet. "Unfortunately, you broke his neck, which prevented us from interrogating him, but based on what we found in the apartment he rented, there was no way we would have gotten anything from him. Two of our best rogues scoured that room and found a few traps. Each missed a trap, but the other managed to discover it before it was set off. It seems he was prepared for this attack and did not expect to return."

As Kaen scanned the sheet, he was amazed to hear there were a few needle traps and an igniting trap inside that man's apartment. Neither would spread among other buildings due to the bricks, yet it looked like they would have killed others.

"Where was he from?"

"There is no record, but we can make assumptions," Hess stated before Herb cut him off.

"We know what assume spells . . ."

"Yes, we do," Hess grunted as his voice became gruff. "However, he had a lifestone and was very skilled in the art of deception. He lived a lie for a year as he planned and waited. Everything he did was meticulous, leaving no room for anyone to notice anything was off."

Both men watched Kaen as he read the few details they had collected. It was a sheet with nothing to go off of. A ghost of a man that had only one purpose, it seemed, to kill him.

"Bren says in this report that the man had mentioned he was from Pensworth, trying to escape the turmoil there and was hoping to get good enough to become an adventurer here."

"Kaen," Herb said as he tapped the table with his fingers. "The man pretended to be just good enough to use Bren's place and slowly increase his ability so as not to raise suspicion. This means he knew the art of combat well enough to deceive even someone of Bren's skill level."

Leaning over, Herb pulled a pouch from the floor next to him and opened it up. There was a cloth wrapping that he set on the table, and he slowly unrolled it. Inside was the dagger.

Two finger holes were at the base below the blade. The blade was simple—a punch blade. Two sharp sides with a small three-inch blade. Perfect for close work.

"This thing is sharper than most blades one will ever find used by an adventurer. It is a testament to your stats that you managed to actually stop him from piercing your chest," Herb declared as he slid the dagger toward Kaen. "It is perfectly balanced and the only details we have about this individual is that he was part of a very secluded assassin guild. They almost never fail. The fact that they did will give them some pause."

His fingers tugged on the two holes and slid the blade over to him. Lifting it up to his face, he saw that the blade's edge almost seemed to disappear and yet was still there.

"This is an amazing edge. Worthless in combat but perfect for what you just told me. How do they get it this sharp?"

"That is a guild secret," Hess butted in as he pointed at the dagger. "Hold it out, blade up, and drop the paper on it."

Scrunching his eyebrows, Kaen smirked and shook his head. Picking up the paper, he did as Hess instructed, and his hand almost trembled as the paper cut cleanly without any force but its own weight pulling it down.

"Wow . . ."

Herb's head was bobbing, and Hess was biting his lip.

"I still don't know how you survived, even with Pammon's help. That poison could take down a dragon his size if a wyvern's tail pierced him."

"We both have our ideas on how it happened, but that means you are far beyond what we had hoped," Herb stated as he pointed to the second paper. "This is a list of the antidotes given to you and the healing you received. On the record, there are less than a handful of documented cases of someone surviving wyvern poison. That goes back for a long time, and all of those were hunts aimed at them with the proper potions and ointments to help treat them. The ones who survived were not the same after that encounter."

Tsking his teeth with his tongue, Kaen read the list, amazed that they had invested so many different potions on him.

"When did they figure it out? What it was?"

"That was Lord Hurem's doing. He is a master of poisons and potions. They personally took note of what you were suffering from, and it took some time to prepare what you needed. In the meantime, they made sure to help you as much as they could."

"Herb won't ask, but I will," Hess cut off his counterpart. "You have to have a forty or higher in constitution to survive something like this and still come back looking the way you do now. The only thing you have lost is your body's fat. Even with Pammon doing whatever he did, you should have wasted away, and yet, that isn't the case. You are probably stronger because of all this."

Chuckling, Kaen flashed his boyish grin and shrugged.

"What you're asking me is what had I planned on telling you later, but I figure it is better to get it over with. I have gained the poison resist skill, which is now a sixteen."

Both men let out a whistle, and each glanced at the other, their eyes wide and eyebrows almost touching the tops of their heads.

"Poison resist skill," Hess muttered. "Impossible."

"He has no idea, Hess. None at all . . ."

"What is it I don't know?" Kaen asked, confused at how both men were reacting to this news.

"Kaen," Herb started to say as he leaned across the table. "Men who deal in the art of assassination will slowly poison themselves with weak poisons, trying to gain that skill. There is no guarantee it will work; some die before they ever do. Getting it above a ten is unheard of for most, except the sect leaders. It isn't like most normal skills. Just getting the skill is a major hurdle. How to best compare it . . ."

"It's like the dragon riding skill," Kaen interrupted him. "Even though Hess has flown with Pammon before, he doesn't have it. I do."

Snickering, Hess smiled as he nodded his head.

"That is a good example," admitted Herb. "Some things may never come for someone, no matter how many times they try. For you, it seems Fiola was right."

A scowl flashed across Hess's face before he realized it and relaxed.

"My family genealogy . . ."

"Exactly. Everything you seem to experience comes faster and stronger compared to the rest. Added with a dragon . . ." Herb trailed off.

"So what is our next step?"

"Nothing. There is nothing you or Hess or anyone else can do right now. You will go and make yourself known in a few days. You will show yourself to the people in the city, and word will travel that you are alive and well. That will send a message far and wide to those who intended to harm you that you are tougher than they expected."

Herb's chest shook as he suddenly laughed, surprising the both of them.

"Imagine, Kaen, what this will do to the resolve of someone thinking just because you are young and your dragon is only a few years old. You were attacked by the best with the strongest weapon they could think of, and you came out unscathed. It will make them reconsider their movements against you. They know eventually it will lead you to move against them, and I doubt anyone wants that after this failed so horribly."

Hess began to chuckle and nodded in agreement.

Someone knocked on the door, and when it opened, Kaen smelled the aroma of more soup.

"Food! Finally!"

Both men laughed as the servant brought in the porridge and broth, setting it before Kaen as he attacked it like a wild animal.

Sitting on Pammon in the courtyard, the sun felt warm and amazing on his skin.

Pammon was anxiously moving as Kaen strapped the harness around him.

Are you sure you are ready for this? We don't have to do this today.

I'm fine, and it needs to be done. We must send a clear message that we are both fine and that their attack against us failed. I have no doubt there is probably another person or two in this kingdom waiting for news of how I am doing. Today is the first day we send fear to those who thought we would be easy prey.

Pammon began to thrum, the courtyard echoing as it reverberated off the walls.

Spoken like a true Dragon Rider. You are making me proud to be your dragon. Many might rest and relax, saying they were not ready, but a true rider does not hide behind excuses.

Pride washed over Kaen, strengthening his resolve and belief that this was the right decision.

Well, let's get it over with. I'm ready to feel the wind in my face and fly with you again.

A trill escaped Pammon as Kaen clipped himself in.

Let's go!

Kaen thumped Pammon on the neck as he leaped into the air, sending plumes of dust around the courtyard.

A cheer broke out from one of the training grounds they flew over as Kaen waved at the adventurers training below.

Elies was right, you know. Strength is not just measured by how strong you are. It is also measured by how you encourage others around you.

13

Making the Rounds

Kaen spent the next two days interacting with people around town and making up for his absence at the ceremony for Phillip and Frederick.

"Keep that arm up and bend those knees more," Kaen shouted as he demonstrated a spear thrust again for Phillip. "Remember, distance and speed are your friends!"

Phillip nodded and assumed the stance as best as he could with the training spear. He thrust at the target, picking different angles and dancing around the straw-filled dummy. He rolled as he had been taught and came up in the guard position, giving multiple thrusts to ward off invisible attackers.

"Shield up! Don't let it drop like that!" Kaen called out as he tossed bean bags with accuracy that always pelted Phillip in the head and the feet. "Block! Move and block!"

The eleven-year-old obeyed and never flinched, absorbing the hits and adjusting, soon blocking the onslaught that rained down upon him as he advanced on his target.

Two quick lunge steps had him in position, and he pierced the ring on the target.

"Nice!" Kaen declared as he moved forward, clapping his hands. "You have improved much more than I would have imagined."

Phillip beamed at the praise and stood there, spear up, holding the shield and breathing hard from the exertion.

"Thank you, Sir Kaen! I managed to earn a point in my spear skill!"

His voice was cracking from the hormones flooding his body and the knowledge of having gained a point in a training session with his idol.

"That's good," Kaen replied as he walked over and roughed up the boy's wet and matted hair. As he saw Pammon approach, he continued, "It looks like our time is done. I hope you can still forgive me for missing your ceremony."

"We understood. All of us," Phillip said, motioning to the rest of the training field. Students who weren't actively training were watching him and Kaen practice or Pammon flying with Frederick. "Knowing you are ok means more than a ceremony."

Snorting, Kaen bobbed his head as he smiled at the young boy. He had matured so much in the last two years. Muscles were showing from his hard work and the food he was eating. There was no doubt both boys had earned their lifestones.

"Well, keep being the example I know you can be. These other students might be jealous of what I have given you, but know that means I expect you two to lead. Don't flaunt the gifts, but instead show them the results of hard work. Soon enough, I know we will need more students like you, ready to carry the mantle of adventurers."

Grinning, Phillip stood at attention. Transferring the spear to his shield hand, he put his fist over his chest and gave a slight bow.

"It is my honor to protect our kingdom and serve the Dragon Rider."

Wincing, Kaen returned the salute and sent Phillip to join his friend, who was just getting off of Pammon.

Those boys seemed to enjoy themselves. Thank you for this.

A thrum echoed from where Pammon and the two boys were, and they laughed, scratching Pammon's head as they had many times. Kaen watched as they both gave a bow and grabbed their gear, running to join the other students, waiting to hear what it was like.

They remind me of you. Young and prone to acting like an eggling, yet committed.

What are you talking about? Kaen asked as he walked toward Pammon, who was staring at him. *I was never that young when we met.*

Age is not a requirement to act like an eggling. We both know that.

Laughing out loud, Kaen glanced around the area, ensuring no one was looking before he lifted a hand and gave Pammon the finger.

Careful, someone might bite that off one day . . .

Oh, making threats, are we? Perhaps I'll just keep from scratching those spots at the top of your head for a while.

Pammon snorted at him, sending small flecks of snot in his direction, which Kaen easily dodged.

Someday, I will find a comeback for that, but for now, we have another stop to make.

Grunting, Kaen stopped and glanced at the courtyard filled with all the kids. Over fifty students were training, practicing movements, doing exercises, and learning the art of combat. It was scary and yet impressive. How many really understood what they had signed up for? A chance to be an adventurer sounded so cool and special as a child, but knowing what it was really like was the hard part.

Come on, let's plan for what we know is coming next.

"Kaen! It has been far too long!" exclaimed Lord Hurem as he strode toward Pammon and Kaen. They had landed in a part of the family *garden*.

It was actually a small area of manicured grass and rare flowers that was nothing like a garden. No fruits or vegetables grew here. Just another reminder that the life they lived was very different from the average person in Ebonmount.

"Lord Hurem," Kaen replied as he gave a slight bow, "I owe a lot for the assistance you gave while I was sick. Guild Master Herb told me you requested to see me sooner rather than later."

"Yes, yes! Now come close and shake my hand, and I promise not to try and bind you for that comment."

Both of them laughed, knowing that even if he tried, it would not succeed.

As they shook hands, Kaen spotted Lady Hurem coming across the grass toward them, carrying a few things on a tray. Behind her was Ava, wearing a yellow dress that hugged her in all the right ways. Her hair reflected light in the afternoon sun, and her eyes held him even from this distance. She smiled at him and he smiled back, missing whatever Lord Hurem had just said.

"Lady Hurem, you look just as lovely as I recall from last time."

She shook her head, her eyelids fluttering at his compliment. A slight smile appeared on her face as she set the tray down on the table near where he and her husband were standing.

"I do not think I have properly thanked you for saving our daughter's life all that time ago. I would say anything within my power is yours, yet I know that might not mean much to one like you."

Lord Hurem flinched as his wife spoke those words, barely noticeable, except Kaen was right next to him.

"I would ask nothing in return, Lady Hurem. I am just glad I was able to make it in time. Losing her would have hurt all of us. Besides, any debt one might have thought I could claim was easily paid for by your husband and Ava's help curing me."

Her face was almost a perfect image of calmness and dignity if it was not for that slight movement of her lip that Kaen recognized as her biting it ever so gently.

"Well, my offer still stands if the need arises. I will support you in anything you might request."

A slight cough from her husband brought the attention back to him.

"Kaen, I summoned you here because I want to ask you and Pammon for something. While Ava and I scoured the books these last few years, I found a few old notes for potions we can make that will assist you. They require some of your blood and his, and I wanted to ask if you would be willing to give some to us."

Glancing down at the tray, Kaen saw two daggers, one with a long, thin blade and the other appeared to have a hollow blade in a round shape. The cup and pitcher he first noticed were actually vessels to hold his and Pammon's blood if they were willing.

"Can I ask what the potions would be?"

Grinning, he nodded and motioned to Ava, who stepped forward smiling.

"We would attempt to make a few potions that would cure you of most ailments. Poison or other things that might affect you. It would require your blood and Pammon's and will only work for you," Ava informed him as she picked up the hollow blade. "We would need a little more than required because we would have to practice a few times. Most of the necessary ingredients are on hand; if you are willing, we will have the others within a week. The other option would be one that should hopefully heal Pammon, similar to the ones Hess had given you. There are not many of those left, and the fact that he had a stash surprised my father and a few other merchants."

Kaen heard a chuckle from Lord Hurem, bobbing his head and smirking.

"Those potions are not as common as they once were. Materials are not as available anymore, and most adventurers have forsaken gathering them. That has changed over the last year as Guild Master Herb and our family have entered an agreement to give a portion of the potions back to the guild to help with the necessary materials."

What do you think? Willing to bleed a little?

I'm not afraid to bleed if you are worried about me. I am interested, though, in what they get out of this. Would they really do this for you and me out of the kindness of their own hearts, or is this a payment for saving Ava?

"Pammon was wondering why to do this for us at no charge?"

"An excellent question," Lord Hurem declared as he turned and gave a slight bow to Pammon. "Research is the main reason, but also knowing we can help prevent another problem like last week. No one has had the chance to work with dragon blood in hundreds of years. Elies and Tharnok did not give any, and we never pressured after the first request was turned down two generations ago."

Lord Hurem was pacing a little, waving his hands in the air, and his voice had gotten higher.

"Imagine what a single drop of dragon blood could do! We could outfit the guild and the adventurers with potions that heal better, find cures for different diseases, and more!"

So all the blood they would be taking would not be just for us?

"Pammon wants to know how much of the blood would be for potions for us and potions for you and others."

Clasping his hands behind his back, he motioned to Ava.

"Our . . . my hope is that most of what we acquire would not need to be used for potions for the two of you. Pammon's would be harder to gather down the road. A single drawing now could possibly serve for hundreds of potions if we figure out what they did so long ago," she stated as her voice matched the pitch of her father's.

"We would work on what we have promised you two first, and once successful, take the knowledge we have gained and apply it to the other potions we would like to make for the kingdom."

After she stopped talking, Kaen turned and gazed at Pammon.

What do you think? Are you willing to let them take your blood for what they have offered?

A slight huff of air came from Pammon's snout as he gazed at the Hurem family. He saw them all staring back at them, faces attempting to remain calm. He could see their slight trembling as they waited to hear what he might say.

Very well. I will bleed this time because they were honest and had something to offer for us. If they prove themselves trustworthy, I may be inclined to bleed again.

Letting the breath he had been holding out slowly, Kaen smiled.

Thank you for not making me ask you to do it.

I knew you would have, and you know I would have given in for you. Why not save the trouble and sound like I am a gentle dragon and not one who will do terrible things to protect you? Besides, I owe Ava a little blood, at least. I have easily eaten a hundred cows by now.

Unable to control himself, Kaen laughed out loud, gathering the attention of the other three.

"He says you may take his blood. He will trust you and what you say and also feels he may owe a little blood to Ava for all the cows she has given him."

The three of them all clapped their hands and laughed.

Pammon began to thrum as he joined in.

The thrumming stopped when Ave moved toward him with the hollow dagger.

"I'll try to make this hurt as little as possible," she said, her voice squeaking a little.

14

A Request of Pammon

Looking at his hand where they had cut it, it amazed Kaen how fast it had stopped bleeding. Even before Ava had applied the salve, it had started closing on its own.

Her parents had watched, shaking their heads and murmuring to themselves.

You know, if I had known they would look at me that way, I might have said no.

Pammon thrummed as he flew toward the guild hall. He had laughed until Ava put that dagger in the gum of his mouth. He still had not admitted how much it had hurt.

At least she said they would not need any more for a while. I would hate to see you cry.

Slapping that scale he always abused, Kaen let out a chuckle as the wind whipped through his hair.

Well, I for one, am excited to see what they may be able to do. Knowing they could create a potion that would heal you was worth it.

Walking around Herb's office, Kaen noticed the subtle difference since Herb had taken over. More paintings and darker wood furniture now furnished his office. A larger desk with more space to hold all the stacked paper dwarfed him when he sat behind it. Three brown couches made of some type of hide sat in a *U* shape with a small table in the middle.

"I am almost done if you will stop pacing," Herb stated as he finished signing a few more pages. "You can help yourself to any of the drinks on the table over there. Just stay away from the ones with the orange lids. I would hate to have you carried out of here."

Ignoring the smile Herb was wearing, Kaen walked to a picture hanging on the wall. It looked just like Fiola except somehow more . . . regal. Herb had insisted on having it in his office. A reminder, he said, of sacrifice and commitment to the job. Unlike Hess, who still sometimes had issues with her and what had transpired, Kaen understood what she had done.

The scraping of the chair got his attention, and Kaen saw Herb stand up and stretch his back.

"I never appreciated all she endured for this job. The long hours spent bent over a desk, forms, and things to sign. So much paperwork."

Kaen laughed as Herb motioned to the stacks all over his desk.

"Every day I come in, more have appeared. I didn't know we had this much paper in our little kingdom."

Herb walked to Kaen's side and stopped to stare at the photograph of Fiola.

"It looks just like her. I think she would appreciate the small gesture."

Nodding his head, Herb sighed as he shrugged his shoulders.

"Only the spirits know where she is now. I pray that I do justice for the office she left me," he declared as he motioned to the couch. "Sit for a moment. I need to ask a favor as Guild Master to Dragon Rider."

Cocking his eyebrow, Kaen followed Herb as he sat down.

"I'm going to ask something, and you can tell me no. Do not think you owe me. I will gladly reimburse you or find some compensation."

"Is this the honey you offer before you tell me there is a frog waiting to snatch me when I come close?"

"That is a great trap to remove pests. The frog is patient," he replied with a chuckle. "No, I want to ask if you will fly two adventurers over the mountains to the south and scout the swamps and the land to the east. Rumors from a few scouts mention that some orcs and goblins have been moving there lately. I need to find out if that is true."

"Moving since I got here a few weeks ago? We saw nothing when we flew around the edge of the swamp."

Leaning back on the couch, Herb nodded as he crossed his arms.

"I have some solid intel that tells me they are moving from somewhere in Luthaelia back to their homeland. If this is correct, it means we have found where they are currently."

Studying Herb's face and how he sat there, Kaen realized there was something he had not shared yet.

"What is the part of this request you have not told me about yet?"

Chuckling, Herb smirked as he leaned forward, resting an arm on his knee.

"I want you to take Selmah and Ava. They would be your greatest allies in this adventure, and Selmah has been on that side of the mountain before. She knows exactly what to look for and where."

Kaen felt his face get a little red. Riding for days with Ava sounded great, but having Selmah there almost felt like they were being parented. If Selmah was coming, why was Ava needed?

"What is wrong with Selmah? Why send Ava?"

Sucking air in through his teeth, Herb grimaced as he massaged his eyes with a hand.

"Only a handful of people know of the damage she experienced the day you saved her life. She was prepared to die and had burnt a large portion of the mana channels that run through her body. Even with the potion you gave her that kept her alive, she burnt out most of her magical ability. Now, she is weaker than a silver token adventurer when it comes to mana. Her knowledge is her greatest asset, and she is training Ava to learn everything she can."

He paused as he pulled a mithril token from his pocket.

"She was due to earn this, but now I cannot give it to her. Doing so would be a lie; I know she would not accept it. The guild would also push back on it. She doesn't want to retire and is not ready to sit in a hall, teaching the next generation."

Kaen understood that. He's had talks with Bren discussing how some adventurers were able to make the change from the field to the hall, but many could not. That failure often resulted in their death and, sadly, sometimes others' deaths as well.

"I will take them with me if Pammon is willing."

Herb nodded and closed his eyes, obviously waiting for Kaen to tell him the news sooner rather than later.

Herb wants to know if you would be willing to take Selmah, Ava, and me to the swamp over the mountains for a scouting mission. He can't offer it as a quest but would compensate us for doing so if we are willing. I told him I would ask you since this all falls upon your back.

Literally, Pammon said with a hint of sarcasm. **Do you feel it is something we need to pursue? Does he know we found nothing a few weeks ago?**

He does. Apparently, some intel came in recently that shows how they might be moving back to the swamp from Luthaelia. It would take us a day to fly there and maybe one more to scout before we fly back. You can even tell me what you would want to ask for payment for the services.

I am willing, and you already know what I would want in return.

Kaen did and he smiled to himself.

"Pammon is willing to do the heavy lifting for payment in different animals to eat," Kaen informed Herb, who had opened his eyes when he chuckled. "The exact amount and variety has yet to be determined, but I am sure he will give me a list when we return."

Smiling, Herb nodded his head and began to stand up.

"If I said I anticipated such a request and have already put in an order for a few exotic beasts from Tanulivar, I might sound presumptuous that I expected you two would be willing."

Rising from the couch, Kaen nodded and extended his hand to Herb.

"When do you want us to leave?"

"Tomorrow if you can. It isn't a lot of time, but I will have everything you need ready in the morning, and my hope is none of you will need to engage any creatures on this trip."

Studying Herb's stance and how relaxed he appeared, Kaen could tell this was just a scouting mission. Perhaps an easy scouting trip with Ava would be just what they needed to work out some of their recent problems.

"Tomorrow it is then. Anything else?"

Herb shook his head and Kaen turned to leave.

"I'll try to keep Pammon from breaking the guild's bank with his lunch order," he joked as he walked toward the door. "I have no idea how he keeps eating everything he does."

He heard laughter coming from Herb's office as the door shut. Both of them were well aware of how much livestock Pammon was consuming.

"Tomorrow," Hess muttered as he sat in the booth with Kaen. "Seems a bit quick for a scouting trip, but perhaps I'm just the overprotective parent."

Setting his cup down, Kaen nodded as he glanced around the room. It had taken a good ten minutes to make his way through the crowd gathered inside. He had been on edge but tried to hide it. He saw possible threats everywhere he looked, and it bothered him that he was so jumpy. He had almost hurt someone who came at him from behind as he spun, seeing danger that wasn't there.

"You look a little high-strung. Settle down and relax. The guards out front are making sure everyone who comes in is known, and right now, I doubt anyone would attempt the same thing again."

Kaen nodded, willing his leg to stop bouncing and keeping himself from scanning the room for the hundredth time.

"It's hard. I didn't think it would be this hard," he admitted with a grunt. "The moment I started walking down the street from Bren's place, I felt my heart take off. Pammon almost didn't let me leave when he realized how I felt. When everyone came up, it took more strength to smile and nod without keeping them an arm's length away."

"I figured that is why you have the sword."

Glancing at the sword resting on the table, Kaen bobbed his head and let out a sigh.

"Tell me this is normal."

Kaen's voice was a higher pitch than usual and it spoke volumes.

"Son, let me be honest. I struggled when I got back. Sure, I put on a smile and pretended to be ok, but Sulenda will tell you I cried many nights," he stated as he held up his left arm. "While I am grateful to be alive, I know I am not the man I once was. My days of adventuring are over. If Herb would let me resign, I would, but we both know I need access to the guild, and staying on his injured list allows me access without having to deal with more paperwork.

"Training the kids at your academy has been a blessing. It lets me use the skills I have and teach those who are willing to learn. I don't feel worthless."

Pausing a second, Hess lowered his eyes, and a shudder ran through him.

"I don't feel like less of a man," he whispered. "It is hard seeing my left arm shrink and become weak. There are days I would consider trying to find healing, far worse than what Cale experienced."

Shuddering, Kaen nodded. He had inquired about that when he was in Roccnari, and the elf healers there had discussed how difficult and painful it would be. All with no guarantee it would work and might require the loss of more of his arm.

"Forget all this," Hess stated as he reached into his vest pocket and pulled out a ring. "This is yours. Consider it payment for many things, but mostly for the horns Pammon gave me."

As he slid it across the table, Kaen saw the bone ring with etching and marks on the outside of it.

"This is from those horns? What does it do?"

Smirking, Hess gave him a wink as he pulled his hand back from it.

"At the time, I was an idiot and traded more than I should have to get it done sooner than later. After our talk the other day with Herb, I realize now that it won't be something you will use. You have become far stronger than I had ever hoped and imagined, and we both know you aren't done yet."

With a slight sigh, he motioned to the ring Kaen now held in his hand. He lowered his voice as he leaned across the table.

"It will give a bonus point to melee weapons and shields. However, with where you stand now stat wise, I think you would be better focusing on getting your numbers to that sixty range I believe you are closing in on."

"Wow," was all Kaen could say as he held the ring in his hand. He knew such a ring would have cost a fortune and taken considerable time to make. What had Hess traded to have this done?

"Perhaps you can use it as a prize for your students. That ring would be a blessing to any of them at the academy," Hess stated as he leaned back in the booth. "Regardless, it is yours."

"Thank you. I'll make sure it is put to good use," he replied, slipping it into a pouch on his hip. Picking up his cup, he drained the last of his milk and began to slide out from his seat.

"I need to finish a few more things tonight before I prepare for tomorrow. Give Callie love from me and Pammon?"

Snickering, Hess nodded and exited the booth as well. They embraced and patted each other on the back three times before breaking the hug.

"Be safe, son."

"I will, Dad."

15

Living like a Dragon Rider

These two seemed to have more stuff than you normally bring on a three-day trip. Is this normal for women?

Trying his best not to laugh, Kaen hid his face as he put yet another pack from Selmah and Ava into the large saddlebags he had secured on Pammon.

Yes, usually, women do require a few more items, but not all. Don't forget about all the arrows I need to carry when we plan on fighting a lot.

Grumbling, Pammon snorted as he shook his head and stayed as close to the ground as possible. He knew the weight of all of them would not be an issue, but climbing on and getting them secured would be the tricky part.

"Just two more bags," Selmah called out as she handed one of them to Kaen. "After that, we will be ready to go!"

He saw the look of excitement on her face. She had hesitated to touch Pammon when she was told she could, and her hand had shaken more than he expected from someone of her rank. With that obstacle removed, her behavior now reminded him of the first time Hess got a chance to ride Pammon.

"Remember, both of you are connected to each other and me. There should be no risk of falling, even if we end upside down, which Pammon will resist the urge to do," Kaen stated as he patted Pammon's neck, and a low thrum came from under them. "Relax, try to remember to breathe, and if you need something, put your head close the person's ear and speak loudly. The wind will carry it away. Any questions?"

He saw both of their faces, and their eyes were wide, grinning from ear to ear. They shook their heads and gave the thumbs-up signal he had made sure they learned.

Turning around, he smiled and took a deep breath. He felt Ava's arms wrapped around him. Both women wore thick cloaks and long pants with some gloves. The cold never bothered him, but he knew from experience that others would feel it as they got higher in the sky.

OK, it's all you. Try to remember to be nice.

I'm always nice. Pammon took one quick stride and leaped into the air, bringing out a small shriek from one of the two women behind Kaen.

Pammon thrummed as he flapped his wings, easily gaining height and clearing the walls within the training area of the guild hall. The sun was barely over the eastern mountains, and Kaen wanted to be off before everyone and their mother came out to watch and gawk as they left.

How far are we going before we will stop?

I'll let you know when they let me know. A break for all of us won't be a bad thing. You shouldn't be hungry for a while, either. Right?

Not till tonight. The pigs they provided were not bad. They were not as tasty as the wild ones, but these had a lot more fat on them. I will say they tasted a little better after I cooked a few.

Groaning, Kaen turned his head back and saw the two women, eyes as wide as apples as they looked at the city below. They were lost in the magic of flying.

Well, choose the path you want. I'm going to sit here and ignore the stuff I feel coming from you.

The flow of frustration and resentment lessened, but Kaen knew it was still there. Having Ava with them meant competition for Kaen's time. Pammon was worried about him making stupid choices because of her. It was like Pammon had forgotten how many stupid decisions Kaen made that didn't require Ava to muddle his mind.

Every two hours or so, they had stopped to allow each of them a chance to stretch their legs, use the restroom, and recover from being in the cold air. Both women had red faces, and Kaen had fetched a cloth and tied it over their faces, helping to cut down on the wind that had left its mark.

As they neared the base of the mountains, memories of the fight from two years ago sprung up, and Kaen glanced around, noticing that none of the caves they had sealed were in this spot.

Did you pick this path purposely to stay away from the caves, or was this just random?

Why would I force any of you to relive what you all experienced? I might be mean on occasion, but that would be too much even for me.

Gently rubbing Pammon's neck, Kaen knew he was right. His heart had quickened some as they got closer to the mountains. He was nervous about how both of the women might respond.

A group of deer up ahead near the base of the mountain. Would you like to show off and shoot one, or would you prefer it if I caught one?

Looking where Pammon was gazing, Kaen knew they were still miles away, but fresh meat sounded great.

Let me do it. I'm not sure how they would handle the ride if you swooped in and ran one down.

Pammon snorted, being kind enough to point his head down so that nothing came back and hit his passengers as he angled to the right a little.

Even with hours of sunlight left, it was safer to camp here tonight and fly over tomorrow. Camping on that side of the rocky barrier would be far more dangerous.

As they decreased their altitude, Kaen unhooked the bow near his leg and pointed to the pack of five deer that were eating shrubs near the mountain base. It was a berry bush that only grew along the mountain. Against most predators, they would be able to escape. Against Pammon and Kaen, they never knew what was coming.

With a single arrow, Kaen fired a shot off, and he felt the pats on his back when his arrow struck true, hitting the deer from a solid hundred yards right in the heart.

The pack scattered as Kaen fired two more shots, dropping two more deer.

I hope you don't mind that I got a few for you.

You would have climbed the mountain tomorrow if you had not.

Licking her fingers, Selmah let out a sigh as she leaned against the log Kaen had brought over for them.

"You are a pretty good cook for having nothing more than a campfire and a few spices," Selmah proclaimed as she reached for her waterskin. "If dragon riding doesn't work out, you can always look for a job as a cook's assistant."

Ava started choking on the bite she was swallowing and glared at Selmah after she finally got the piece free.

"You waited to say that on purpose," she said through a raspy voice after coughing a few times.

"Perhaps."

Selmah was all smiles, and it appeared she was enjoying herself more than Kaen had expected. Her hair was whiter than he remembered, and wrinkles that were not there the last time he had seen her had begun to mar her once smooth complexion.

"I'm glad I could achieve something good enough for someone with so many years of adventuring experience," Kaen fired back as he cleaned up the cooking area. "I have no doubt you have enjoyed far greater food when you were traveling the world."

"I wish. Most of our food was not near as good as this, or as fresh. Finding time to go hunting was a luxury, and I lived off more dried fruit, nuts, and meat than I want to talk about. Besides, I still want to thank you and Pammon for being willing to let me fly with you two. It has been a treat that surpasses most things I have ever experienced in all my years."

Ava nodded in agreement as she wiped the last tears from her eyes, from her near death by choking on meat.

"It makes me very jealous that you two can see the world like that. Not to mention how easy it is to cover long distances so quickly."

Chuckling, Kaen shot them both a grin as he motioned with his head at Pammon, who was dozing behind him.

"We actually did not fly as fast as he can. Pammon flew a little slower so that you two did not get too wind-burned. I had forgotten that would happen."

He had already gotten in trouble once for mentioning the red line from the ridge of their nose to their scalp where the wind had buffeted them.

"Tomorrow morning, Pammon will go hunting, and when he comes back, we can set out for the other side. Based on the clouds we saw today, there might be some moisture at the top of the mountains, so you two will want to wear all of the clothes you had on again."

"You don't feel the cold, do you?" asked Selmah.

Shaking his head, Kaen slid the knife he had just cleaned into his sheath.

"I never did. Elies told me that it happens once one bonds with a dragon. They resist the cold and the heat better than most. Even way up in the sky, above the clouds, the air gets thinner, but a bonded Dragon Rider does not experience it like you two would."

Tapping her lips with her finger, Selmah nodded as she took in all the information.

"Well, if we are done eating, Ava and I need to go and practice a few things before we can call it a night. Would you care to watch?"

Smiling, Kaen moved and offered a hand to each of them, helping them up from the ground.

"I would be honored to watch and learn."

Ava burst into laughter until she saw the look on Kaen's face and realized he was serious.

"Do you really hope to learn what she is teaching?" she asked as her voice warbled a second. "I have been training with her for years, and none of it has been easy."

As Kaen grinned at her, all he could do was shrug.

"I didn't say I would succeed. I just said I wanted to see what I could learn. She is, after all, the oldest and wisest caster in our kingdom."

A grunt and the sound of a foot tapping against dirt with effort caused them both to turn and look at Selmah. Her arms were crossed, and her eyes were narrowed at the two of them.

"If you are both done calling me old," she stated as her voice sounded gruffer than Kaen could ever remember, "we will start, and I promise it will not be fun for either of you."

Wincing as he sucked air in through his teeth, Kaen nodded.

"I'm sorry?" he pleaded, unsure if that would make a difference.

Scoffing, Selmah turned on her heel and began to walk away.

Groaning, Ava pushed Kaen to follow the upset caster, who was now going to ruin their night.

"Remember, this is all your fault," she whispered.

Both of them were sweating, and Kaen glanced at Ava, who was breathing hard.

For two hours they had been attempting to mimic the lightning spell that Selmah had easily cast, hitting all six of the wooden sticks she had burnt on her first demonstration.

Neither of them had managed to accomplish the same thing.

Kaen could see the power wanting to come out, yet unlike the fire spell, he had learned nothing wanted to work. Even when calling upon his lifestone, it sat there, just out of reach.

"Focus and stop trying to figure it out!" snapped Selmah as she watched both of them struggle with the spell. "It requires your mind to see it and activate it. Feel the energy in the air, call upon it, harness it, and release it. You cannot will it from nothing."

Ava had managed a few small single-lighting shots, but none of them had split like Selmah wanted. Kaen could see the scowl on Ava's face as she could not figure out how to get it to split its path.

Are you going to listen to me or keep obeying that woman who forgets you are not like the two of them?

Kaen had ignored Pammon for an hour as his dragon had watched him fail at every attempt.

What am I doing wrong, oh wise and powerful dragon mage, he finally replied, the sarcasm dripping from their bond.

A huff came from where Pammon lay, and Kaen snorted himself, knowing that was not lost in translation.

Think. How does all of your magic work? Why try something different?

Standing there, trying to make lightning leap from his fingertips, Kaen paused and considered what Pammon had said.

Dropping his arms to his side, he let out a sigh as his head bobbed. Turning around, he began walking over to where Pammon was lounging on the ground.

"Giving up so soon?" Selmah taunted as Kaen walked away.

Seems you aren't as foolish as I thought. Figure it out finally?

There is no guarantee this will work. If it doesn't, I'm still unable to do this spell.

Who cares? So what if you can't shoot lighting from your arse. No one will think less of you. I doubt there have been any Dragon Riders in a thousand years who can do what you can. Stop trying to be everything, and just be you.

Easier said than done, Kaen replied as he fished his bow out from the pile of items stacked near Pammon and grabbed his quiver. *I still don't know what I can and can't do. Not knowing might cost me or someone else their life.*

Then, do what you can with what you know. Don't allow them to force you to be like them. Selmah has had a lifetime of learning magic her way. She has trained Ava to be like her. She has never trained you or anyone like you before.

Selmah had grunted and shaken her head when he rejoined them with his bow and an arrow drawn.

Ignoring her, Kaen drew the arrow back and focused on the tip. He could easily imbue it with mana and fire off an explosive shot, but that was not what he was supposed to do.

He felt the energy in the air like Selmah had talked about. That wasn't hard at all. It was everywhere. He just had no way to focus it. Now, he could feel that possibility.

Slowly, he drew the energy in the air around him.

From the ground up into his body, through the air and the vastness of nothing was the charge she was talking about.

All around them were electrical charges, waiting to be harnessed and focused.

He stamped out his lifestone and made sure it was all him. Elies had drilled him to learn how to do things on his own. The lifestone was a tool, but it should never become a crutch. He had depended on it too much.

This would be him, nothing but him, as he focused all that energy to gather in the tip of his arrow. It felt alive, and when he opened his eyes, he saw small sparks dancing on the tip. He could feel it flowing through the shaft and into his hand that held the string.

Narrowing his eyes at the stick only fifteen yards away, he smiled.

His mana was flowing into the arrow and, with it, a storm.

Freeing the grip he had on the string, it bolted toward the stick, and upon striking it, the arrow burst into a lightning storm, traveling through ten of the fifteen branches she had set up for them to practice on.

[Lightning Shot Acquired]

"Impossible," Selmah gasped as she watched the finished product of his attempt.

"Ungghh," moaned Ava as she stomped her foot and shook her head. "It's not fair, you bastard!"

She playfully swung at him and gave him a smile as she let out a sigh.

"How . . . how did you do that?"

Turning to face Selmah, Kaen saw the bewilderment in her eyes.

"All the magic I do is through my bow. I can sense and see everything you said, but I couldn't find a way to focus it like you described. When I hold an arrow, ready to shoot, everything is focused on one point."

Using his finger, he motioned to Pammon, who had raised his head and appeared to be smiling.

"It is actually Pammon who told me what I was doing wrong. He told me I was trying to do it your way instead of mine. It made me wonder if everyone has to learn magic the same way."

Nodding her head, Selmah glanced at Pammon before turning her eyes back to Kaen.

"You impress me even more, Kaen Marshell. In fact, you have just taught me there might be more I still have to learn that even I do not know."

"Yes!" interrupted Ava. "He needs to stop showing off!"

Selmah and Kaen both chuckled as Ava took a deep breath and turned back to the targets, trying to figure out what she was doing wrong.

16

Shelter in a Cave

Ava seemed to still be a bit jealous that she had not learned the lightning spell Selmah was trying to teach her. She had played it off that she was tired, but everyone recognized the frustration she felt from watching Kaen succeed.

They were flying over the top of the mountains now, and the mist that was rushing at them slid off Pammon's scales and stuck to their clothes and faces. It was like standing next to a waterfall and the mist constantly coming over you.

Ava had tried shouting something, but Kaen shrugged, unable to hear her over the noise.

There is no movement, Pammon informed Kaen as they began their descent on the other side of the mountains, letting the cold wind nearly freeze their wet clothes. **It looks safe to land if you want, so they can dry off or even change.**

It's probably for the best. No point in them getting sick or chilled to the bone.

They flew down the mountainside, and once they were about halfway down, Pammon found a section of it where he could land.

Both women were shivering as they started to dismount.

"You really aren't cold, are you?" asked Selmah as she stripped off the wet clothes she had on and started changing into some from the pack she had tossed off.

Looking away, Kaen felt a little heat in his cheeks, but Selmah simply chuckled.

"Forgive me if I'm not modest enough to want to stay in those clothes. I assumed you have seen enough or would be willing to turn as you have."

"It uh . . . caught me a little off guard," was all Kaen admitted. The truth was he had not really seen a woman strip before him. A few had tried; Huethea was one of them, but he had always turned or left. None were the one he was interested in.

"Keep your head turned," snapped Ava as she followed Selmah's lead.

A minute into the shuffling noises behind him, a rush of wind came across the mountains, almost blowing him off, and he heard a cry from the ladies behind him.

"Don't you dare!" Ava shouted as he heard Pammon thrumming.

"My eyes are closed," he stated, groaning a little. "I can't help it if your stuff flies off the mountainside."

They are stuck against me. I should have probably let them off the other side, but I didn't realize the wind would come like that. Would you like me to describe what I am watching?

No! I don't need any help in that department.

Are you sure? I mean, both of them look exceptionally fit.

Kaen groaned again, knowing his cheeks were redder, and he felt the thrumming of Pammon increasing.

"Do I want to know why he is laughing?" Selmah inquired.

"He thinks he is being funny, but I know he is not."

He heard Selmah chuckling and kept his eyes firmly focused on the swamp below them.

You need to focus on scouting, not making things weird or harder with the women.

Oh, we both know I am just making it fun. Besides, I can see nothing out there besides the occasional rare animal.

Shaking his head, both knew that someone must intentionally be keeping the swamp clear.

"We are done," Ava announced, breaking his thoughts about the swamp.

When he turned around, he noticed both women were changed and that their hair was almost dry.

"Magic?" he asked while tapping his head.

A corner of Selmah's lip rose as she bobbed her head.

"One of the early spells a mage learns. It has many uses, but I would like to think not flying with a wet head would be at the top of my list."

Nodding as he walked over to pick up their bags, he slung off his pack and dropped it at their feet.

"Go ahead and get a little bit to eat and drink. We will be flying for a few hours, and I would prefer not to stop unless we need to."

Without waiting for a reply, he grabbed their bags and turned to Pammon, his head darting around as he scanned the forest.

There is a cloud coming from the east. It might rain again while we are flying.

Are you saying we should stay on the ground or what?

I have no problem flying in the rain with you. It is those two who would be the ones to suffer. We can see how things go, but we have maybe an hour before it will be upon us, and then I will need to fly lower if I want to see anything.

Grumbling to himself, Kaen began to secure the bags.

Never easy, is it?

Thrumming, Pammon shook his head even though he knew Kaen wasn't paying attention.

Pammon had been right. The rain started as a slight mist before turning into pelting drops of water. He wasn't flying fast, yet it was moving toward them as they flew east.

Selmah and Ava had their cloaks pulled over them and they were pressed against each other. Kaen had offered his cloak to Ava, shielding her from both directions as the rain ran over him with no mercy. He felt the sting of the rain, but it was not the first time he had flown in it.

Keeping his eyes mostly shut, he could see nothing.

I am as low as I want to be. We are less than half a mile above the trees, and it is a mess down there. Nothing is moving if they can help it. Even all the birds are roosted at the moment.

Is there anywhere we can land and wait this out? Other than perhaps in the forest?

There are a few spots, but none that I think you will like.

The caves . . .

Kaen felt Pammon as he agreed through their bond. Neither of them knew what might still be in the cave, and camping out on the edge of them would only act like a beacon from the fire. They would have to go deep inside a cave, and neither liked that idea.

The swamp isn't a good choice either. There are too many creatures in there that might consider us a snack worth trying.

They would not bother me, but you and the other two would be at risk. You already know the options. We can fly, hoping the storm will end some-time before night, or find a cave and camp there. I cannot tell you when it will end, but I doubt it will happen soon.

Sighing, Kaen wiped his face, feeling the growth of hair on his chin and cheeks. It had only been a few days since he had last shaved, and already it was getting scratchy.

Lightning shot through the sky, and thunder boomed as they flew into the storm. The wind had picked up considerably, and the sky was dark and ugly. Pammon could see without a problem, yet neither Selmah nor Ava could see anything but the blackness around them. Kaen could barely make out the trees thanks to his improved vision that came from being bonded with Pammon.

We need to land, and we need to find a place to wait this out.

Even if it means a cave?

Dread came from Pammon, and Kaen knew he was sending that same feeling right back. There was no doubt it was the only option they had.

Yes. We cannot stay out in this forever.

Another hour went by as Pammon flew around the base of the mountain. By the time they found a cave, Kaen could feel Ava shaking a little bit as she leaned into him.

Pammon landed a good distance away and made them dismount, letting Kaen follow with his bow out and his sword on his hip.

A few minutes of Pammon scouting into the cave resulted in an all-clear sign, and the women rushed in to get out of the rain.

Both looked like cats who had been dunked in a barrel multiple times. Their outfits were spilling massive trails of water as they moved inside the cave. Water was running inside the cave for a few yards, the wind tossing it inside before it slowly rolled back to the entrance.

If you stay inside, I will go collect some trees.

Chuckling, both women glanced at Kaen as he held the light orb and illuminated the large opening of the mountain.

"Pammon will get us some firewood. We need to go a little deeper inside, but he said it is safe," he informed them as he walked ahead, leaving wet footprints with every step. "We will get situated, and then I will let you two change as quickly as possible."

"Can't you feel it?" asked Ava, her teeth clacking together as she hugged herself.

"I can, but it doesn't bother me. I have experienced worse cold for far longer. A perk of being bound."

Both women were shivering, and Selmah did her best not to let it show, but it was too much for her.

Ten minutes later, a crash echoed outside the cave, and Kaen smiled as he heard Pammon coming through the entrance.

That is a whole tree you dropped outside, isn't it?

Forgive me if I didn't take the time to chop it up into smaller pieces, but yes, I grabbed a tree and brought it with me.

No, I am just impressed. I knew you had gotten stronger, but I had forgotten just how strong.

Pammon came into view, carrying branches that were bunched together in his jaw, easily hundreds of pounds and longer than fifteen feet in length. He was thrumming as he came, proudly showing off his strength to Ava and Selmah.

He dropped them on the ground and turned, heading back into the rain to gather a few more pieces.

"That was remarkable," muttered Selmah between clattering teeth as she watched Pammon. "I know he is as tall as most houses in Ebonmount."

"And he eats enough to feed most the families in just one meal," added Kaen as he took out his axe from a pack he had been carrying. "You should ask Ava just how much he has eaten."

Ava smiled and chuckled. She knew firsthand just how much Pammon ate.

Within a few minutes, Kaen had a pile of wood stacked up, and Ava had turned it into a roaring fire. The wet wood snapped and popped, but it burned warm, and the smoke rose into the top of the cave, spreading out and traveling deeper into it.

The lights it cast off created a dance of shadows on the walls.

"You two can go ahead and change and try to get dry. I'll keep working on this wood and wait till you both are ready."

As he turned, he heard a *thank you* from both of them.

An hour later, they all sat around the fire, enjoying the warmth of dry clothes and some food in their stomachs. Pammon was not back yet but should be soon. He had gone hunting, hoping to find something, but after a solid half hour of searching, he resigned to the fact that finding anything in this downpour would be impossible.

Upon his return, he shook off the water at the entrance of the cave and then created a barrier between them and the outside.

Kaen had returned from setting a few small traps deeper in the cave. Nothing that would kill anything but simply create noise, alerting Pammon to their arrival.

"I have not been in a downpour like that in ages. I will admit the wind from flying made it much worse than I could have imagined," Selmah stated.

Pammon thrummed as he lay near them, his head against Kaen's leg.

Both women watched as Kaen absently scratched the base of one of Pammon's horns.

"What is it like? Having a dragon and something connected to you always?"

Raising his eyebrows, Kaen grinned at Selmah and then glanced back at Pammon.

"For me, it is something more than I can describe in simple words. I was lost. I was lonely. The pain of losing my father and trying to find my way to who I wanted to be was overwhelming. He called out to me the day I found his egg and changed everything."

Kaen scratched a little harder. Pammon trilled and huffed as he shook his head gently.

"I found joy I had forgotten was possible. I was afraid when I learned how dangerous it was for people to know about him. There were times it hurt because we had to be apart."

"Hurt?"

"We learned that Dragon Riders are meant to be with their dragons. Separation from each other actually causes pain and can lead to death over prolonged absence. For us, it felt like an itch we couldn't scratch and a pain in our chests. Now I know what he thinks most of the time, and he knows what I think. Even in battle, we know what the other will do without having to say it."

"That must be . . . different," Selmah replied with a small chuckle. "I guess there is no way to describe it. And is it true he makes you stronger?"

Swallowing the saliva that formed in his mouth, Kaen chewed his lip for a moment before answering.

"We make each other stronger. Sure, there are stories of how powerful a Dragon Rider can become, but together we are better. We keep each other from making stupid decisions."

Tell them you only sometimes listen to my advice.

Laughing out loud surprised the women, and Kaen patted Pammon's head.

"We can speak without words, and he wanted me to make sure I mentioned how often I ignore his advice."

Both of them laughed, and Ava opened her mouth to say something but closed it suddenly.

She grinned at Kaen and just shrugged.

Letting out a yawn, Kaen got up, moved a few supplies around, and stacked some items near Pammon.

"You two need to come here tonight and sleep next to him. He will help you to sleep and keep you warm. The added perk is that anything that gets close will have to deal with him first."

Both of them looked at the other and smiled, rising from the wooden stumps Kaen had created for them to sit on and moved to where he had created a spot for them.

"You going to join us?"

Kaen smiled at Ava and nodded.

"Yes, but I want to explore a little first."

"Alone?"

"I'll be fine," he answered as he picked up the shield sitting beside him. "I'm probably an idiot for saying I would love to run into something, but I won't go too deep. I just want to explore a little more."

Snorting, Pammon moved his head where both of the women could see and nodded it before encircling them both.

"Be safe," Ava said as she watched him start to walk away with a lightstone in his hand.

"I will. I have a promise to keep."

As he moved into the cave, he heard the sound of the rain outside and Selmah mutter, *What promise?*

Smiling to himself, he resisted asking Pammon to tell him what they said.

17

Investing in the Dark

While exploring for about two miles, Kaen learned a few things about the cave. Part of it was natural, and the goblins, orcs, or something else had mined the other part. Drag marks created by rocks and wheels could be seen on the rocky floor. It wasn't smooth, but it had been smoothed out from the amount of traffic it had seen. There were actual grooves in some spots.

Wooden beams had started deteriorating, but they held up any possible cave in that had maybe been once considered.

The eerie part in all this was there were no tools, no leftover carts, or anything else showing that a presence had once been there. He imagined he would find trash, at least. Instead, it had been picked clean.

A thin layer of dirt and dust carpeted the cave floor, yet no footprints were noticeable. Surely, an animal of some kind would live in here. Why would they not use the safety of the cave?

So many things felt off.

The orb was bright enough to see thirty yards in every direction, and as he walked, the sounds of his footsteps echoed in the silence of the caverns. The wind made noise but not loud enough to hide any other movements. The echoes of his traveling were the only sound he heard.

I can sense your concern. You still have found nothing?

I have found nothing at all. I should have found something! Bones, tools, old torches, trash. Something! It is beyond abnormal.

Should we leave? Would it be better to brave the storm?

Kaen stood still in the cave, closing his eyes and listening.

No. They need to sleep and rest. I could see they were nearly blue from the cold and rain. A good night's sleep next to you is what they need.

Why is it I sense you are going to do something stupid?

You noticed I put on my armor, right?

Yes. You are wearing everything you own. I almost said something, but I was hoping what I felt was you *not* being an eggling.

Holding back the smile he felt forming, Kaen took out the second lightstone he had and activated it but put it on a very low setting.

Turning the other one off, he activated his sneaking ability and quietly crept along the cave floor, making no noise as his eyes adjusted to the lower light. Once they were, he turned the other orb off and stood still for a moment. His eyes allowed him to see—not far, but a good twenty yards—as he activated the skill he had learned from the elves.

[Night Vision Activated]

The mana drain was nothing, thanks to his regen rate that came from being bound to Pammon. It only gave him a little bit of room to work with, but he needed to make sure he was right.

Sitting against the wall of the cave tunnel, he listened as he sat in the dark, waiting for what might come.

An hour had passed, and no sounds had come from the cave.

Perhaps I am wrong. I would have expected something to have come by now, if it was there.

I know you do not stink. The water has washed that away, and I doubt you were heard. How long are you going to stay?

Resisting the urge to grunt in frustration, Kaen slowly stretched, flexing his muscles and shifting his weight. Practice had taught him how to do this without making noise, but the effort was almost as much as sitting still. Slow, controlled movements were required, which was more of a physical demand than not moving.

When another hour had passed, and Kaen had determined it was time to go, he kept the lightstone off and slowly snuck back toward Pammon.

Four minutes into his slow and steady trip back, he froze.

What was that? Your heart just spiked.

Kaen had heard a clatter deep inside the cave. It had only happened for a moment, but it was the sound of something falling.

Something fell in the cave. It could be anything, but what would the odds of that be?

You don't believe that for a moment. I can feel that coming from you.

Pammon was right. The sound was something he expected to hear if someone had dropped a broom handle or some other wooden object. Could he have stopped just deep enough into the cave that he missed finding something for the first time in miles?

I'm going to be stupid again.

Should I wake the others?

Weighing that option, Kaen knew if it were nothing, he would have disturbed them when they both needed rest. He was fine. He and Pammon were stronger and could last far longer than the others without sleep. If they pushed it, they didn't need sleep for days.

Let them rest. You will know if I need help.

Frustration floated through their bond as he snuck back into the cave.

It had been almost another half mile, and Kaen realized that there was something in the cave, deeper but there. Occasionally, a small sound would echo ever so slightly, but he knew something was there. It could be an animal, or it could be something else.

He studied the floor again. No tracks present, even with his night vision.

There is something here, but I still see no tracks. Whatever it is has to be deeper. I'm going to keep searching. We both know I can't let this go.

We both know you are a fool, but just be safe. What could live in a deep cave without needing to come out and hunt or find water?

I have no clue. That is why I cannot let it go. Which cave are we in, in relation to the original seven?

He knew what Pammon was thinking, and he sat still and waited, listening to the small sounds that were coming through the cave now. Ticking . . . no tapping . . . something softly tapping the stone floor.

This is the second farthest one from the east. The one after Fiola's cave.

The second oldest cave . . .

Yes.

Resisting the urge to shudder, Kaen slowly began moving again. Avoiding the small rocks he saw on the cave floor. Creeping along in the dark, trying to stay near the wall, he stopped and realized what he was moving through.

It's a rock trap! These rocks are small and set in tiny piles, just enough to grind under someone's feet if they are walking along them!

How old are they?

Concern hit Kaen through their bond, and it almost bowled him over. He knew Pammon was not happy with him being that far into the cave, away from him, and realizing there was a trap.

Studying the floor, he saw the dirt again and the fine layer on top of the small rock piles.

They are using magic to hide their footprints! Just like in the woods!

Pammon had moved, and Kaen felt him growing anxious through their bond.

You need to return. I have woken up the women. They are looking around and are anxious because you are not here.

We both know that's not going to happen. Get them on your back and get the stuff stowed, and let me focus on where I am. I'm fine.

Pammon growled at him through their bond. He could only imagine what it sounded like where Ava and Selmah were.

How am I going to tell them to get on me and pack the stuff up if I can't talk?

You're a dragon . . . You're smart. Use your claws or something and point to what you want. For now, let me focus. I need you to trust me. We might not get another chance to find out if something is here.

I swear, when this goes wrong, I am not going to stop talking about it for a decade.

Kaen didn't care that he knew Pammon was probably right. It had been hours, and he finally felt like he was close to figuring out something and wasn't going to turn back.

There were more of the stone piles now, only a few feet between each of them as he wove around them. It was apparent that someone or something was smart enough to create these. That was the part that made him hesitate just a little bit.

The tapping sound stopped, and the cave became quiet again. A few more minutes passed as Kaen froze in place. There was an opening up ahead, and with the cave being a good twenty to thirty yards wide in some sections, he couldn't make out anything on the other side as the spell did not grant him vision across that distance.

Another ten minutes or so passed, and the tapping started again. It was random, and as it grew just a little louder, he realized what it was.

Whoever was on guard duty was bored! He sat there nodding his head in the same rhythm. It wasn't loud, just a fidget one would have after standing or sitting on something for long hours on end.

There is something or someone deeper in the cave. I think I have figured out the sound. I'm not sure how much further it is, but it can't be more than a few hundred yards at best.

Kaen could almost imagine Pammon closing his eyes and snorting right now. The wave of frustration coming from him was stronger than it had been in a long time.

You realize that I cannot get to you near as fast with these two sitting on me.

Nice work! I knew you could get them to understand you.

Stop patronizing me. This is foolish, and you know it.

Ignoring Pammon and his complaining, Kaen kept sneaking through the cave. Another hundred yards later, the tapping stopped again. It felt like a bend in the cave was coming up, and he noticed the small stone piles ended in about ten yards. The dust that had covered the floor basically ended, and footprints were noticeable.

Goblin and orc footprints.

Controlling his breathing, he focused on listening even more. The sound inside caves was weird. Normally, there would be wind, noise echoes, and the sound of something. It was eerie just how quiet it was.

There was so much about magic he knew was still unknown to him, yet something made his skin itch. Something had to be stopping noise from coming down the cave tunnel. Why have a lookout if there was no one else to warn?

I can see goblin and orc footprints, and I know there must be something really close. Do you know of any magic that can stop sound?

A tinge of fear hit him as Pammon considered what Kaen was saying and asking.

I'm not one to ask about that kind of stuff. I would assume there is magic for everything. Sound would be close to controlling the wind; since we know the elves do that, it would make sense to expect someone else to control sound.

A moment passed, and Kaen waited for the tapping to resume.

You're still going to go in, aren't you?

Yes!

I promise you I will—

Quiet! I hear something!

Kaen cut Pammon off as he heard a grunt and a shuffling sound not far off.

Ignoring the concern Pammon was radiating, Kaen resumed his path along the cave wall. He drew closer to the sound and saw a spot where the tunnel pinched together, barely fifteen yards apart. As it came into view, he noticed hundreds of orc, goblin, and cart tracks, as well as other things in the dirt.

Just around the edge of the opening, he saw something move, and the tapping started again.

A soft leather boot was gently tapping the wall. Something was sitting right on the other side of the opening!

Kaen took a slow breath, making sure he was as quiet as possible. Even though his heart wanted to race, he forced it to calm down. Slowly, he unhooked a knife from his belt and pulled it out of its sheath.

With no idea what was around the corner he was coming up on, his first concern was what must be a goblin or a hobgoblin. The boot was too small for an orc.

Each step he took was perfectly timed with the creature's heel tapping against the cave wall. This close, it was too risky to try moving without making a sound. An orc or goblin could see farther into a cave than he could. His spell only allowed for so much distance in this absolutely dark cave. Outside at night, he would be fine, but in here, they could easily see twice as far as he could.

Seven steps from the edge of the opening, the tapping stopped, and Kaen waited. No movement came, no noise. A light breathing, almost like a person sleeping. The gentle breathing of a creature not concerned with anyone close by.

He wanted to rush around the corner and kill this creature, but doing so was dumber than what Pammon had accused him of. There was no telling what was over there, and he saw nothing that warned him of others.

Minutes trickled by, and soon it was ten. Then, the tapping began again.

The last few steps before the edge felt like they took forever when it was, in fact, just a few seconds. Timing the taps as the next one came, Kaen swung around the opening, dagger flying, and saw the head of a goblin resting on his hands as he sat in a small alcove in the wall. He moved so fast that the goblin had no time to react or even make a sound before Kaen's dagger plunged into its eye socket, causing the creature to shake.

It dropped a wooden horn it had been holding as it spasmed in death.

Not hesitating, Kaen bent down and snatched it inches before it hit the floor of the cave. He felt the goblin fall on his shoulder, and he absorbed the impact, glancing around the dead body to see what was nearby.

Squinting, he saw a few other shapes lying on cots at the edge of his distance. Four of them and just a few feet beyond them was some type of shimmering wall. It was black but almost glowed as it shimmered in the air.

Taking the goblin he had just killed and the horn, he slowly moved back around the edge and laid it against the cave wall.

I found some goblins. Killed one, and a few more are here. There is a black barrier of some kind. It almost looks like water or a mirror.

What are you going to do? Do we need to come?

Considering his options, Kaen was torn. He could try and kill the other four and investigate the wall. There was no telling what it was blocking, but deep down inside, he had an idea. Doing so would require him to kill the other four, and the element of surprise would be his.

Not investigating and instead going back with the one he killed might throw them off, wondering where their scout had run off to. Doing so might allow him to figure out what was going on without the orc army knowing that he knew.

Then he remembered the fire they had built. There would be no way to dispose of all that evidence. They would know something had happened.

Wait there. I am going to have to scout it out. Our camping in here has ruined any chance of hiding we were here.

Retrieving his dagger from the goblin socket, he cleaned it off.

He had no idea what he was about to discover.

18

An Enemy We Can't See

Slaying four sleeping goblins was much easier than Kaen had realized. The art of killing someone or something in their sleep had never been a skill he had practiced, yet now he knew exactly where to plunge his dagger while holding his hand over their mouth. No sound beyond the squishing noise.

When the fourth one was dead, he slipped the dagger back into its sheath, after having cleaned it off, and drew his sword. Unhooking his shield from his back, he knew that a dagger would not be enough.

The wall shimmered as he moved closer to it. Like water on a stream at night, even with no moon or stars to reflect on it, it rippled in the darkness of the cave.

The goblins are dead, and I am going to touch it and see what this thing is.

Another grumble and wave of frustration hit him, but Kaen had to block it out. As he began to reach toward the wall of liquid, he stopped and saw a sword from one of the goblins he killed in the room next to him. Putting his back in his scabbard, he retrieved it and moved back to the edge of the shifting wall.

Putting the tip of the goblin sword into the inky substance did nothing as it wrapped itself around the blade. Pulling it out, it looked just as it had before. A pock-filled and worthless blade for any real combat but great for shanking someone in their sleep.

Snorting, Kaen put it back on the goblin's dead body and drew his own. With one last breath to settle the nerves he had, he pushed his sword through the barrier and pressed until his hand made contact.

A cool tingling effect began to spread over his fingers and wrist, but no pain was evident.

Holding his breath, he pressed his entire arm and chest through until his head popped out on the other side.

As he strode through, he felt heat and was assaulted by noises and a smell that reminded him of the first cave they had found.

Stumbling through, he saw a massive cavern inside the mountain. There were buildings made of rocks, small and tall ones. Forges and other sounds of tools against rocks echoed throughout the cavern, and the noises of a busy army were everywhere.

Somehow, that wall behind him stopped all the noise and light. Inside this cavern was an army building and waiting.

We are in trouble, Kaen called out to Pammon. *There is a whole army in here. Far larger than any of the ones we faced two years ago.*

You need to come back now! Do not argue, and do not be foolish! Return while you can!

Kaen knew Pammon was right. Even though everything in him wanted to scout and see what he might find, the path that led down into the cavern below was empty. No one seemed worried about a person stumbling in on them.

A sea of orcs, goblins, and a few other creatures, like trolls, moved like ants below. Lights were present from great fires, and he saw carts and other wagons bringing what must be more to some of the fires off in the distance.

This cavern must be at least a mile wide he thought as he counted the number of creatures he could see.

You aren't moving yet! What are you doing?

Bending down to blend in more with where he was, Kaen sighed as he tried to take in all that he saw. Everything he could report back would be important. Scouting around, he paused as he looked at a few lines of movement a ways off. Squinting, he realized his eyes had not tricked him.

There were humans in there, pushing and pulling carts right next to orcs. They did not appear to be chained or forced.

"Humans are working with them . . ." he muttered to himself.

Wishing he had brought his bow, Kaen could have at least caused some damage. Not as much as he knew would be needed. Pammon wouldn't be able to get in here as the section of the cave he came through was too tight. He might fit, but it would take a while, and that would mean none of them could get past while he did. Yet if Pammon was in here, he could easily fly around with how tall the cavern was. It had to be at least eighty feet high, maybe even a hundred in most places.

King Aldric and Herb had guard stations outside the original caves and rigged explosives. Yet, looking at this collection here, they could easily dig a tunnel somewhere else. Perhaps that is what they were doing.

Why aren't you moving yet? The two women are just as anxious as I am. They have been tied to me for a while!

Backing into the black wall behind him, Kaen felt himself drift through and saw the corpses at his feet.

He needed to go, and he had to do his best to hide his actions.

Fetching the goblin he had first killed, he took the blade from it and used it on three of the goblins, widening the holes in their eye sockets.

On the fourth one, he took the blade and cut a mark on its cheek, acting like he had missed, and used the blade of the first one he had killed to plunge a few times into the scout's chest and stomach. Leaving the scout's dagger in the eye socket of the fourth and the other blade in its chest, he left it on top of the one he hoped would think had killed the traitor. Blood did not flow like it should have since they were dead, and anyone with any skill should figure it out.

I'm coming; be ready. We need to leave and make it back to Ebonmount. The mission is over.

He felt Pammon agree and, forgoing stealth, quickly returned through the stacks of warning rocks, sprinting once he was past them.

"Kaen!"

He waved at them as he slowed down some, taking a breath and wiping the sweat from his brow. The moisture from the rain combined with the cave and running in full gear for miles had made him a bit slimy under his armor.

"We need to go!" he announced as he got within range of the others. "I'll explain on the other side, but time is important, and I do not want to waste a moment."

Ava started to speak when she felt a pinch on her waist from Selmah.

You smell. Both goblins and sweat.

I know, but now we know what they are doing. The real question is, how can we stop them?

Shaking his head, Kaen felt Pammon acknowledge the problem but had no answers. Knowing he would not fit inside the cave prevented him from helping at all.

Kaen glanced at the fire, and without having to say anything, Pammon smothered the flames with his foot. Darkness engulfed the cave, and his lifestone appeared in his hand, causing both women to flinch for a second at the light.

"I need you two to listen to what I am about to tell you. Make sure your harness is tight around you. Pammon will use a skill, and we will fly much faster than we have before. If you feel you need to vomit, make sure you turn far enough to the side that it doesn't hit you in the face or the one behind you."

Ava glared at him for a moment, wondering if that was directed at her.

Are you sure you want me to use that with them? We both know it may be harder on them than we realize.

Cinching his harness around him, Kaen considered that once more. The wind would be extremely brutal. He could sit up a little more, absorbing some of the wind.

We will have to see how it goes. There is no time. Aldric and Herb need to know what we found out.

He tossed the light globe to Ava as he started to climb up on Pammon. Selmah coughed, and he turned around to see what she wanted as he fastened himself in.

"I assume this is worse than what we are supposed to be finding out?"

He saw the look of concern on her face. She knew he wouldn't call that off unless it were that important.

Nodding, he pointed to the darkness of the cave that led under the mountain.

"Thousands of orcs, goblins, and I am not sure how many humans are in there building something. If the other caves are like this one, we are looking at an army of easily twenty thousand."

Ava gasped as she weighed the news against what they had thought before.

"What will you do?" Selmah asked, her face set like stone.

Shrugging, Kaen turned around and picked up the reins sitting on Pammon's neck.

"For now, I warn the kingdom. After that, whatever I must do. This is bigger than anything else right now."

Pammon turned the moment he had the reins, moving toward the entrance of the cave. The sound of a pouring storm was gone, but as they got close, gentle rain echoed off the walls.

"Cover yourselves," he warned them. "This is going to get much worse once we cross the mountains."

Pammon had flown hard and fast to gain the altitude needed to cross over them. The rain was colder and stung more as he flew over the peaks.

The sun was gone; it was nighttime, yet only he could see what was before them.

Dozing in the rain, Kaen had closed his eyes, waiting until Pammon told him to prepare.

I am going to drop a little bit down the mountains, and then once over the forest, I will use my skill. We are too high for them to handle this air and temperature.

How long till we get home? Kaen asked, choosing not to bug Pammon with endless questions as he wrestled with the knowledge of what he had found.

I will see how long I can hold on, and if they can manage. Perhaps in less than four hours. Maybe three.

Even though they had practiced this skill multiple times in Roccnari, knowing Pammon thought he could manage to keep it active the entire trip home amazed Kaen. He had grown a lot, and with how large he was now, Kaen knew Pammon would have easily destroyed that fort of bandits without help.

[Flight Burst Activated]

Yelps had come from Ava and Selmah when Pammon rocketed forward. Even before he had used the skill, he used the descent from the mountainside, gaining speed as he plummeted toward the forest.

Like an arrow loosed from a bow, he surged forward.

Ava's arms clenched tightly around Kaen's waist, and he would have smiled if it had not been for the air that was buffeting his face. It took effort to keep his mouth from flying open, and he had to squint to be able to see.

This is much faster than before!

Yes, because I sense the need is that great. Now, hold on and just close your eyes. It will get faster if you lend me your lifestone.

That could be harmful for so long. I do not want to risk you for this. It is not that important.

A wave of confusion came across their bond from Pammon. **If you say so. I am willing if need be. For now, just let me handle this part. When we get there, I will want to eat and sleep. Some of us did not get a full meal.**

Fighting the wind, Kaen rubbed that same scale as always and chuckled, letting the wind steal it from his throat.

Closing his eyes, he let the stinging wind remind him of how much he loved being on Pammon's back. Alive like this.

19

A Last Goodbye

Herb was tapping his fingers against the small table as they waited for Aldric to arrive. The sun was finally starting to climb the peaks, and Kaen was trying not to sleep in the chair as he sat there waiting.

Both Selmah and Ava had returned to their homes, and Pammon was off hunting. It had taken less than four hours for them to return, a feat that impressed Herb and Kaen both.

"I still cannot believe how fast he did that," Herb stated, continuing his assault on the table with his fingers. "Four hours from bottom to tip. That is a feat I could not begin to fathom."

"The real truth is that we would not have time to react if a dragon used such a tactic against us."

Grunting, Herb saw the truth in what Kaen had already realized. They were not as safe as they once thought they were.

"Forgive me," Aldric said as he waved both men to take their seats. "I was not expecting the message, and it took a minute for them to verify the truth. I am intrigued and nervous for what it is I am about to hear."

Kaen waited for him to sit down and then stood up, pointing at the map on the table with the seven caves they had sealed still marked. He had sketched a few spots on the other side of the mountain where he felt the cave entrance might be for two of them.

"I already told Herb some of what I have found, and he has his people researching the magic I encountered, but let me tell you everything I know."

When Kaen sat down, done with his report, Aldric just sat there, eyes closed as he slowly rubbed the ridge of his nose with a finger.

Neither Herb nor Kaen interrupted his thoughts. Both of them had time already to think about what this meant.

"They say bad news comes in twos or fours. I pray this is twos."

"What's the other bad news?"

Opening his eyes, Aldric grunted at Herb's question and reached into his vest, pulling out a letter and handing it to Kaen.

"This came yesterday. It bothered me greatly, but now . . . "

Kaen leaned over and took the letter from Aldric and saw that it was still folded and sealed. The wax seal bore a dragon on it. On the opposite side was his name. The writing was shaky, letting him know that Elies himself had written it.

"Elies? He sent a letter?"

"One to me and that one for you. I pray your letter has better news than mine."

Realizing both of them were waiting for him to read it, Kaen broke the seal, watching it shimmer for a second before dissolving.

"That fool sealed it with magic," he realized as he watched it melt away.

Opening it up, he saw lines of barely legible chicken scratch. It must have taken Elies a long time to write this, knowing how badly his fingers worked.

Kaen,

I sent Aldric a letter so he knows this part.

I have left with Tharnok on a trip to the land of the dragons. My time is ending, and I pray I make it before I pass. We needed to leave before Tharnok unleashed the anger and rage he had held in for over a century upon these elves. Perhaps I should have let him.

Havannath is a fool. He took advantage of me when he bound me. A friendship I thought had led me to being stupid one day and making a promise. A promise that left me bound to him and unable to escape. I fought it for a bit but realized it would hurt the world more if I tried to escape it. In time, I grew used to my collar and believed I was free even when I knew I was not.

When you freed me, I had forgotten what the freedom to choose really felt like. Any path I wanted was mine to take. Sadly, I am too far gone to enjoy this, so now I have chosen to ask for the dragons to help you. It has been almost two centuries since I have been there, and you will need to come at some point and present yourself to their council. You will need allies like them for what is coming. We both know you and Pammon alone cannot win . . .

I want you to know that if anyone can succeed, it is you. You are the last of us. You alone can forge a new path for this world. Since the day I heard about you, I prayed a new day would dawn for Dragon Riders. Every day that I saw the effort you put into learning and growing stronger, I knew the spirits had chosen you two for a purpose. You and Pammon are one soul, even before the bonding. You may rise to become the greatest Dragon Rider since the days of old.

Protect yourself. Havannath has sent emissaries to Stioks. I have yet to tell Aldric this. Havannath does not know I was aware, but I have old friends in the elven court. Many are upset with him and Huethea for their attempt to bind you. Had he succeeded, you would have been married to her. I am thankful you somehow resisted what I could not.

If he does join an alliance with Stioks, I have people here who will seek you out. Come and remove him and his daughter from the throne. The elves will stand behind you and break away. I cannot see how you will win in the coming days if you do not do this.

Remember what we talked about. Remember the lessons you learned. Your ability to inspire others and your commitment to protecting them has taken root here, even though the king tries to pull them out.

Forgive me for not saying goodbye in person. You deserve that, but time was limited. Even now, each word I write has required Tharnok's strength.

Be safe, Kaen. Trust Pammon and free this world from the darkness that threatens it.

—Elies

Kaen sat there stunned as he read the letter once more. When finished, he glanced up at Herb and Aldric, who were both watching him intently.

Ignoring their stares, he folded the top sheet and began to put it in his vest as he noticed the second sheet had a metal disc attached to it.

There were only a few lines on the second page.

Kaen,

Present this page and that disc to the guild master, and they will give you access to my vault in the adventurers' guild hall. There are only two things in there, but they are yours. You will need them in the coming battle.

—Elies

Plucking the disc from the paper, Kaen felt how light it was but also knew it was stronger than any metal he had held before. On one side was a dragon, and on the other side was an image of a man.

Coughing, Herb leaned forward, and his voice was a bit higher than usual as he spoke.

"He gave you his vault . . ."

Nodding, Kaen leaned over and handed the paper to Herb, who quickly read it as his head bobbed.

"With that token alone, you can access the vault in any guild hall. It is keyed to a specific vault, and most would not question your having it. With this letter, they might even make you a new disc if you lost it."

"How many vaults are there?"

Chuckling, Herb stood up and handed the letter back to Kaen.

"There are vaults for many things, none of which I can discuss. Just know guild halls are warded, and it would take you and your dragon a long time to hope to breach most of the defenses."

"Forget the vaults," Aldric interrupted, his voice turning gruff. "What did the first letter say?"

"He told me that he was headed to the land where the dragons live," Kaen began as Herb started to talk and stopped as he shook his head at him. "He mentioned that he would implore them for help but that at some point, I would need to come and present myself to them."

Grunting in frustration, Aldric looked around and spotted the cups and pitcher on a table nearby. He went and retrieved one and brought back the pitcher, filling up Herb's cup before sitting down and pouring Kaen some.

"That is not good. Why would Elies leave? Surely, he knows the odds are against him, and this weakens our position greatly."

Ignoring Herb's comment, Aldric drained his cup and filled it again.

"What are you not telling us," he asked as he held the cup from his lips. "I have spent a lifetime reading men, and I can tell you are hiding something."

Kaen felt their gazes on him as he sat there, trying to remain calm.

Returning their gaze, he held his voice steady and did not waiver as he spoke.

"He did, which is why the letter was written to me and not you. Some things are best kept between Dragon Riders and the obligation we have to protect the world."

Aldric finally grunted and bobbed his head before setting his cup on the table.

"I will trust you then to tell me when I can assist with those things. Do not forget I have been honest and entrusted the defense of my kingdom to you these last few years. The rest of the world will fall based on our actions. We stand alone, so they attempted to attack us two years ago. That is why they are building an army in the mountain as we speak."

"But what can we do?" Herb asked as he thumped the table, shaking the cups. "Your troops and my adventurers are standing guard, but with the news Kaen has shared, they would be overrun in moments. We could set up more charges and attempt to hold them off that way but how long would that slow them down? Twenty thousand troops would march across our southern flanks, eating everything in their path!"

"We have defenses now!" Aldric shouted back, slapping the table with his hand and causing Herb's cup to fall over and spill. "We cannot stop them there!

We must defeat them here, pulling all the people in and fighting the fight we are prepared for!"

"And what if Kaen is gone when they come?" Herb fired back, pointing at Kaen and ignoring the wine spilling on the ground. "We are weaker without him."

Kaen noticed Aldric had lost his usual cool temperament and now had a vein in his forehead that throbbed like Hess's used to when upset.

"Both of you, stop!" Kaen barked as he saw the two men getting flustered at each other.

"What would you have done had I never found Pammon? None of us would be here today! We would be living in another land or dead."

Both men snorted and huffed, turning their attention back to Kaen and acknowledging the truth he had spoken with their silence.

"I am unsure when or if I will visit the dragon council. For now, I must do many other things before that is even an idea I will entertain. We must consider all options and figure out what magic they use to hide their presence. I am certain the bandits Hess and I wiped out years ago are using the same magic to hide in the cave. This points to not just Stioks being a part of this, but his kingdom must be engaged in it now."

"That is why the guild hall there was shut down," Herb stated. "They no longer have adventurers there. Some ended up here and only after swearing by the orb."

Resisting the urge to shake, Kaen remembered that encounter when they found the mole.

"I will talk with my generals and advisors and see what they recommend," Aldric declared as he stood up suddenly. "I do not want to seem like I am storming off, but I need to reach out to a few other kingdoms and see if I can acquire some help and possible troops."

"Do not ask Roccnari," Kaen said with a sigh. "Havannath is not thinking right and I would not trust him with any knowledge of our weakness right now. Especially since Elies has left. There is no telling what that elf might do."

Kaen noticed how Aldric's gaze shifted as he spoke. His head slowly started to bob in agreement.

"You have grown in not just size but in understanding," he admitted as he paused for a moment. "I had not considered that Havannath might make some poor choices if he felt he had no other options."

"I would not trust that king with anything. A king who will force a Dragon Rider not just once but twice to be bound to them is dangerous. It tells me that he cares more for his own hide than anyone else."

"Very well," Aldric finally declared as he considered Kaen's opinion. "I will inform you both on what I decide we can do. Let me know what you two find out or decide."

With that, he strode toward the door he had entered, walking with purpose.

After Aldric left, Herb stood up and picked up his empty cup.

"Would you like to check Elies's vault, or do you have something else that is pressing right now?"

Sighing, Kaen shook his head.

"Let's see what is there so I can figure out what Elies thinks is so important I will need it. Any idea what it might be?"

Laughing, even though it felt wrong with their recent conversation, Herb smiled at him and shook his head.

"I do not, but I will not lie. I am excited to find out."

20

What's in the Vault?

Herb stopped in the hallway, putting his palm on a black, twelve-by-twelve-inch stone block that was recessed in the wall. The hallway was like every other one except for a row of black stones lining the middle. Dim light from the orbs filled the wide hallway as Kaen stood near Herb, wondering what would come next.

Moments after his hand was placed on the panel, a grinding noise began, and a stone doorway appeared next to it.

"How many of these doors are there?"

Chuckling, Herb grinned as he waited for the door to move. It slid sideways into the wall.

"I cannot share the complete truth, but know that there are more doors here than you can imagine. Endless vaults were built back in the great days of Ebonmount, and if your academy produces the number of recruits that we hope it might in a generation, I may have to order more to be built."

When the stone door had disappeared into the wall, a small hallway led to a metal door with a dragon engraved on it.

Herb motioned for the door.

"You're up," he stated, moving back and flashing a grin.

The door loomed larger than life, though it was only about ten feet tall and five feet wide. Kaen could only imagine why it was so much bigger than the others. It had a silver sheen, but he knew it wasn't silver. The dragon on the front had a circular hole in its body, located in the middle of the door. Pulling the disc out, Kaen could swear it tingled in his hand.

You are at the door; I can tell.

Nodding his head, Kaen grinned.

I wish you could see this . . . I mean, this door is amazing, and all I know is something is behind it that Elies felt I should have.

Well, stop wasting time, and let me know what you find.

Grunting, Kaen put the disc on the circular spot, but it wouldn't stick or do anything. He looked at it and realized he was putting it dragon-side out. Turning the disc over, he put it back against the spot, and it stuck to the spot and clicked. The disc began to turn, making a full rotation until the dragon image was facing its head up. A popping noise sounded, and the door shook free from the wall.

"You ready?" Kaen asked as he glanced over his shoulder at Herb, who was shifting his head from side to side, hoping to see something.

"More than you know!"

Nodding, Kaen pressed on the door, and it swung open without any effort. As the door opened, lights flickered and turned on in the room.

The room was as large as the inside of Sulenda's inn. Rows of weapon racks stood empty; armor pedestals were nothing more than wooden stands. Cases had nothing in them.

"It's empty," Herb murmured as he came to stand next to Kaen.

"No, it's not," he replied as he pointed at the end of the room. "Look down there."

They started walking across the stone floors. There were no rugs, no tapestries, no decorations. The room appeared like an empty armory.

"Why would this be empty?" Kaen asked as he glanced around the room. "It looks like it should be filled with stuff."

"This has been here for a thousand years," Herb replied, his voice low. "No one but a Dragon Rider has been in it that I am aware of."

Kaen heard the disappointment in Herb's voice. He felt it, too. His eyes focused on the rectangular standing box and the item on the ground next to it.

Both were covered by a cloth of some sort, hiding what was under them.

Herb slowed down, letting Kaen finish the last few yards by himself.

Standing before the cloth, he hesitated. What would be here that Elies felt he would need?

I'm still waiting. This isn't fair . . .

Ignoring Pammon and his frustration, Kaen grabbed the cloth and pulled it down from its hiding container.

His chest tightened, and he felt it hard to breathe as the covering fell to the floor.

There, on an armor stand, hidden behind a metal and glass box, was something words would fail to describe.

"Is that . . ."

His voice cracked. He couldn't believe what he was looking at.

"Dragon armor?" Herb answered, even though the question wasn't for him. His voice was a whisper.

What is it?! Demanded Pammon as he felt the awe and disbelief washing over him from Kaen. **Tell me!**

It's armor . . . made with dragon scales . . . It's beautiful.

Not many things shocked Pammon anymore, but Kaen could feel that his words had caused Pammon to experience it now.

From a dragon? What color is it?

Kaen moved forward and ran his hand along the glass, looking for some way to open the case.

Small scales were somehow woven underneath larger scales. Where the joints for movement were, the tiniest scales, no bigger than his thumb, were woven together, appearing to allow for the wearer to bend and flex without issue. He realized why Elies had never worn this suit. It was too big for him but should fit Kaen almost perfectly.

There are different color scales. A giant red scale sits on the center breastplate with a dragon emblem on it. The shoulders have a gold scale on each corner and the hands have a silver or green scale on the top. The knee pieces are purple, I think. The rest of the set is made with black scales. There is even a helmet made with black scales as well.

Pammon said nothing else, but Kaen sensed that he was still in shock. Giving up one's scale like that would mean something, and both knew it had to be well over a thousand years old.

"Kaen, do you realize what this is?"

"I have no idea what this is, but if I had to guess, it's something created just for Dragon Riders. Tell me what you know."

His fingers drummed against the glass as he considered punching it or using his sword on it. Even as he spoke with Herb, his mind struggled not to attempt something he knew would not work. It seemed to call to him, wanting to be worn.

"That is one of the original Dragon Rider's armor," he informed Kaen as he struggled to keep his voice from spiking. "The armor depicted in the rare paintings that are kept within guild halls and treasure rooms for kings. I have only seen one picture in my entire life, and it showed a warrior of old and his dragon. He was wearing one of these."

The way Herb was speaking sounded like he was almost in a trance.

"Pull the cloth on the item next to it!"

Having forgotten about it, Kaen reached down and yanked off the smaller cloth, gasping when he saw what was under it.

"A shield . . . a dragon scale shield . . ." he stated as he bent down and picked it up.

A single brown scale that was over four feet tall and nearly three feet wide was set with straps to attach to one arm. No handle to hold the shield. Instead, it could be used with any weapon or bow.

"Why did Elies leave this?" Herb demanded. "He should have worn this when he faced Stioks!"

Ignoring Herb's question, Kaen felt the shield's power as he held it out before his face. He doubted anything he threw at it right now would even scratch it.

His thumbs rubbed the scale on both sides, wondering how old the dragon must have been to make a scale this size.

"I don't think he could get it out of the glass. When I touch it, something is stopping me from being stupid and trying to smash it with my fist."

Turning around, Kaen saw Herb looking up at him, shaking his head with a look he had not seen before.

"I . . ."

Herb couldn't finish what he was about to say, moved up next to Kaen, and motioned at the glass case with his hand.

"Touch it," Kaen said as he flipped the shield around and started to strap it to his arm.

Even though it appeared this had been in the vault for a long time, the straps moved with no cracks or stiffness. It felt like it had been just serviced and prepared for battle.

Slowly, Herb reached out, and as his finger got close to the glass, a *zap* was heard, and a small spark leaped from the case, causing him to flinch and recoil as he held his finger in his other hand.

"Holy mother of goblin shite!" Herb cursed as he shook his hand from the pain.

"It shocked you," Kaen stated, even though it was obvious. "I wonder why it didn't shock me?"

"Really? You wonder?" Herb asked as he glared at Kaen. "It somehow knows you are a Dragon Rider, and I am not. The real question is, how do you open it?"

Finished buckling the shield, Kaen motioned for Herb to back up.

"Let me try something stupid," he stated with a grin.

Moving back a few feet, Herb waited to see if Kaen was really going to attempt what he thought was about to happen.

Moving back a few feet, Kaen held the shield out before him and lunged at the case. When the shield came in contact with the glass, Kaen was stopped as if he had run face-first into a wall. A grunt escaped his throat, and his movement was halted completely.

Snorting, Kaen shrugged his shoulder, and he checked the scale shield.

"I guess that would have been too easy."

Chuckling, Herb nodded as he rejoined Kaen at the case.

"So, what will you do?"

Turning and smiling at Herb, he tapped the shield and motioned toward the door they came through.

"I'll keep this for now and figure out another day how to open the case. Right now, I need to get some food, take a shower, and start working on a few more things I have in mind."

Sighing, Herb nodded and turned to leave the room.

"Who would have believed it," he said with a slight groan. "One of the greatest treasures for a Dragon Rider in our guild hall, and no way to access it."

Laughing, Kaen increased his stride, caught up to Herb, and paused momentarily. He reached out and messed up Herb's hair, as he had seen Hess do so many times.

"Bah, stop that!" he yelped playfully. "I finally got used to Hess not doing that anymore. I don't need you starting up."

Feigning innocence, Kaen waved his hands in surrender as Herb glared at him playfully.

Fixing his hair, Herb pointed at the disc when they passed the door.

"Don't forget that, and whatever you do, don't lose it. I don't want to have to wait to produce another one of those."

That is very impressive, Pammon stated as he ran his talon across the shield. **I cannot scratch it.**

"Think you should try and hit it a little harder?"

Pammon's thrum vibrated through Kaen as his dragon shook his head at him and rolled his eyes.

Why would I want to do that? Sounds risky.

Glancing around the courtyard, Kaen turned back to Pammon and smiled.

Inspect Dragon Shield
Dragon Shield - + 5 to all stats. Steadfast. Impenetrable.

I inspected it and wanted to see what the steadfast thing meant. Besides, you know what my stats are right now. I can take the hit, provided you don't go all out on me.

Just because you are over forty in strength and constitution does not mean I should attempt to hurt you. What happens if I injure you? Imagine how bad I would feel.

Stop whining and just do it.

Grumbling, Pammon turned and snorted, getting a few feet between them and setting himself in a position for a solid strike.

Remember, you asked for this. I don't want to hear about it later.

Setting his feet and preparing for what he knew was coming, Kaen lifted the shield up and braced himself.

Go for it!

After one last snort, Pammon lifted up his front claw and swiped at Kaen, striking the shield with a solid hit.

Kaen grunted as he slid back a few feet but never gave up any real ground. Pammon blinked a few times as he saw Kaen smiling at him.

That should not have happened!

How hard did you try to hit me?

Pammon thrummed for a moment. The frustration he felt not seeing Kaen get knocked across the courtyard answered that question.

You tried to launch me across the yard!

Yes . . . I did. I wanted to teach you a lesson . . . Now, I will try harder.

Sensing what Pammon was about to do, Kaen braced himself even more, digging his feet into the ground and bending his knees. He leaned into the attack as he saw Pammon swipe the shield with intent.

When his talons connected with the shield, Pammon drove through the strike, causing Kaen to slide back about eight feet.

IMPOSSIBLE! You should have been knocked clean across the courtyard!

Why would you do that? demanded Kaen. He started flinching his shoulders and arms. He had felt the force wash through him. The shield had somehow absorbed all that impact and barely sent any through him like he had expected. If the steadfast effect provided this kind of protection, it would change so many things. He could easily go toe-to-toe with some of the larger orcs without fearing the impact of their swings.

Kaen glanced at Pammon and saw him snorting in frustration.

It's good to know you got serious. Now, we just need to figure out how to get inside that container. I can only imagine what the rest of the armor will offer.

21

Always Training

Kaen felt Pammon watching him while he lay in bed staring at the ceiling.

It's too late to stay in bed. You need to get up and start working on what we discussed.

Turning his head sideways, he stuck his tongue out at Pammon and extended his middle finger.

Do you think I want to lay here? I'm weighing everything in my head. We have too much to do, and I'm not sure what to do first. Besides, we have two days before we can head out anyway. Ava said her dad is almost done creating what he believes will be a successful potion.

Keep showing me that finger, and unlike Hess, I will bite it off and swallow it. I'm sure you don't need that one to shoot a bow or swing a sword.

Kaen sat up, laughing and rubbing his eyes with his offending finger before dropping out of his bed.

The servant who kept this place clean for him needed a raise. The floor was free of dirt, and he wondered how much work it took to keep it all out, especially with the large sliding doors that opened so Pammon could get in and out.

If you keep growing, we are going to need a bigger place to stay. You're almost too tall to fit in here.

Says the Dragon Rider who has kept tailors in business for the last two years with how much you have grown. Hess is barely a few inches taller than you now, and you could easily beat him in a fight, and you know it.

Flexing, Kaen admired his body and ran his fingers over his abdominal muscles. There was almost no fat on his body, and everywhere he looked, he rippled with the rewards of his hard work these last two years.

Regardless, we need to discuss our next plan. Are you still ok with us hunting the griffons near the dwarven kingdom? Rumor has it there are some there, and we both know you need to try and find a few creatures to eat that will help you grow faster.

Pammon thrummed as he lifted his head and started to smile.

I am always game for eating something new. You never need to ask that question.

Kaen walked over, reached up with his hands, and scratched the scales on Pammon's neck. He studied their size and shape, following them down toward the base of his chest.

Comparing my scales to the ones you saw on the armor and the shield?

"I am," he answered as he stopped at the largest scales on Pammon's lower breast area. "The shield would have had to come from here, and the size of the dragon would have been at least three times the size you are now. It would have been even bigger than Tharnok."

Pammon's chest heaved suddenly, catching Kaen off guard. The dragon lowered his head and began pushing Kaen down, playing with him.

Kaen pressed up on his dragon, able to hold his head up, even if it required him to give everything he had.

Now stop that before you hurt me, you fool. Then I won't be able to help you eat something new.

Lifting his head up, Pammon started trilling once Kaen began scratching his scales again.

Fine, but let's stop talking about pulling scales off. It hurts to imagine.

Four attacks came at him simultaneously, and Kaen knew he couldn't block all of them. Time was on his side as they were slower than him, but still, he needed to choose the best path.

The spear was going to force him into the sword coming at his head. The mace that was on his left was a solid wide swing, preventing him from choosing that path lest he get caught by the attack. That left the staff on his right. The reach was good, but the trainer using it was not providing enough speed to prevent him from escaping it.

Rolling to his right, he lifted his wooden shield, absorbing the staff's blow as it came down on him, letting him continue forward to tackle the trainer, knocking the wind out of them and giving Kaen space once again from the other three.

They had all shifted and pursued but knew their one chance was gone.

Glancing at each other, they nodded and held up their weapons.

"We surrender; we will delay the inevitable."

Kaen had successfully defeated six trainers, and the sound of clapping and cheering echoed off the walls as the students cheered for him. The area they had been given to duel provided too much open space.

That was too easy. Where is Master Bren? He should be challenging you.

Glancing at Pammon, he noticed Callie trying to climb his tail as Hess stood by, watching her play.

He is at his place in town, dealing with some things there. He is still upset after what happened, and even though I told him not to worry, he has pulled back some from here.

You people get upset about stuff like that. If I make a mistake, I will fix it. I won't whine about it after the fact.

Shaking hands and patting the shoulders of the trainers he had sparred with, Kaen smiled, ignoring the fact he knew Pammon had indeed whined about things before.

"You all did great. Just remember to work together as one. A stronger opponent who is faster will require you to be smart. A few more feints, a double feint, and a better use of your range will help win a fight like that."

Each of them bowed and nodded before heading back to the students who cheered for them.

"Kaen!"

He turned and saw Racha, the headmistress, coming toward him.

As he handed the shield and mace to a young boy who was grinning up at him like a fool, Kaen waved and began walking toward her.

"What can I do for you, Headmistress?"

She covered the space between them, holding her gray skirt off the ground as she strode quickly across the dirt. She was biting her lip, and her usual well-kept hair was a bit undone.

"This contest of yours is causing me more grief than Finn will admit," she declared, her voice tense as she threw her hands up in the air. "These children are pushing themselves too hard!"

"Too hard? What do you mean by that?"

She grunted and motioned at the crowd of a hundred children who had just finished watching him spar and had now moved to pick up practice weapons and repeat what they had witnessed.

"Look at them! They will not stop. Every day, they push themselves to the limit. They are tired, bruised, sore, and exhausted. They are fighting as if their lives depend on it."

Kaen noticed she was wringing her hands, and he put a hand on her shoulder, feeling her flinch.

"Racha," he said in the softest voice he could muster at the moment, "you are not caring for children. These *children* are training this way because their lives and those who live in Ebonmount depend on them. Soon, a day will come when we need children who are hard and prepared for pain. It saddens me that this is true, but they see that. Why can't you?"

Tears welled in her eyes, and a heavy sigh escaped her lips.

"But what about when some of them die?" "I feel that weight. Trust me. I know that burden more than anyone else here," he said, sighing and squeezing her shoulder. "If there were any other way, I would take it, but I know what is coming. You know what is coming. They must be prepared this way. Remember, each of them chose this path and passed the interviews. Every child whose parent made that choice for them was sent back home. Only those who are choosing this path are here."

Moving to stand beside her, Kaen pointed to the children and the sounds of wooden weapons clacking together. "We are building walls because something is trying to get in and destroy any future they will have. I just pray that we have time to prepare them to help against it."

"It's just . . ." she began to say as she paused, watching the students as they played at fighting.

Turning to face Kaen, she gave a slight bow. Her lips were drawn tight, but her eyes held his gaze.

"I'm sorry, last night was hard. A few children required . . ."

"Students, Miss Racha. Students," he interrupted, his voice firmer than it had been the last time he spoke.

"Students," she stated, bobbing her head. "A few students required healing for injuries received while sparring. They are all fine, but it bothered me. No one felt they were abused or bullied. Just injuries gained in the process. Even Phillip required some healing a few days ago, suffering a nasty crack to his head from one of the other students."

"Good!" exclaimed Kaen. "I know this might bother you, but Hess never took it easy on me when he trained me. I had bruises from rocks that he threw at me. He did not take it easy on me because I was young or because I was his charge. Remember, we are in a race against time. You, of all people, know what next month will bring."

She nodded and grimaced.

"You understand the pressure you have put on Finn and myself. Having over thirty lifestone students will change everything. Even your mentor, Hess, has mentioned how things will change for that group. This is why the older ones are fighting so hard."

Laughing, Kaen nodded and thumped his chest where his lifestone was.

"They are being given a future and a chance to pursue their dreams. It will be six months before the next batch of lifestones comes in. I have paid a fortune to secure this many, as has the king and others. They will be the ones on the frontline someday. For now, only those who are strong enough to push past the pain and focus on their goals will be chosen to get one."

She grunted, and Kaen spun around, hearing laughter coming up from behind him. He saw Hess and Callie laughing as he chased her toward Kaen.

"If you will excuse me, Miss Racha, I will continue to entrust these students to your care. You are doing fine work. Keep loving them and pushing them."

Striding off, he left her standing there, still wringing her hands, but her head bobbed. Being in charge was never going to be an easy job.

"Callie!" Kaen shouted as he dashed toward her, snatching her off the ground and tossing her high into the sky.

She laughed and giggled as he caught her, dipping her low before throwing her once more into the air, watching her red hair bounce in the wind and her eyes sparkle.

"Kaen!" she squealed. "Again!"

Tossing her once more, he caught her before bringing her in and giving her a hug.

"I missed you, little sister. Are mom and dad being nice?"

Hess groaned as Callie turned and narrowed her eyes at him.

She nodded her head sharply and smiled.

"Yes! See Pammon!"

Bouncing her on his hip, he nodded and pointed at his dragon, who was watching the three of them.

She likes to grab my tail. I have mentioned I don't like my tail being grabbed, haven't I?

Oh, you have, and yet not once have I heard you growl at her when she does.

Pammon remained silent, but Kaen saw his tail get tucked under himself as he laid his head on the dirt floor.

"Pammon loves you, but remember, don't tug on his tail. It hurts the dragon. He isn't strong like your brother."

Laughing, she punched him in the chest, and Kaen growled playfully, tipping her upside down and tickling her.

"Remind me why I wanted kids when those punches she throws start to hurt," joked Hess as he smiled, watching the two of them play.

"They hurt," he answered as he dipped her down again, causing another cascade of laughter to fill the space around them.

Lost in that moment, Kaen tried to ignore the conversation he'd just had with Racha. He hoped that Callie could grow up without having to be that hard, but Kaen knew the odds were not in her favor.

22

The Cost of Potions

"I cannot promise these will work completely, but they should heal an injury for Pammon," Lord Hurem declared as he handed the two fist-sized potions to Kaen. Each of them was a black color, almost as if they were sucking the light from around them. "Remember, he needs to break them in his mouth before swallowing them. Do not worry about the glass. The notes I followed said they would dissolve without problems in his stomach."

That does not look appealing, Pammon stated as he gazed at the two potions Kaen was holding. **Perhaps you should try one first.**

Chuckling, Kaen shook his head.

"Pammon wanted to know what would happen if someone besides a dragon tried to drink these."

Lord Hurem's voice rose as he barked out forced laughter. "I would not try that as I think it would probably kill someone. Dragon blood is slightly acidic and, if not treated properly, can cause damage."

"I understand. Don't drink unless I want to die" Kaen responded.

"Let's move past this whole potion side of business and talk about other matters, if you would," Bridgette said as she motioned to the table and chairs behind them. "Ava will be here in a few, and I have some servants coming with snacks for all of us. Pammon included."

Licking his snout, Pammon flashed a toothy grin, which made Lady Hurem smile.

They had been sitting together for a few minutes when Ava came into the courtyard, wearing a simple dress that took Kaen's breath away. As she walked across the courtyard, he moved her chair next to his and pulled it out for her.

"Thank you."

He nodded and smiled as she pulled her hair back in a simple ponytail. Her black hair was shiny and smelled like flowers that might be in a field during the springtime. No one commented on the redness on her face from having endured the wind on Pammon's back.

She always looked good no matter what she wore, but the dark green dress she had on really seemed to suit her well. It showed off her curves and reminded him why it was so hard to focus sometimes when she was around.

"Kaen?"

Realizing Lord Hurem was calling him, Kaen turned and saw her father motioning for the small bowl filled with fruit next to him.

"Mind passing that to me?"

Bobbing his head, he handed it to him, then turned his face in time to see Ava blush a little.

"Are you allowed to share what you learned while on the quest with Ava?" Lady Hurem asked.

"Mom!"

Narrowing her eyes at Ava, she cut off the complaint before turning her smiling face back to Kaen.

"I'm not at liberty to share much, Lady Hurem . . ."

"Call me Bridgette, please."

Kaen heard the disdain in her voice. He had forgotten how much she disliked him calling her *Lady Hurem*, believing it removed the familial bond she felt they shared.

"Forgive me, Bridgette," he replied, glancing at her husband and noticing he was watching how this played out while eating an apple. "We scouted out some areas as requested by the adventurers' guild and reported our findings to them. Right now, due to the nature of the mission, we aren't really allowed to speak about it. Perhaps, if you would like, I could ask Guild Master Herb if he could share some details with you. No doubt you are asking so you can prepare for any potential need for more potions."

A cough was heard coming from Lord Hurem, who appeared to have choked on the bite he had taken.

"No need," she declared as if dismissing the need with a wave of her hand. "I just wanted to make sure my daughter was safe. She barely even mentioned how amazing the trip must have been, getting to fly with you and Pammon."

Pammon grunted as he looked back at them. He was currently enjoying the fresh sheep carcasses that had been dropped off before Ava had arrived. Hearing his name had gotten his attention, but seeing there was no specific question, he returned to enjoying his snack.

"As you might have noticed, flying on a dragon is not always easy. The wind can be very fierce and cold. When you consider the rain we flew into, it can quickly make a trip miserable."

Nodding her head, she picked up her glass and took a drink.

"Did Father give you the potion he created for you yet?"

Glancing at Ava, he saw a smile pulling at the corner of her lips, hidden well from her mother's watchful eyes.

"I had not yet given it to him," Lord Hurem stated as he set his nearly finished apple down. "I figured we would give it to him before he left. After all, what better way to send him off than with a potion made just for him?"

Rolling her eyes at her father, Ava let a sigh escape and motioned at him.

"Father likes to be a little bit more dramatic than my mother sometimes. The truth is he could not stop talking about it once he was able to fuse your blood and Pammon's together successfully. Eventually, he will be unable to resist and tell you that nothing like this has happened in probably over three hundred years."

"Ava!" he exclaimed. He shot her a fearsome look and then laughed.

"It sounds like you truly are a master at potion making. I had heard Guild Master Herb sing your praises a few months back, and I can see it was not just mere words."

One might have thought Lord Hurem was part peacock as he shifted with his chest out and his shoulders back.

"Oh, I will never hear the end of that," groaned Bridgette before taking another drink from her cup.

Kaen and Ava both laughed as the servants brought in trays of food.

"They like you," Ava whispered as she and Kaen lounged against Pammon on the grass in the courtyard.

"I assumed, since she only asked me about seven times if I was ever going to consider joining the family," teased Kaen, who received a sharp elbow in response.

"Pammon, how do you put up with him and his big head?"

A thrum came from the massive body they leaned against, shaking them from the vibrations. Pammon lifted his head and adjusted his neck till he was staring at both of them.

Tell her it is not easy, but thankfully, I am strong enough to support the weight of your head.

"Pammon says it's not hard at all."

Shaking his head, Pammon took in a deep breath, and Kaen knew what he was about to do.

"I lied!" he shouted. "He said it's a good thing he is so strong that my big head doesn't bother him."

Ava laughed as Pammon shifted his neck and snout, blowing out the air through his nostrils and coating a section of the courtyard with his phlegm.

"That is disgusting," Kaen said, grimacing. "Worse is he would have gotten that on both of us if I hadn't told you exactly what he said."

"I doubt that," Ava replied as she leaned over and scratched a spot on Pammon's chest where his front leg met his body. He trilled and moved so she could get between the scales at the joint.

"I don't suppose I can ask you if I can come when you leave next?"

Shaking his head, Kaen drew her close to him and breathed in her scent, doing his best to lock it in his mind.

"It is going to be a long and dangerous trip. We are hunting for something to help with his growth. We will need to find it first before we can actually engage it. I'm hoping to be gone less than a week."

"A week," she said with a grunt. "That seems like an awful long time to be gone."

If she thinks a week is a long time, what will she do when you are gone for months at a time again?

Well, we will not tell her about that right now. Let's just focus on the task at hand. I don't want her to think I don't care, but there is still so much to do.

Glancing around the courtyard, Kaen saw that it was empty except for the three of them. Turning, he put his finger under Ava's chin and lifted her face to his.

He leaned over and kissed her, feeling her soft lips against his. Her hand reached up behind his neck, and as she started to pull him tighter, Pammon shifted, rolling backward and sending the two of them to the grass.

His thrumming began, and Ava scowled as she poked his hard scales.

Kaen couldn't help but laugh as he lay on his back, looking up at his dragon, shaking his head from side to side.

"He did that on purpose!" she exclaimed, her face turning red.

"Yes, yes, he did," Kaen replied, putting his hands behind his head, looking at her as she glared at Pammon.

"Why?"

"We aren't old enough for that yet. He says we can think about it in a few more decades."

Climbing to her feet, Ava smoothed out her dress, pointed at Pammon's snout, and shook her finger.

"If you keep that up, I might have to reconsider how many *treats* arrive at your place from me. Rumor has it the king may only supply him with pigs since nothing else can keep up with his belly."

She paused when she saw Pammon watching her, his eyelids not moving, and those golden eyes stared her down.

"Perhaps a cow might be hard to come by for a while."

She doesn't play fair, does she? Pammon asked as he shifted his body, tearing clumps of grass out as his weight and scales dug furrows in their manicured lawn.

No, I doubt she does. Besides, we need to prepare to leave soon. I was just getting a goodbye kiss for the week. Nothing else would have happened.

That is a lie, and you know it. I can feel how you felt during that kiss. If you want to do that, do not do it next to me. The last thing we need is for your passion to awaken something in me that should still be a long time away.

Kaen erupted in laughter and couldn't stop, holding his sides. Pammon and Ava watched him.

"Should I ask what is so funny?" Ava finally asked.

"Pammon said we cannot do that when we are next to him. Not because he doesn't want us to enjoy ourselves, but because doing so might make him want to seek out a female dragon."

Kaen started to roll, sensing what was coming, but he was too slow. Pammon's tail flicked his side, sending Kaen tumbling along the grass and into Pammon's side.

"Mother of elf . . ." Kaen began to curse before remembering Ava was there.

"You didn't need to stop on my behalf. I have been around enough adventurers to have heard my fair share of colorful language."

Shaking his head, Kaen got up, massaging the side where Pammon's tail had caught him.

"Maybe another day. For now, I think this is a good time to call it a night. Pammon and I must finish preparing a few things before we leave in the morning."

Letting out a breath he had been holding, Kaen moved over and winked at Pammon before giving Ava another long kiss.

A snort broke their embrace, and both laughed when they saw Pammon's snout just a few feet away.

"Is he always like this?" she asked while she laughed.

"Yes . . . yes, he is."

23

Always Finding Trouble

"Three days, maybe four. It really depends on how the weather is," Kaen informed Hess as he continued packing his bags with supplies. "I'm not sure how long it will take for us to find what we are hunting once we get there. Then I still have to try and meet with the dwarven king if I can."

Hess simply nodded, lost in the awe of the shield Kaen had let him hold.

"Whatever you do, do not show them this shield. In fact, keep it with you at all times. Something like this . . ." he trailed off as he spoke in a hushed tone. "People would kill their own mother for it."

"That is why I have kept it hidden in one of the baskets on Pammon. It would not be easy getting that from him."

Nodding his head, Hess ran his one hand down the shield again. He had enjoyed it when Kaen put it on his good arm, amazed at how light it was, and allowed him to hold a mace without getting in the way.

"I plan on being back in two weeks. I need to start traveling more, and people need to get used to me being gone for random amounts of time."

Letting out a sigh, Hess picked up the shield and moved closer to Kaen, handing it back to him.

"I must say, boy, you are getting smarter. That time with Elies did you good."

Please do not make his head any bigger. It will be hard to carry him any-where if it keeps growing.

Laughing at Pammon's joke, Hess turned and moved to where Pammon was lying in their home. He held out his hand, and Pammon brought his snout to him, getting to enjoy a rough scratching of his scales.

"I'm sorry you must parent him now. I'm just glad that I got a chance to learn from him. A girl is far worse."

I'm surprised that you didn't bring your daughter. Not that I care either way.

"Don't pretend I don't see how you two interact," Hess stated with a chuckle. "If I didn't know any better, I would believe she has her tiny claws embedded in your heart."

Snorting, Pammon shook his head free of Hess, but both of them could see the smile from the curve of his mouth.

"He likes her more than me sometimes," added Kaen as he bent back over, putting extra clothes and boots in a pouch. "He complained last time Sulenda came for a visit and didn't bring Callie. That reminds me. Why did she come?"

"School stuff," Hess answered as Kaen cinched up the pack. "Always something I need to sign and spend money on. Perhaps someone should remind her how long it takes to earn a gold coin."

Seven coppers a day . . . not even enough to get out of bed for.

Both of them laughed, agreeing that Pammon was right. No dragon would waste their time for such a small amount.

With a map in hand, Kaen and Pammon took off a few hours later, knowing they wouldn't get as far as they wanted, but both had somewhere else to be. Neither had mentioned to Hess that they wanted to scout the northeastern border past the area where they had once fought the bandits.

I know it's a bit dangerous, but we won't be going anywhere near Stioks's border. I just want to see if we can spot a large gathering of troops, orcs, and goblins.

I understand. I will stay high in the clouds. Besides, it is a good thing we are leaving today. It should rain for the next few days in Ebonmount, and I would rather not always be wet.

Chuckling, Kaen rubbed that familiar scale and let himself get comfortable. He leaned back against the pad that Hess had brought him. It was his first attempt to try out this addition to his saddle. He could lean back against the raised part and relax a little more. It came loose easily from two small clasps so that if need be, he could still spin around and fire behind him without it interfering.

They reached the eastern edge of the Ebonmount mountain range, and Kaen marveled, as always, at the massive lake. Water piled up in a huge lake near the base of the mountain, stretching for miles before becoming open farmland and trees. All this water would move slowly to the south, creating swamps on the southern end of the mountain range. Here, showers would drop their water, and as it rose, the water rolled down the natural incline. Fish were plentiful, yet there were not as many boats as there had been in ages past. It would make breaking into the eastern side of Ebonmount difficult.

Nothing but the occasional small ship down there using nets. I think most of them are aware of the coming storm and are staying off the water.

Kaen saw the clouds above him and off to the east. They were dark and looked ready to deposit all of the water they held. The seasons were changing, and soon rain would be a common thing before it changed even more. They wouldn't get much snow, if any, but it would get colder in about three or four months.

Let's head north then. This is far enough. I know we are still a day from being deep enough in Stioks's land, but I would rather not risk a random encounter.

You're afraid. I can sense it.

I am . . . and I know you are as well.

Pammon didn't reply. Both of them knew he had done damage to Elies. They had mentioned the damage done by Stioks, and Juthom was more than they had expected. Tharnok had also dealt some damage, but in the end, both riders and dragons had pulled away, neither feeling they had the upper hand.

How will we ever get to the other kingdom if we can't go through Stioks's?

Pensworth was northeast of Luthaelia; the cold weather and constant snow were a barrier most could not handle. While it was not a heavily populated area, the people who lived there were strong and sturdy. They were considered some of the strongest warriors when faced with solo combat. No one ever tried to conquer the land because living there was not pleasant for a non-native person.

I'm not sure. We should be fine with the cold, but it would require us to fly way north and then turn east. That would add days to an already long trip.

Pammon grunted as he flew, keeping them just below the clouds that were in the sky. No need to get wet from the mist if they did not have to.

Hours passed as they occasionally talked, and Kaen studied the map he had been drawing on his leg.

Herb had been a genius, not that he would ever tell him that.

Wrapping some leather around his leg and fastening it with a few straps kept it from moving in the air. The charcoal pencil allowed him to sketch out the things that he saw, and he began to make sense of the mess of trees, rocks, hills, lakes, streams, and other land features they flew over.

While all the maps he owned and checked were nice, learning this skill would prove much more valuable as he traveled. He could glance down and get a general idea of where they were. It let him know how far they should be from any given place. The best part was he could mark down something of interest for himself or someone else to check out later.

He and Pammon were both content to just simply fly. It was what they were supposed to do—be free with nothing holding them back.

As the sun began to set, Pammon found a spot near a lake and dropped Kaen off to set up camp while he went and hunted. He had seen a few animals and knew that the lake would draw them in.

Kaen had set to the task of collecting firewood and, after having gotten it going, pulled out the map he had been given by Herb and the one he sketched today.

He compared them and saw similarities, but other areas were different. Tree lines had shifted from either forest fires in the last two hundred years or people cutting them down. Some areas had expanded as growth took place with no one to hold it back.

A lake that was marked on Herb's map was gone. Not sure if something had happened to drain it or there had simply not been enough water in the last few years to keep it full.

All those things spelled lessons to remember.

Depending on something that was this out of date could cause problems during battle. Landscapes would be different, and showing up somewhere, expecting a tree line and an elevated position might leave an army exposed to the elements and an attacking force who knows the land better.

As he worked, listening to the fire and enjoying the view of the setting sun's reflection on the lake, he sensed something from the trees.

Where are you?

Sensing Kaen's apprehension, Pammon shifted from where he was and turned to head his way.

I'm not far, maybe five minutes if I don't use my skill. What is it?

Kaen pretended to keep looking at the map as he shifted his body slightly and looked out of the corner of his eye.

Something or someone is in the woods. I can sense it. Like, I know from a sound I heard and the fact that the insects and birds are quiet near me.

Pammon was south of him, and he knew the trees were thick but not so thick that he couldn't see through them. He was not as high as he would be if he weren't hunting. That meant the angle was off and would be a limiting factor.

Kaen's sword and mace were on his hip, but his bow was a few yards from him. Not knowing what was out there, he hadn't expect to be in trouble if attacked, but his bow made him feel more comfortable.

Listening, he continued to scan the tree line as he moved the pencil along the leather, not leaving marks but pretending to.

A few seconds later, he saw the movement and realized it was a person.

Thankful it wasn't an orc or a beast, Kaen let out a small sigh as he rolled up Herb's map and slowly put it in his bag.

"I am afraid you are not as stealthy as you thought you were," Kaen almost shouted, his voice echoing into the woods. "Come out and show yourselves. I mean you no harm if you mean me no harm."

Pammon was still a good three minutes away, so Kaen waited until they came into view so he could see what he was up against.

A man and a woman stepped out from behind the trees. They wore leather armor and had sticks in their hair and leaves attached to their armor. Each were holding a bow and had a knife or sword on their hips. Seeing their pointed ears and fine features, Kaen knew what he had found.

Wood elves.

"How did you get past our sentries?" the woman asked as she held her bow with an arrow pointed at the ground.

Smiling and holding his hands in the air, Kaen noticed the difference in their skin color. Darker than the elves in Roccnari. Where the elves there were fairer and taller, these elves were shorter and more muscular.

He realized the female elf was speaking the common language, which sounded rough and under pronounced. The odds that most of them actually practiced it meant they might not understand everything he said.

It's wood elves. There are two of them showing themselves, but I know there are more.

The woman scowled. Kaen had not answered her question yet. She grunted and raised her bow at him.

"Tell me, human, why you are here and how you got here, or I will not hesitate to make you a corpse."

Chuckling, Kaen smiled and then spoke in the elf language he had learned in Roccnari.

"I mean no harm. I'm just spending the night as I travel to the dwarven kingdom."

Shock, awe, and anger flashed over both of their faces as the bow now trembled in her hands.

Perhaps using the elven language was not the best idea . . .

Pammon flew faster.

24

Elves in the Forest

The female elf spat on the ground as her scowl deepened and she pulled the bowstring back more to aim at Kaen.

"You would be wise to tell us who you are and why you know that language!" she shouted as her male companion turned his head and whistled toward the woods.

Sighing, Kaen felt where Pammon was and knew he needed another minute before his backup arrived.

"I am Kaen Marshell. I am a Dragon Rider and on my way to the dwarven kingdom."

"Lies!" she cried, motioning at Kaen with her bow. "There are no young Dragon Riders. You are still wet behind the ears."

Kaen watched as four more elves appeared from the woods, each with a bow and arrow ready.

"Would you be willing to wait a moment so that I can prove myself? He will be here soon, and I would prefer him not to be upset if you all started attacking me."

The woman stared at Kaen, a confused look on her face. Why would a man be so calm with so many arrows pointed at him? The fact that he spoke the elvish tongue was problematic enough. No elves would consider teaching a human their tongue unless they had a good reason.

"Thistle, look at him," the male elf whispered as he glanced around the spot where Kaen was standing. "No tracks, supplies that would have been difficult to carry this far, and no boat. His attitude says he is telling the truth."

Grunting, she shook her head and gazed at what her partner told her.

"There are no Dragon Riders except the old and cursed ones. We both know the rumors we heard last year are just that. Rumors."

Kaen smiled at them as they stood arguing, and they both narrowed their eyes, wondering why he was suddenly smiling.

Pammon's roar echoed across the waters and the treetops, causing the elves to take a step back in shock.

"A dragon!" the male elf shouted as he quickly began to move back toward the tree line.

The female, Thistle, remained where she was, slightly lowering the bow some but staring at Kaen in disbelief.

"It's true," she muttered, seeing Kaen nod his head when he heard her.

A few seconds later, a massive shadow emerged over the tree line and swooped down along the shore, turning sharply. Pammon was now in full view, flapping his wings and sending waves of water and dirt toward the shore and the elves.

He glared at them and snarled, causing them to raise their bows toward him absently.

"I wouldn't do that," Kaen shouted as the elves stepped back toward the trees.

Thistle began to slide backward, tripping over a branch and sending her arrow up into the sky, thankfully away from Pammon, as she fell onto her rear.

Pammon landed on the dirt near Kaen, sending a cloud of dust at those still brave enough not to hide behind trees, while Kaen slowly moved toward the elf woman, who was sliding on her backside on the ground.

Behind Pammon was the setting sun, its light reflecting off the water and onto him, creating a majestic image of a bronze dragon silhouetted by the sun.

"We mean you no harm unless you attack us," Kaen informed them. "We had no idea you and your people were here. We just stopped here so we could rest for the night."

The woman stopped moving backward as Kaen got closer and held out his hand.

"How?" was all she could say as her mouth hung open, and she glanced at Pammon, who was eyeing her, his mouth slightly opened as he bared his teeth.

"It is a long story but one I would prefer not to share with you and your friends. I promise you that unless you mean me or Pammon harm, we will not hurt you."

Kaen was still a few feet from her, holding out a hand and offering to help her stand. Thistle jumped up on her own, dusted herself off, and did her best to regain some composure.

"We . . . we would be honored to converse with a Dragon Rider," she declared, trying to hide how many different octaves her voice had cycled through. "Rowan! Bring us some food and water and fetch the others!"

The man who had been beside her hesitated a moment before moving, and when her orders finally registered, he nodded and whistled a few times, directing those hiding in the woods.

She is lucky she did not shoot me. I might have had to eat her.

Grinning, Kaen resisted the urge to laugh and turned and beckoned her to join him at his fire.

"They call you Thistle, if I heard right?"

She nodded and slowly moved toward the fire, keeping an eye on Pammon, who was moving closer to Kaen.

"Nice to meet you, Thistle. Again, I am Kaen. I promise he won't hurt you unless you shoot at him again."

Even with the smile that Kaen was flashing and how his dragon had stopped baring his teeth, Thistle was struggling to move closer to the fire.

I guess you really did scare them.

They threatened you. They pointed arrows at you!

And we both know that I was never in danger. Unless that woman is better than me, we both know I would have been fine until you made it here.

Snorting, Pammon caused the woman to tense up again and watch him.

"Ignore him," Kaen informed her as he bent over and pulled some dried meat from a pack. "He was not happy because he thought I was in danger, but he is fine now."

"If you say so."

Thistle finally made it close enough to the fire, keeping a wide berth between her and Pammon. A few minutes passed as she turned down Kaen's offer of food. The one she called Rowan arrived with six other elves, who all stayed closer to the tree line.

"Would you two like to hear about Pammon and me, or would you prefer to continue sitting there, staring at us in silence for a little longer?"

Rowan coughed and elbowed Thistle gently, and she nodded.

"Sorry, we are . . . caught off guard. A new Dragon Rider, one who speaks the elves' language, is here in our forest. None of us would have imagined these things possible when we set out this morning."

Smiling, Kaen tossed a small log into the fire and glanced at Pammon, who lay down, resting his head near Kaen and closed his eyes.

"Well, let me share with you what has happened in the last few years, and then we can go from there."

Putting the waterskin down, Kaen watched the two of them as they absorbed all the news he shared with them. The other six had gotten closer and were seated on the ground, legs crossed.

"We know of the black Dragon Rider and of Elies. It pains us to know he is sick. He had protected many in the years before," Rowan stated as he put his hand to his chest. "We, too, have seen increases in the orc and goblin forces. We have had more incursions over the last few years but so far have kept them from gaining ground in our homes."

Kaen nodded as he listened. He had his map out and had shown them what he had drawn versus the old map he had.

"Where would you say the last few fights with them have been?"

Rowan moved over and glanced at both maps, noting the differences between them.

"Here and here," he stated, pointing to two spots off to the east and south. "They have come in a few other areas, but those were smaller scouting parties."

Kaen marked the two spots on both maps and blew a raspberry as he sat thinking, causing the eight wood elves around him to laugh. he realized what he had done and grinned.

"Sorry, I did not mean to offend."

Thistle waved her hand and smiled.

"It is good for us to see that you are not . . ." she paused, trying to think of the word in common. "Stick up?"

"I believe you mean *stuck up*. Not uptight or someone who walks with a stick up their rear?"

Rowan started laughing, and Thistle's face flushed a bit as she nodded her head.

"Yes. Sorry, my use of common is not that great. Not many speak it anymore in our village. Even your elven is considered a dialect we don't use. We don't hold onto every vowel as long."

"I noticed but figured I would do my best. Now, are you all ok with Pammon and me staying here for tonight? I would offer to let you all stay with us unless you need to head back somewhere or patrol the woods."

"Do you need us to keep watch for you? We would be honored!" exclaimed Rowan as he stood up and began motioning to the six, who were almost immediately on their feet.

"I would not ask that of you," Kaen stated as he stood up, holding his hand out to calm them down. "Pammon can easily sense things that are happening around us even when sleeping. I would prefer not to make you all give up your sleep if there is no need."

One of the scouts behind them whistled and made some hand motions. Rowan nodded and held up three fingers. Four of the scouts gave a slight bow and rushed off into the woods.

"I have sent them to go looking for some food for your dragon. It is the least we can offer since we pointed our weapons at him. Our elder would not forgive us if we did not make some effort to repay that debt."

When Rowan mentioned food, Pammon's eyes opened, and he lifted his head and grinned.

I like these wood elves. Perhaps they finally understand the honor I am due.

Groaning, Kaen shook his head.

"Pammon says he would appreciate that. Only a few, though, or I'm afraid he might get spoiled."

Pammon leaned his head forward, bopping Kaen in the side and knocking him off the log, and then he began to thrum.

Kaen stood up, laughing, and rubbed Pammon's head. The elves joined in once they saw the two of them playing and laughing.

After they settled down, Kaen noticed Thistle was glancing at his bow.

"Do you want to see this?" he asked, holding it out to her.

"That string. Do you know where you got it from?"

Shaking his head, Kaen watched as she took the bow and examined the string that was wrapped around it.

Rowan leaned over her and watched as she ran her fingers over it.

They mumbled something in their elvish tongue that Kaen didn't catch as Thistle unwound the string from the wood.

"I believe the word is the same . . . a shimmering mare," she stated as she held the string close to her eyes. "Very rare to find. Where did you get this from?"

"It was a gift from my father."

Kaen stood there, wondering what the fuss was about. He had wondered before what made the bow so powerful, and how they were reacting to it confused him.

"A very special gift . . ." she murmured as she wrapped it back the way it had been and extended the bow to him. "Tomorrow, could you spare a few hours to meet our elder? I think he would like to meet you and hear the story you told us."

Taking his bow back, Kaen slowly nodded his head. Getting a chance to meet the wood elves he had heard of but had never imagined meeting was an opportunity he couldn't pass up, even if it put him a day behind.

"I would be honored."

Smiling, Thistle motioned at one of the two elves who were still behind them, sitting on the ground.

"Go tell the elder that tomorrow we will bring a Dragon Rider to visit."

The man jumped up and took off like a rabbit into the woods.

"Tomorrow, we will honor you and your dragon the way we should have the first time we met," she declared with a slight bow.

25

City in a Forest

Thistle and Rowan stood in awe as they watched Kaen and Pammon take off over the lake that morning, choosing to follow them by air. Rowan had marked a grove of trees on Kaen's map that would stand out as a landmark for their village's location.

As Pammon tracked them through the air, Kaen studied the forest they had been flying over and noticed the difference in the trees here versus some of the other forests.

If I had to take a guess, there is magic in how these trees grow. The wood I burned yesterday . . . the rings were wide apart compared to a normal tree. Something tells me this forest has been made to grow faster somehow.

Would forest magic be hard to believe? You saw what the elves did in Roccnari.

Kaen considered what Pammon was talking about. The elves there had made crops grow with magic and produced far more than should have usually been possible. The fields in Ebonmount, or even in their own village, never produced that kind of growth. The only thing that had was when Pammon's crap had been used to fertilize the plants.

What would be the reason for this? I knew wood elves existed, but no one would say where. I had expected a village, not a kingdom. There are countless wooded areas all over. They could easily form a kingdom. Right?

Pammon huffed and shook his head as he watched the elves darting through the forest below.

I do not deal with kingdoms. If they are happy in small groups, let them be happy. Why force a path they will not survive?

Rubbing the scale he always did, Kaen smiled, wondering when Pammon had become such a thinker.

With countless miles of forest and land around him, knowing that most of it was not inhabited and that the wood elves were keeping back the spreading forces of the orcs and goblins gave him some peace. A partner in the days to come was always welcome.

They saw the ten trees that Rowan had talked about, and when they got closer, Kaen saw a small opening that would allow Pammon to land below.

As he drifted toward the opening, Kaen noticed the bridges and rooms that occupied the trees. Staircases ran up the outside of trees wider than the house he and Hess had lived in.

That is impressive. More impressive in some ways than the wall at Ebonmount.

Pammon was right, and Kaen could only imagine how they had built such things.

Elves were waving, and Kaen couldn't help but smile as he saw younger ones hiding behind who he guessed were their parents.

In the center of the ring of trees was one taller tree, and a group of wood elves gathered in a semi-circle ring near the base.

Looks like that is the place. I'm guessing I can't roar . . .

Let's hold off on that for now.

Pammon grunted, and Kaen knew one day Pammon was going to get them in trouble with how he liked to announce himself.

Slowing down, Pammon gently glided to a place where it took a few beats of his wing to stop himself a few feet above the ground. He barely made a sound when he landed, yet the wind he generated from his flapping sent many flowers and other decorations flying across the clearing.

Great . . . now they're going to get mad that we messed up their welcoming party.

It's not my fault. I tried not to damage the ground or land really hard. You try flapping wings this large and not creating windstorms when you try to hover.

Grinning, Kaen slid off Pammon's back and landed on the ground with ease. He saw the gathered elves with their brown skin and dark hair. So many things that are different from the elves in Roccnari.

As he moved forward a few steps, a trio of younger elves, two boys and a woman, came forward and bowed. One had a necklace of flowers for him, and the other two carried a larger necklace of flowers tied with vines for Pammon.

They spoke at the same time, impressing him with their use of the common tongue.

"We greet you, Dragon Rider and dragon and offer a gift of the forest."

Kaen bent down and lowered his head for one of them to put the flowers around his neck. The other two were hesitant as they approached Pammon, but once he lowered his head, they were smiling as they laid the flower necklace around his massive head.

Giggling, they all ran off, joining the ranks of the others who were watching and waiting.

An older elf, whose hair was solid white and back was bent forward from years of living, smiled and bowed as he approached them.

"Dragon Rider Kaen and Dragon Pammon, we welcome you to our village. I am Queleth, the elder of this village, and I welcome you."

Grinning, Kaen gave a slight bow and chose to use the elvish language he had spent time practicing.

"Thank you for the honor and gift of the forest. May the branches of your trees always provide shade and food as long as you live."

The elder's eyes sparkled, and he smiled when Kaen used a greeting he had learned from his time in Roccnari.

"It seems the report that you had spent time with our distant cousins is true. You speak their language well and know the honored greeting. For now, let me welcome you and invite you to sit at our table and relax."

He clapped his hands together, and some servants arrived with carts, holding a variety of animals that looked freshly slaughtered from the forest.

"A gift for the dragon. I heard he enjoys eating the animals of the forest. Normally, we would not kill so many at one time, but since I know a dragon needs his strength, the forest will forgive us for doing so."

The forest will forgive them? Do they believe there is a god who protects the forest?

Kaen felt Pammon's confusion as he eyed the animals in the back of the carts.

Just enjoy the food, and we will talk later. Rumor has it this is one of the many reasons why wood elves and the other elves split.

Pammon bowed his head when the elves with the carts began depositing the animals near him and started eating them after they had backed away.

"Come, let us retire to the table I have set up near the base of the tree. I look forward to hearing what you might tell us about the world and how a new Dragon Rider has been chosen."

Holding back a slight groan, Kaen knew he was going to repeat a lot of what he had told Thistle and Rowan last night. Both had yet to make it here, but then again, running through a forest and flying above it greatly affected one's travel time.

Kaen watched the looks on the faces of all the elves as they listened to him share the details of the last few years. Some had grunted, and a few had wanted to ask questions, but Queleth had kept them all quiet until the end.

"War . . ." he muttered when Kaen finally stopped talking. "Another war is coming. The trees were right."

"The trees?"

Nodding, Queleth motioned to the forest around them.

"The trees have been telling us that is why the orcs and goblins have been invading the land, more than they have in generations," he replied, his voice taking on a somber tone. "We wondered and prayed that the forest was wrong, but all the other villages have reported the same things. Foolish groups were burning down trees, trying to forge a path through our homes. They have not succeeded yet, but they have cost the lives of many of my brothers and sisters."

Queleth stroked his chin with one hand as he crossed his arms and leaned back in his chair.

"Tell me, Kaen Marshell, what do you intend to do to stop this?"

Leaning his head forward a little, Kaen scratched the back of his head as he grimaced.

"Lots of people keep asking me that question, and I have no solid answer right now. I am seeking alliances with those who would stand against the coming darkness. My dragon and I are doing everything we can to get stronger and help the other nations fight against what we all know is coming. I know Stioks will make a move one day, and I pray that we are strong enough to stand against him."

"And the other Dragon Rider. The older one . . . Elies?"

Kaen grimaced, and the air rushed from his nose louder than he wished.

"I take it that is not a good topic."

Leaning against the table, Kaen interlocked his fingers and rested his chin on them.

"I won't lie to you, Queleth. Elies is dying, if he is not already dead."

A gasp rose from those at the table, and whispers broke out in their native tongue.

"Yet your face tells me all hope is not lost. What else about him did you not share?"

"He and his dragon have gone to the land of the dragons across the sea to ask them to help in what is coming. He told me I would need to go at some point and seek their help," Kaen paused as he took two pieces of fruit and set them on the far end of the table. "It is a long journey, and I will be gone for most likely almost a month, if I go. That leaves a lot of time for the kingdoms to be unprotected. Even now, I am not where some might expect me to be, but I have a mission to accomplish before I can even begin to think about that. There are many things I must do, none of which are going to be easy. Each time I depart, I risk leaving the kingdom that stands in the way of his desire to sweep away all those who stand against him."

Queleth nodded as he watched the younger elves around the table converse quietly with each other. None spoke out of turn; it was not permitted.

"How would you ask us, the elves of the forest, to help in this fight?"

One of the men at the table stood up and started to speak before seeing the glare from Queleth. Standing there with his mouth open, no words came out, but his frustration was evident by the red hue it now bore.

"Sit down or lose the spot you have, Varian!"

The elf glowered at Kaen and his body shook, but he forced himself to take his seat.

"Forgive this one for his behavior. Some of us have not lived long enough to remember we owe a debt to the Dragon Riders and are obligated to help if we can."

Trying to hide the surprise on his face, Kaen nodded and took a drink from his cup. He was thankful they had water and had not pressed him to drink wine. The last thing he needed now was a cloudy mind.

"When the time comes, I might ask for your best warriors to fight where help is needed, if they are willing. A strong bow is a great weapon, and I have no doubt you and your people are gifted with them."

Queleth grinned at Kaen's praise.

"You have a bow on your dragon, I see. Are you skilled in using it or carrying it around like a trophy?"

Chuckling, Kaen knew what was about to take place. He had heard about the rivalry that existed between the wood elves and the elves of Roccnari.

"I'd like to think I'm one of the better archers in the kingdom."

Queleth's grin grew wider as he stood up and motioned to a few elves at the table.

"Seems like we might need to see what kind of aid your kingdom could use. Perhaps a shooting contest to see just how gifted you are."

"I would be honored," Kaen replied as he stood up and gave a slight bow.

26

An Archery Contest

Five archers stood near him, three women and two men. By now, Thistle and Rowan had made it back. Both were covered in sweat, and it was obvious they were not excited to miss out on getting a chance to go up against Kaen.

Queleth had examined Kaen's bow and praised the maker. The detail and strength, combined with the magic he knew that lay within it was amazing.

"I guess we should skip the simple shots?" he asked. "We have a course that changes and will test each of you equally, if you are up for it."

Pammon was behind him, thrumming as he watched the crowd of elves who were lining the area and up in the trees.

Are we betting that you lose?

We could, but don't forget how much I won the last time people bet against me.

Queleth led them all to an area where various objects and obstacles were placed over a range of one hundred fifty yards. He motioned to one of the men who stood ready.

"In a moment, they will show you one of the possibilities of the course. Each target will only be visible for a short period of time before disappearing. You will have six targets. The course will remain the same for each contestant. So that no one gets an unfair advantage, no one will watch the other, and each person will get to see the course one time before they then must shoot. Any questions?"

Kaen realized that the question was for him. It was obvious from how the other five were standing that they had done this many times before.

"I get to see what it will look like now?"

"Yes. Not the actual course, but since you have never participated, and I doubt anyone has done a course like this with you before, I want it to be somewhat fair."

Grinning, Kaen nodded, and Queleth waved at the man who would be demonstrating the course in action. He held up some cards, and Kaen noticed there were other men and women along the course.

A bell sounded, and a target sprung up twenty yards away with a small one-foot section. It hovered for only three seconds before dropping down, and another target popped up on the other side of the field, fifty yards away or so. It was slightly larger and stayed for a little longer before dropping down. Two more targets then came up in the middle of the field about seventy yards off before disappearing. There was a pause, and then a target shot up on the far left one hundred yards away, and before it dropped, a target on the far end, at around one hundred thirty yards popped up. Both dropped after about seven seconds each.

"Huh," Kaen said as he watched the course targets disappear; he was grinning. "I won't lie. This seems like something I could do all day just for fun."

Laughing, Queleth waved his hand, and the workers of the course began moving.

"Does that mean you want to go first?"

Laughing, Kaen nodded. "I wouldn't have it any other way!"

Three rounds had passed, and only one of the female archers and one male were left, and Kaen. They were the only three to have perfect scores on each of the courses, and it was obvious the crowd had a favorite.

Sedel was a well-built, female wood elf, whose muscles might intimidate most men. She carried herself well, and her dark hair was braided all the way to her lower back. Kaen had gotten to watch her shoot all three rounds since he had already gone and saw that every movement she made was exact and without flaw.

The male archer, Vadaac, had almost lost the last round on the second target. He was just as well built as Sedel and was a few inches taller than her. His finger twitched occasionally when he was about to let go of the string; not a lot, but enough that Kaen realized his skill with shooting was at its limit.

As they waited for the crew to replace targets and make a few changes, Queleth stood with the three of them, smiling and making light jokes.

"Dragon Rider Kaen, I must admit you have impressed me. Even when you lose, we will tell stories of how great your skill is!"

"Why do I feel like you are going to make things almost impossible for me to win?"

Queleth motioned to Sedel with his head.

"She knows what is coming up next, as does Vadaac. I will tell you. The next course will require you to use your skills. It will come fast and hard. You won't get to see the targets like you did before. That means you will get to view it only as it happens. We have found this best simulates the real combat experience, minus things being thrown at you."

Kaen began to chuckle, and Queleth gave him a peculiar look.

"Sorry, I had a mentor who used to throw rocks at me while teaching me to shoot."

A grin broke out on his face, and he nodded.

"Sounds like my kind of trainer. Now, since this is your first time, I will let Vadaac go first. The course will be different for both of you, but know it is fair to use your skills whenever you desire."

Vadaac nodded and moved to the ready position. Kaen watched as he moved his arrows around in his quiver, getting them positioned how he wanted them. It seemed like a smart move that he could use for his turn.

When he nodded, the course started, and two targets popped up, one at thirty yards and the other at forty-five yards, both right behind each other. Vadaac grinned as he rapidly shot off two arrows, the second one barely clipping the furthest target as it began to fall. As soon as they dropped, two targets popped up on either side of the field, each at seventy yards. He fired off one shot, and by the time his second arrow was released from his bow, it had missed the target.

Two more targets then popped up closer to each other, around one hundred twenty yards away. He fired his shot, and before they were halfway there, the arrow split into two, hitting both targets. A single target popped up at one hundred fifty yards, and Kaen saw the arrow glow for a second before it leaped across the field, destroying the target with ease.

Headshot . . . What was that other one?

It was a splinter shot. A level thirty skill. It's like a multishot but only requires one arrow. If you had to choose between the two at twenty, splinter sounds better, but the cooldown, I hear is a lot longer.

How do you think you will do?

I have no clue, Kaen answered honestly. *Hopefully, I won't embarrass myself.*

The crowd clapped, and Vadaac gave a slight bow and shrugged.

"I only manage to pass this every now and then. My skill choices are good for some things and not for others."

Kaen nodded, understanding what he meant.

Sedel stepped up and began to mimic what Vadaac had done, adjusting the arrows in her quiver. She smiled at Kaen and motioned at his bow.

"That seems a little small for you. Is there a reason you haven't gotten a bigger one?"

Chuckling, Kaen shrugged as he held it up.

"I've only had it for about three years now. I don't think my dad would have imagined I'd grow as much as I have. I'm not sure I could find something out there that I would want to replace it with."

She nodded as she held out her bow for him to inspect. Kaen took it in his hand and found it to be perfectly balanced. It was a good foot longer than his and was made of a very dense redwood. He could feel the power in it. The string she used wasn't hair like his but a kind of sinew. He wondered what creature would be so strong that it would have sinew thick and strong enough to hold the kind of power he knew this wood produced.

"This is an amazing bow," he said, knowing it was an obvious statement. "Family heirloom?"

She laughed and shook her head.

"I won this years ago at a competition like this one. Each year, I have to defend it."

Her voice was confident and not bragging. He realized now that he was walking into a whole different world of competition.

The workers signaled they were ready, and she turned back to the course. Taking a single breath, she nodded.

Two targets came up at thirty and forty-five yards, each near the edges of the field. The arrows were already in the air when they began to rise, striking both before either one had begun to drop.

Sedel grabbed two arrows as the next two targets popped up simultaneously. They were close to each other—about sixty-five yards away—so no time was lost. The arrows flew true, breaking both targets at the same time.

The next two targets began to rise at around one hundred fifteen yards, each on opposite sides. Before the first one had reached its maximum height, the arrow was gone. A second arrow was already loaded and released, striking the second target as it began to drop down.

Kaen marveled at the archer, as she already had another arrow nocked when she saw the final target at one hundred fifty yards begin to rise. She let her arrow go, watching as it flew straight. Kaen saw the target begin to drop but knew what she had done. As it fell, almost disappearing from view, the arrow caught it two inches before it would be hidden forever.

The crowd around her roared in applause and cheers.

She turned and gave a slight bow, and smiled at Kaen.

"That was . . . impressive, to say the least. I take it this isn't your first time."

She laughed and shook her head.

"I have been shooting these since I was a young girl, and let's not worry about how many years that has been.

Nodding, Kaen walked up to the starting spot and began to stretch his neck and shoulders as he waited for the course to be reset.

Queleth moved up next to him with a large smile from ear to ear.

"Nervous?"

"If I said no, would you believe me?" Kaen joked.

"Maybe, but I'll tell you after I see how you do."

Nodding, Kaen returned his gaze to the course and thought about what he had seen and needed to do.

Seems like you might need to cheat.

Kaen felt Pammon and his laughter coming through the bond, even though he had not done it where the others could hear.

No, this time, I don't think I will. I want to see how far I have come.

A wave of approval came from Pammon.

When the workers gave the ready sign, Kaen took a breath and nodded.

The first two came up at thirty-five yards, near each other.

Having seen what Sedel had done was important, and he owed Queleth for letting him watch the other two archers before his turn. Sedel had sprung into action the second she saw movement. Vadaac had waited, and it had cost him.

The moment the first target was rising, Kaen's arrow was away, and then the second one obliterated its target. Once destroyed, the next two popped up at ninety-five yards and one hundred five yards, on opposite sides of the field. Kaen had already released the first arrow and was letting go of the second one before the other target had reached its maximum height. Both were destroyed before they began their descent.

Kaen grinned as he drew two arrows and put them on the string. When one target popped up, he groaned inside, knowing what was coming next, but had no choice.

[Twin Shot Activated]

He couldn't waste time trying to free an arrow from the grip he had. Both arrows sped across the field and struck the single target that had risen at one hundred thirty yards.

Kaen drew one arrow and knew what he had to do. He didn't want to give away too many of his tricks, but there was no time. Pouring mana into the tip, he charged the arrow, letting it rocket off at the first target as it rose. Wasting no time, the second arrow was on his string, and another trickle of mana flowed into it. As the string slipped from his fingers, he saw the arrow streak across the field, striking both of the one-hundred-fifty-yard targets, blowing them up, along with the small area.

[Archery Skill Increased]

The crowd stood silent for a moment before erupting in cheer and applause. None were sure what skill Kaen had just used, but he had succeeded at something most would not have been able to.

Queleth and Sedel both walked up to Kaen and were applauding.

"Magic?"

The way Queleth asked was as if he didn't believe it was even possible for an archer to do that.

"Perhaps," Kaen answered with a wink and a grin. "It felt dirty since I figured both of the last two were like that, but it serves me right."

Sedel laughed and nodded as she patted Kaen on the shoulder.

"You have outdone yourself, Dragon Rider Kaen. I'm sure we could go another round if you wanted. We have many different games we can play."

"Are you up for wagering something?" Kaen asked with a grin on his face.

Sedel flashed a toothy grin at Kaen. "What do you have in mind?"

I don't like being used as a bargaining chip . . .

I did ask first, didn't I? You said yes.

Grumbling, Pammon had agreed but being offered as a ride felt beneath him.

Are you sure she will give up the bow if she loses?

I guess I will have to win to see.

Baskets of arrows were lined up near the starting point, and Sedel was about to begin when Kaen raised his hand.

"Before we start, can I ask if we can up this a little bit more?"

"Trying to back out already?" Sedel asked, grinning at him again.

"It's more that I want to leave no doubt about who is better. If we break the same amount in the allotted time, all we are doing is wasting arrows and targets. I think with one small change, we could easily solve this problem."

Queleth stood by watching the two of them and was listening intently.

"Let's do this blindfolded. Each of us shoots the best we can with one attempt while blindfolded. Most targets down wins."

Sedel stared at Kaen.

"What makes you so certain you will win, or is this your way of losing gracefully?"

"I know you have an archery skill of forty," Kaen stated, and when he saw how she reacted, he knew his guess had been right. "By the way, you have the baskets out here. That means you probably have a fan shot. This means you will have a chance to reach more targets with a higher skill. Obviously, you're wondering what my skill level is and what skills I possess. This provides you a chance to possibly find out. However, if I'm not using the same skills as you, I am at a disadvantage to begin with. That is why Vadaac can rarely make it past a certain stage. He will struggle at the multi-targets. "So let's make this more about skill and technique and who we are than about what skills we have."

Kaen watched Sedel and Queleth exchange looks and saw something curious pass between the two of them.

"I accept," she said with a grin. "Something tells me you are making this work in your favor, but I'm interested to see how it plays out."

Laughing, Kaen motioned at the people gathered along the course.

"Perhaps we should move them away from the sides?"

Laughing, she and Queleth both nodded.

27

An Impossible Contest

Sedel stood prepared. A timer would be set, and after twenty seconds all targets down would count. She had a red sash tied over her eyes, and Kaen marveled at how calm she seemed to be, even though she couldn't see.

"She has done something like this before, hasn't she?"

Queleth nodded and flashed him a playful smirk.

"She has been the winner for the last ten contests in a row. There isn't much you can do to faze her."

Letting a groan escape his throat, Kaen heard Pammon thrumming behind him.

"Even my dragon thinks I may have shot myself in the foot."

Sedel laughed and took a few breaths to recenter herself.

Drawing five arrows at once from a quiver on her back, she loaded them all, uninhibited by the blindfold.

"Go!"

The timer flipped over, and she released *fan shot*. Four waves of five arrows leaped from her hand, racing toward the targets, mowing down the ones closest to her. Each shot took out a target, dropping twenty in just moments of starting.

She launched a multishot, followed by a split shot, all striking targets and bringing her up to a total of twenty-four. From there, she began firing arrows methodically, listening to the sounds of the arrows hitting the targets and calculating the distance between each of them. One would have thought she had no blindfold on the way she hit target after target.

Kaen saw her lips moving as she fired, counting each and every target and shot. He had been wrong, and he knew it now.

Time was ticking down, and she was letting an arrow go every second. Her speed and skill was amazing. He knew his dexterity was higher, but her actions were ones that were practiced every day. What she could accomplish was hard to fathom.

"TIME!" shouted Queleth as the last grain of sand fell in the hourglass.

Sedel held up her bow, and the crowd cheered. She took her blindfold off and gave a slight bow to the onlookers before turning and bowing to Kaen.

"Thirty-seven!" one of the men shouted.

The crowd roared even more, and Kaen let out a whistle and his eyebrows raised.

"You didn't want to tell me this isn't your first time?"

She walked over to Kaen, handed him the sash, and smiled.

"Does the spider tell the fly where they hang the silk, or wait for it to find out?"

Pammon began thrumming, and Sedel gave him a slight bow, too, and grinned.

"It seems even your dragon agrees with me."

Pammon flashed a toothy smile and nodded his head.

"Time to face the music, I guess," Kaen announced as he walked up to the starting spot. It would take a few minutes to replace all the broken targets.

Putting the blindfold over his eyes, Kaen grinned.

Are you ready?

This feels like cheating, and she seems like someone I could enjoy watching kick your rear.

It isn't cheating. I said we would show what each of us could do. You can look for me, and I can follow your vision.

Even then, how do you expect to win? Your two skills will only strike seven between multishot and twin shot.

You know what I'm going to do, and don't pretend you don't.

A groan came from their bond, and Pammon snorted.

Kaen loaded the two arrows for his first shot and then considered why he was doing what he was doing. He had seen these families and their children. He knew if the kingdoms didn't get united, even these outlying villages and other small groups of families would die. He couldn't lose. He needed to unite them all, and this was the first step.

He felt his lifestone grow hot, and it began to burn.

Pammon focused on him, and he felt his vision shift to what Pammon was seeing. It took a moment, but he worked out the angles. He could see the targets and knew where he needed to shoot, even from where he was right now.

"When you are ready."

Kaen nodded and took a breath.

Ready?

Always.

"Go!"

Kaen let the two arrows go, and they took out the first two in the middle closest to him.

He activated multishot, and arrow after arrow streamed out in a split second, dropping the next five in a straight line. Without hesitation, he fired off arrow after arrow for the next seven seconds.

He pushed mana into the next arrow he pulled. Sparks began to glow, and Kaen could feel Pammon smiling. He pushed more mana into it, letting it crackle and pop. The heat of it felt warm against his fingers.

Three seconds!

Kaen let the arrow fly free, a bolt of lightning striking from his bow, igniting the target at eighty yards away, unleashing a lightning storm that erupted in a full circle around it, taking down targets and boxes that held targets. Mayhem was unleashed as Kaen destroyed most of the course for forty yards in every direction.

"Time!"

When Queleth shouted this time, it was more in disbelief than with pride.

Again, when Kaen took his blindfold off, he saw the crowd staring at the carnage before them. No one knew what to say or do. He had not only defeated their champion, but he had destroyed her completely.

As everyone stood there in silence, Kaen felt a hand grab his arm and lift it high.

He saw Sedel holding his arm high into the sky.

"The winner! Dragon Rider Kaen!"

With her affirmation of the win, the crowd began to clap and cheer. It wasn't as heartfelt as the first time, but they acknowledged that he had done the impossible. He had won.

I think you have just crushed their spirits and stolen their treasure.

Have faith in me. I'm not a heartless dragon who eats all their animals.

Pammon thrummed as he snorted and laid his head down on the ground to watch what was about to unfold.

"This is yours by right of the contest," Sedel stated as she held out her bow. Her voice cracked a little, and Kaen saw her hand tremble as she held it out.

Putting his hand on her hand and the bow, Kaen smiled and shook his head.

"I'm afraid I cannot use it. It is much too big for me, and besides, I would dishonor the gift my father made me. Perhaps you can keep it until next year's champion can claim it."

She looked up at Kaen's face and he could see her eyes well up, but she did not allow any tears to fall.

"I would be honored to guard that which belongs to you until the next champion can claim it."

"Good!" exclaimed Kaen as he patted her on the shoulder and smiled at Queleth, who looked like an approving parent. "Now that this is settled, Pammon and I need to depart and continue our journey north, but I want to say I look forward to the next time I stop through here."

The ones who had gathered to watch Kaen claim their champion's prized treasure all bowed as Queleth came up next to Kaen, dropped to his knee, and touched his head to Kaen's hand.

"We are honored to have met you and are blessed to have provided you shelter and food. May the forest watch over you as one of her own."

Kaen smiled when he heard Queleth speaking in the common elvish language.

"I am honored to be considered one of its children and will do what I can to protect it from those who seek to harm it."

Standing up, Queleth clapped him on his shoulder and gave an affirming nod.

Hours after having left the village, Pammon was still thrumming from his enjoyment of Sedel's joke.

They did not realize the Dragon Rider had set such a large web to ensnare them all. Perhaps they will warn the others of how dangerous he is to bet against.

Kaen laughed and didn't care that the wind carried the sound away. Pammon was right. He had managed to survive a bad moment and won the hearts of another group of people in the world he was trying to protect. There would be many more he would have to try and win over, and he knew there was no promise all would be successful.

The next two days were consumed by mapping and marking the two maps he had the best he could. It was a chore as Kaen saw more and more of the landscape had changed in the last two hundred-plus years.

Roads were gone. Other ones had sprung up. He had seen the signs of a few villages that were new along even newer roads, and he saw a few clearings where fields had been cleared. They kept away from others, as neither wanted to waste more time or have to deal with the possibility of running into someone hostile.

When the cliffs of Tanulivar came into view, Kaen and Pammon felt relief as they knew they were closer to their goal.

We are not stopping and talking with the dwarves first? What changed your mind?

Our stop with the wood elves has added a day, and I would prefer to keep to our original schedule. The longer we are away, the more I worry about what is happening at home.

Do you really think he will make a move on the kingdom like that? He hasn't for two years.

That is because Tharnok was still around. He wouldn't make a move like that even with Elies being injured. Now that we know Elies and Tharnok are gone and that Havannath may be trying to align with them, word will travel, and they will know the kingdom is unprotected.

Pammon grumbled as he did when frustrated. Kaen knew that Pammon often felt he worried too much about things he couldn't control. It was that part of him that drove Pammon crazy. Focus, train, do. Easy for a dragon who only had to worry about a handful of people.

If we manage to find what we are looking for and succeed in hunting the griffons, then we can visit the dwarves. Hess told me not to expect much help besides the occasional adventurer.

You realize dwarves do not like dragons . . . Tharnok mentioned that multiple times.

Ignoring Pammon and his constant negativity, Kaen focused on the map he had out. It was his second piece of leather, and he was reaching the end of the map that he had copied from Herb. No maps went past the peaks of Tanulivar.

As they flew slightly beneath the clouds, Kaen noticed that the land beneath them was cleared out farther than he had expected from the dwarven cliffs.

It is as if they harvested all the trees for miles and miles.

Kaen saw it. There were farms all over, and Kaen began to understand what he was seeing.

They are planning on hiding in their mountains. They are stockpiling food to see how everything works out.

How can they expect to survive if they do that?

Kaen considered that question as he saw the massive change in the landscape.

They might survive, but they won't really be living . . .

28

Hunting Griffons

They camped near some trees away from the dwarven border, and Kaen found himself eating another meal of dried meat. He was tired from a long day in the air, and even though Pammon had offered to find food for him, it was far easier just to chew what was on hand and rest. Tomorrow was a big day. He had an idea of where to look for their prey, but they would still have to fly and search through a lot of the mountain areas hoping to get lucky. If they traveled the wrong way, they would have to backtrack and search again. There was also no guarantee they would be flying today.

During their studies of griffons, Herb had mentioned that they sometimes stayed in caves for weeks at a time.

Quit being so depressing. You are making it hard to enjoy my dinner.
Kaen chuckled.

I'm sorry, but I feel like time is running short. Seeing what the dwarves have done really upsets me. I dreamed of being an adventurer all my life, and now I see that kingdoms are petty. Men, dwarves, elves, it doesn't matter. They all seem to only care for themselves and are willing to allow others to suffer.

He felt Pammon grumble as he swallowed whatever it was he had caught.

Listen, we are the same way. You will protect me first and then those closest to you. If need be, you would sacrifice others to save Hess, Callie, and Sulenda, right?

Well, yeah, of course I would. They're family.

And every other group looks at it the same way. They will sacrifice friends to save their families. How much easier is it to sacrifice another kingdom? We haven't even talked about those who desire power over anything else. You saw firsthand what Havannath was willing to do. Why do you still doubt it?

Frustrated, Kaen tossed a rock into the woods, listening to it bounce a few times.

It's . . . it's just hard to sit back and watch others suffer. You know how I am.

I do, which is what I find most frustrating and admirable about you. You care because of how you were hurt. I care because of what I was given. Together, we can only do so much. Stop worrying about what you cannot do now, and focus on what you can.

Taking a few deep breaths, Kaen let each of them out slowly.

Is it too late to ask for you to bring me something fresh to eat?

He felt laughter from Pammon and joy from his request.

I'll gladly find something for the both of us to share.

The next morning, they went east, avoiding the main area of the dwarven kingdom, and flew over the multi-colored mountains that were their domain. Some mountains were higher than the ones surrounding Ebonmount, with snow on them year-round. Frosted peaks could be seen, and the dark rocks that promised ore and metal ran for miles upon miles in every direction.

The map he had was worthless at this point. Everything they crossed and covered were new areas. The moisture in the air required him to keep things sealed up tight, and now both of them were fully armed and prepared for battle. His new shield was equipped, and his bow was on his back. He was wearing every piece of equipment he owned, as he had no clue what these creatures would be like.

Simple Status Check
Kaen Marshell - Adolescent
Age - 19
HP - 1225/1225 (25%)
MP - 400/400 (25%)
STR - 40 (25%)+8
CON - 41 (25%)+13
DEX - 44 (25%)+36
INT - 31 (25%)+6
WIS - 26 (25%)+6
Blessings:
Dragonbound Complete - 25% current bonus to all stats
Dragon Shield - +5 to All Stats
Hunters Tunic - +3 to Str / Con / Dex
Blessed Vambrace - +1 to Dex / Int
Blessed Vambrace - +1 to Dex / Wis
Bonded Bow of Archer - +5 to Dex +3 to Archery *Locked*

King's Belt - +2 Dex
Eagle Pendant - +2 to Dex
Blood Ring - +5 to Con
Silver Ring - +1 Dex
Dexterity Ring - +2 Dex
Dexterity Ring - +2 Dex
Dexterity Ring - +2 Dex
Dexterity Ring - +2 Dex
Dexterity Ring - +2 Dex
Dexterity Ring - +2 Dex

Kaen marveled at the realization that he had an eighty in dexterity. He was well beyond what he and Hess had considered possible, but there had been no major change since he hit sixty. Perhaps one could only push so far with items before they lost the advantage they gave. Maybe he could test some things out with Hess or someone else he might be able to trust with his items.

Stop comparing numbers and focus! Pammon snapped as they flew over another mountain range. **This is the third zigzag we have done, and nothing has been spotted in the area they said it might be.**

Do you think we are too high? Perhaps we need to fly along the mountains so they see you as a threat and attack.

Why don't we tie a rope around you so you can dangle beneath me? Perhaps then they will think you are a treat I am delivering.

Kaen ignored the joke as Pammon began to fly lower toward the cliffs. They had seen a few caves, but nothing flew out; no creatures wanted to risk getting pursued by Pammon. He had found no real game besides the occasional mountain goat or rare mountain leopard.

Hours passed, and boredom took hold as they continued crossing miles and miles of rocks and cliffs, trying to find something that was believed to be there.

Halfway through the day, they stopped and took a break on one of the mountain peaks that was not covered in snow. The rocks they sat on had been pounded by rain, wind, and ice, leaving no shrubs on their surface.

Using Pammon as a windbreak, Kaen glanced at his map.

He was scanning the area they had traversed while Pammon kept watch around them.

"I have no clue where we should look," Kaen informed Pammon as he glanced out over the landscape.

Herb's information hasn't turned anything up yet, and there was so much mountain area to cover. It could take weeks to search all of it.

"How about if you handle the searching? Where would you live if you were a giant griffon that ate animals and people dumb enough to enter your domain?"

Pammon thrummed as he glanced down at Kaen and back over the area they had covered.

If I am honest, I think Herb and his information are wrong. There is nothing to eat here. The small goats are not worth the time because they are scrawny. How old was that information he was using?

Pulling out a stack of papers that Herb had given him, Kaen began scanning them.

Groaning, Kaen found the date and realized that the information was over a hundred years old with regard to where they were believed to live. It had been ten years since the last sighting.

"So yeah, none of this information is going to help us. Other than there have been griffons, where they are, who knows."

Pammon sniffed the air, then looked to the south momentarily.

Climb on, and let me see if I'm the better hunter.

Kaen shrugged as he put the papers back in their tube and slid them into his pack.

Lead on, oh mighty hunter.

Pammon had been flying low along the first ridge of the mountains between the woods and the massive cliffs for a solid hour, taking his time and letting the current help glide as much as possible.

Kaen continued marking his map as Pammon scouted their area. It was at least a half day of flying from where he had originally been told they would be.

What are you looking for?

Think like a predator. If you are a flyer and want food but also to stay near your home, you need somewhere that animals are going to be. There is no water, no real habitat for game. I have seen very few deer or even hogs out here. I cannot see a creature you described living near here. Perhaps before the dwarves did what they did to the land near their home, there was game to keep them here. Now . . . they have had to move elsewhere, if they are even still alive.

Glancing at the forest below them, Kaen realized Pammon was right. There would be no way for Pammon to survive out here without moving constantly. They would need a place where a creature they were hunting could thrive.

So lead on. I'm glad you figured it out; otherwise, we would still be searching the mountains.

Pammon thrummed as he gained a little bit more altitude and kept going east.

Trees and rocks passed beneath them, winding like a snake for countless miles. Pammon would occasionally circle slowly over an area before continuing his path to the east.

We are getting closer, I think, to a possibility. There has been more game, and that stream south of here has been winding in the same direction for a while. There might be something coming from the mountain ahead that feeds into it.

The sun was beginning to set by the time Pammon reached a spring that was coming out of the mountain they had been following. Up ahead, a small oasis sprung up with a small lake that branched out and turned into streams of water leading south from its base.

This is where we will need to hunt. If I were one of them, I would call this place home, but not on this side of the mountain. That would be a bit pretentious.

Do you think they are that smart?

Pammon didn't speak for a moment as he beat his wings and gained more altitude, rising higher in the sky.

Maybe, but they wouldn't be stupid either. I'm not sure how intelligent they are, but if they have survived for all this time, they understand the nature of . . .

Pammon suddenly dropped both wings and dove straight to the ground, sending Kaen's pencil into the air. He found himself pressed against Pammon's back, and before he could ask why Pammon what was going on, he saw the reason.

We are in trouble! Fire at them!

Fighting the force of the decent, Kaen used all the strength he had in his core and leaned forward as Pammon twisted and weaved.

Four griffons, each a quarter the size of Pammon, were about forty yards behind them, coming at them from different angles. They had obviously approached from higher in the sky behind them, using the setting sun to hunt the very creature that did not expect to be hunted.

Finding his bow, Kaen pulled it to his hand and reached for one of the arrows in the special quiver Elies had given him. They were held tight, compressed with padding to keep them from falling out accidentally.

You need to get them off my tail before we reach the ground, or things will go badly!

Kaen knew what Pammon was talking about. Elies and Tharnok had shown them this maneuver, and being under the attacker put them in a world of hurt, especially against four attackers.

Kaen drew back the arrow and let one go, surprised when the griffon he had shot at spun mid-air and dodged it with ease, not losing the distance it had on them.

Twenty seconds tops!

Pulling two arrows, Kaen cursed and called on his lifestone, surprised that it took so long when he needed it to answer his request the most.

[Twin Shot Activated]

Two arrows sped toward their target above them.

"Hairy dwarf . . ."

Now! We don't have time!

Kaen felt the fear and frustration in Pammon's call for help. It had never been this bad before.

There was only one thing left he could think of to try.

29

When We Are the Ones Hunted

He knew the ground was coming fast, but there was no other option.

Flight burst now!

Pammon grunted, and Kaen knew he was not excited but felt when it engaged.

[Flight Burst Activated]

Kaen felt Pammon's body surge forward. The speed at which they were dropping, the angle of the approach, the griffons behind them—everything spelled doom if Pammon couldn't pull this off.

His wings adjusted for the sudden shift in the direction he was about to attempt. The force he felt was horrible, far worse than he had ever felt before. His brain struggled to keep him awake, and he squeezed his legs and his core tight. He pleaded with his lifestone that this was life and death and felt it get hotter, a white flame burning in his chest. He sent his power to Pammon, knowing he was asking for more than he had ever asked before.

Mere feet from the ground, Pammon surged in line with the ground before beginning to angle toward the sky.

Kaen unleashed his attack as the griffons began to shift in speed and angle.

Kaen charged then released an arrow infused with mana. When it struck the griffon's wing, the magical energy sheared it off, sending the creature tumbling toward the ground.

The other three shrieked in defiance, and amazingly, their speed did not seem to let up at all.

A pop sounded from Pammon, and Kaen felt the pain as he roared.

[Flight Burst Expired]

Pammon immediately slowed down, and his left wing seemed to flop wildly compared to the right one.

I tore something, Pammon cried as Kaen felt the pain surging through his friend's body. **I can't stay in the air much longer.**

Each beat of the wing sent tremors through Pammon, and Kaen had to block out the pain so he could focus.

Spinning around in his harness and saddle, he saw the other three closing in fast, with Pammon now floundering in the air. The ground was quickly approaching them again, and Kaen knew Pammon was doing everything he could to prevent them from crashing headfirst into the rocky ground.

[Multishot Activated]

Kaen sent five arrows after one of the griffons closest to him, amazed that it was somehow dodging shots. He was grateful when the last two pierced its chest and wing, sending one more tumbling toward the ground below.

The last two griffons approached from both sides. They opened their mouths, and Kaen heard them shriek. Pain surged through his head from the noise, and he felt dizzy momentarily. It was like someone stood beside him with their hands cupped around his ear and yelled into it. Pammon seemed to shrug it off as he approached the ground. As he slowed, the one on the left came for Kaen, swooping down with his claws extended at him.

He held the shield and saw the one on the right approaching Pammon's injured wing.

Dodge down!

Pammon flared both wings wide. The pain he felt from his sudden speed decrease caused his wing to flap like a ribbon in the wind.

The sudden action caused the griffon going after his wing to rip out a chunk from the top part of Pammon's web, sending them spiraling to the left.

The griffon attacking Kaen scraped its claws against the shield and was bounced back when Kaen was able to resist the attack.

I'm going to crash!

Kaen felt the panic in Pammon's voice as he saw the ground fast approaching. There was no time for anything. The griffons were circling, and he knew this next part was going to be dangerous.

I'll jump! Protect yourself!

There was no time for discussion, and Pammon tucked his wings, putting his feet out and preparing for the coming impact.

Kaen undid the straps that kept him on his saddle and prepared for the last few feet as the ground blazed toward them. When Kaen was about twenty feet from the ground, he stood on his saddle and jumped, feeling an eerie reaction as he seemed to hover where he was instead of leaping up or out.

Pammon fell below and to the side, sliding into the rocks and dirt, tumbling repeatedly.

When the ground came at him, Kaen bent his knees, absorbing the blow and rolling once before standing up and seeing the griffon that was coming at him.

Drawing his sword, he crouched low, scanning the air for the other.

Pammon was up, but he was hurt, and Kaen knew if it came to a battle on the ground, Pammon would be limited in what he could do with that injured wing.

Left!

Kaen rolled to the left as claws raked from where he was seconds ago. The second one came at him, its claws spread wide, ready to rip his body in half.

Kaen waited, a smile on his face, knowing how often Master Bren had complained about this next choice.

[Shield Charge Activated]

Kaen leaped through the air at the griffon and saw its eyes widen as it tried to adjust its wings. He came forward, shield out and his sword on its side, dashing between its massive claws and planting the blade right in its chest.

He plowed through its ribcage, crushing it completely and lodging himself inside the cavity.

The creature screamed in pain as it fell toward the ground, rolling and coming to a stop with Kaen deep inside it.

Bursting from the carcass, Kaen sent bloody gore everywhere as he heard Pammon roar and saw him sending flames at the griffon, who had decided it would attack head-on at the injured dragon.

The smell of burnt wings and flesh filled the air as the final griffon crashed into Pammon, sending flashes of pain coursing through his body.

Not wasting another second, Kaen ran to his friend, who was trying to push the burning corpse off him.

Pammon! Let me help!

I'm . . . I'm sorry, Pammon cried as the left side of his body struggled to respond.

Kaen ignored his apology. When he got near Pammon, he surveyed the mess before him.

Hold still a moment, and let me handle this!

[Shield Slam Activated]

Kaen slammed the shield against the flaming bird, ignoring the heat coming off its engulfed body, sending it flying yards away from his friend.

Pammon limped toward him, making a sound Kaen had never heard before.

Clear liquid streamed from Pammon's eyes as he dragged his injured wing out from under him.

Let me help! Slow down!

Kaen moved to the other side, gently touching Pammon and making sure there was nothing broken that he could feel.

It's just my wing. It's torn and broken. It's my fault for not paying attention to what might have . . .

Stop it! Please! Do not blame yourself, Kaen implored as he began pressing with all his strength. He wished he had brought a set of strength rings to help move Pammon's weight; the sheer mass was challenging to move.

Focus on turning to the other side. We will get you settled and then try to fix everything.

Pammon winced as Kaen pushed. He took a large breath and stood up, almost buckling on an injured hind leg.

Between the two of them, Pammon finally freed his pinned wing, and Kaen's eyes saw the extent of the damage.

The middle outside joint on the wing was bent backward, causing the wing to almost fold over on itself, and he knew Pammon was trying to move it back into position but couldn't. Large chunks were ripped out from the edge of his wing, and the flap where the griffon had sent its razor-sharp claws through the membrane.

Gently running his hands along Pammon's scales, Kaen felt a lump in his throat. As much as Pammon felt guilty and like this was his fault, it had been Kaen's idea. He had made the decision that they should hunt these things.

Stop that. Do not blame yourself.

Coughing, Kaen saw Pammon looking at him. His head was lying on the ground, tilted sideways as he tried to take weight off his left side.

We chose to do this. I should have known the griffons might attack like that. I am the one who flies, not you.

Neither one of us knew that would happen. Now stop blaming yourself, and let me check the contents of the containers.

Pammon winced and closed his eyes. Kaen saw Pammon squirm as he climbed to the smashed containers. The dark liquid was already leaking out of the one on the left, and he prayed that the potions he was looking for were not broken.

Cutting the straps and releasing the bent and twisted fasteners took a few minutes.

"These aren't going to make the trip back," he muttered as his knife sawed through the thick custom leather straps he had built to resist rubbing against Pammon's scales.

When the basket finally came free, he lowered it to the ground and got off on Pammon's right side to help minimize contact on his injured side.

No matter what you find, you realize you must bend my wing back over.

Kaen nodded and began pulling out the different pouches and containers. He had not considered them ever crashing, and Elies had never mentioned it before. Water flasks had burst from the pressure of the impact, and everything was a wet mess.

Halfway through digging around, he found one of the two potions he was searching for, smashed and empty.

How is the other one?

Kaen could feel the despair in Pammon's question. He had tried to hide what he found as he lifted out the broken glass pieces. The thick black liquid was still stuck to the inside of the container.

"You could try and swallow this," Kaen said as he held it out. "Lord Hurem said it wouldn't hurt you, but I'm not sure there would be any gain from this."

Pammon grunted, and Kaen noticed there was a wheeze along with it.

We don't even know if it will work, Pammon reminded him as he steadied himself on the ground. **Hurry up, look for what you are trying to find, and then help me with my wing. I need to get it turned right.**

Ignoring Pammon's pessimistic attitude, Kaen began digging through the basket again. Pouches of meat and other things were tossed in a separate stack, ruined by the water and broken vial.

Reaching the bottom, he found the pouch he sought and felt the leather wet and slick.

His heart broke as he carefully pulled it out, watching black liquid drip from the pouch.

"Eat this!" Kaen implored as he held out the leather pouch, black liquid running down his fingers and arms as he held it up toward Pammon. "Quickly!"

Pammon turned his head, saw the pouch, and knew it was broken inside. He moved his head closer and opened up his mouth.

Toss it in.

Kaen's steps were rapid as he moved to get next to Pammon's open mouth, ensuring he got the pouch inside.

As he watched his friend close his jaw, Kaen jogged to the other side of his body and looked at the wing folded back on itself.

I can do this fast, or I can do this slow. Which way would you prefer?

Locking his jaw tight, Pammon put his head down on the ground. He was waiting to swallow the pouch until after Kaen did what he must.

Do it fast. It will hurt, and I will survive.

The taste of bile was noticeable in Kaen's mouth as he stared at the wing again and began planning the best way to do this. He knew it was going to hurt regardless. Moving around the side, he carefully put his hand on the outer bone that was bent over and took a deep breath.

On three.

When he saw Pammon nod and gulp down the pouch, he never got past one before he felt a wave of pain wash over him as he lifted the wing up enough to get a good grip on it.

One!

His strength was more than enough to flip the wing back into position. He felt the socket next to him pop and make a noise. It was like trying to turn a cart over, or some giant sail, if he had to envision something else. The long span of the wing was moving air across it as he folded it back into position.

It only took a second, but every fraction felt like an eternity.

Pammon roared as he did what he had to, causing his whole body to shake and birds to scatter from nearby trees.

What felt like it took forever was done, and the wing was how it was supposed to be.

His chest heaving and snot flaring from his nostrils, Pammon groaned as he let his wing rest against his body and the ground.

You said on three, Pammon complained weakly before he closed his eyes and laid his head on the ground.

30

Standing Watch

Kaen and Pammon had waited for a while after he had swallowed the wet pack with the spilled potion in it, hoping to see some magical healing take place. Nothing had happened like when Kaen, Hess, or anyone else had drank one of the potions.

I'm hungry. Will you bring that closer to me so I can eat?

Sighing, Kaen pulled out his sword and moved to the burnt carcass of the griffon. He started hacking pieces of it off and then brought the main body closer to Pammon.

"I'm going to get one of the others for you. I need to harvest a few trophies if I can."

Already digging in, Pammon grunted, taking giant bites from the burnt carcass and swallowing them.

The work required to chop up the corpses wasn't that difficult. Kaen's sword and strength made cutting them easy. The one he had killed when he charged its chest was missing all of its organs, turning them into a paste when he hit it.

Taking the beak, claws, and a few feathers, he proceeded to quarter the rest of it and carry it over to Pammon, who had already managed to consume most of the first one.

I will only eat two for now. My ribs are hurting, and I don't want to overeat. You will need to stand guard tonight. I am tired and unsure if it's the pain or the potion.

I'll always protect you. Eat and sleep. I got this.

Not sure if he was trying to convince Pammon or himself, Kaen fetched the second large basket off Pammon and set it to the side. From the looks of it and the sound it made when he set it down, many things inside were also broken.

* * *

Pammon was asleep by the time he got the other two griffons dragged closer to them. He had decided against butchering them for the moment. Any more blood would only attract predators, and while Kaen doubted any would pose a problem, he searched through the second container.

Most of the arrows inside it were broken or bent. Less than ten were worth keeping; the few in the quiver were not in much better shape. Fifteen total arrows at best.

"Makes me wish I had some glue," he whispered to himself as he collected all the broken arrows and wrapped them in a cloth.

His axe and bow had made it through the crash, and he was thankful neither broke nor impaled Pammon in the landing.

With Pammon out completely, he moved his sword to his left side, brought his bow and the few arrows he had, and went off searching for wood.

The forest area they were in had a lot of game trails. He managed to shoot one deer that had gotten close to the water and cleaned it along the edge, bringing just the meat he would eat tonight. For the rest, he dug a small hole and buried organs and all.

After testing the water and washing off, Kaen moved further up the area and found a place where the water tasted sweeter and was clearer. Filling up two waterskins, he took the meat and drink back to the camp before returning to get the wood he had found.

With a fire going and food cooking, Kaen could tell that Pammon was out completely. Usually, he could sense a little bit of consciousness when his friend was sleeping, but this time, nothing was coming through their bond. The occasional wince of pain was the only thing he could pick up between them.

He walked around Pammon, checking the rest of his body in the fading light, and saw that his scales were intact, and none had been lost.

Stooping down, he took out a stick and drew an outline of a dragon, spread from snout to tail and wing to wing.

Glancing at the image, he considered what had happened and where their weak points were. Pammon was still young, according to Tharnok and Elies, and the fact that he had a skill most would not get for a few more years proved how dangerous it had been to use. His body could not handle the force it experienced during that maneuver. He still wondered if it had been the wrong decision to attempt it.

Shaking his head, Kaen glanced at the two griffons waiting to be consumed, knowing it was their only option. Had they not gotten the little bit of room they had gained from that maneuver, three or four of them would have descended upon Pammon, tearing his wings apart and sending both of them to their deaths.

Tapping the wings on his artwork, Kaen considered what that might mean for a fight against another dragon. If they could come in from behind and above, they might be able to attack these weak points. Doing so would allow them to win against a foe they might not be able to easily defeat.

"Do all dragons keep checking behind themselves?" Kaen wondered, realizing they had never considered themselves vulnerable like this before.

When they had dueled with Tharnok, they always knew he was around and, as such, were constantly looking for him.

They would need to consider how they viewed themselves and where they were as potential battlegrounds from now on.

Setting another log on the leaning stack, Kaen realized he was smiling as he remembered learning this trick from Aubri long ago. Tonight, it would serve him well since Pammon was clearly out.

The night had been long, and Kaen had spent most of the night reading one of the books his father had left him. The book *Tactical Warfare: Land Use* was different from what he had initially considered reading, but he felt it would be necessary with the threat of orcs and goblins in the mountains again. He had sketched a map in the dirt of the walls in Ebonmount and considered the view he and Pammon had seen, and how they helped consider some of the weaker points in the defenses.

They would need to fortify a few spots along the mountain areas as well as a few choke points along the road. A section also mentioned the weakness of the stream and river that flowed through part of the wall.

It wasn't the most exciting topic he had considered reading about, but it had passed the time, and it would be beneficial when the actual fighting took place.

Kaen stretched and checked on Pammon, who was still sleeping soundly. He went over and checked the spots on his wings and saw that they were knitting together nicely. The joint on his wing that had bent backward was not as swollen, and it looked like everything was healing. He wanted to wake up Pammon, yet if he was sleeping this soundly, it was either due to him needing to or the effect of that potion bag.

Walking to the water, he cleaned himself up while watching for any possible game. He wasn't hungry, but eating was always essential when one could. There was no telling when he could go hunting again.

As the afternoon passed, Kaen realized Pammon was not awake yet. A solid night's sleep like this was unusual. In fact, he was trying to remember any time Pammon had slept this soundly or this long.

Realizing this might last longer than he had intended, Kaen gathered more wood and prepared a bonfire. The meat from the griffon corpses was beginning to spoil, and if Pammon was not awake by tomorrow, he would need to burn it all to prevent it from rotting and becoming a problem.

Kaen washed himself off again. The sweat from working had made him stink, and he needed to rest before night came if he was going to stay up all night.

Back at camp, Kaen added more wood to his fire and scraped away a few coals before snuggling up against Pammon and closing his eyes.

A few hours after falling asleep, Kaen woke up when Pammon started moving around.

You're awake!

Just for a moment.

Kaen could feel Pammon talking slower as if his mind was cloudy or dull.

What's wrong?

I don't know. I'm just tired, and my wing is still not healed. I need to eat and sleep again.

Getting up, Kaen watched as Pammon shifted his body slowly, meandering like a cow in a field without much purpose. He made it over to the pile of griffons that Kaen had stacked up and began consuming them without regard for chewing. Huge bites followed by him swallowing everything in his mouth almost made Kaen wonder if he would choke on them.

Before Kaen knew it, both corpses were gone, and Pammon had turned around and moved back to where he had been earlier.

I'm sorry, but I cannot keep my eyes open. Thank you for watching over me . . .

Pammon's voice trailed off in his head, and before Kaen could reply, he knew that his friend was out again.

Kaen moved over and rubbed his friend's snout, seeing him press into his hand even though he was still asleep.

Turning back to the remains that Pammon had left on the ground, Kaen sighed. He tossed a few logs into the area and fetched a few lit coals from his fire. Better to burn what was left than let the stink draw birds or other creatures.

The second morning, Kaen found himself bored. He had already worked over the walls and defense adjustments for when he got back to Ebonmount and had considered other things to work on at the academy. He was filled with days that involved watching Pammon sleep and nothing else to do.

Leaving him felt fine as long as he was within a mile or two, but anything further left Kaen feeling uncomfortable. He had faith in his speed and stamina to return to Pammon if something happened or he woke up.

* * *

The third day had left him realizing he had no idea how long Pammon would be out. With that in mind, he started doing what he needed to take his mind off the concern he felt for Pammon.

The days became filled with setting traps, finding food, feeding himself, checking on the wood pile, and slowly building a makeshift shack. All those years living with Hess and the practice he had building Pammon's sleeping area back then helped. He cut down trees and began digging out a section of the ground, placing beams and fastening logs with the leather he knew would not be worth using on the trip home.

By the fourth day, he had built a solid lean-to shack and had begun putting mud he fetched from the lake in the wall gaps. It didn't have a door, but with the way he had it facing and the natural tree line, it cut down on some of the wood and provided him a chance to start putting his things out of the sun and wind, as well as providing a place for the food he had been drying out.

The next thing he worked on was an outhouse. During the past few days, having to go in the woods was a reminder of how spoiled he had been lately. Sure, it was part of life, but having a sheltered place to sit was much nicer.

His mind was trying to give him things to do on the fifth day since they had crashed here and Pammon had gone to sleep. Kaen was struggling with what was happening. Everything was going differently than he thought it should. That potion should have healed Pammon, even if it was left spilled in that leather sack. Surely, some of it had to have been good. When he examined Pammon's injury, everything looked like he was okay. There appeared to be no more damage, and the clawed sections had closed together nicely with a freshly healed scar.

Sitting on a wooden chair he had built, Kaen started modifying the broken arrows. With only nine full-size ones that worked, he cut off the tips of the ones that were broken or bent and carefully sawed off the sections he needed from ones that would be shorter but still work. It was long and tedious work, but it gave him something to focus on besides Pammon.

He was tired, lonely, and concerned. When sleep took him late in the afternoon on the fifth day, it was filled with dreams he had not had in a year.

31

Awake at Last

"It seems your best still isn't good enough," mocked Stioks as he broke the fourth arrow Kaen had just fired at him. "I would have believed you would be more of a challenge."

Fear filled Kaen's heart, and he could feel Pammon's beating fast as well.

We need to run! Perhaps Tharnok can buy us time!

Glancing at Elies and Tharnok, Kaen was shocked to see both of them gone. They were alone, facing Stioks and Juthom.

Stioks's black dragon grew larger, and smoke began to billow out of his teeth and snout.

Fly Pammon! Fly!

Pammon dropped down toward the ground, trying to gain speed as the laughter of Stioks and the thrumming of Juthom filled his ears.

Glancing back, he saw both of them coming after them, faster than they had been. Kaen saw both of them laughing and smiling as they stayed just a few yards off Pammon's tail.

No matter how he turned, twisted, dove, or climbed, they couldn't shake them.

I can only try one thing! Hold on!

Grabbing the reins, Kaen leaned against Pammon as he dove straight at the ground.

[Flight Burst Activated]

Lurching forward, Kaen felt them diving right at the ground.

It's too fast!

It's our only hope! Pammon cried back, not holding back as he made himself as streamlined as possible.

Fighting the wind that was buffeting him, Kaen glanced back and saw that Juthom was still right there, close enough to reach out at any moment and snap at Pammon.

Faster! I trust you!

With those words spoken, Kean felt Pammon gain even more speed as the ground rushed to meet them.

Hang on! Pammon screamed in his mind as his wings went out to change their direction.

Gripping the leather tighter, Kaen felt his entire body press into Pammon's neck as he arched his back and wings, spreading them out to catch the wind, and they began to curve away from the ground.

Finding the angle needed to make that turn, Pammon began to climb, letting out a thrum as he knew he would make the turn.

A crunching noise, followed by Pammon shrieking filled Kaen's ears as he glanced to the left and saw Juthom's teeth next to him.

In his mouth was Pammon's wing, sending them into a corkscrew and plummeting toward the earth.

I'm sorry I wasn't strong enough . . .

Those words right before they stuck ground echoed in Kaen's ears as his eyes closed, prepared to join Hoste wherever he was.

Stop thrashing! Wake up!

Kaen jerked himself awake, smacking his head against the wooden shelf he had built in the cabin.

Holding his head, he glanced outside the door and saw Pammon's eyes, open and staring at him between the wooden frame.

You're awake!

Getting to his feet while rubbing his head, Kaen dashed over and embraced Pammon's neck, running his hands along his scales and listening to him trill softly.

I am. I needed to sleep to recover, and I'm not sure if it was the potion, the griffons, or the injury. Either way, I feel fine. Now stop that crying and get me some food.

Laughing, Kaen leaned back and realized he was crying. Tears were streaming down his face, and he didn't care. The last five days had been brutal on his mind and heart.

"I just . . . I was afraid you were never going to recover," Kaen began to explain as he hugged Pammon's neck once more. "Don't do that again!"

Thrumming, Pammon nodded his head and slowly folded his wing around Kaen while curling him into his neck.

I will do my best not to. Now stop crying and go find me some food. I really am hungry.

Taking a deep breath and letting it out, Kaen nodded as he rubbed his arm once more across his face and slowly backed up from Pammon.

"I'll go get whatever I can. Are you able to fly or . . . ?"

Pammon lifted his wings a few times and gave them some solid flaps, sending air gusts around him and showering the area near the fire with sparks.

I can, but I want to rest it a little more and stretch some. How long have I been asleep?

Turning to the shed, Kaen began walking to retrieve his bow and quiver.

Five days. You only woke up once to eat the other two griffons before returning to sleep.

Pammon lifted his head and stared up at the sky, not replying for a moment.

Five days. That does seem like an awful long time. I do remember eating something, but it is still fuzzy to recall completely.

Laughing, Kaen grabbed his bow and attached his quiver to his hip.

Just relax. I'll be back as quickly as I can.

Watching Kaen run off toward the woods, Pammon smiled until his belly rumbled.

His eyes went wide as he realized what was about to happen.

Kaen was already in the woods when he felt relief and contentment wash over him.

Seems like you are feeling better. What has you so happy?

A tinge of something Kaen had not really felt before hit him. Embarrassment?

You aren't going to be happy, but we will probably need to move camp.

Did you knock down the cabin? It will be fine. I can rebuild it.

No. That isn't it. I think it would be better if I just found us a new spot to stay until we leave.

Confused, Kaen tried to focus on what would require them to move.

What happened? Why do we need to move?

I'll just wait for you to get back. It will be better that way.

Pammon was laughing, and Kaen started laughing, too. He had no idea what Pammon had done, but there was nothing to worry about. Kaen was just glad Pammon was awake.

HOLY GOBLIN SHITE, THAT SMELLS HORRIBLE!

Kaen was almost gagging, and he was still about a hundred feet from camp.

Why did you do that there?! Why couldn't you move somewhere else?

It just happened! I hadn't gone in seven days, and after eating all that food, it just hit me. I was just glad I was able to get it out. Imagine if you had to help me.

Choking down the bile in his mouth, Kaen dropped the deer he had killed and brought back.

You can come and eat this one here. I'll be going back out and looking for another, but you will need to try and bury that! Why didn't you do that already?

Thrumming, Kaen knew precisely why the moment he heard and felt Pammon laughing.

You are such an eggling!

Moving to where Kaen had dropped the deer, Pammon smiled.

Ignoring the grin and the laughter, Kaen shook his head as he sought the safety of the forest to cleanse the stench that had assaulted his nostrils.

Find us a new place. Somewhere, I can't smell that. And don't forget to collect my gear. I don't want it to smell like that!

It had taken about four hours to gather three deer, but with half a moon out, they were coming to the water to eat and drink. Thankful that the smell from Pammon had not come this way, Kaen returned to wash up after he had given Pammon more food at their new camp.

He was down to five arrows, two of which were not in the best shape.

Wishing he had finished the adjustments to the ones he had been working on, Kaen had no desire to return to the old camp and dig around for them.

That smell would last for days, and Pammon's load was at least the size of a small wagon.

I don't know why you are so upset. It isn't like you didn't build a place to go to the bathroom.

Mine is built near the trees and away from the camp. I also cover mine up with dirt and wood chips after I go. You didn't even cover yours up!

Thrumming again, Pammon just lay there as he waited for Kaen to return and set up a few things around the camp.

I am glad to see you missed me. I am sorry again that I caused you pain and angst.

Grumbling to himself, Kaen walked in the direction where he knew Pammon was. It had been hard, and he was glad Pammon was okay, but that smell had been overwhelming.

I now know what Hess meant when he told me once that adventuring was not glamorous. Who knew my whole camp would be destroyed by a dragon's bowel movement?

That night, they relaxed and chatted about nothing in particular. Pammon was glad to be awake, and Kaen was just as glad to see him moving around and acting normal.

With Pammon active, Kaen enjoyed the best four hours he had sleeping in almost a week.

I am fine! Pammon stated again as he did another slow pass over Kaen. **Stop being a mother hen, and let's fly out of here. We don't need to waste any more time.**

Fine, but we are going to stop by the dwarves. I would rather stop there, try to find some rope or leather, and get you a few animals to eat. It will be a long trip, and I am out of all my basic supplies.

Fine, fine. Now move out of the way before I crash into you and have to sleep again.

Ignoring Pammon, Kaen gathered the last of his supplies and put them into the only basket that would work. He would have to tie it on somehow, but he didn't want to leave all the harvest materials he had taken from the griffons.

You've grown. I need to let out two notches on the saddle.

Stepping back, Kaen looked at Pammon and reached around with his arms. He had gotten bigger.

I haven't noticed. Two notches? That is faster than usual.

Tightening the straps for his saddle, Kaen nodded as he felt how tight it still was. Not time for three yet, but soon.

Does that mean a whole new set of straps before long?

It does. I wonder if the amount of sleep combined with the number of griffons you ate had anything to do with this growth.

Maybe almost dying and killing you was worth it, after all.

Ignoring the jab, Kaen finished cinching everything into place, climbed on, and got in his spot.

Enough blabbering. Let's get moving. I want to be at the dwarven place before nightfall.

Would His Highness like anything else to go with that request?

Laughing as he rubbed that same scale as always, Kaen smiled.

Yes. I'd like a promise from you to never crap in camp again.

I wish I could make that promise, but we both know I'm not nice.

Thrumming, Pammon leaped into the air as Kaen and he both laughed.

Pammon was right, and Kaen knew it. Sometime in the future, it would happen again, but next time it would be because his dragon thought it was funny.

32

A Dwarven Ally

Are you taking it easy, or are you trying to fly faster? What are your stats?

Kaen had been judging how fast they were going by the land moving beneath them, and it felt like Pammon was covering more ground, even with a steady beat of his wings.

I am not trying to fly faster; I just am. I think the griffons have played a role in this. In fact, let me see something.

Simple Status Check
Pammon
Young Dragon
HP - 4000/4000
MP - 600/600
STR - 50
CON - 55
DEX - 65
WIS - 30
INT - 35

It would appear that I have grown during these last few days of rest. Perhaps we should restock and see if we can find any more griffons.

Not on your life.

They were already higher in the sky than usual, but both of them had learned from that last encounter that staying low was not a smart move when traveling in a zone with flying creatures.

I am glad it appears there was some gain from all of this, but we are way behind on time and need to restock.

Even worse is the clouds off in the distance. It will rain in a few days, and we may be flying back in a storm.

Glancing behind them, Kaen noticed the clouds off in the distance but it was too far for him to tell if they had rain or not. Flying home in the rain was not fun and flying above storm clouds was not easy.

I know what you are thinking, and my answer is no. I will not attempt that again.

Grinning, Kaen knew it wasn't a good idea. The air was too thin even for him and that kind of time. Had he not been strapped in he would have fallen from Pammon's back. The headache it had given him lasted for hours, but it was a valuable lesson to learn.

Well, judging by the map, we should get to the dwarven gates an hour or so before sunset. Here's hoping no one mistakes us for the other dragon.

The sun was barely over the trees in the west as Kaen and Pammon slowly flew up the main road leading toward the massive metal gates built into the mountain. The dwarves had cut the mountain flat, and a large stone bridge connected the gap that was dug out before coming to the entrance to the mountain.

Small openings were set within the rocky face, and massive ballistas and launchers that housed harpoons looked like they could easily strike them down and were pointed in their direction.

Pammon was telling Kaen all of the defenses long before they got close. He could only see the two giant dwarf statues they had carved in the mountain on both sides of the gate. One was a dwarf with a shield and a hammer, outfitted in what he guessed was plate armor, and the other was a dwarf in a robe holding a staff. Even a mile off, one could make out them.

The dwarves under us have noticed, and that sound you heard echoes from the fortress. It appears the door is closing on the keep.

We expected all this. Elies told us where to head and to stop. You are almost there.

Snorting, Pammon slowed down his approach and turned slightly, aiming for a section to the west of the city toward a large building and a field.

The one with the red, white, and yellow striped flag?

That's the one. Hopefully, the dwarf we are looking for is there.

A crowd had formed, and torches were lit as the two of them sat in the clearing, waiting for the chaos to end.

Initially, armed dwarves showed up with weapons, pointing bows and crossbows at them. They had been nervous and kept a distance from Kaen, but word had reached them about a new Dragon Rider over a year ago. He was still amazed at how fearful they really were.

Your friend . . . the dwarf with the beard. Gertrude, I believe, was not this fearful of me.

You also saved her life. That goes a long way to earning someone's trust.

Snorting, Pammon watched as a group of three dwarves came through the makeshift crowd and approached them.

One female and two male dwarves. I don't know if I should be proud of myself for being able to tell the difference.

Snickering, Kaen unhooked himself and slid off Pammon, taking a few steps toward the three who were approaching him.

"Dragon Rider Kaen, I assume?" asked the older-looking dwarf.

"Lady Elnidith, if I am correct?"

She nodded and chuckled as she stroked her red and white beard. Her age had turned most of the beard and her hair white but a few red streaks still ran through it. Her face was marred by a scar on a cheek and weathered skin that did not hide her age at all.

"It would appear Elies spoke of my beauty to you," she replied with a slight bow. "I must say rumors of your appearance and size do neither of you justice. We are honored to have you visit us finally."

One of the men next to her gave a sharp whistle and all those who were still standing with their weapons pointed put them away and began to disperse.

"These two are my right-hand men. Brabrel is the ugly one with the dark black hair and my number two. Kirus is the better-looking one and my third in command."

Glancing at the two dwarves, Kaen realized they looked exactly alike, and each was smiling and not saying a word. The two of them had dark black hair and beards, both braided exactly the same way. The only difference was their eyes. Brabrel's left eye was green and his right eye was brown, while his brother Kirus's left eye was brown and right eye was green.

"Oh, that's right," Kaen stated as if he could tell a difference. "Elies had told me that Brabrel had the ugly eye while Kirus was much better looking."

The dwarf on her right scowled while the one on her left began laughing.

Hearing Kaen's comment and how they responded, Elnidith groaned before smiling.

"Those two knuckleheads can't keep a straight face if their life depended on it. By now you know which one is which and I see that Elies either shared some of his wisdom and tact with you or you come prepared."

"I'd like to think a little bit of both."

Nodding, she motioned to the building behind her.

"We should move inside if you are ok with it. If you would like, I will have a guard stay near your dragon, Pammon. I will also call for some food to be brought to him. Any idea how long the two of you are planning on staying?"

"Only for a day or two if I can help it. I need to resupply and head back to Ebonmount, but if the king were willing to see me, I would like to at least present myself before him."

Elnidith studied Kaen's face, running her hand along her beard braids. After a moment, she nodded her head and snapped her finger at the one who was Kirus.

He gave a bow and a slight smile before taking off in a jog.

"He will see if the king is willing to see you. Perhaps he will, but for now, let's move inside and take care of other things."

Are you going to be ok out here? I can stay if you want.

I have no fear of these dwarves. I doubt any of them could pierce my scales when I am on the ground, and a good blast of flame would send them running. Not that I considered any of that.

"Pammon says he would be happy to stay here and appreciates the kindness of the dwarves for bringing him food. I may have to pay if he eats too much."

Laughing, Elnidith waved off his comment and motioned for him to follow her.

As they walked toward the building he would be staying in, Kaen watched the dwarves staring at him.

"Why is everyone giving me a weird look?" Kaen whispered as he bent down to her ear.

"Most had not believed it was true. A new Dragon Rider," Elnidith answered, her own voice was hushed and low. "I would have struggled to believe if Elies had not sent me a letter himself. Many believed Aldric was just making things up for a while when the report of the Ebonmount attack occurred."

Glancing around her and looking at the faces in the crowd, she frowned before she turned back.

"I had hoped one who owes you much would have been here, but most likely, he will arrive tomorrow."

"Who owes me? No one owes me anything."

Cackling as she walked, she put her hand on Kaen's back and smiled.

"My dear boy, you know nothing of a blood debt."

Sitting at their table, Kaen noticed how much taller he felt when everyone was gathered in Elnidith's main room. The ceiling was slightly lower than what he was used to. Since most dwarves were a good six to twelve inches shorter than him, it made sense that all their tables and chairs were shorter.

The chair he was sitting in was one she had said was for when Elies or others had visited, and it lifted him higher so that his legs were not scrunched.

The table was right against his legs, and he smiled as they began bringing out lots of different meats, cheeses, bread, and a few different ales as well.

"Could I bother you for milk or water instead?"

Raising an eyebrow, Elnidith glanced around the room, and the assortment of half a dozen dwarves who were at other tables winced at his request.

"No ale? I mean, that seems almost like an insult," she stated as she snapped her finger and motioned to a young dwarf who ran off to fetch what he had requested. "I don't know of any dwarves here who drink milk except those on their mother's teats."

A raucous laughter echoed around the room as dwarves slapped their hands on the table.

"Let's just say that I don't handle alcohol very well, and I would like to keep my mind clear tonight and for the next few days."

"It's your reputation," she replied with a chuckle. "Most here will give you grief, but I understand your desire to keep a clear mind. If you change your tune, let me know, and I can have one of the boys fetch the stuff we give the two-year-olds."

A dwarf nearby started coughing and choking as ale flowed from his nostrils and down his beard. Elnidith's statement had tickled something deep inside him, and his table mate was slapping his choking friend's back while cackling at Kaen's expense.

Brabrel leaned across the table, took the tankard of ale that had been sitting before him, and gave a wink.

"Since you won't be enjoying this fine vintage, I shall suffer through it," he declared before lifting it to his lips and guzzling the frothy drink down.

Tsking at him, Elnidith just smiled as she sat in her chair and motioned for Kaen to begin eating.

"I won't tell you how special that ale was, but perhaps one day, when you grow a real beard, we can talk about trying to get you some more."

Rubbing his hand on his chin, Kaen felt the stubble that had turned into a thicker patch. He hadn't bothered trying to shave at all the last week, and now he wondered if he should keep it or shave it off.

Kaen loaded up his plate by grabbing some of the roasted boar they put before him and a few pieces of bread.

He could sense that Pammon was also eating, and a content sigh came through their bond.

While he ate, Kaen glanced around the room and saw all the different shields and the colors that decorated them.

"What's with all the shields?"

Elnidith motioned to Brabrel, who smiled as he paused his stuffing of some meat into a roll.

"Those are all shields representing families that have served in the elite squad that Elnidith is responsible for. This outpost handles all threats inside and outside the city walls. If there be a fight, she is like your adventurer guild but without all the drama."

"But you do have an adventurer guild," Kaen stated between bites. "I know that some of our best warriors have come from your kingdom."

Grinning at the compliment, Brabrel nodded as he pointed his meat-filled roll at Elnidith.

"Aye, we do, but they have nothing on the core squad that follows her command. I doubt you would find a better mind in all the land, though she won't brag on herself."

Grinning, Kaen turned to look at Elnidith, and she shook her head.

"Something tells me you are going to ask me about something, and I doubt I want to know what it is."

Taking another bite, Kaen nodded.

33

A Possible Partner

Elnidith stared at the map Kaen had drawn and listened to his description of the walls and land changes. He had shown her how it was currently designed and laid out and then pointed to the few things that he felt needed to be changed and upgraded.

A small group of other dwarves had gathered around, listening and watching as he spent a solid twenty minutes going over the different wall systems and what he knew was in the mountains to the south.

"Sounds like you know more about defenses than most of these knuckle-heads around us," she stated, sighing. "The problem isn't just your land issues or your defenses. The real problem will be how many troops you can muster and the length of your wall. With the numbers you say you have and the amount of area you have to cover, a solid attack in a few places will easily overwhelm your wall and prevent your troops from retreating."

She marked a few spots based on the map he had of the forests and streams and pointed out a few weak points he had missed.

"You really need at least another five thousand troops. All the stuff you are doing sounds great, but it won't matter once the real fighting starts because you can't defend it."

She glanced up at Kaen and saw the frown on his face.

"Did you come here to ask for troops from the king?"

Shaking his head, Kaen marked a few more notes on the map before turning to look at her. He saw how her eyes were narrowed and her forehead furled.

"I wasn't, but judging by the excitement on your face, that wouldn't go over at all."

A small grin cracked her face, and she nodded.

"Right now, the king has only one plan for whatever is coming. Store food and continue carving out more room in the mountain. The amount of rock we have off to the west could build houses for tens of thousands of people, but I won't get into politics with you."

She turned and motioned to the men and women gathered around her, and they all turned and left. Even Brabrel gave a slight bow and walked away.

"Roll up your map and sit with me. We need to talk."

She turned and moved to two chairs in a corner of the room. They had furs and other pelts draped across them, and there were no other chairs nearby. Only a small table between them.

"What did Elies tell you about us?" Elnidith asked as she folded her hands on her chest and leaned back in her chair.

"About you or the dwarves in general?"

Chuckling, she smiled and shrugged. "Both, but mainly the dwarves as a whole."

Sucking some air in through his teeth, Kaen grimaced as he looked around the room and saw only a few dwarves were still downstairs and as far away as possible from them.

"The truth is, Elies mentioned that the way the king was acting seemed typical of his behavior. I know he does not always like to get involved in the things of the world. It has taken a lot of money and other items to convince him it was worthwhile in the past."

Pausing, Kaen studied Elnidith to see if anything he had said yet was upsetting, but her face was like stone, giving nothing away.

"Bosgreth is old. Perhaps that is why he has the nickname *Lightbeard*."

Elnidith scowled and shook her head. "Do not let him hear that name from you," she said, her voice like cold water poured down one's spine. "He would ignore what you are and treat you as a criminal."

Holding his hands up, Kaen feigned innocence.

"I didn't mean it as an insult but . . ."

"It is an insult, and he will take it no other way. I know what you mean, but we don't speak that name. Ever!"

The way she accented that last word drove her point home.

Nodding his head in understanding, Kaen gave a slight bow.

"I appreciate the instruction. Forgive my ignorance on the matter."

She waved his comment away and motioned for him to continue.

"I know he is older and does not want to risk much. This means we can do very few things to convince him to join the fight against Stioks. I don't see how hiding in a mountain can be the best solution for the dwarves. Do you believe that I am wrong?"

Gently biting her lip, Elnidith sat there a moment and studied him.

The way Kaen was sitting and the tone of his voice spoke to the fact he believed what he was saying.

"I am in a difficult position," she finally answered, lowering her voice. "While I protect the king and the kingdom, my opinion on recent developments has been ignored. One of the reasons the forest has been taken back as far as possible is to help control the potential advance against us. I doubt you noticed it, but the land slopes downward as well. No dragon would be foolish enough to attack our main gate, and the cost of crossing our bridge would make any army regret that decision."

"But that isn't the problem," Kaen interrupted. "You will seal yourselves in a tomb, unable to leave until you are either too weak or are willing to give up."

Snorting, Elnidith nodded as she closed her eyes a moment and rubbed them with her fingers.

"I'm not sure if Elies told you that or you figured it out alone, but that is the truth. The day we call to seal everyone inside is the day we sign our death certificates."

Her face sagged, and there was something about how she looked at him that Kaen had seen before.

Defeat.

"What other options do you have? Can you convince Bosgreth to change his mind? Is there no one that can?"

Kaen's voice was getting louder, and she raised her hand to silence him.

"No, there is not. His son is not going to go against his father, and he believes it is the right path as well. There is nothing you can do, not even as a Dragon Rider, that will change the way dwarves are. This is something we must figure out on our own."

Groaning, Kaen rubbed his whole face with his hand and leaned back in the chair.

"I am going to sound ugly and probably piss you off, but you are sounding just as bad as the elves."

Her head snapped back at that insult. He had not done it to be mean or ugly but to prove a point.

He saw how it burned her, but she did not respond.

A rush of air escaped her nose as she huffed at him.

"You are taking great liberty with an insult like that, but I know how you mean it. Tell me what you would have me do, Dragon Rider Kaen."

Her voice had changed. Gone was the casual tone she had been using, replaced with one reserved for diplomatic discussions.

He crossed his arms and traded stares with her momentarily while considering what he might request.

She was a tactical genius and better prepared for war than he would be for many years yet. Their people were caught between a literal mountain and a hard place.

"How many people do you have under you?"

"Battle-hardened or that I provide for?" she asked, her eyes twinkling at his question.

"Both. If you had to move today, tomorrow, in a year, how many lives would you be responsible for?"

Grunting, she motioned to the shields on the walls.

"I have over twenty shields here, and each of those shields has from fifty to one hundred warriors that will answer my call if the need arises. Beyond that are at least four thousand who depend on me for jobs and more. I have a lot of lives I am responsible for."

Her tone was grim, and he knew she felt the weight of each of those lives.

"If I asked, as a Dragon Rider, could I count on you and yours to come to Ebonmount and provide assistance defending against the threat?" he asked before leaning forward and tapping the arm of his chair with his finger. "I would ensure jobs and homes were available for each who come and defend the kingdom."

Leaning against the arm of her chair, Elnidith began stroking her beard braids as she considered what Kaen had proposed.

"Perhaps a quest request?" she finally asked after sitting silently for a moment. "Something from the adventurers' guild even?"

"Would that be better than a request from me?"

"Both of them together would be hard to resist. It would put much more pressure on the king to allow such a move, and I could propose some reasoning. Once there, the length of the contract could be adjusted. How long will it take before Stioks makes his move?"

"He could be making a move now. I have been gone longer than I wanted, and while I am away, there is limited protection for Ebonmount."

Kaen began to say something and stopped. He saw her puzzled look when he did.

"There are things I am not at liberty to speak on yet, but know that in the coming months or even years, things will most likely get worse for a while. For now, all I can do is make decisions based on what I believe will save the most lives and stop Stioks from getting what he wants."

"What do you think he really wants?"

Leaning forward, Kaen made sure his voice was even and calm.

"He wants a dragon egg. One he can bond with so he can live a lot longer."

Elnidith's eyes widened, and he saw her face turn a lighter shade.

"So the rumor is true," she said, shaking her head and gazing at the floor. "We believed those were impossible things, but he wants another dragon?"

"He does, and for whatever reason, the three dragons he has right now have not laid any eggs. I believe he will become less cautious the longer this goes on. If he gets an egg of his own, we are looking at the potential of another hundred or more years with him."

Turning, she spat on the floor and let out a curse.

"I would rather eat a hairy goblin sack before I live under the fear of that," she exclaimed with a growl. "Make your request. Tomorrow, go and see the adventurers' guild and turn in a request there as well. When you return, make sure to do the same in Ebonmount."

Standing up, she glanced around the room at the few dwarves who had stayed downstairs with them.

"I cannot promise it will happen fast, but if you make those three requests, I will do everything in my power to bring my men and women and their families to help prevent such a thing from taking place."

Kaen smiled as she extended her hand. He shook it, impressed by the strength in her grip.

"Now, let my men show you to your room. I need to take care of a few details after discussing this with you," she stated, letting go of his hand. "Try to get a good night's sleep, and I will let you know in the morning if King Bosgreth will see you."

She motioned to one of her men, who came over, and gave a slight bow to Kaen.

"If you are ready, sir, I will show you to your room. Is there anything else you need?"

Ignoring the ability to be discreet, Kaen nodded and motioned to himself.

"I'm sure I do not smell the nicest; a tub or at least a lot of water would be appreciated. I may need some clothes washed tonight as well."

Grinning, the dwarf nodded as he motioned to the stairs.

"That will all be taken care of for you, sir. If you please."

The man began walking toward the stairs, and Kaen followed him, grabbing his pack from the table.

"Sleep well, Dragon Rider Kaen. I will see you in the morning," Elnidith called out as he walked away.

34

Making the Right Request

Stretching, Kaen lay on top of the bed, having slept in just his underclothes and no blankets. The room he was in was furnished with a soft chair and a desk, a fireplace he had not added any wood to since he entered last night, and the tub they had left in the room after filling it with water. He had passed out, exhausted from watching over Pammon for so long.

You are up early.

It isn't early, you fool. The sun has been up for hours. The dwarves have already brought me food, and I am trying to decide where I want to leave a gift.

Groaning, Kaen sat up and turned so his feet were on the floor.

Wait . . . please wait. Let me speak with Elnidith first and see if they might want that somewhere specific. I would prefer not to get chased off because you ruined their property.

Even though he couldn't hear or feel Pammon's thrum, he knew that his dragon was laughing, probably scaring the dwarves who were outside *guarding* him.

Moving to the door, Kaen poked his head out after cracking it a little and saw that his clothes were on the floor, folded neatly and sitting on a cloth with a washing basin next to it.

Smiling, he bent down and picked up the pile and moved back into his room. There were perks to all this Dragon Rider stuff.

"You look rested," Elnidith declared as she looked up from her small stack of papers. "Come, sit and eat as I tell you what is in store for you today!"

Nodding, Kaen sat down in a chair near her. She flashed a small grin before stroking her beard braids and motioning to a servant who was waiting nearby.

"Get this man some milk, and make sure it's cold!"

Laughter echoed in the room from the other dwarves, who were going over paperwork of their own. Each lifted a tankard at him and grinned before draining it dry. The sound of at least ten cups being set down at the same time made Kaen chuckle; he knew they were playing around with him.

"I have a question I need to ask sooner than later. My dragon would like to know if you have a place you would prefer his load to be dropped off."

Narrowing her eyes at him for a moment, they suddenly went full size and Elnidith bust out in laughter as she nodded.

"Oh yes!" she exclaimed when she finally settled down. "I will get someone to show him where. Sometimes Tharnok was kind enough to give us a *load* and I would appreciate it greatly if he did not do that right outside."

"Durlan, I got a job for you!"

A round male dwarf with fiery red hair and a beard split down the middle waddled over and gave a slight bow. Kaen thought for a moment the man might tip over from how round he was.

"Whatz canz Iz du fer da rider?" he asked, his accent thicker than porridge.

"Go outside and lead his dragon to the field where we want him to take a crap and be quick about it! I don't want him doing that foul mess in my yard, or you and your brothers will be cleaning it up!"

A horrified look flashed across the dwarf's face and it almost appeared that he turned a little green.

"Iz gut it ma'am," he declared as he saluted and quickly waddled to the door leading outside.

There is a fat red-headed dwarf coming to show you where to crap at. Be kind to him.

A hint of amusement came through their bond as Kaen could only wonder what Pammon was thinking.

Chuckling, Kaen watched as the man hurried away and turned to see Elnidith watching him.

"His uh . . . speech. Why was it so . . ."

"Thick? Rough? Hard to understand?"

Nodding, Kaen scratched his facial hair as he glanced back at the man scurrying through the door.

Tsking her teeth, Elnidith grabbed her cup and took a swig before returning it to the table.

"He took a hit to the head from an orc. Should have died, yet somehow he lived. He isn't fast when it comes to thinking now, but in a fight, he is like a wild animal," she stated, tapping her temple. "All fear goes out the window for him. He once ran into a pack of three orcs with his war hammer, spinning like a top. They were in shock, to say the least."

"Glad to hear he is ok. How long ago was that fight?"

Leaning back in her chair, she folded her hand across her chest and played with her beard as she studied Kaen's face.

"It's been a good decade at least. I have lost a lot of warriors since then. More than I would like to admit. There were years when the orcs and goblins pestered us every month at least."

She paused as the servant showed up with Kaen's milk and waited till he had moved away.

"Since we started the path the king is on with retreating to the mountain, the number of raids has dropped drastically. Only one small group came this past year, and it was nothing more than twenty goblins. I can only imagine what they are planning."

He could see the frustration on her face as she watched him. A slight scowl showed behind her beard, and her brows had drawn together, letting him know she wasn't happy.

"So what have you and your warriors done in that time?"

She grunted and glanced around the room, blowing wind out her lips.

"Gotten fat and soft. It is hard to keep them motivated when there isn't anything to kill."

Kaen took a drink from his cup and appreciated that the milk was chilled. He knew it was colder up here where the dwarves lived, but it was hard for him to always notice the slight temperature change.

"So tell me, what is the plan for today?" Kaen asked, changing the subject.

"Eat, and I'll give you a quick rundown."

Not wasting time, Kaen grabbed the bread and meat and focused on forming a pile on his plate as Elnidith started listing the things she had set up for him.

"I may need some better clothes for King Bosgreth. Even with these washed and pressed, I am down to one other pair of traveling clothes, and they are not better."

Elnidith chewed on her lip as she bobbed her head up and down.

"I don't think that would be possible, even if a group of tailors worked together," she finally answered. "Perhaps we can make a coat of some sort, but I would not worry that much about it. The King knows you are a Dragon Rider and that you did not originally plan on coming here for an audience."

Scratching his chin, the itch from the hair was affirming he should shave it off.

"I won't worry about it then. For now, let's deal with the other two items. I have like six hours before I meet the king. You said the adventurer's guild is inside the mountain?"

She nodded as she extended a piece of paper to him.

"Read it, but I think if you turn this in as an actual request, it will speed up the process so that me and my warriors can help you with your problem."

Kaen scanned the document she had given him and began smiling.

Elies had commented many times on how sharp Elnidith was, and this quest request was proof of that. She must have stayed up a good chunk of the night drafting it for him.

"I'm assuming you have a copy for me to turn in at Ebonmount as well?"

She winked as she handed him a folded copy in an envelope.

"Why Dragon Rider Kaen, what would give you the impression that I wasn't prepared?"

He laughed as her voice attempted to sound innocent and sweet, spiking higher than normal, but she joined him in a quick laugh as she handed him a third piece of paper.

"Sign that one and give it back and I will have that one to turn in later. With three different requests asking for the same thing, it will be hard for Bosgreth to say no."

Accepting the pen and the letter she gave him, Kaen read it quickly before signing and returning it to her.

"I guess all that leaves now is this Marfo I am supposed to meet?"

Sliding her chair back, Elnidith stretched and winced as a few audible pops came from her shoulders.

"Old age does take a toll," she said with a grunt as she winced and popped her shoulder once more. "If you want, we can walk, ride, or you can fly to where we need to go. I would choose horseback or flying if I were you."

The gleam in her eye told Kaen that walking was not the option he should pick and he scooted his chair back, tucking both papers she had for him into his tunic before grabbing one more roll from the table.

"I will choose flying, as I'm called a Dragon Rider and not a horse rider," Kaen joked as he began to follow her.

She laughed and nodded as she motioned to three of the dwarves who had stood up when she did.

"It is only an hour from here by horse. Let me get you a map and we can meet you there."

Brabrel waved at him as the dwarf jogged to the door and opened it up.

"Looks like you slept well, Dragon Rider Kaen," the dwarf stated as he held the door open. "Rumors were we had two dragons here last night. One snoring inside and one snoring outside."

Kaen grinned and shrugged as he walked outside.

"Sleeping on the ground is not as nice as the bed you all let me use last night. I don't think I moved much at all."

"I will make sure the housemaster knows. He will consider that an honor and be happy to hear that."

Kaen hadn't realized that his statement would carry so much weight. It was almost like the elves, except his words carried more weight here than they did in Roccnari.

"Are you going to need to summon—" Elnidith cut herself off when she saw Pammon sitting outside waiting for them. "Did you tell him to be here?"

Chuckling, he shook his head and pointed at Pammon, who was almost the full height of the two-story building with his head held high.

"He had returned from his business, and I think, based on the feelings I am getting from him, Pammon is trying to show off his size and stature."

Elnidith saw the smirk on Kaen's face and nodded.

"He is rather large for one so young. It does make me wonder how big he might become when he reaches Tharnok's age."

Snorting, Pammon spread his wings and shook his body, causing a few stammers and shouts from the dwarves on the edges of the area watching him.

Slowing his step, Kaen glanced at the horses, which were a good five minutes away and then back at Pammon.

Elnidith furled her brows as she saw the smile on Kaen's face.

"Elnidith, have you ever flown on a dragon before?"

Her head snapped back a few inches as she flinched, and her eyes were as wide as saucers. Her tan skin took on a slight white tone, and a collective gasp was heard from the dwarves, who were escorting them.

"On . . . on . . . on a dragon?" she stuttered, having lost all the dignity and confidence she typically portrayed.

Still grinning like a dragon who had eaten an entire herd of cows, Kaen nodded and pointed at Pammon.

"If you'd like, we could fly together on Pammon and you could see what your kingdom looks like from up there. Besides, it is the least I can do for all the help you have given me in just one day."

Pammon was watching Elnidith and started thrumming loudly. The air radiated even from thirty yards away as Pammon laughed, his chest walls flexing with the effort.

"Do it," whispered Brabrel from behind her. "Do it!"

She turned around and saw him nodding his head so fast one might think it would fall off.

"Thousands of years since it was done last! Think of the honor!"

Elnidith quickly regained her composure, turned to Kaen, and gave a deep bow.

"I would be honored to ride with you," she said, her voice quivering.

He wasn't sure if it was excitement, fear, or a combination of both.

Smiling, Kaen motioned for her to follow him.

One point for me! Kaen declared, laughing at the victory.

Bah, that is only because you wouldn't let me breathe fire! Otherwise, she would have said no for sure!

Pammon stopped laughing as he watched the dwarven woman approach him. He saw her eyes twinkling at the realization of what she was about to do.

Snorting, he lay down on the ground, knowing he was about to make some dwarf's life.

35

A Debt Paid, a Price Set Low

Kaen grinned as he felt Elnidith squeezing him tight when they came in to land at the place she had pointed at.

The entire trip had only lasted twenty minutes since Pammon had taken his time and flew around to show off more of their land. There were a few times it felt like Elnidith was trying to break a rib from how tight she squeezed his chest and abdomen. He had laughed each time and she had loosened her hold. A little.

The fields looked mostly empty as the time for their harvest was nearing an end. The property they were coming to was, like many, tasked with growing a barley crop. Useful for many things, including alcohol, it was a staple in the kingdom.

A decent-sized house sat in the middle of the property with stone walls leading from the main road back to it. Each field was sectioned off with stone, which appeared to be coming from inside the mountain they were cutting out at a breakneck speed.

People in the fields and near the home could be seen running to the safety of the house, gathering in a large group and pointing up as Pammon circled a third time.

He finally landed on the wide road that led to the house and stopped fifty yards from the gate leading to the main estate.

You two will have to walk. I have played the kind dragon role long enough. Tell her I hope she enjoyed her only trip.

Patting his favorite scale, Kaen chuckled as he untied the rope that held him and Elnidith together.

"Sorry, I don't have a better system for staying connected right now. I don't think it would make you feel better if I mentioned we crashed almost a week ago when fighting a pack of griffons."

He felt her go stiff and laughed harder than he should have after untying the last knot. Sliding down to the ground, he held his hands out and helped her dismount with some dignity.

She chuckled as it took a moment for her legs to get used to the ground.

"Thank you, Pammon," she quickly blurted out as she turned and bowed to him. "I am honored more than words can ever begin express for what I have experienced. If there is anything I can do to repay that debt, just tell me."

Kaen started to laugh before Pammon even had a chance to reply.

"Before he bombards me with requests, he likes to be repaid in things to eat. Something new is always a treat, but at the end of the day, he loves a cow."

Elnidith burst out laughing so hard she coughed a few times. "That I can do! Tonight, you will eat every different creature I can provide!"

Pammon started thrumming.

Perhaps I should start offering a dragon traveling service to wealthy individuals who can provide me with food choices.

Groaning, Kaen moved over and scratched Pammon's scales.

Yes . . . let's find ways to get you even more food so that when you don't get what you want, I have to listen to you complain even more.

Pammon gave a gentle push with his snout against Kaen, causing Elnidith to laugh again, while she watched the two of them wrestle for a moment.

"Should I ask what he said?"

Letting out a sigh after breaking his embrace with Pammon, Kaen smirked and shrugged his shoulders.

"He asked me if we could open up a dragon transport service that required rare and exotic animals as payment."

Two minutes later, they walked toward the gathered group of dwarves, who were watching the strange scene play out with a dragon, a human, and a dwarf laughing.

Elnidith was still wiping tears from her eyes, and Kaen might have had a few tears needing to be wiped away.

"Up ahead is a dwarf named Marfo, the father of Gertrude. I am sure you remember her as the warrior you saved a few years ago."

Nodding that he did, Kaen looked at the man, clearly her father, standing before everyone else gathered. His body shape and demeanor all reminded him of Gertrude. He even had a few beard braids with metal rings spread throughout it.

"When word reached him that you were here, a messenger came to me last night demanding that I bring you so that he could honor a debt. I have no idea what he might offer, but please remember this is something serious for our people."

Kaen recalled the number of times he had been approached over the last few years by dwarves he had saved. They all had offered their lives and service to him, including Gertrude and Brazuc.

"Perhaps I can just swing a few cows and call it a day," he joked as he watched Elnidith wave at the crowd before them.

She snorted and spat on the ground after clearing her throat.

"He would offer you all his cows and more if you pushed, but I would not recommend that. Let him offer what he wants and you can ask for less or more as you feel led."

When they reached the gate, two dwarves opened it wide and gave deep bows as Kaen and Elnidith moved through it. Both held their heads lower than Kaen had expected.

"Dragon Rider Kaen!"

The shout rang out over the yard as the one he knew must be Marfo approached them, holding his hands wide and a smile etched on his face.

Kaen saw the wrinkles on Marfo's face and knew this man must have seen a few things in his lifetime. When he flashed Kaen a smile, the two gold teeth on the bottom row caught him off guard. His hair and beard were salt and pepper, with an equal amount of white and black in each.

"I am honored you have come to visit me," Marfo called out as he covered the ground quicker than Kaen had expected with his stubby legs.

He gave a deep bow before standing up and extending his hand to Kaen.

Shaking those well-worn and calloused hands, Kaen smiled back and gave a slight nod with his head.

"I am honored to be invited to your property. I have heard many great things about it from Brazuc and Gertrude," he said as scanned the fields. "I am trying to figure out, though, which part of this belongs to Brazuc so I can tell him it is not as big as I think he led me to believe."

Marfo started laughing and pulled Kaen in for an unexpected hug.

"My daughter was right, it appears, when she spoke of your quick wit and fine sense of humor! Now come inside and let us relax inside where I can get to know you a little better before letting you get back to the schedule I know Elnidith has set for you."

A cough came from behind him, and when Kaen looked over his shoulder at Elnidith, he saw her wink at him and shrug.

"I would be honored to enter your home and spend time with you."

"Excellent!" exclaimed Marfo as he clapped Kaen on the back and pressed him toward the entrance to his house.

He looked Kaen up and down as they walked and shook his head in disbelief.

"I'm not sure which of you is a finer specimen. You or your dragon," he joked as they walked. "You both look like you eat well, and judging by your clothes, you are still growing."

Kaen let out a cough as he knew his outfit was tighter than he wished.

Waving his hand in the air, Marfo kept talking, ignoring his reaction and explaining who they were passing by as they made their way to the house.

"So tell me, Dragon Rider Kaen, if you know what a blood debt is, what can I give to fulfill my obligation?"

Kaen heard the struggle in Marfo's voice as he leaned against his chair, running his fingers along the lip of the cup he held in his hands. After the few minutes spent showing him around the house and his two pictures of Gertrude, one of her as a young girl and one now, he had led them into a room with just a few cushioned chairs.

Setting his cup on the small table near him, Kaen leaned forward and tried his best to not appear frustrated.

"The truth is that your daughter is a valiant warrior and provided me with great protection during our battle against the orcs and goblins we faced. Both she and Brazuc honored their family names with how they fought and defended our entire squad. I know you feel that I am owed something because of what my dragon, Pammon, did, but I feel that I cannot ask for anything myself in good faith."

As Marfo began to respond, Kaen held up his hand and stopped him.

"I will ask any obligation you feel toward me to be given to Pammon instead. He is the one that sent the horde running and provided us with the means to defeat the cave troll."

Having closed his mouth, Marfo slowly nodded his head as a grin appeared on his face. He let out a small snort, reached up with one of his hands, and scratched his beard.

"Honor a dragon for saving my daughter . . . That is . . . different."

He glanced at Elnidith, who was sitting quietly, sipping her drink as her eyes drank in everything taking place before her. Marfo noticed the glimmer in them and how she gave a slight nod with her head.

"I assume you know what your dragon would want as payment for this debt?"

Kaen leaned back in his chair and chuckled, running his finger through his hair.

"He likes to be paid in things to eat. As you have seen, my dragon does not miss many meals; I find that his love language is food. He would not ask for more than one meal as payment as we both know the cost of quality animals."

Still playing with his beard, Marfo gave a nod as he considered what Kaen had said.

"That is an interesting proposition. I guess I should not mention I was ready to offer my daughter's hand in marriage to you or up to half of my estates if you asked."

"While those would be considered great gifts," Kaen stated, not showing his shock at what Marfo had been willing to give, "I already have someone I am bound to, and I would never feel comfortable taking land. I live too far away to manage the day-to-day requirements of such a thing as this."

Setting his cup down on the table, Marfo stood up and stretched for a moment.

"So, no daughter and no land, just animals for your dragon to enjoy?" he asked, keeping his gaze steady.

Kaen stood up as well, nodding his head as he kept his eyes on Marfo.

"Very well," he stated as he clapped his hands together. "Elnidith will bear witness to the repayment of the debt I owed, ensuring that I have restored honor to my family."

He extended his hand once more, and Kaen shook it and smiled. He saw that Marfo visibly relieved at how the deal had transpired.

"If you will give me a moment, I will inform my servants to prepare for the agreed-upon repayment."

He gave a slight bow again before exiting the room, leaving Kaen and Elnidith alone.

"That was very kind of you," Elnidith stated as she stood up from her chair. "I wonder if you realize just how much you have indebted yourself to him."

"I'm not sure what you mean," Kaen replied as he turned and saw how Elnidith was looking at him. "He gets to give Pammon the credit, and all he has to do is give up a few animals for it."

She chortled and nodded her head.

"All . . . you still don't understand, but then again, I guess you wouldn't."

Motioning around the room, she pointed to the weapons and shields on the walls.

"This room represents the true power of that man and his family. These shields are a testament to how important they are and the number of *favors* he could call in at any moment. His daughter is one of his greatest treasures. Tell me, Kaen, how many other pictures did you see in this house?"

His eyes shifted from side to side as he considered what she had asked. Other than the picture of Marfo and his deceased wife, the only other pictures he had seen were the two of Gertrude.

"You already know there were just three pictures in the house."

She nodded and moved to one of the shields on the wall, slowly running her hand along the base of it.

"Yes. She has two pictures compared to the one he keeps as a memory of his wife. She is the greatest treasure he has. He would have offered her hand to you for saving her life, even though he knows nothing about you or the quality of your character. He would have also offered you half of his land. And you really don't know how much land that is."

Her voice was like a teacher giving a lesson. Clear and sharp, each point was accented, and her steady voice echoed in the room.

"You have allowed him to keep both when many had wondered how weak he might become if you asked for either of those two things. He can marry off his daughter and gain much for her hand. Instead, he will be looked at as a shrewd and crafty man. He will earn honor for paying off the debt he owes at a fraction of the cost, and also because he pays the debt to your dragon."

She paused as she chuckled and shook her head.

"Sometimes I wonder if the gods must love you, Kaen Marshell."

"Why do you say that?"

Turning around, she let out a sigh before giving him a grin.

"Marfo is akin to Bosgreth, and how you have handled yourself with Marfo will pay off when you meet with the king."

36

Dwarven Guild Master

Kaen glanced along the short counter as two dwarven attendants worked with a set of dwarven adventurers, counting coins after weighing the harvested plants they had taken a quest for.

When he first entered, he had been surprised by how empty the building was. The complex was slightly smaller than the guild hall in the capital of Roccnari. He had learned from Elies that most halls were not as active or as big as the one in Ebonmount; other races preferred to stay within their own circle. Elves, dwarves, taxabi, gnomes, and a few of the other races joined the adventurers' guild, but they had a wandering itch.

He had only seen two other humans in Tanulivar so far. One was a trader and the other was an adventurer providing security and protection.

"Thank you for waiting," a dwarven man who was moving toward the counter called out to him. "I apologize for keeping you waiting but it is not every day a Dragon Rider asks for a meeting with the Guild Master. If you will follow me, I will gladly take you to him."

Nodding, Kaen followed the man as he led him to a hallway that was off to the left of the counter.

"Is everything here made of stone?" Kaen asked when he noticed there was very little wood used, even for decoration.

The stocky, black-haired man laughed, not bothering to turn around as he tapped the stone hallway.

"We don't waste wood for that with all the stone that we have. Besides," he informed Kaen as he tapped the stone wall again, "this building can stand against almost anything. Wood burns and takes a lot more magical enchanting to prevent that."

It made sense, especially after all the work they were doing in Ebonmount to prepare the town to resist a dragon attack. The stonework was exceptional with detail that rivaled most wood crafters. He eyed the scenes carved into the stone wall and you could feel the waves moving as he ran his fingers along the different depths someone had done in the masterpiece.

They passed a few more doors and came to a set of stairs leading down. A quartz-like material was used for the handrails, polished and smoothed beyond any stonework Kaen had ever seen. He knew his eyes were wide; hiding his shock at how well everything was crafted was difficult.

Reaching the bottom of the stairs, they entered a room similar to the one outside of Herb's office, with a large stone desk and a set of massive stone doors with runes carved all over it. Each door had a matching stone carving like the one in the mountain by the entrance to the city in the mountain.

Twelve-foot-tall sculptures, each with tens of thousands of lines depicting hair, folds in their armor or cloth, wrinkles, veins, and more. Each face conveyed power and fortitude.

A slight cough got his attention, and Kaen turned to see his escort smiling at him.

"Sorry, I was just lost for a moment. These two sculptures are so lifelike."

The dwarf stood a little more erect and puffed his chin out.

"We have been gifted with some of the greatest stone masons. These doors are almost two thousand years old and have not aged at all."

Nodding his head in appreciation, Kaen motioned to the door with his hand held out.

The man smiled and nodded.

Running his fingers along the carved dwarf on the door, Kaen felt a world of lines and carvings with his fingertips. Leaning closer, he saw just how detailed everything was. How they had ever crafted something like this was beyond his imagination.

Shaking his head again, Kaen scratched his hairy chin and smiled.

"Now I see why so many talk about the stonework skill of your people. This is far greater than any painting I have ever seen."

The man gave a slight bow and grinned from ear to ear.

"I will make sure to let our current stonesmiths know. They will find the praise of a Dragon Rider a great thing, spurring them on to improve their skill."

Giving a slight bow back, Kaen watched as the man tapped two runes, and the door shimmered and swung open, providing a small opening into the Guild Master's office.

"Dragon Rider Kaen, I apologize for making you wait, but I had a few things to attend to. Please have a seat!" exclaimed a blond-haired dwarf, who was probably a good four inches taller than most dwarves Kaen had ever seen. His shoulders were massive and his beard glistened, letting him know the man had just oiled it before seeing him.

"Guild Master Galdin, I appreciate you taking the time to see me. I must say, your guild hall is a testament to the stonework of the dwarves."

The man smiled and motioned to the stone chairs, each outfitted with cushions that mimicked the colors of gems. Bright red, orange, yellow, green, and blue cushions all turned a hard surface into an inviting place to rest.

Sitting down, Kaen watched as the Guild Master took a seat across from him.

"I would offer you a drink but word has reached me that you do not partake in most alcohol."

Kaen noticed the gleam in the man's eyes and the slight smirk at the edge of his lip.

"That is true," Kaen admitted as he settled down, shifting to get comfortable. "I had a run-in with some Dragon's Fire or Goblin's Piss once, or whatever one might want to call it. Needless to say, it let me know quickly that I am not meant to drink alcohol."

Galdin chuckled and nodded as he slowly stroked his beard.

"I have known grown dwarves who have thought themselves able to handle Dwarven whiskey and learned the folly of their beliefs. Now tell me, what can I do for you?"

Reaching into his tunic, Kaen pulled out the paper Elnidith had given him this morning and slid it across the stone table between them.

"I have a request for your guild hall, asking for assistance with a current need in Ebonmount."

Nodding, Galdin picked up the paper and unfolded it.

His fingers tightened when he reached the part of the request that specifically asked for Elnidith and her warriors and families to come. Kaen saw the paper crinkle slightly.

Kaen heard a faint grunt. His hearing was better than many might realize, so he smiled, knowing that Galdin was going to have a hard time with this request.

"This is . . . a very specific and difficult request," he finally declared as he folded the paper and put it back on the table between them. "You know that the king might not want this to be approved?"

Nodding, Kaen intertwined his fingers and rested them across his body as he tried to look relaxed.

"None of what we are dealing with right now is easy. You know the problems Tanulivar will face in the coming years. Allies are an important thing to have, and we will need to work together if we hope to overcome the darkness that is threatening us all."

A frown appeared on Galdin's face and he stood up, moving around his chair and going to a stone shelf with a variety of cups and containers with drinks. He poured some into a cup and paused, adding more to it before setting down the glass container and quickly guzzling what he had poured.

Galdin set his cup down harder than Kaen figured he'd meant to and came back to his chair. He closed his eyes, rubbing them with his thumbs as he sat quietly for a moment.

"I'll come back to the request in a minute," Galdin finally said when he opened his eyes. "There is no offer of a reward here. How would I prove there is value for those who answer the call?"

Smiling, Kaen watched as Galdin took in every movement he made.

Leaning forward, he tapped his chest with his finger.

"I personally told Elnidith that we would give them land to live on and jobs for their people. They would also be paid and opportunities would be given. I, however, did not yet share that I would allow the children to join my academy, if they so desire, free of charge."

His eyes widened at the mention of the academy.

"I have heard some things about your academy. Tell me more."

Almost half an hour later, Kaen could see the difference in Galdin's face. Perhaps it was the alcohol he had consumed, but he would like to believe it was what they had discussed. The knowledge that there were opportunities for the dwarven children to attend his school and possibly earn a lifestone was huge. Families would sign up just for that chance alone. Getting a lifestone here was impossible unless someone came from specific bloodlines or somehow earned it.

"You are a shrewd negotiator," Galdin finally admitted. "There is no doubt you know what we need and want and have tailored your request to make turning it down difficult. I could ask for more, but we both know you are at the limits of what you can promise. We also both know what you are offering is far beyond what most people here would ever hope to attain."

He paused and unfolded the paper again.

"I have heard of your exploits and how you have treated Marfo today."

Kaen sat there, still like the two figures carved on the outside of the doors to this room.

Galdin gave in first, snorting and letting out a sigh.

"I will do everything in my power to make this work. Knowing Elnidith has already signed off on this and desires it will make this easier. It may take us half a year or more to relocate everyone. I am assuming this won't be an issue?"

Kaen shook his head and grinned.

"I am honored and grateful that we will be allies. I understand the logistics of moving that many people and the necessary materials over a distance like this. Just know that you need to be careful in the coming year. I have seen people working from Luthaelia who are involved in a variety of subterfuge and more. I would not put it past them to try their best to sway others here, or even attack you in your own homes."

Galdin narrowed his eyes, sensing what Kaen was saying had something behind it. He watched the young man across from him and noticed that Kaen gave no other hints.

"I take it by your silence that you are unwilling or unable to go into more detail?"

Leaning back in his chair, Kaen tapped his finger against his chin for a moment.

"It shouldn't surprise me that word hasn't reached here, or perhaps Guild Master Herb did not share the findings of what happened in Ebonmount. Are you saying you did not hear about the attempt on my life?"

A coughing fit replaced Galdin's casual demeanor, and it took him a moment to get it resolved.

"Someone attacked you?" he gasped. "When? How?"

Grunting, Kaen tapped his arm where the dagger had barely cut him.

"An assassin, most likely from the secret assassin guild that every Guild Master seems to know about, came after me. He cut me with a blade covered in wyvern's poison."

"Yet you survived!"

Chuckling, Kaen nodded as Galdin realized how his statement sounded.

"I mean you survived, of course," he muttered, "yet you do not look at all how one who typically gets poisoned by a wyvern does."

"I owe most of that to Pammon and Lord Hurem," Kaen stated. "It basically took a week for me to make it through, and without them I wouldn't be here today."

Galdin jerked on his beard a few times, apparently unaware as to how hard he was pulling it.

"I am grateful for your warning, then. I will make sure to inform the king of what transpired. After you leave, of course."

"Speaking of the king," Kaen said as he stood up, "I need to go and prepare for my meeting with him later tonight."

Rising from his chair, Galdin moved around the stone table and held out his hand to Kaen.

"It has been a pleasure and an honor, Dragon Rider Kaen."

Shaking the man's hand, Kaen gave a slight bow.

"The pleasure has been mine."

37

A King in a Mountain

Kaen had felt flustered, shifting on his feet from side to side after getting off of Pammon before the bridge to the mountain entrance.

I'm not a fan of all those weapons that are still pointed at you. Surely, the king must know I would notice such an act.

Pammon huffed and snorted, causing the dwarves who were near them to back up. He flashed a toothy grin and turned, preparing to fly away from the bridge.

Just because someone feels they need to show their power does not mean they are smart enough to know when to use it. Something tells me that this was done for a reason, and a foolish one at that. Regardless, I will go back to Marfo's property and finish consuming the gifts he has for me.

Seriously? Kaen chuckled as he watched Pammon take off, heading south from the gate. *How can you still need to eat? I am impressed you are even able to fly after the dozen or so things I know you enjoyed already.*

Pammon laughed, his thrum unable to be heard by Kaen, but both of them knew he was laughing through their bond.

How do you think Marfo would feel if I did not accept all of his gifts? I wouldn't want my actions to bring him shame or dishonor.

Kaen gave up trying to debate with Pammon, knowing that part of his mindset was correct.

Just don't make yourself ill. I'll try to give you some notice before we are done so you can come back here for me.

He felt Pammon's acknowledgment but could also feel his anticipation about getting to eat more.

Smiling, Kaen moved to where his escort was waiting, giving a smile and a slight bow.

"Dragon Rider Kaen," said a stocky dwarf, who was dressed in a nearly golden set of chainmail. He stepped out from the other dwarves waiting in line and continued. "I am Dagan and will escort you to King Bosgreth. Are you ready to proceed?"

"I am," Kaen replied.

Each of the twelve dwarven warriors wore a set of chain armor and carried a shield and a sword or hammer. Their armor glistened, appearing to have been freshly polished, and an emblem was emblazoned on each of their chests—a hammer and a sword crossed in gold. Only Dagan had a silver version of that crest on his.

Dagan grunted and snapped his head to front position as he turned on his heels and proceeded to walk toward the bridge.

With no instruction given, Kaen quickly strode ahead, moving in beside Dagan, who gave him a side glance. He could hear the twelve dwarves fall into position behind them.

Kaen marveled at the stonework of the bridge and how a few lines ran every twenty feet or so across the entire bridge. Huge chains were taut and connected to massive metal rings on the sides of the stone bridge.

"Do these pieces hinge?" Kaen asked as he studied the bridge.

Not giving more than a small nod of his head, Dagan kept his brown eyes forward, walking in a steady and sharp pattern, matched by the entourage behind them.

The bridge was at least sixty feet wide, yet they were walking down the middle of it for some reason, causing all the carts or people traveling either way, to move to the sides and stop as they walked toward the entrance.

Some dwarves waved and gave greetings, but most remained quiet. Kaen guessed it was because of the expression on Dagan's face and that of the dwarves behind him.

Kaen took in everything he could about this quarter-mile walk. The stone the bridge was cut from massive blocks larger than him, and he had no idea how much each one weighed. The way they all fit together perfectly was even more impressive than that stonework he had seen in the guild hall.

The two statues flanking both sides of the bridge appeared to be just as impressive as the two on Galdin's office door. Kaen walked in silence as he gazed upon the stone work, wondering how men and women had cut them from the rock. It must have taken a long time. They were so lifelike, it felt like the statues could come out of the mountain and start moving on their own.

The giant thirty-foot-tall gate that stood open beckoned them inside. Each of the stone doors appeared to be over five feet thick, yet somehow they could be opened and closed with ease from the inside.

Kaen took everything in. The knowledge of stonework had either been lost or was still kept a secret He had no doubt the dwarves who had built this place were also responsible for the castle and walls in Ebonmount. Too many small things looked exactly alike.

Once past the massive gates, long tunnels and walkways began to appear inside the mountain. Kaen had wanted to see the ramparts and defending areas, but Dagan had told him they were not for viewing, and keeping Bosgreth waiting was not an option.

For miles, they walked deep into the mountain, taking massive stairs cut right into it and down long tunnels, lit with countless light orbs.

A huge market was off to the side on one of the levels they were passing, with hundreds of dwarves shouting and haggling over prices.

He saw young dwarves running and playing in one of the tunnels they passed, tossing a ball and hitting it with a stick before running to a safe point, while the other team tried to pelt them with a smaller ball.

He was amazed at how much life thrived inside the mountain. Perhaps Bosgreth might be right and the dwarves could survive for a while. Taking the bridge and breaking down their defenses would be difficult.

If an army camped out on the other side of the bridge, leaving the mountain would be just as difficult, with no way to get out except to push through the barricade that would seal them in.

Dagan ignored his questions and continued walking, leading him deeper into the mountain.

A sudden shift in the amount of carved statues of dwarves let Kaen know he was coming upon the throne room.

There were massive, thirty-foot-tall statues on each side of the hallway he had entered. The hall had to be at least forty feet wide and just as tall. A dozen statues on each side stood watch over him and the others as they walked across the polished stone floor.

People stared and pointed, yet none said a word as they moved to the side, allowing them passage to a room he could see past all this.

At the far end of the hall was another set of double stone doors, but these were coated in gold and had a mural depicting multiple scenes of dwarves fighting goblins, orcs, trolls, and other foul creatures. At the top of the right-hand side of the door was a mural showing them defeating a dragon.

Doing his best not to chuckle, Kaen wasn't sure if this was an actual event or just something they believed they could do.

Dagan was watching Kaen as they drew close to the final set of doors. He saw the look on Kaen's face shift and finally spoke. "These are the stories of when our kings were so fierce that all the other races came to us, begging and paying for help," he stated, his voice about as soft as sandpaper against skin. "There was a time when we were considered the greatest race."

Kaen nodded, smiled, and tried to seem impressed. Replying was not an option.

With no reply, Dagan increased his stride as they moved to where Bosgreth awaited them.

It felt weird to Kaen as he strode into the throne room that after being inside Aldric's and Havannath's castle and keep, neither was as ostentatious as King Bosgreth. Everywhere he looked were stone or gold statues and carvings. Some as tall as the thirty-foot ceiling in the throne room, others only ten-feet tall. Most were decorated with gems and other fine stones. A long rug that was finer than any he had seen in the other two kings' courts ran the entire length of this fifty-yard-long room.

At the far end was a throne easily eight-feet tall, nearly dwarfing King Bosgreth as he sat there in a full set of gold-colored armor.

What the heck is with kings and their need for golden armor?

As they entered, all gathered inside hushed, watching Kaen as he moved along the carpet, and finally believing that a new Dragon Rider had been found. He could see the men and women as they pointed and whispered to each other, but he kept his face focused on Bosgreth, who was rigid like a rock on his throne.

Each of their steps echoed through the massive room, regardless of the carpet they were walking on.

When they were ten feet from the king, Dagan held up his hand, stopping and causing Kaen to stop behind him while the twelve guards escorting him continued past him and spread out before the throne.

Once everyone was in position and facing Kaen, Dagan bowed to Bosgreth before turning to face Kaen.

"Dragon Rider Kaen, you have the honor of being in the presence of King Bosgreth."

Noticing the movement in Dagan's eyes, Kaen bowed deeply.

"It is my honor to meet you, King Bosgreth," he declared as he stood up. "Thank you for allowing me to finally meet you."

A small smirk appeared on the face of the wrinkled and aged king. It was evident where his nickname *Lightbeard* came from because most of it was missing, having been drawn together in a single braid, ordained with more ornaments to help give it size. His black eyes still had a glow of intelligence and wisdom behind them, but everything else about the dwarf looked tired, weighed down by the responsibilities and length of his life.

"You honor me with your words," Bosgreth called out, his voice almost rasp like even though it was deep. "What brings you to our kingdom besides seeking our aid and supplies?"

Grateful for years spent with elves who had often tested his patience with the curt way they spoke, Kaen kept his face calm, not expressing the frustration he felt.

"I know you are aware of the coming darkness and the changes across the land that I have seen, and I have heard of how you are preparing to protect your people."

Pausing, Kaen watched for a moment as Bosgreth shifted on his throne, but when he did not reply, Kaen continued. "I witnessed firsthand how great your warriors are when they helped defend the mountain of Ebonmount from a surprise invasion by the orcs and goblins. I was grateful for their swords, maces, and shield skills as we stood together to fight back the invading force."

Seeing Bosgreth begin to open his mouth, Kaen waited.

"Some might be grateful for the way you speak about our warriors," he declared, shifting slightly in his throne as he watched Kaen. "What I heard is that your dragon protected the entire kingdom of Ebonmount while our people were cut down by the army before them. How many of my people might have been saved had you not hidden your dragon?"

The silence in the room was almost deafening after he stopped speaking. Kaen felt every eye upon him as they waited for an answer.

38

A Dangerous Offer

"I wish I had an answer for that, King Bosgreth, but I do not have one that would make everyone happy. As I had no Dragon Rider to teach or train me, I could only listen to the advice of the man who raised me and obey his teaching. He told me how many would gladly kill me or my dragon, happy to use him for parts. That advice seemed true even recently, as someone attempted to kill me with wyvern poison just a few weeks ago, and yet here I stand after having been cut with a dagger covered in it."

Gasps erupted from the dwarves standing before him and around the room. Kaen even noticed the eyes of Dagan and the other dwarves near him widen. Bosgreth never flinched.

"It seems many would consider my dragon, Pammon, and I a threat, even though we have risked much to protect Ebonmount and Roccnari. Even now, I am here to pledge homes, jobs, coin, and land for those warriors from Tanulivar willing to join in the defense of Ebonmount. I have even pledged there will be spots available in my academy where dwarven boys and girls can earn lifestones."

Gasps rang out across the room again, and the shifting of steps came from all around as Kaen's words reached the ears of everyone in this room for the first time.

"I have not heard of such an offer yet!" Bosgreth called out, his voice booming across the hall. "Why should I allow my people to risk their lives for you and a problem that doesn't concern us?"

Kaen tried to decide how to play this moment. His mind and heart were wrestling with what he could say that wouldn't poke this bear more but also prove his intent.

He felt his lifestone surging on its own, offering its aid as a tool at this moment.

"I will answer that question in a moment, if you hear me out for a second, King Bosgreth. Tell me, do you enjoy hearing when King Havannath makes a dangerous mistake?"

Bosgreth's eyes narrowed, his white eyebrows almost touching in the middle of his face.

"What dwarf doesn't enjoy hearing of a pointy ear falling on their face?" he asked, his tone a bit more cautious.

"Perhaps you might like to hear that Havannath made a mistake. He underestimated me. He attempted to bind me to him."

The sound of wind rushing into the gathered collective told Kaen he had hit home, especially when a few chuckles and some hard laughter could be heard in the hall.

Even Bosgreth coughed momentarily, straightening in his seat as he struggled to not laugh.

A moment passed without either of them speaking, murmurs circulating around the room. Eventually, Bosgreth raised his hand, the room going quiet. Resting his arm on the edge of the stone throne, he tapped his fingers against it for a moment.

He opened his mouth to speak and then closed it, a grin appearing. Snorting, he shook his head, and Kaen watched as the grin grew bigger, teeth eventually appearing as his lips parted.

"Dragon Rider Kaen, I must say there are not many things that bring a smile to my lips anymore, but even if what you said is not true, you have managed a rare feat."

Kaen smiled and nodded his head, glad to hear the tone in Bosgreth's voice lighten, almost cheerful.

"It would make sense that he tried, as rumors have made their rounds for generations about why Elies has always stayed in that kingdom."

The weight of Bosgreth's gaze could almost be felt as Kaen watched the king stroke his beard almost without realizing he was doing it, seeing the twinkle of delight in his eyes.

"Tell me, how did that go once he failed that attempt."

Nodding his head slowly, Kaen did his best reenactment of the moment.

Everyone was quiet as Kaen told them the story of how the last time he had been in Havannath's presence, he had forced the king to break the bond he had over Elies.

"After that, I strode from the room, leaving the king in disgrace, and went to pack my bags, never to return, if I can help it, while he still sits on the throne."

A raucous cheer broke out from those along the edges of the crowd, and even King Bosgreth clapped his hands, nodding his head in satisfaction and smiling the entire time.

[Story Telling Skill Increased x3]

Applause, whistles, and more went on for a good twenty seconds till Bosgreth held his hands up, and it died down quickly.

"Two treats in one day," he stated, his voice no longer gruff or stern. "I cannot tell you how much I enjoyed hearing such fine descriptions of that pompous fool finally paying for his actions."

Murmurs and nods came from the other dwarves that Kaen. Even Dagan had nodded in agreement with his King.

Bosgreth let out a deep breath and collected himself.

"I guess this brings us back to our original discussion. You have spoken of promises. I assume you have a way of guaranteeing the safety of those who might take up your request?"

"I wish I could guarantee the safety of every man, woman, child, dwarf, and even elf," Kaen replied, accenting each one as he called them out. "We both know that no one can promise that. An unexpected plague can overcome even the greatest walls that an army cannot defeat."

A few grunts circulated throughout the room, and Bosgreth nodded his head.

"I offer only what I can promise. My academy has already handed out twenty lifestones, and I plan to increase that number to thirty or more a year. King Aldric and the adventurers' guild in Ebonmount have already partnered with me to ensure that happens."

Turning around to face each of those in the hall for a second, Kaen focused again on the king.

"I have spoken with Elnidith and Galdin, having turned in a formal request with both, outlining what will be offered in compensation for all those who answer the quest I have put out. It may seem difficult to consider, with them not being here, but with fewer people to protect, feed, and house inside these walls, it may be better for both kingdoms and strengthen the alliance between you and Aldric."

When Kaen was finished speaking, he stood there, almost as if he was at ease and not surrounded by a collection of dwarves, most fighting the temptation to let their mouths hang open in shock at his declaration.

"That is . . . " the king paused momentarily as he glanced around the hall, "an actual solid point."

Grunting and then chuckling for a moment, Bosgreth rose from his throne, creating a stir of sound in his people.

He slowly stepped down, taking each of the steps carefully and intentionally as the guards all shifted their positions, and even Dagan looked surprised to see him leaving the throne.

When he had reached the base of the hall floor, his soldiers turned and saluted as he walked past them. Bosgreth gave them a nod, and Dagan moved aside, allowing his king to stand before Kaen.

When he was just a few feet from Kaen, Bosgreth looked up at his face, studying the young man, who seemed unmoved in the least by how he had given up his place on his throne and joined him here.

"You are a peculiar boy, I must admit," he declared after a moment of taking Kaen in. "I will make you a deal if you are up for a game of chance."

Kaen saw the mischievous twinkle in Bosgreth's eyes and had no idea what the dwarf wanted to do but was left with only a few choices. It was worth at least hearing the king out.

"I'm not one to shy away from a game of chance. What do you have in mind?"

He motioned for Kaen to lean down, and once Kaen's ear was near the king's mouth, Bosgreth spoke, making Kaen's breath rush out at once.

"I will try to bind you to me. If you resist, I promise to let my people do as you have asked. If you fail to resist my binding, then you will serve me as Elies did him."

Kaen stood there, unable to breathe. He saw the smile on the old dwarf's face, and while he had complete confidence in his skill, there was a nagging in his heart that beckoned him to be cautious.

Clasping his hands behind his back, Bosgreth backed up a step, his smile never leaving his face.

"Take your time, think about it, and let me know."

What is wrong? I can tell something is troubling you?

Bosgreth told me that if I could resist him attempting to bind me like Havannath had tried, he would do what I asked. If I fail, I will be forced to serve him as Elies served Havannath.

Anger, rage, and white-hot fury erupted through their bond, and Kaen could only imagine that if Pammon was here right now, fire would be coming out of his mouth.

You cannot risk your life like that! It is not worth it! I would burn them all down if that happened.

Please settle down, Pammon! I cannot think straight with you like this.

Think straight?! There is nothing to think about! This is not something you can even consider! Why would you even begin to pause and allow your mind to believe this might be the best course of action? That is something an eggling would do!

It was hard for Kaen to think straight with Pammon yelling in his head and Bosgreth staring at him, waiting for an answer.

He knew there were only a few options. If the King said no, it would leave Ebonmount weak. His family and all those he promised to protect would be at risk. His choices were limited, and the longer it took to shore up the weaknesses at Ebonmount, the more he would be pulled in too many directions.

Hold that fury you have. We are going to need it.

WHAT?!!

The fury Kaen had just mentioned exploded through their bond, and Kaen knew that Pammon was now in flight, upset and coming in his direction.

If you do something stupid, I swear I will burn this place down to the ground!

Relax Pammon! Trust me! This is the only way, and we both know it. If you lend me your strength and fury, combined with my skill, I don't see how we can succumb to an attack we know of beforehand. Havannath managed to get Elies when he wasn't prepared and still failed against me when I wasn't expecting it. There is no way we can lose.

The frustration simmered just a little but did not go away completely.

You will owe me for this. I'm not sure what, but one day, I will do something just as rash and stupid, and when you complain, I will remind you of this moment.

Unable to stop the chuckle that escaped him, Bosgreth cocked his head at him.

"I will take you up on that offer, but I want to propose a second part of that bet."

Rubbing his hands together in front of his chest, the king smiled, more teeth showing now.

"I can't wait to hear this," he stated with glee.

39

Bound or Free?

Kaen watched as Bosgreth leaned forward, anticipating what Kaen would say next.

"If I'm going to risk my freedom, I want more than just a promise to help. I want complete access to the kingdom's forges, weapons, and armor crafters. Obviously, I will pay for or supply my own materials, but I do not want to wait in line unless a request from you alone is made."

A smirk with a look of consideration flashed across Bosgreth's face. Slowly, his head began to nod as he considered Kaen's proposal and what it might mean.

"That sounds like a reasonable request," he finally admitted as he held out his hand.

"As I am sure you are aware from my dealings with Marfo, I am not one to ask for anything too great or costly," Kaen replied, extending his hand to grasp Bosgreth's.

Snorting, the King nodded and motioned to Kaen with his head.

"Make a promise."

Giving his best smile, Kaen nodded as he willed his lifestone into a roaring fire.

Now Pammon. Let your rage and anger fill me for being an eggling.

With those words, the fire that burned within Pammon flooded into Kaen, causing his skin to break out in goosebumps as his lifestone flared even hotter.

"I promise to protect all those who rally to my call," Kaen declared, grasping Bosgreth's hand tightly.

The king squeezed back, his eyebrows drawing close as he took a breath and seemed to will every fiber of his being into this next moment.

[Charm Resisted]

A look of amusement flashed across the older dwarf's face. Shaking his head slowly from side to side, a small sigh could be heard.

"Want to go for double or nothing?" Kaen asked, his eyes blazing from the power of his dragon and his lifestone.

Freeing his hand from the grip, Bosgreth tsked as he took a step back.

"Never in my life," he muttered in awe. "You have a formidable will, boy."

"A single purpose is all I have," Kaen replied. "To protect those that I can. To ensure that families will never be forced to live without a father or mother if I can help it."

For a brief moment, his face betrayed him as Bosgreth's eyes went wide, and his mouth hung open for just a second. Quickly catching himself, he set his face back to its normal stony appearance and took two steps forward, smacking Kaen on his arm as he smiled.

"Dwarves of Tanulivar," he belted out, his voice echoing across the room, "Tonight we celebrate an agreement to help Dragon Rider Kaen. We will help defend Ebonmount from the goblins and orcs that seek to attack it, causing them to once again fear the dwarves!"

Shouts and stomping of feet echoed throughout the room as Kaen let a small sigh of relief escape his lips during the noise.

I survived, Kaen informed Pammon.

A wave of frustration and thankfulness came through their bond as the rage Pammon had been channeling, and the fire inside his lifestone, faded.

I would have made you suffer to no end had you not.

The shaking of his shoulder and arm brought him back to the moment, where Bosgreth was turning him around to face those who were cheering.

"Tonight, we will eat here, and then you will depart tomorrow. Elnidith had already informed me of your need to return to Ebonmount."

Kaen shook his head and groaned as he saw a grin cracking the wrinkled face of the old king.

"You were playing with me?" he asked, waving to those still cheering and shouting.

"Up until the moment I tried to bind you," he admitted with a sigh. "Marfo told me that if I didn't do justice for the debt he owed and you let him off the hook, he would collect a debt from me."

Cocking his eyebrow at the king, Kaen smirked, his face asking the question he hadn't voiced.

"No, I won't tell you what I owe him. Just know I would rather do what I know is right even if people think I am too old and cautious." He tugged on his beard and shrugged. "I have heard the rumors, and while I dislike the name given to me, it allows me great room to navigate those who think they can outsmart me or try to push me around."

He motioned to a few dwarves around the room that had not cheered as much as others.

"There are a few here even now that will not know how to react when I let certain details about our wager slip out."

Unable to hold back, Kaen began to laugh out loud, realizing he had bought into the rumors himself and underappreciated the wisdom of the dwarf who had risked much at a chance for a Dragon Rider to command.

"All this was a farce just to see if you could bind me?" Kaen asked, knowing the answer before it was given.

"It was," he admitted with a shrug as he motioned to a door on the side of the throne room. "Once you told me what Havannath had attempted in secret, doing things dishonestly, I figured why not try and do it to your face. Either you proved you are a man worth following, or I win a Dragon Rider. You would have to agree it would be hard to complain since you gave me permission to try."

Walking next to the king as they moved toward a set of open doors, Kaen couldn't help but nod. Had he lost and the king bound him, he could only blame himself.

"Forgive me for doubting the wisdom you possess," Kaen said with a wink. "I had not realized you were outmaneuvering me even before I stepped onto the playing field."

Laughing and smacking Kaen on the back, Bosgreth patted him a few more times as he grinned.

"I would like to think I still play the game well, even with the lack of hair on my chin."

Reaching up to scratch his growing patch, Kaen motioned to it, sending the King into a fit of laughter.

"It appears we are both lacking a little hair."

Glancing behind him, Kaen saw Dagan looking relieved as Bosgreth and he laughed and joked all the way to the dining area.

It was late when Kaen went outside to where Pammon was waiting, and he was feeling slightly tipsy because he had finally relented and had a small taste at the king's request. Dagan was walking him carefully toward Pammon, keeping a hand on his back, unable to lose the smile that ran from ear to ear.

"You really can't handle alcohol, can you?" he asked for the twentieth time.

"No . . . Itz hard fur me," stammered Kaen, well aware that his tongue did not want to work right. "Never havez."

Chuckling still, Dagan motioned to Pammon, who appeared to be glaring at the two of them.

"I have returned home a few times, drunker than I had anticipated . . .

the misses was not very happy, to put it mildly," Dagan stated, chuckling for a moment as he took in the number of teeth in Pammon's muzzle. "You might end up in a worse spot than I ever did."

Kaen laughed and then stopped, leaning over, emptying his stomach for the third time.

I swear if you vomit on me, I will make you wish you were dead.

Holding his head in his hand, Kaen groaned as his dwarf escort helped him get moving again.

Why must you shout . . . it hurts . . . You know I didn't have a choice. The king insisted.

Oh yes . . . the king forced you to drink by having every guard there hold you down and empty the barrel into your throat.

One sip! That's was all it was.

Pammon snorted, visibly showing his disgust at Kaen's appearance.

"So . . . I'm going to let you make it the rest of the way, if you don't mind," Dagan muttered. "Not interested in getting on the bad side of a dragon. Good night, Dragon Rider Kaen, and thank you again."

Feeling the gentle pat on his back, Kaen staggered the last twenty feet and fell against Pammon's scaly neck.

"I'm sorry," Kaen blurted out as he belched, his face turning green from the smell of his own bodily function.

I promise you, I will find a way to make you suffer if you throw up on me.

Holding up his hand, Kaen turned and took a few steps away before sticking his finger down his throat and making himself bring up the remaining contents of his stomach. As he wiped his finger dry on his pants and tried to give a thumb up, Pammon shook his head.

You look awful. Your eyes are bloodshot, and tears are running down your face. You look redder than an apple.

I'm fine . . . now stop being a mother hen and let me get on you.

Growling again, Pammon finally lowered himself and turned to the side so Kaen could get on. Once seated, Kaen got himself harnessed in before laying across Pammon's neck.

"I owe you one," he muttered as Pammon stood up.

More than one, but I'll collect later. For now, just remember what I told you twice already.

Kaen nodded as he patted the scale he always did and closed his eyes.

The following day, Kaen's head felt like someone had used it as a punching bag. Having been hit before by Hess when they trained, it was perhaps worse than the occasional hard strike.

Tell me I didn't throw up last night.

Not on me, but you did once we reached Elnidith's place. She didn't look happy to see that either.

Muttering, Kaen got up and slowly made his way to the wash basin, glancing in the mirror and shaking his head in disgust at his reflection. His eyes were still bloodshot.

I'm not sure what was in that drink, but I promise that no matter what, I won't drink again.

Even though Pammon wasn't there, the sensation he felt through their bond was like the dragon was rolling his eyes at that comment.

With no more complaining from Pammon, Kaen dunked his head under the cold-water pitcher and got ready for the day.

"You look like someone put you in a sack and went a few rounds on you," teased Elnidith as Kaen sat at the table near her.

"I feel like it," he groaned as he massaged his temples with his fingers. "Bosgreth said this was his special brew and only gives it to a few select people, and it would be a dishonor if I didn't at least taste it. What the heck is that stuff?"

Trying to not laugh too loudly, she shrugged her shoulders as she poured him a glass of water.

"I have no idea. I'm not *select* enough to get a taste. You managed to escape better than some who attempted to drink a whole glass. I hear it is pretty potent."

Snorting, Kaen took the water and drained the glass.

"You heard the news, I take it," he asked after setting down his cup.

"I did. I am still amazed that you managed to get him to agree to all that, but I will gladly take it. This will help both kingdoms."

Kaen nodded and reached over for a slice of bread, tearing off a small piece. After swallowing it and taking another drink, he sighed. "Six months?"

"Maybe less, but let's plan on six months," she answered, her face turning serious. "I have a lot to accomplish, but with Bosgreth's backing, it will be much easier."

Taking another bite, Kaen closed his eyes, savoring the taste and the short victory they had achieved.

"I'll inform King Aldric and Guild Master Herb. Some things will need to be done to prepare for your arrival."

As they sat there, Kaen slowly eating, Brabrel came in after about ten minutes and motioned to Elnidith.

"It appears all the supplies you requested are outside, bound, and ready for you to load onto your dragon. Is there anything else I can get you, Dragon Rider Kaen?"

Snorting, he glanced at her and noticed she was smiling.

"Are you kicking me out?" he asked jokingly.

"Yes and no. You have work to do, and so do I. Sitting around watching you suffer after drinking too much is not part of my job description. As a hostess, it would be bad form for me to leave you, though. So the only way we can both get to what we need to," she stated," is for you to get on your dragon and let the kingdom of Ebonmount know they have an ally coming to help."

Grabbing two more rolls and stuffing them in his pocket, Kaen took one last swig from his cup and stood up.

"Elnidith, I am grateful to you for sharing your roof with me."

She smiled and gave a bow.

"Providing a roof for a Dragon Rider is always an honor."

40

An Unexpected Find

Kaen felt the fear and concern through their bond before Pammon said a word.

Focus on where I am and tell me if you see him.

Dread and anger billowed up from Pammon, and Kaen closed his eyes, letting his lifestone burn, shifting his vision to Pammon's.

Is that—

It is. That is Stioks and Juthom. What do we do?

Flying to the west over the forests were Stioks and Juthom. Kaen and Pammon could not believe they had stumbled across them.

Kaen and Pammon had been flying for over two days now, headed back toward Ebonmount, and based on the direction, it looked like Stioks and Juthom were headed toward Roccnari.

They haven't seen us yet. The clouds and our altitude have us hidden.

Kaen felt his heart racing. His hands shook from fear and rage at the man and dragon beneath them. Part of it was coming from Pammon, but the rest was all his own.

What should we do? If we engage, what chance do we have?

Pammon had stopped beating his wings as often, allowing himself to glide as much as possible to minimize all movement that might catch Juthom's attention. He was taking in everything he could.

I'm not sure what would happen if we attacked. We might get a few shots in before they turned on us. We never really got to practice much against Tharnok, and we both know Stioks favors close combat with Juthom and his breath.

So many possible ideas ran through Kaen's head. If they could strike a blow and cause significant damage, or somehow win, they could end all of this right now. Yet Kaen wasn't foolish enough to believe he could take down a dragon that large after hearing Elies share how bad it had been for both dragons.

He had seen the scars on Juthom's body, scales that had taken time to heal from where Juthom had ripped them off with his talons. Both dragons had resisted most of the damage from their breath attacks, but Stioks and his spells, combined with Juthom's breath, brought the end to Elies two years ago.

You're scared, and so am I. Pammon spoke while Kaen felt his mind wandering. **We have the advantage of altitude. We can stay above the clouds longer than Stioks, using the altitude to shoot at them if they follow. That doesn't mean they have to give up chasing us. They can stay back, waiting for when we begin to descend. If we do that, it would be two or three days until we made it to Ebonmount, and I am not sure if they would turn back.**

But we would have defenses, help to fight against them if they came.

Pammon shook his head but made no other sound. He wanted to laugh but didn't risk it, even though the two were miles away from them.

We need to decide. Soon, it will be hard to catch them if we wanted to try. They are flying away from us.

Kaen couldn't shake the fear in his heart.

He would attack Juthom's wings if they engaged, using every spell and skill he had to unleash holy hell upon them, but he had no idea if they would make a dent.

Can I injure his wings?

Kaen felt Pammon considering the question. It's the attack he would recommend if they chose to attack. Knowing the power of his arrows, he felt it would work or at least scare Juthom into landing or flying away. The damage they could do from a distance was their strongest attack, and if they struck first, it would put them in a position of power.

If we can sneak up from above and you get a few powered shots on his wings, you could control the battle. However, if you miss or cannot damage them enough, we would need to turn tail and run.

All the advice Hess had ever given him echoed in his ears, namely, "Grow stronger, live longer." It was hard not to acknowledge how much Pammon had grown in the last two years or how strong he had become.

Kaen knew that this chance may never come again. The lesson with the griffons had taught him this. Those who considered themselves the strongest often needed to remember to be on the lookout for an attack from where they least expected it.

Let's do this. How long till we are close enough to engage?

As Pammon turned, angling toward where Stioks and Juthom seemed to be lazily flying miles beneath them, Kaen could feel the growing rage from his friend.

It will be a few minutes, but you will know. I have no doubt.

Resisting the urge to grin, Kaen cleared his mind from every stray thought but one.

If we do this right, we can possibly end this war before it starts.

Pammon didn't respond, yet his rage began to boil inside, the base of his scales turning warm as the fire inside him grew.

Either we end this or let them know we will not be easy prey.

[Multishot Activated]

Arrows that burned with power flew from his bow as Pammon dove down from above.

Once the descent had begun, they had gotten close, but were not seen. Yet, somehow Juthom had noticed less than ten seconds before they were in the perfect position.

His arrows flew, two striking the back of the black dragon's massive right wing, tearing holes in it and causing him to veer to the right.

I cannot catch him! Keep shooting!

A white-hot fire burned in his chest as he saw Stioks turn for a moment, a dangerous gaze staring at him as he held his hand out toward them.

Juthom's direction suddenly shifted, his wings flaring hard as he filled them with the air he was rushing against, slowing down momentarily.

A green lance of something shot out from Stioks's hand, burning toward them as Pammon dove to the left, dodging the attack, channeling his speed from the descent into a corkscrew maneuver.

Kaen tightened his core muscles, leaning back against Pammon and scanning the sky, watching Juthom twist to the left, flapping his massive wings to turn and come in the direction they were.

Turn right! Now!

Even before he had finished giving his commands, Pammon banked quickly to the right, sending unbelievable pressure on them as another green bolt of power came for where he had been heading.

Climbing, hold on!

Kaen's eyes were watering as he felt the rapid change in direction, his body pressed against Pammon's back as his dragon rose higher in the sky, now turned away from Juthom, who was coming at them.

Leaning back, Kaen's lifestone filled him with rage, anger, and hatred. Even though he didn't want to let it overcome him and distract him, knowing the man and dragon behind them were the reason his father had died sent emotions he had not dealt with in years straight to his heart.

How many people have lost fathers, mothers, and children because of this man's greed?

His lifestone's burning fire made him grab his chest, losing an arrow as Pammon twisted again, dodging another attack from Stioks, who was leaning around Juthom's massive neck as they pressed toward them from behind.

Clenching his jaw, Kaen spun on his saddle and drew another arrow.

It burned white and then blue, a deep blue he had not seen before. A moment later, it was black, almost as dark as Juthom's scales.

The arrow sped across the sky, striking Juthom's shoulder, drawing a roar from the black dragon as his mouth flung open.

You hurt him!

Pammon felt joy and pride and did everything he could to keep his lead on the massive black dragon, who was easily a third bigger than him. Even with Juthom's wing injured, it was a struggle to keep their distance as each time the black dragon beat its wings, massive amounts of air were moved, propelling him at a blazingly fast pace.

They are gaining!

Keep shooting!

It took three seconds for each shot to reach that same dark color, and Kaen let another one go, catching the dragon in one of his front talons as he tried to dodge the arrow, sending a spray of scales into the air.

Juthom roared again; he could barely dodge the next shot Kaen sent toward him. His black wings paused for half a beat, leaving him slightly out of position, and Kaen took that moment to attack.

[Twinshot Activated]

Two arrows glowed, each of them blue when he let them fly. There wasn't enough time to risk this moment in hopes of getting them charged completely, but Kaen didn't care as one of them struck the same wing that he had hit earlier, this time on the bone near the mesh, sending a shower of flesh at the ground.

[Archery Skill Increased]

Kaen wanted to enjoy the moment. It felt like ages since his skill had increased. Unfortunately, now was not the time.

A massive ball of green light hovered above Juthom's head, and Kaen let his mouth hang open as the light grew. It was easily five feet wide now, and it was growing.

We need to go!

Pammon dove down immediately, adjusting his angle, and Kaen knew what was coming the moment he changed directions.

Spinning as quickly as he could, he grabbed the reins with his free hand and clenched his legs around Pammon's neck.

[Flight Burst Activated]

The world shifted momentarily as Pammon poured every ounce of strength he had from his body and the power that came from Kaen's raging lifestone.

The speed they took off in was faster than the time they had saved Hess, the tree line below them coming at them at an alarming rate before Pammon adjusted the angle enough to no longer be in danger of crashing into them.

A roar and a cry came from behind them, and as Kaen leaned back, squinting his eyes to see what they had left behind, a ball of green magical energy flew behind them on a direct course with the ground.

We dodged it! Can we turn back and engage?

Pammon couldn't respond, and Kaen realized why. The pressure of what they were doing was overwhelming him.

Slow down! They aren't pursuing us!

[Flight Burst Expired]

Almost slamming into the back of Pammon's neck as the speed decreased, Kaen felt Pammon shudder for a moment.

That was faster than I had thought it would be.

A hint of exhaustion came across their bond as Pammon turned back and glanced toward where Stioks and Juthom hovered in the air.

I'm going to climb back into the sky, but it looks like they will not pursue us.

Hairy dwarf balls . . . look under you at the forest.

Pammon shifted his head and took in the sight.

The area where Stioks had attacked was burning and rotting with a green power like neither had ever seen before. Trees were falling over at an alarming rate. A circle of at least fifty yards was already gone up in green flames.

Is that what Elies was hit with?

I have no idea, but if so, it is a miracle that he survived, if even a tiny portion of that hit him.

A minute passed as Pammon flew higher into the sky, constantly checking behind him.

Any change?

It appears they are leaving. They turned back to the west but are flying much higher now. I think they realize we are a threat.

A smug satisfaction came from Pammon.

Did we really accomplish anything with that attack?

Yes! Kaen, you injured Juthom enough that both rider and dragon are unwilling to pursue us, even though we are almost two hundred years younger. Can you imagine hurting Tharnok enough that he would prefer not to fight?

Mulling that over, Kaen turned back, staring at where they had just fought, unable to see the black speck that had been Juthom as they flew away.

We may have bought ourselves some time. I'm not sure we could have won that fight as we are now. I only have about thirty arrows left. Then what?

Then, it would come down to me.

Kaen could feel Pammon's concern, knowing that if they had no arrows, he was somehow supposed to overcome the size and strength difference between him and Juthom. That dragon's head was twice his size, and one bite would most likely crush him.

Let's not worry about that right now. We survived and know they took more damage than either could have expected. Head home, and we can plan on how to win next time.

Pammon snorted, angling toward Ebonmount as he rose higher into the sky. He would not risk them suffering the same attack they had just inflicted. From now on, they would push the limits of how high he could fly.

41

No Time to Relax

The last two days had been hard because they couldn't light a fire to stay warm, and they slept inside a thick canopy of trees.

Neither Kaen nor Pammon knew if Stioks and Juthom might turn around and try to track them down, but when they finally had to sleep after flying for another solid day, it was still better to be prepared.

As the mountains of Ebonmount came into view through the clouds, they let out a small sigh of relief, happy to be home and possibly get some real rest for a few days.

"Hairy dwarf balls, Kaen!" shouted Hess when Kaen was finally finished sharing what had happened. "You two actually damaged Juthom! Do you have any idea how huge that is?!"

The way Hess was waving both arms . . . well, his stub and undamaged arm, and how red his face was from shouting, Kaen had a pretty good idea how big of a deal it was.

Kaen glanced across the yard, watching Sulenda, Callie, and Pammon playing together. Turning back to Hess, who had gotten out of his chair, Kaen motioned for his mentor and friend to sit again.

"Don't get worked up, or I won't be able to calm down for a while. Yes, I do have an idea how big a deal it is. No, I couldn't have won that fight without more arrows. I still don't know what Stioks sent at us either. Whatever it was destroyed a forest, and I have no idea how Elies survived it if he and Tharnok got struck by it."

Hess plopped into his oversized chair with a massive sigh and grunted as he mindlessly rubbed his arm stump with his hand.

"Regardless, this changes so much. You are not just a threat. You are now a challenge to Stioks. Everything he believed up until this moment changes."

Hess turned, narrowing his eyes as he pointed his fat finger at Kaen.

"Until a few days ago, he most likely believed he could end your life without any real issues. He probably thought he was buying time till Elies died before he did that."

Hess stopped talking as he chuckled and then started to roar in laughter.

Kaen sat there confused as he watched the grown man start to cry momentarily as his whole body shook. When he finally calmed down enough and began taking a few breaths to regain control, Kaen interrupted him.

"What was that funny?"

Snorting, Hess dabbed the corner of his eye with his thumb and displayed a toothy smile.

"Can you imagine the conversation between Juthom and Stioks? Oh, the rage and frustration they both must feel! The two of them thinking they are, or I guess were," Hess said with another quick snort, "the top of everything. Now, they will be blaming each other. Kaen, you have done something none of us could have imagined was possible."

Juthom and Stioks fighting amongst themselves?

That thought struck Kaen in a way he had not expected.

Could I put a rift between the two of them?

"Do you think they would ever stop working together?"

Tsking his teeth for a moment and creating a small whistle as he sucked air in through them, Hess squinted and squirmed.

"Split them up? I doubt that. They have been in bed far too long, and I have no idea what drives that dragon."

"And the man?"

The way Hess's gut jumped with the grunt he gave almost looked like he had been punched.

"That man is the most dangerous thing we have seen in ages. He wants to be like the Dragon Riders of old, living hundreds of years and building a world in his image . . . " Hess trailed off as he leaned back in his chair and closed his eyes. "Did Elies ever mention the evil Dragon Riders to you? The ones that made most dragons vow to never work with men again?"

Leaning forward in his chair, Kaen shook his head no, realizing after a moment that Hess couldn't see him do that.

"No. What happened?"

Slowly opening his eyes, Hess gazed at Pammon and smiled as he saw and heard the laughter and thrumming coming from the two of them.

"A Dragon Rider had more than one dragon."

"What? How?!"

Turning his eyes to Kaen, he frowned as he shook his head.

"The *Destroyer of Nations* was the name he gave himself. Most don't know the story because history books have it removed. I only know of it because of my time with Elies and your father. Stioks killed more Dragon Riders than one can imagine. Some through strength, others through treachery. Eventually, he killed his dragon right before another egg hatched and bonded with it. His mind was evil, warped by many things, and the madness that followed was unimaginable."

A hole began to grow in Kaen's heart as Hess continued to share these things. *Who could imagine killing their own dragon?*

"He fed his hatchling dragon his old one, allowing it to grow faster than it should. Like its rider, it came to love the power it gained from their bond. Both were content to do anything necessary to get stronger."

Hess paused a moment as he turned his attention back to Callie.

"It took most of the remaining Dragon Riders working together to kill him," Hess finally said, his voice low and somber. "The remaining ones destroyed everything he owned and burned the dragon's corpse, none of the dragons wanting to even eat it. After that, the number of riders decreased, and kingdoms struggled to give that kind of power again. Alliances were made, and with the number of dragons decreasing in the kingdoms, the riders slowly began to die out. Elies was the last one to get a dragon. I'm sure he told you about that."

Kaen nodded.

"He told me how the two Dragon Riders who trained him were impressed by him. He had risen decently through the ranks of the adventurers' guild and had a reputation for only taking quests that involved helping others, regardless of what kingdom they were in. The two dragons had mated, and a single egg had been born, something that hadn't happened in a hundred years. They gave him a chance with that egg."

Laughter came from Kaen as he smiled and sat up in his chair.

"I remember when he described Tharnok as an eggling. It seems their personality is often already formed to a great deal while they are in the egg."

Hess shrugged and pointed at Pammon.

"He has changed. Mature, just like you, but both of you are still alike. You care for others no matter how tough you talk or present yourself. Each of you has a weakness for children. How many times has he said no to an adult but gladly let a child touch, scratch, or even fly on him?"

Looking at Pammon, Kaen felt his heart beat differently for a moment as he realized Hess was right. He saw Pammon turn and look at him, those golden eyes twinkling as they held his gaze.

You are talking about me, aren't you?

All good things, I promise.

A snort came from Pammon before he turned his gaze back to Callie, who was tugging on his wing. He carefully poked her with his snout as she laughed and ran around him again for the hundredth time.

"She will sleep well tonight," Hess said as he stood up and stretched. "Perhaps we both should go and play with them?"

Standing up, Kaen nodded but moved over a few feet, grabbing Hess and embracing him momentarily. He smiled as he felt both arms encircle him and the familiar pat of his hand on his back.

"My gosh, you have gotten thick!" exclaimed Hess as he pulled back and stared at him. "What have you been eating to get this wide? Where is the scrawny teen boy I had to make eat back in Minoosh?"

Laughing, Kaen gave him a gentle shove, almost bowling Hess off his feet.

"We can compare numbers if you want," he said with a wink.

Shaking his head as he smiled and chuckled, Hess finally groaned.

"No . . . let's not and say we did. Somehow, I doubt I'm the stronger of the two of us now."

Giving one more wink, Kaen motioned to where the others were and started jogging.

"If you try, I might let you win."

Laughing, Hess took off, smiling as they ran to the others.

A moan escaped his lips as he felt Ava's fingernails gently massage his scalp.

"Stop that, or people will get the wrong idea," she hissed as she glanced around the people sitting at tables near them.

The Dragon Rider Inn was packed as news had spread that Kaen had returned and was relaxing inside. The steady stream of parents whose children were at the academy never seemed to end. One came up and thanked him again for the hope he had given their children.

He smiled and thanked them each time for entrusting their greatest treasure to the kingdom and the school. It wore on him as the hours passed, but he knew it was vital for them to express their gratitude.

"I'm sorry," he whispered, flashing her a smile. "I'd much rather be relaxing with you elsewhere, but Sulenda informed me that I had a duty to fulfill, so here I am."

Giving him a kiss on the cheek, Ava laughed and then poked him in his ribs with her free finger.

"I'm just glad you were smart enough to invite me. I was a bit nervous about you being gone for two weeks. I assume your promise to tell me later means it's not common knowledge?"

Rolling his eyes, he turned his face to hers and scrunched his nose.

"For the fourth or fifth time, yes . . . I will tell you later and not in public. Now, behave yourself, please. I can't have the townspeople thinking the love of my life is trying to get me in trouble."

Ava felt her cheeks turn red at that comment and cocked her head as she gave him a slight smile.

"And what exactly would the *love of your life* be doing that would get you in trouble?"

Giving a playful growl, Kaen kissed her back on her forehead and shrugged.

"That remains to be determined."

Shaking her head, she snuggled a little closer and sighed.

"I'm just glad you are safe. Father will be a bit flustered at how the potions turned out. I can't say I'm not surprised, though, as it was our first attempt at something like that."

Nodding, Kaen held up his glass as someone came close, giving him a slight bow before walking off.

"Speaking of that, I need to tell you something you aren't going to like, and I'm trying to decide if I should tell you where it's safe or somewhere private."

He felt her flinch and saw her look up at him with a perplexed look on her face.

"I need to leave soon," he whispered in her ear. "I don't want to, but there is something I have to do, and I have no idea how long it will be before I return."

He paused as he felt her tense up and shook his head slowly.

"Before you ask, I cannot take you. We will be flying as high as possible and with no rest," he said as he lowered his lips to her ear and spoke so quietly she almost missed it. "Pammon and I have to travel across the sea to seek help from the dragons."

42

The Problem with Duty

The only thing that prevented Kaen from getting a face full of Ava's hair as her head snapped up was his dexterity stat.

With her eyes bulging and her mouth hanging open, she exclaimed, "You what?!" forgetting the need to be quiet as heads turned to see what caused the outburst.

Kaen's eyes darted across the tables. He motioned towards the others in the room with his head, aware of how they were staring.

"Mother lovin', dwarf humping, goblin shite, dragon balls," she cursed under her breath.

Taking a deep breath, she calmed herself, letting the redness of her face slowly subside as she reached over with her right hand and grabbed his shirt, pulling him close to her, ignoring how he was bumping into the booth.

"I swear you are impossible," she growled, glaring at him. "You just got back and shared how close to death Pammon was, and now you plan on flying off across the sea."

With a grunt, she pushed him and sat back against her seat in the booth, crossing her arms as she glared at the table.

"Ava," he said, trying to get close, but she shook her shoulder when he tried to put his arm around her. "I told you I would be honest. I promised I would keep you informed of everything possible."

Closing his eyes briefly, he breathed in her scent, holding onto it before letting it out slowly through his nose.

"If I could take you or stay longer, I would, but you must trust me. Once we get somewhere, I can tell you why this must happen. Then you will understand."

The moment he finished that statement, she turned, her hands on his shoulders, pushing him almost off his seat.

"Then we go now, and you better be right about that last part."

Catching himself before he fell on the floor, Kaen held his hand to her, feeling her grip as she let him help her out of the booth.

"Let's use the office," he said as he motioned to the door with his head. "Something tells me you don't want to wait."

She shook her head, and they walked briskly, ignoring the looks they got from the patrons who picked up on the change in their temperaments.

"You picked a fight with Stioks?" she shouted, thankful the room had wards to help cut down on the noise she was making. "What in a goblin's tit is wrong with you?! Do you two have wool for brains?"

Kaen leaned back on the new couch Sulenda had put in there, content to watch Ava pace around the room, waving her hands in the air as she yelled.

"Juthom is an ancient dragon! Why would you even try?!"

She continued her rant for a few more moments, glancing at him and realizing that Kaen was still sitting there, quietly, not replying but had a slight smirk on his face.

"What?!" she demanded, her breathing rapid from how worked up she was.

"Are you finished yelling yet?"

Obviously, that was the wrong question. Ava launched into another tirade about how much of an idiot he must be. After another minute of her finger-pointing and yelling, and even a foot stomp, she turned on him again, her nostrils flaring and her face red.

"You aren't going to yell back, are you?"

Shaking his head, she threw her hands up and grunted.

"Why in a goblin arse not?"

"Your parents yell, don't they?"

She jerked her face back as if he had slapped her across the cheek.

"What?" she sputtered, stammering for a reply.

"Your mom and dad. They yell, and the loudest wins."

Ava's entire body language changed. One moment, she was sputtering, caught off guard by his statement and how true it was. The next, she shuffled her feet as she adjusted the collar of her dress and went speechless.

Kaen stood up, crossing the room in a heartbeat, putting his arms around her and drawing her close.

"I don't want to yell at you. I never want to yell at you," Kaen whispered as he felt her tremble under his embrace. "When we are married, I want you to know that I will gladly discuss the choices we have in a calm voice, as best as I can. I made a choice. We had the high ground. Pammon agreed it was the right decision, and it was. Was it risky? Yes, but there are times when we must risk everything. Like the time I told you I loved you."

He began to slowly push her away to look her in the eyes, but she wrapped her arms around him and wouldn't let him.

"I love you, too, you big oaf," she grunted, squeezing him tight.

"Pammon and I achieved something far greater than I could have dreamed. In fact, I shared with you that dream that haunted me for so long. Now, I know it was just a nightmare. Now I know we can actually do something to them."

Ava leaned back, smiling when she heard the excitement in his voice.

"I'm just glad you are ok," she whispered and squeezed him again.

Leaning back, she flashed her fantastic smile and then let out a small laugh. "Tell me again how you injured Juthom."

Kaen pulled Ava in, resting his chin on her head as his whole body shook from laughter.

Both of them jerked up a bit as they heard the knock on the door, adjusting their clothes as it opened slowly.

"You two decent," came Sulenda's sweet and playful voice as she held the door open just a few inches.

"Yes," Kaen replied, his voice cracking, which brought a chuckle from behind the door.

A few seconds later, Sulenda and Hess came in, smiling and watching as the pair stood up at the edge of the couch.

"It's a wonderful seat, isn't it," Hess teased. "Very soft and yet firm at the same time. Perfect for all kinds of naps."

An elbow from Sulenda caught him in the ribs, eliciting a grunt. She rolled her eyes at Hess and smiled even more.

"Now, ignoring the crass man I love, you two look in better spirits than when you stormed out of the dining hall, scaring half the patrons."

"Sorry about that—"

She waved her hand, cutting him off.

"Don't apologize. Most of them weren't spending enough coin for me to worry about. You did what I asked, and everyone knows you have a lot on your plate. Now Hess told me what you plan on doing, and judging by how both of your clothes look, you are well aware of the plan also."

Kaen glanced at Ava, who held her chin high, not reacting in the least to Sulenda's statement. Kaen had begun adjusting his clothes a little better, earning him a smile and a wink from Hess, who was behind Sulenda.

"I leave in three days. Should I ask what you *need* from me now?"

Raising her eyebrows for a moment, a smirk appeared on Sulenda's face, and she began nodding. "Tomorrow, I will tell you what you need to do before you go. After that, I expect you to return as quickly as possible. There is much to discuss and do with what Hess has informed me of. Knowing I will receive an influx of dwarven children in the coming years will require more buildings and changes, but I think I can manage it. Any chance I should be expecting a horde of elvish children at the same time?"

Snorting, Kaen shook his head.

I just hope the elves aren't doing what I think they are.

"Fine then. It is late, and Hess and I need to turn in for the night, but I wanted to make sure you stop by before you visit Aldric and Herb tomorrow. You need to take something to them for me."

Kaen felt his eyebrows furl as he tried to imagine what she would need him to do.

"School business?"

She nodded and motioned her head to her husband. "Tell your father good-night. It's time I got his lazy body to bed."

A huff came from behind her, and she flinched slightly when Kaen saw Hess pinch her backside.

"Night, Dad. Don't let Mom keep you up too late."

Sulenda rolled her eyes and turned.

"You two are just alike," Sulenda muttered, exasperated

"Aye, he is my love."

Hess gave a slight bow to Ava as he turned and chased after Sulenda. Over his shoulder, he added, "Night, you two. Don't stay here all night; word might reach someone's mother, and you will find a collar around your neck."

Ava coughed, her cheeks flushing as she glanced up at Kaen, who was smiling.

"He is right, you know. I need to get you home. You have work to do!"

She groaned and playfully elbowed him, and then he drew her in for a quick kiss.

"If you keep doing that," she gasped after their lips parted, "I may not make it home at all."

Reaching up to his neck and pretending to tug an invisible chain, Kaen pretended he couldn't breathe for a moment. "You're right. Best get you home quickly; I wouldn't want to be collared too soon."

With a groan, she pushed him away, rolling her eyes and turning for the door.

"You and Sulenda must be related with how well you both roll your eyes," he called out as she started to walk across the room.

"Oh, just you wait and see," she said, her voice a little throaty as she looked over her shoulder and raised her eyebrows.

Kaen darted for the door, barely reaching it before her.

"I look forward to that day," he whispered as she walked past him and out the door.

She simply nodded and smiled.

* * *

You seem to be in good spirits, and I can only imagine why.

Pammon was not amused, and he could tell by the wave of frustration that came through their bond.

I didn't do anything overly wrong.

No, you didn't, Pammon stated as he glared across the room, watching Kaen as he lay in his bed in the dark. **Yet I could feel everything you felt, and it is hard to enjoy a nice meal when one isn't sure if they want to swallow the cow or do other things to it.**

Kaen started laughing so hard he choked, having to roll over and grab his glass of water still sitting on his nightstand from earlier.

Pammon thrummed momentarily, his better mood hitting him through their bond.

Yes. I, too, feel the passion you profess to feel for her. Imagine how bad things will be for you when I find a mate. You might need to lock yourself in a room and hide, lest you injure your poor wife.

The coughs that had just subsided came back with a double amount of force, and Kaen couldn't help but laugh at the thought.

"You're bad," he wheezed as he poured himself another glass of water. "Sometimes worse than Hess."

Who do you think I learned all this from? When you are off having fun or doing something, I have to hear the stories he doesn't want to tell you.

The water in his mouth sprayed out over his blanket, and now Kaen was ready to die. Between choking on water, hearing that Hess was telling Pammon his sordid details with Sulenda, and a dragon threatening to go into heat and cause his life to be upended, the peaceful night's sleep he had planned was not happening.

"I'm going to go take a quick dip in the tub," Kaen muttered as he climbed out of bed, tossing his wet blanket on the floor. "Someone has ruined the mood."

Pammon thrummed as he watched Kaen walk toward the open doors into the night air.

I tried to tell you. Some of us don't like feeling turned on and aroused for hours at a time.

Kaen didn't reply but instead just took a deep breath and let it out. There were no instructions given about this part of being a Dragon Rider.

What else is there I need to know about this?

43

Planning for the Future

"Are you sure I can't give you a medal?" Aldric asked again, his face beaming with excitement. "I mean, Herb and I have told you already how amazing it is you did what you did!"

Having not stopped his head from shaking side to side, Kaen rolled his eyes once more as he fidgeted with his mug.

"We don't have time for that, and I don't want the attention. I'm sure Stioks and Juthom aren't going to announce it to anyone. There is no need to poke the dragon by celebrating what I did. Right now, I need to take advantage of the time this may have bought us."

Herb started roaring with laughter, and Aldric just grinned.

"What is so funny?"

"When did you get so wise?" Herb finally replied after settling down. "Where is that kid that stood before me just a few years ago, ready to rush head first into any challenge, believing he could overcome it all?"

Kaen shrugged as he pointed to the stack of papers they had discarded on the table after reading. "This boy has learned through blood, sweat, and tears that real success doesn't come from always beating one's head against it. I still risk everything sometimes, but usually only if Pammon says I can."

A chuckle came from Aldric as he thumbed the papers Kaen had pointed to. "I owe you a lot for what you have done, Kaen."

His voice had gone from playful and bantering a minute ago to his serious *king* voice. "With the dwarves coming to help shore up our defense, I honestly believe we might have a chance. I knew what we were doing would most likely fail, and it would be catastrophic when it did. The kingdom needed a reason to not cower and waste away. Your original plan gave us that."

He paused, pointing at the map he and Elnidith had marked along the walls that needed more fortification.

"You improved on that plan. Somehow, you found a person not only smart enough to help make it better but willing to move a portion of the dwarven people here. You have summoned a small army; all it will cost me is some land, money, and jobs. Things I would gladly give up if it means we have an actual chance of not losing everything."

Kaen could see the glimmer of hope in Aldric's eyes. They almost seemed brighter, and his face was relaxed, not the usual hard stone where he clenched his jaws too much.

"I still need to ask forgiveness for offering up a portion of your kingdom without your consent. It wasn't my—"

"Nonsense," he said, waving off Kaen's apology. "You did what a Dragon Rider should. You made a decision based on what was best for the people. All people. Not only were we at risk, but so were those at Tanulivar. Now, they have a place to defend and hope to start a new life here. Will it be hard? Yes. Will people complain about the weight of five thousand or more dwarves? Yes. Will they accept it because it gives them a better chance of making it through what is coming?"

Kaen waited for the next word to come and watched as Aldric just sat there smiling.

"Yes," Kaen finally said, watching the older man nod.

"Don't forget the wood elves," Herb chimed in. "How long has it been since they were willing to stand with us?"

"Too long. Way too long."

That comment sparked something Kaen had forgotten to show, and he grabbed his pack off the ground and began pulling out rolls of leather.

Picking up the papers from the table strewn about, he stacked them neatly in a pile at the corner of the table and then began to unroll the leather maps he had drawn.

"These aren't perfect, but I made them while we traveled. A lot has changed since—"

"You made these?" gasped Herb as he looked over the maps.

Kaen nodded, turning his head to see Herb's mouth hanging open as the shorter man scanned the crude drawings.

"Incredible," Herb murmured as his finger ran along the edges of some of the forests. "Hundreds of years . . . "

"Goblin shite!"

Both men turned and looked at Aldric, whose unexpected cursing had caught them off guard.

"Excuse me?"

Shaking his head, a look of frustration on his face, Aldric winced as he turned his attention to Kaen.

"Sorry for cursing. Not very kingly, I'm afraid. Herb is a bad influence, as is Hess, but still."

He pointed to the maps leading to Luthaelia and said, "All of our maps are way out of date. I had tried sending teams out for a while, but they never returned, even with help from the adventurers' guild. It was far too dangerous."

Aldric tapped three different spots before running his finger along the eastern edge. "These changes are proof of just how much Stioks's kingdom has been pushing into our area. The changes in the forest line," he said as he tapped closer to where the wood elves lived, "the advancement to this section of the forest. All this tells me our count on his forces is completely wrong. In order to accomplish all this . . . "

He frowned as he looked up and saw the men staring at him.

Taking a breath and letting it out slowly, Aldric forced a smile.

"Ignore that for now. Let's rejoice in the victory we have. With your maps, the dwarves joining us, the news we have of the caves to the south, and how you managed to injure Juthom, there is much to celebrate."

"About that," Herb almost interrupted. "The advisors say it must be a higher-level spell than what you described. There has to be a high-level caster or two who has somehow found a way to cast that spell and keep it going. There were rumors of the guild hall in Luthaelia having seen magical development beyond what we have."

Moving back to his chair, Herb sat down and intertwined his fingers across his chest.

"Stioks has been spending at least a decade channeling all the magical ability of his kingdom into magical gear and equipment. Even with a barebones crew in Luthaelia, we heard reports of all casters being forced into his endeavors."

Tsking his tongue for a moment, Herb began to chew on his lip. "We have already seen what he has helped the orcs to create. Suicide bombers are rigged with a device that only detonates when their wearer dies or they are caught up in another explosion. Goblins and orcs shouldn't have been able to develop that on their own. If he provides them with magical gear and training, it will be something we have never faced before."

Leaning against the table, Kaen considered this and asked, "How far behind are we? I mean in magical item creation and advancement."

Shrugging his shoulders, Herb turned and looked at Aldric with a questionable expression and answered, "Very far behind. We have poured everything into the material for the wall and the roofs."

Rubbing his eyes, Kaen nodded as he considered what all this meant.

"I think we should stop worrying about the roof tiles for now. Do you agree?"

He saw both men nodding and crossed his arms. "You have adventures collecting materials and supplies, right?"

Herb nodded.

"Give me your honest opinions. Other than finishing up the two walls and the extra defenses that are going to be erected in the pass, does anything else matter?"

Aldric shook his head first, and Herb a few seconds later.

"So what do we need to turn our attention to enchantment-wise?"

A snort came from Herb, who smirked and said, "Definitely Hoste's son."

Grinning, Aldric nodded and sat back down in his seat. "Do you want answers now or later?"

"I don't care. I'm leaving in two days. You two need to figure that part out. I remember the people in Fiola's party mentioning she had wands. A dozen or so of those with the right spell could change the direction of a battle. I have to believe that Stioks has considered that and has created, or is creating, some. That kind of power is a trump card for the undefended."

"I can draw up a list of ideas and share them with Aldric in the coming days. What else, Dragon Rider Kaen?"

Rolling his eyes, Kaen almost gave Herb the middle finger but stopped himself.

"You two must ensure Sulenda has her request by this week."

Aldric shifted in his chair. "That will drain most of what we have created, and they are still taking a while to make."

"Then focus the mages on that task for a while. We need more lifestones. Those fifty students are at the right age, and if we want them to progress how they must, they cannot wait any longer."

"The results speak for themselves," Herb chimed in. "Those two pillars of your academy are shooting stars. Their results are beyond anything anyone could expect."

Kaen's smile ran across his whole face.

Frederick and Phillip had already reached level ten in a melee weapon and shield. Their physical stats were also growing as Finn enlisted Hess's help in constructing a training area like the one he had used in Roccnari. The other students were lagging behind, their bodies not able to adapt and grow from normal development. It was time for a boost.

"I know you have them, and I know it will take most of what the town has, but if we are honest, a lifestone in the hands of a merchant or a noble will not mean as much compared to these children in a year or two."

Kaen stood up, pulled out the talisman he wore around his neck, and gave it a tiny flick.

"Between their stats, skills, and all the gear I have in my father's vault, we can outfit a small team to help at the walls. Imagine getting five or ten years before the enemy throws everything at us. What kind of army could we have then?"

Aldric and Hess nodded. They could hear the excitement and hope in Kaen's voice. He had done something on a whim, knowing it might never last long enough, but now, the truth was there might be enough time. If they could go from one or two classes to sixteen or seventeen, those boys and girls would be assets far more significant than anything imaginable.

"Fine," Aldric conceded. "I will give all but two that I have in my castle. If Herb does the same, we can give her ten more than she requested. Any noble or merchant that wants to complain about this choice can talk to me personally."

Herb chuckled and nodded that he would do likewise.

"Thank you."

Both stood, sensing that Kaen was finished.

"Anything we can get you for your trip?" Herb asked as he extended his hand.

Shaking it, Kaen nodded. "I'll take any information either of you have on the council of dragons and relationships with them. I need to be as prepared as possible to deal with them."

Herb's face contorted, considering what they might have on hand. "Check in before you leave. I'll see what I can find, but it won't be much off the top of my head."

Aldric's hand appeared before Kaen, and he shook it, watching the older man smile. "I'll get my people scouring every bookshelf we have. Anything we find is yours and will be dropped off at the adventurers' hall, so you don't have to make multiple stops."

"Perhaps you two could say a few prayers to the spirits for me," Kaen joked as he motioned to Pammon, who was about to land on the other end of the courtyard. "Dealing with Tharnok and my own dragon has been an adventure. Dealing with dragons that don't like men and are most likely older than Tharnok is nothing I have ever imagined."

"I'll say multiple prayers," Aldric replied, putting his hand on Kaen's shoulder and squeezing it. "Just know I have faith in you. We all do. For some reason, you and Pammon were brought together, and I have to believe it was for this moment. Trust in that."

Giving the best smile he could muster, Kaen tipped his head as he walked to Pammon.

I can tell you are frustrated. Where do you need to go?

Take me to the sky. I need to be with you up there where I can clear my head.

Pammon thrummed as he waited for Kaen to climb on his back.

Spoken like a true Dragon Rider.

44

An Unexpected Trip

Most of the afternoon and evening were spent in the air, above the rain clouds that were forming, noting the change in season.

Dark clouds loomed to the east, absorbing water from the lake on the opposite side, a forbidding sign as they drifted over the mountains.

Tell me the truth. You are afraid.

Kaen couldn't hide the fear of what this journey would bring. The trip itself was going to be long and hard. The map he had received from Elies compared with the ones he had drawn told him it would most likely be a week and a half of flying. They would need to stop at the city on the edge of the Great Seas. A kingdom most never engaged with outside of trade.

Golden Edge was far to the west of Roccnari, and they disliked the attitude of the elves, not that Kaen could argue against that point. They were content to slowly grow and expand, eating into the miles of land and forests that separated them from the other kingdoms.

Since it would be at least a solid day of flying to cover that distance, neither kingdom fought over that expanse, as Roccnari didn't have the forces or will to fight.

We both know how long and hard this journey will be. Most of it depends on you getting there and flying for days without rest unless we find an island or something. If you want to eat, you will have to try and find food in the sea, and we both know how well that went last time.

Pammon's snort was more of a reflex than a sense of hurt pride.

You try grasping at something tiny while water shoots up your snout.

Kaen just laughed, rubbing the same scale as always and smiled.

Tomorrow would be a hard day. He had a lot to do, and saying goodbye to Ava would be rough. Even Callie seemed to be growing like a weed, talking more and getting around quickly; it had only been two weeks.

Life was passing by so fast, yet he felt he was missing out on it.

Looking at the city below for the past few hours brought everything into perspective.

There was a world that he didn't belong in. He needed to stay somehow in both. Each of the lives of the people on the ground was important to him. Flying today reminded him that the lives down below would go on. People would pass, and he would age slower, living longer, burying friends and family.

I'll always be with you until your dying breath.

Laying against Pammon's neck, Kaen hugged his hard scales.

I just accepted the truth of all this. Every day, we risk ourselves for a belief. For a purpose. My reason for all this hasn't changed, but it feels heavier. How long will the people love us and support us? Will the next generation despise or envy us to the point of trying to take away what we have? Are we really making a difference?

Pammon, as always, gave Kaen a hug that felt comforting through their bond.

You couldn't live with yourself if you didn't try. I see how you light up when you engage with those students. Your heart is happy when you play with Callie and your family. I can see that. I can feel it. The truth is you are scared about returning. What lies across the ocean is an unknown we are unprepared for. Elies and Tharnok gave us as much information as they could in the time he had, but he trained us more to be fighters. Perhaps he knew that was what we really needed to become.

I must say you are not an eggling anymore. Tharnok really taught you how to be a wise dragon.

Flaring his head and neck back, Pammon tossed Kaen into his saddle.

I'm not the one who is scared. You are ready for this. We are prepared for this. If anything, our moment with Juthom and Stioks proved that we can be a threat and we are not weak.

Then let's go home. I know you are hungry. I have listened to your stomach growl for the last hour.

Thrumming, Pammon leaned forward, starting the descent as the setting sun glistened off his bronze scales.

Remember that when you see Ava tomorrow, no running off and doing certain things. I don't want to have to endure that again for a while.

Laughing, Kaen leaned back, letting the wind rush over him.

"Kaen!"

He glanced over and saw Lord Hurem shout as he dismounted from Pammon, doing his best not to ruin the grass they always seemed to destroy when they landed in their courtyard.

"It has been only a few weeks, but it still feels like it has been forever!"

When they finally drew close, Kaen extended his hand, only to be surprised as Lord Hurem took it and pulled him close, giving him a small hug and three taps on his back.

"I'm sorry to hear that the potions we made for Pammon didn't work as anticipated. I have been working nonstop on a few others, and they will be brought up here before you leave."

"It's ok; you had said—"

"Nonsense! I can't be responsible for not caring for you or your dragon when both of you mean so much to us."

Kaen glanced at the man, who seemed way friendlier than usual. His facial expressions, the hug. It was all weird.

If he is so concerned with me almost dying, perhaps he will give me a hundred cows in return.

Kaen almost choked, holding back the laughter as Lord Hurem glanced at him before shifting his gaze to Pammon.

"He says do not trouble yourself with how the first batch worked. A few animals will be more than enough to compensate for your concerns."

Lord Hurem smiled and gave a slight bow before turning and snapping his fingers at a servant standing off to the side.

As if waiting for permission, teams of individuals brought in various animals, all butchered for Pammon. Pigs, sheep, a cow, and something else Kaen couldn't recognize.

"A treat for you!" the man stated as he saw Pammon eyeing the different carcasses. "A bird that runs fast because it cannot fly."

A chicken?

Pammon thrummed, saliva dripping from his mouth as he watched the servants set down the wooden boards that carried all the animals.

If it is, we will need to get more of them so I can take revenge on their leader back in Minoosh.

Kaen laughed as he gave a slight bow.

"Pammon is very thankful for your gift and special treat."

Motioning to the chairs around the table behind him, Lord Hurem waited for Kaen to sit before joining him.

"My wife and daughter will join us in a moment, but I need to ask you something before they arrive."

Like a statue, Kaen didn't allow his face to change, a slight smile on his lips as he gave a slow nod.

"My daughter told my wife the other night," he whispered as he leaned in, "that you professed to my daughter that you love her. Needless to say, my wife is ecstatic, and while we both have considered you a part of the family if you ever need to ask me specifically how to join the family, I will be happy to say yes."

A low thrum came from Pammon as he swallowed the meal provided for him.

It appears someone has just stumbled into a trap. Oh, how the mighty have fallen.

Shut it . . . what the heck am I going to do?

Pammon laughed louder, distracting Lord Hurem from Kaen as the man smiled and watched a whole side of beef slide down Pammon's throat.

"I'm glad you like it!" he stated, ecstatic at the show. "I can have more brought in a while if you need."

Pammon thrummed louder, nodding as his tongue cleaned the outside of his snout.

Without hesitation, Lord Hurem turned to the same servant and nodded, and the man gave a quick bow before dashing off into a servant's door.

I have given you a moment to think. Use those brains you spoke highly of the other day when you spoke with Herb and the king.

Kaen reached for the glass and took a long, slow drink. Lord Hurem was almost giddy, bouncing his leg under the table and leaning forward.

Setting his cup down, Kaen straightened himself in his chair.

"I believe that time will come, but I have a few things to take care of first. I'm sure your daughter informed you of my need to leave for a place across the sea?"

Lord Hurem nodded his head in excitement.

"Yes!" he said, louder than he had intended. He leaned closer and then whispered, "Dragons! Can you imagine? A land filled with them!"

Kaen's smile wasn't very believable, but that was because the two of them obviously considered the situation a bit differently.

"Yes, well, as you know, I cannot ask you that question until after I return. Imagine how I would feel if I . . . " Kaen paused, feeling Pammon's eyes on him as he spoke. "If I made that commitment and something happened. I could never bring myself to put her through the added or extra pain that might bring."

A slight frown formed on the man's face.

"You are saying you love her, and yet you are worried about how she might feel if you didn't return after having professed your love? I don't want to be mean or sound disrespectful, but Kaen, you are missing out on what love is all about!"

The man stood up suddenly, almost tipping his chair over from the force.

"To be in love is a marvelous thing. It shouldn't be put off," he explained as he began to pace before spinning on his heels to face Kaen while pointing a finger at him. "Just look at Hess and Sulenda! They didn't waste time with what had been or could be! They gave themselves fully to each other, and now look at how happy they are, even with the injury he has sustained."

Kaen began to open his mouth, but Lord Hurem shook his head and didn't let him interrupt.

"Imagine if Hess had waited until you and Pammon were announced. Would he have fought with the same zeal? Would he have wanted to return that badly?"

Moving to stand over Kaen, Lord Hurem bent down, putting his arm on the table as he leaned in close.

"Would you have fought so hard if you didn't know Sulenda was pregnant? Could Hess have given himself like did, had he waited till he returned, missing an arm?"

The stern gaze he was enduring, combined with the barrage of well-thought-out questions, left Kaen speechless.

"I—"

"Act, Kaen, act! Tell me right now, do you want to marry my daughter?"

Kaen froze, caught between Lord Hurem's gaze and Pammon's gaze. He wasn't sure which one was harder to endure.

Tell him. You and I both already know the answer.

Kaen swallowed. His hands were sweaty, so he wiped them on his pants before answering. "I do, but—"

"No buts! You have my permission."

Kaen shook his head in disbelief as the man's face softened immediately, going from a hard gaze to a soft, approachable look. His lips were no longer drawn tight. He was smiling, and those perfectly manicured eyebrows no longer fought for position over his nose, now lazily reclined above his eyes.

A hand appeared near his chest, and a small box rested on it. Where it had come from, Kaen had yet to learn.

"Take it, Kaen. Take it and marry my daughter tonight."

A snort came from behind the man, and Lord Hurem turned and faced Pammon.

"I have done some reading, Pammon, about Dragon Riders and their dragons. I know you are probably unhappy about this, but let me ask you a question and let you decide. If you love Kaen and want him to be happy and give everything he's got to return here safely, why deny an anchor that will hold his heart firm when challenging moments arise? Why not let him declare his love, bind his heart, and do everything in his power, as Hess did, to return to the woman he loves? Would you, as his dragon, not do anything to protect your rider? I ask because I also care about Kaen and want to help him return. Just as I made those potions for you and him, I need him to come home. We need him to come home.

"If that means tonight I ignore my wife's dreams of a wedding that would rival a king so that my daughter and the man she loves can be together for one night and use that moment to plant a seed in his heart that will make him fight with every fiber of his being to return here with you, then so be it. I will endure countless years of a nagging wife whom I love to know that I can possibly fulfill the same desire you have for Kaen. To see him safe every day he is alive."

Kaen was stunned. He felt every emotion Pammon was dealing with right now. Rage didn't come close to describing how he felt. They had been lured and trapped. Resentment at what this change would mean to the two of them. Fear that their bond would become weaker due to having to share him with another. The realization that Lord Hurem was right. Kaen would need all the willpower he had to endure what they might experience, and this small thing might be the edge their bond couldn't provide.

A snort came again, followed by a long breath as Pammon moved across the grass until he was closer to Lord Hurem. He slowly reached out with his head, just a foot from the man's unflinching face.

Tell him I accept but that if he ever tries to control you through her, his life may end quicker than he may wish.

You accept? What do you mean you accept?

Pammon shifted his gaze to Kaen, and his lips curled slightly as a hug came through their bond.

Marry that poor girl. I have been an eggling for trying to keep you two apart. Lord Hurem is correct. I would do anything to protect you and bring you back. She will help with that. Take the ring and begin your life with her.

Kaen rose from his seat, stumbling to Pammon, and put his hand out.

Pammon moved his snout and pressed it against his rider's hand.

Thank you. More than you know, thank you.

Pammon snorted, Kaen believed intentionally, getting some mucus on Lord Hurem's clothes, eliciting a gasp of horror from him.

Take the ring. Wait to ask till I return. I need to do one thing before you do this.

Moving back a few steps, Pammon smiled, watching as Lord Hurem tried to wipe the mucus off with his hands, having no luck.

Remember, wait for me to return and tell that man the mucus is a dragon tradition to welcome a new family member.

Kaen watched as Pammon took off into the morning sky, his thrumming filling the courtyard as he beat his wings quickly.

Turning to Lord Hurem, Kaen saw the man's grimace as his hands were slimy and covered in snot.

"Dragons," Kaen said with a shrug as he smiled. "At least he said yes."

45

A Private Affair

Lord Hurem had sent a servant to tell his wife and Ava to wait a bit longer.

Kaen watched as his soon-to-be father-in-law read a note, his fingers shaking.

"Everything ok?"

The older man chuckled, put the note in his vest pocket, and smiled. Unconsciously, he wiped his hand on the outside of the vest one of the servants had brought him.

"As I am sure you will quickly learn, women are not always the most patient. Especially in regards to matters like these," he said, gesturing to the jewelry box on the table next to Kaen. "Neither of us has mentioned to Ava what is taking place, only that you and I needed time to discuss a few important matters. I told her that things are as they should be, but we are now just waiting for Pammon to return."

Kaen could sense Pammon flying in his direction. He was about five minutes away at most.

"He should be back soon. He won't answer my questions about what he is doing, but sometimes he likes to think he is funny."

Lord Hurem shrugged and smiled.

"Dragons. Not my area of expertise. I'll leave that to you."

When Pammon appeared over the walls, Kaen strained his eyes, and then when the realization of what he saw hit him, he felt tears welling in his eyes.

You ruined the surprise.

Pammon's mood was one of happiness as he felt Kaen figure out where he had gone.

You went and got them! Did you tell them why?

I had to, but Hess promptly had them all on their way once I did. I might have caused a commotion when I landed in the street. At least I made sure everyone got out of the way.

Kaen wiped the tears, and he watched Lord Hurem as he finally noticed the trio on Pammon's back.

"I'm guessing that was his idea?"

Kaen nodded, grinning like an idiot.

"I never even thought of it," he muttered. "You surprised me with what you said, and then how you convinced Pammon to do something he fought against for so long left me a bit dumbstruck. I feel bad now, realizing I had not thought to gather them."

"You are lucky, son," he replied as he touched Kaen's shoulder. "Maybe it's too early for the son part, but know my wife and I will grow to love you as a son. That is the only thing I ask. Love her and protect her."

Nodding, Kaen took his eyes off the man and began waving as Pammon landed, smiles on everyone's faces.

Callie loved that, didn't she?

Pammon thrummed as he lay on the ground, lowering himself as Kaen came forward to help.

More than you can imagine. The squeals were loud enough to be heard over the wind.

Sulenda came down first, giving him a massive hug before turning and gathering Callie from Hess.

Callie was laughing as she spoke. "Pammon, fly me!"

After repeating that a few times, Kaen heard the thud of Hess sliding off Pammon and fell into another embrace.

"I'm proud of you, son," he whispered in his ear. "About time you grew a pair and did what you should have."

Hess pushed him back with one hand before pulling him back in. "I won't mention there is a betting pool on when this would happen. You just made some person's month."

Busting out in laughter, Kaen grabbed Sulenda, and the four hugged. Well the three of them hugged as Callie kept reaching her hand out toward Pammon.

"Kaen!" Lady Hurem shouted as she waltzed into the room, wearing a stunning green dress that complemented her figure and hair. "It has been too long!"

He couldn't remove the small smile on his face as she came in, giving him a hug. "You need to hurry this show up, son. I am paying by the hour for the minister." Her whisper made him chuckle as she leaned back and winked at him.

"Ava," Kaen said with a slow drawl as he spoke and gave her a wink.

"What the hell is going on? You three are acting very weird and secretive, and you all know how I hate it when you act like this." Ava furled her eyebrows and stood with her arms crossed, glaring at the three of them.

A cough and a gentle nod from her father let Kaen know they were done waiting.

"I'm sorry, love of my life, your parents are a bit overprotective and brash sometimes," Kaen said as he walked toward her.

Her eyebrows relaxed, and a smile appeared because he used that phrase again.

Giving her a quick kiss on her forehead, he smiled and motioned with his head toward her parents.

"You can blame them later for being so smart and persuasive."

Confusion filled her face as she glanced past Kaen to see her parents embracing each other and smiling in a way she hadn't seen in years.

Let Hess and the rest out.

Pammon shifted his wing, raising it up to reveal Hess, Sulenda, and a young girl doing her best to play hide and seek.

Looking at Hess and Sulenda, who waved and smiled as they moved to stand by her parents, Ava turned back to Kaen, only to realize he was down on one knee before her.

"Ava Hurem, will you be my wife?"

She saw the ring in his rough hands, a massive white gem set in a gold band. His eyes were alive, drinking her in, and she saw the smile on his face, one she knew he only had for her.

Words failed as her body began to shake, no matter how much she opened her mouth.

It couldn't be happening. Kaen had said it was too soon. Was this a ploy to put her off? To hold her at bay and not suspect a thing?

Seeing her parents, she knew that wasn't the case.

"Ava, will you marry me," Kaen asked again. His voice was steady, calm, and warm.

Nodding her head frantically, she finally managed to speak

"Yes!" she exclaimed, her voice squeaking with the excitement.

Holding out her trembling hand, Kaen slid the ring onto her finger, amazed at how perfectly it fit.

Rising to his feet as she stared at the ring on her hand, Kaen lifted her chin, seeing her eyes lock on his.

"Do you love me?"

"You know I do," she gushed, needing his steady hand to keep hers from shaking even more.

"Then marry me right now," he said, watching her face turn red and finding herself once again speechless.

The minister her mother had hired walked out the servants' door in his official gray robes, holding the marriage rope in one hand and smiling.

"Now?" she gasped as she saw the minister walking across the room. "What about—"

"Your father was right. Why should I miss out on any time I have with you. I would rather be married today and fight with every part of my being to ensure nothing stops me from returning to you."

Kaen paused and moved, pointing at Hess.

"That man showed me the power of that kind of love."

She watched as Sulenda gripped Hess's good arm, smiling as tears rolled down her cheek.

Turning, Ava faced Kaen, reaching her hands up and touching the scraggly beard he had decided to keep, still unsure if she liked it.

"I do," she said, her voice calm and steady.

Cheers rang out from her parents, as well as from Kaen's. Pammon even let out a small roar, causing everyone to laugh.

"Pammon is ok with this?"

"He apologized for being an eggling. His foolishness and selfishness kept him from seeing how powerful your love can be to keep me alive."

Steadying herself, Ava moved across the courtyard, past her parents, and stood a few feet from Pammon. Holding her hand out, she waited.

Pammon didn't wait long before putting his snout against her hand.

"Thank you, Pammon. I promise to love and protect him while doing everything I can to ensure he will always come home to you."

She watched as Pammon's eyes took her in. Those golden eyes seemed to read into her soul and see how she really felt.

Pammon pulled his head back a little bit and put a talon into the back of his mouth. With a grunt and some force, a tooth popped free and was clasped between his talons.

"Hairy dwarf balls," Hess whispered.

The elbow he received from Sulenda didn't faze him, as he knew what was about to happen.

Come close, Kaen. I want you to be here when I do this.

Kaen quickly covered the distance, hearing what Pammon had done. He fought back some tears as the emotion he felt flooded into Pammon and back into him.

Pammon held the bloody tooth out it to Ava, who carefully took it.

Putting one talon against the tooth, Pammon willed his mana into it. He had done this before and knew how it worked, but it would be different this time. The tooth glowed from where the sharp point of his talon touched it. It filled with light and then suddenly vanished, the light of it washing over Ava.

I promise I will protect you just as I will protect Kaen.

Ava's hands trembled as she covered her open mouth. Tears began racing down her cheeks as she stood there speechless.

Kaen's placed his hand on her back to offer a little support and slowly drew her close to him.

Kaen held out his hand without hesitating, and Pammon came to it, letting him draw his snout into the small embrace.

"Thank you," Ava cried, her voice so low only Kaen and Pammon could hear it. "Thank you for sharing him and yourself."

Forgive me. I was a fool to try and keep you two apart.

Ava reached out, putting her hand on Pammon's scales and slowly scratching him as she knew he liked.

A small trill filled the air, and Ava started laughing, causing the others to join her.

"Pammon fly me?"

Callie's tiny voice rang out, sending everyone into a fit of laughter again.

"Come," Kaen said as he kissed her head. "Let's get married so your mom will stop telling me she is paying the minister by the hour."

Ava couldn't help it. With tears of joy running down her face, she laughed harder than she had in years.

"That does sound like my mother," she finally replied after wiping her face.

"Do you take this woman to be your wife? To love her, cherish her, protect her, and put everyone except your dragon before her?"

Kaen smiled as the man spoke those words. Ava had made sure the minister had added the part about Pammon. She knew the truth about Kaen and Pammon. She could never allow that bond to be broken, or both of them would be lost forever.

"I do," Kaen said, sliding the ring on Ava's finger again. As he did, his lifestone burned, the promise sealed by the rope wrapped around both their waists, marking the promise he had made.

She smiled at him, having felt the rope pass that commitment from him to her.

"Do you take this man, this Dragon Rider, to be your husband? To love him, cherish, protect him more than any other?"

Ava gave the same smile back as Kaen watched her eyes.

"Hold out your hand," she whispered.

Kaen's eyes looked at her, confused, but he did. He didn't have a ring, nor did he expect one at this moment.

She reached into a small pocket in her yellow dress, never having intended it to be her wedding dress. She saw Kaen's eyes go wide, and tears began to well up when he recognized the ring.

He glanced at it, at her, and then turned his head to Hess, standing behind him with the others.

Hess smiled, holding up his one good hand, wiggling his fingers, showing the tan line where his ring had been.

Kaen wanted to talk, wanted to ask why. As the tears rolled down his cheeks, he saw Hess smile and motion to Ava. Hess paid no attention to the tears flowing down his face.

A soft and gentle hand brushed his ragged beard, and that drew Kaen back to her.

"A gift for a Dragon Rider and from your dad to his son," she said, her voice struggling to keep calm.

As she slid the ring onto Kaen's finger, holding his hand that now shook almost as much as hers, she felt her lifestone roar in a way it had only done once before. She gasped as it hit, shaking her head when Kaen looked at her through his tear-filled eyes.

"I do," she answered as the ring slid into place and shrunk to fit his finger.

Kaen almost jerked from the force that hit him when the rope sent her promise through the lifestone.

For a moment, both of their lifestones burned, causing the rope to glow a bright white.

The gasps in the room, including the minister, let them both know it wasn't supposed to do that. After a few minutes, the rope returned to its normal color.

"By the witness of those present and the sign of the spirits who watch over us, I now pronounce you husband and wife. Now seal this vow with a kiss."

They stood there, intertwined by the marriage rope, having pledged to be bound to each other in body, mind, and soul. It meant more knowing they shared a bond beyond what most ever would. They had permission to kiss, yet both waited, taking the other in, gently brushing the cheek of the other with hands that each wore their marriage rings.

"I love you," Kaen said, drinking in every part of her with his eyes. "Since the day I first danced with you, I felt myself drawn to you. Now I feel complete in a different way."

Ava nodded and smiled.

"And I love you," she said, finally giving him a small wink as she gently gripped his beard. "Now come kiss me."

They drew close, their lips meeting as he bent his head. As they kissed, the rope grew taut, pulling their bodies together. Time seemed to go on, and neither kept track as they lost themselves in that moment.

Oh, please stop. I can't take it anymore . . .

They suddenly separated, the rope magically coming undone and dropping to the floor.

I swear, tonight I will need to fly far away . . . somehow, I can feel both of you now, and it will drive me to seek a mate.

Their simple laughter grew into a roar as the rest looked on, wondering what private exchange had occurred between them.

I'm sorry, Pammon. Perhaps you are old enough for that after all.

Pammon began to thrum. He laughed harder and harder as the thrumming grew.

When he stopped, everyone saw him smile and nod.

Go and hug the others. They are waiting.

They smiled and nodded, moving to their family, who opened their arms to receive them both.

46

A Hard Goodbye

Congratulations, hugs, kisses, and tears were shared by all except Pammon and Callie, who ignored the adults, choosing to *wrestle* with each other instead.

Lady Hurem had prepared a small meal with only four courses.

Hess and Lord Hurem were taking great delight in their children's marriage, discussing the future and what it would hold.

Sulenda and Lady Hurem were already discussing the announcement of this union and a place Kaen and Ava could call home and raise children.

Ignoring all distractions, Kaen and Ava sat side by side on a bench, fingers intertwined and making the most of their moment together.

"You still have to leave tomorrow, don't you?"

Kaen nodded slowly and kissed her on her cheek.

"I cannot wait any longer. I may never get a better chance for months."

She sighed, wiggling her shoulders and burrowing closer to him and his side.

"Then why are we still here?"

Choking for a moment, Kaen felt his face suddenly become warm, and Pammon let out a thrum at that same moment.

Tell Hess what you still need for this trip. He will take care of it, and I will get you two back to your place.

What . . . why . . .

Kaen could feel the humor Pammon felt at what was going to come next.

Your wife informed me you two needed to be alone for the rest of the afternoon, evening, and night. I was right in letting you pick her as your mate.

Using his finger, Kaen gently turned Ava's chin so that he could see her eyes. Behind those emerald green eyes was a spark, and he could feel the heat from her gaze.

"Did I really have to ask your dragon to help?" she whispered, the corners of her mouth slightly turned upward. "I had thought by now we would be gone from here within the last ten or twenty minutes."

"But . . . your . . . my . . . " words seemed to fail him as Kaen glanced at her and then at their parents, who were now noticing the small commotion where they sat.

"They are waiting on us to leave, you fool. Do you think they expect us to stay with them all day?"

Kaen noticed the smirks and grins from the others as they knew what was coming next.

Can you tell Hess what I need him to do after you drop us off?

If that means you get out of here quickly, then yes. Your mate is not going to wait much longer by the aura I feel coming from her.

Kaen shook his head in disbelief. Somehow, in that moment, he had been content to fulfill a promise to Ava, and everyone else had other things on their mind except him. Even Pammon was well aware of it.

"Well, if you all don't mind, my wife and I will be leaving," he announced as he stood up.

"About bloody time," Hess muttered, loud enough so that all could hear.

A few laughs and chuckles came from the others, and Kaen shook his head.

"Hess, Pammon will give you instructions on what to do. Have them ready by when we leave tomorrow."

Feigning a deep bow, Hess smiled and nodded.

Turning to Ava, he held out his hand.

"Ready?"

"Yes!" she exclaimed, almost jumping to her feet without using his hand.

Waking up the following day, Kaen felt Ava's hair and warm skin against his chest. He was still tired from the long night, but there would be time to sleep down the road.

He moved slightly, eliciting a slight moan as he leaned over and kissed his wife on her cheek.

"If I tied you to the bedposts, would you stay?" she mumbled, not opening her eyes yet.

Kaen chuckled and found a light blanket, somehow only wrapped up around her, and yanked a piece of it free and covered both of them.

"I doubt you could find rope strong enough to hold me, but no, I have to go."

She groaned, rolling to her side as she propped her head on her hand and flung her hair over her shoulder.

They lay there side by side, staring into each other's eyes for a few minutes.

A frown flashed across her face, and Ava gave him a stern look.

"You called him . . . "

"How do you know? Did he tell you?"

Rolling to her back, she lay on her pillow, the only pillow that had managed to stay on the bed.

"No, I can feel him now. He is close enough that I can. Last night, he was too far away."

Moving next to her, he ran his finger through her hair, slowly down and along her cheek.

She smiled, closed her eyes, and sighed.

"You are going to make this difficult if you do that."

Kaen laughed before glancing at the large closed doors. Ava had not wanted them to stay open as the breeze had been too cool late in the evening.

"Give me a moment."

Leaping out of bed, Kaen walked across the floor to the massive doors, not wearing a stitch of clothing.

Turning back before he reached the door handle, he saw Ava smiling and raising her eyebrows in quick succession.

Rolling his eyes, he chuckled before flexing a moment. Hearing her laugh, he grabbed the door handle, twisted the massive lever, and pushed with great force, sending both doors wide.

Right outside the now open doors was Pammon, staring at him in all his glory.

Ack! A worm! Quick, call the healer. My Dragon Rider has been attacked by a tiny worm!

Kaen lifted both hands, proudly displaying the middle finger on each of them while Ava erupted in laughter from the bed.

You think you're funny, don't you?

Pammon thrummed loudly, nodding his head as he came close.

Perhaps I can knock it loose. Hold still a moment.

Kaen darted backward, using every bit of the dexterity stat he had to quickly dodge the massive talon coming for his midsection.

Pammon stopped his attack and thrummed louder, vibrating the room so much that a picture on the wall and the jug of water on the table shook.

"He's impossible," Kaen declared as he moved toward his dresser.

"No, he is hilarious, and I'm glad he is yours."

Ava sighed as she lounged in the bed, covered with the blanket, while Kaen began to get dressed.

"I don't suppose you two would mind if we might put a wall up till I get used to Pammon seeing me like this?"

Kaen stopped, one leg already in a pant leg, the other waiting to go in.

"Like what? With no clothes on like in the cave when we traveled with Selmah?"

It struck Kaen odd that a woman's cheeks could turn red so quickly.

She growled after her initial shock and embarrassment ended, giving him a scowl.

"Should I mention Pammon offered to describe everything he saw?"

You two leave me out of this. I don't want to be a party to this conflict.

Slipping his leg into his pants leg, Kaen pulled up his pants and just smiled.

"You may, my love. Decorate however you want. In the end, all that matters is you are here when I return."

He gave his best smile, watching her reaction.

"It seems Hess did teach you a few things after all. That is a good answer, but never give a woman that much freedom. You may find yourself broke before you know it."

Tying the string on his waist, Kaen moved over to the bed, giving her another long kiss before slowly pulling away.

Opening her eyes, she let out another sigh and flopped back down on the bed.

"You two better be safe and not do anything stupid."

Kaen turned and looked at Pammon, who showed his teeth and started strumming.

Laughing, Kaen just smiled and shrugged. That wasn't a promise he could make.

"I got everything Pammon told me," Hess said as he passed the last basket up to Kaen after he strapped on the third one. "There are only seven of those arrows you commissioned. There wasn't enough time to make more, but I will ensure we get you a few quivers before you return."

Kaen nodded, looking again at the set of arrows strapped next to his seat. Their black feathers marked them as different from the usual white ones he used.

"I'm hoping I don't need to use them."

"Better to be prepared, I always used to say. Now, there is a little extra food for you, and the potions from Lord Hurem are wrapped a little better, and each is in a pouch that shouldn't leak even if they break. He says that was an intelligent move feeding him that one pouch last time."

Putting the last basket in place, Kaen nodded and tightened the straps around it.

You better make sure Callie doesn't forget my name.

Hess chuckled as he moved to scratch Pammon's neck.

"Pammon, I doubt she will ever forget your name. Sometimes, I think I should change my name to yours so that I can pretend she wants to see me."

A low thrum lasted for about five seconds before it ended.

"Take care of him. It's your job now."

Pammon put his head against Hess and gave him a gentle nudge.

I will make sure he is not behaving like an eggling.

"Good enough."

Kaen hopped down from Pammon's leg. He had been standing on it to get everything strapped on.

"She isn't coming, is she?"

Kaen shook his head and gave a wink and a halfway grin.

"It is easier on her this way, she said. I . . . " Kaen had to swallow the knot in his throat. "I think I understand now how hard it must have been for you the day we fought against the orcs and goblins. Leaving her, knowing that something could happen and I might never see her again, leaves a hole that—"

"Never goes away," Hess finished for him.

Kaen nodded as he bit his lip.

"Look at me, son," Hess said as he used his good arm to turn Kaen completely toward him. "You are more than just a Dragon Rider. You are a man with a good heart and some decent brains. Don't go into this planning for the worst. No matter how bad it looks or how hard it may feel, know that you can push past all that. Come home to your wife. Come home to your sister. Come home to see this old and crotchety man."

Unable to hold it back, Kaen laughed as he pulled Hess close, holding him in an embrace for a long time.

When they finally gave each other three taps on the other's back and let go, Kaen heard Hess chuckle.

"I guess you still haven't checked the stats on the ring, have you?"

Kaen's mouth dropped and his eyes went wide as he had forgotten about it with everything that had happened since Ava slipped it on his finger.

"No, but I will," he replied, excitement evident by the pitch and speed of his voice.

Simple Status Check

Kaen Marshell - Adolescent

Age - 19

HP - 2765/2765 (28%)

MP - 460/460 (28%)

STR - 42 (28%)

CON - 45 (28%)+4

DEX - 46 (28%)

INT - 36 (28%)

WIS - 31 (28%)

Blessings:
Dragonbound Complete - 25% current bonus to all stats
Blood Ring - +5 to Con
Wedding Ring - +3% to all stats. Unlocked: Rune of Fortitude - All HP are doubled.

Kaen felt the breeze blowing through his open mouth.

"Impressive, isn't it?"

Unable to close his mouth, Kaen nodded and then shook his head after finally closing his mouth.

"Three percent—"

"I know, and with Pammon, I can only imagine how that helps."

"And the Fortitude Rune."

Hess grunted and nodded, his face scowling a little bit. "One day, hopefully, you can unlock it. It is supposed to be legendary."

Blinking fast, Kaen focused on Hess, who was watching him. "All hit points are doubled."

"Yes, that is what it is suppo— HAIRY DWARF BALLS, KAEN!"

Hess's face turned red as he reached out with one hand, grabbed Kaen's shoulder, and shouted loud enough to be heard two buildings over. "Did you unlock it? How?! That means . . . "

Hess was shaking or trying to shake Kaen, who just stood there, barely moving against Hess's force. He glanced at the ground, his face bunched up as he solved the problem he was dealing with.

"All three of your physical stats are over forty," he whispered more to himself than to Kaen.

Hess turned his vision back to Kaen, who stood there with the slightest smile on his lips.

"Are you asking or telling me?"

"Mother loving, goblin humping . . . " Hess cursed. He spent another few seconds shaking his head before he leaned back and began to laugh. "You never cease to amaze me, son. I should have figured you had pulled that off somehow."

Kaen nodded, motioning his head toward Pammon. "I owe most of that to Pammon."

Lies. He likes to push himself. I just carry his growing body around.

"So, do you want to hear my real numbers without any items?"

Hess groaned as he took a step back and rubbed his face.

Please say yes. Kaen has been dying to show you he is bigger for quite some time. Then, I can make both of you feel tiny after he does.

Scoffing, Hess shook his head.

"Those are your secrets. I am proud of you for how hard you work. Keep them. Maybe one day I'll ask when I'm old."

"So tomorrow?"

Nodding, Hess gave a slight tap with his fist before letting out a sigh.

"It's time, son. Go do what you have trained for."

"I will, Dad."

47

Harsh Lands

You know we will be back, so stop worrying.

Kaen patted the same scale he had thousands of times before as they flew above the clouds.

I won't lie since you will know if I do. What we are about to do differs from what we have trained for. Elies didn't teach us how to interact with other dragons. He didn't tell us anything other than where to travel.

Tharnok did. Every day, he was abrasive. There wasn't a moment that he didn't try to break us with his will. You prevented that. I would have caved under his authority, but your strength and your power are what allowed me to hold my head up and fight against him. I believe Tharnok knew this day would come, so he did everything in his power to push us to be strong enough.

As the wind rushed through his hair, Kaen considered Pammon's words. Tharnok had been gruff the entire two years they had trained with him. He was always calling out their mistakes and pushing them to be better. It wasn't until the day he and Pammon left after freeing Elies from Havannath's binding that Tharnok actually spoke kindly to them.

Kaen shuddered as he let out a groan.

Are you cold?

No . . . I'm just agreeing with what you said and realizing that we are in for a difficult time. Imagine an island full of Tharnoks.

Pammon's head shook, working its way down his back and finally his tail.

That is a horrible thought. Next time, keep that to yourself.

Kaen laughed and felt Pammon's mood change through their bond. They needed not to be downcast if the next few weeks were going to be as challenging as they both expected.

* * *

"You know you're not a bad hunter. I'm still impressed you don't smash everything you kill."

Letting out a snort, Pammon blast Kaen with air from his nostril, causing Kaen to cover his food, lest it get covered in mucus.

"Not fair! Some of us like to eat without bodily fluids blasted over everything."

Perhaps next time you won't joke about how I hunt.

"It was a compliment, and you know it."

Kaen groaned, flinging the wayward snot off his arm and using the log he was leaning against to scrape it off.

Checking the piece of meat in his hand, he gave up and tossed it to Pammon, who snatched it in his mouth midair.

"Let's not waste anymore. I still need to eat a little bit."

Pammon's thrum filled the clearing where they were camped. The fire was going strong, and Kaen moved to procure more meat from the deer Pammon had brought back.

"These things are smaller than usual."

Yes, and quicker. They are much smaller than the ones in Ebonmount. It is probably because they have to forage, and the vegetation is sparse around here.

"We are closer to the desert. How many did you eat?"

Only five. I was tired of having to track them, and we needed sleep. Tomorrow, we will hopefully find some better game.

Sipping water, Kaen nodded and got to work eating the food he was cooking before giving the rest to Pammon.

Putting a few more logs on the fire, Kaen moved over and leaned against Pammon's side, letting out a chuckle as his dragon wrapped a wing around him.

"It's funny. If the world didn't need us and we could do this, I would be happy to camp out every night."

What about Ava? Would she be up for that?

Hitting his head against Pammon's scales, Kaen grunted.

"Really? I was trying to have a moment."

Pammon thrummed and bent his neck so that his snout was facing Kaen.

Consider it a little payback for what I had to experience on your wedding night.

A cough escaped his throat, and Kaen smiled as he cleared it with a few thumps to his chest.

"Wake me up at first light?"

Pammon smiled.

You did an excellent job avoiding the question. Yes, I will wake you up.

Nodding, Kaen smiled and closed his eyes as he slowly scratched Pammon's scales with one hand.

Maybe she would enjoy this.

Another day of hard flying put them below the southern borders of Roccnari. They skated the bottom of the kingdom to avoid any possible conflict or sightings. This mission required no one to know where he was going. If word got out, too many things might happen while he was gone.

You can stop looking for me. I will just eat the dried meat. Finish getting what you need.

A grumble came through their bond, and Kaen chuckled as he lifted a rock and set it near the fire he had built.

I swear this land is barren. I have seen only the tiniest creatures, and the one thing I ate was not worth the taste.

You are fine. I got my stuff here. Get what you need and return.

Digging through his pack, Kaen found his jerky and pulled it out, taking a bite as he stared into the fire.

"Holy elf tits!"

Kaen smacked his neck, looking to smash whatever bug had bit him, only to find himself pushing a small needle deeper into his skin. Pulling it out, he saw that it looked like a dart.

His eyes began to water, and he felt the world shifting slightly.

Pammon . . . someone attacked me . . .

His brain was swirling as he felt like he was lurching sideways, even though Kaen thought he was still sitting on the rock.

Hold on, I am coming!

Turning toward where the dart must have come from, Kaen strained his eyes, seeing a few humanoid shapes in the dark coming at him slowly, holding weapons ready.

Anger filled Kaen, his lifestone answered, and the sensation he had been experiencing began to clear.

[Poison Resist Skill Increased x1]

Drawing his sword, Kaen shook his head as the notification scrolled past, and he focused on the four people he now realized were all women. Clad in leather armor, they seemed surprised at his ability to stand and hold his sword.

Three of them lifted tubes and put them to their mouths.

He tried to dodge to the side and stumbled, his legs not working as they should.

Another prick sent a tiny shock of pain into his cheek.

He winced as he reached up, yanked it out, and tossed it to the ground.

"What are you doing?" Kaen asked. His words sounded like he was in a cave. "Why are you attacking me?"

The right side of his face felt numb, yet he struggled to his feet, pushing himself up off his knee and holding his sword out at them.

They were speaking softly to each other. Kaen could hear the noise yet didn't understand a word they said.

He could hear Pammon trying to talk or say something in his mind, but his brain couldn't register it. It felt cloudy and like one of the times Hess had hit him too hard in the head.

Blinking his eyes, he saw the women slowly moving closer, holding spears toward him.

"Don't do this," Kaen pleaded. "I don't . . . want you . . . to die."

Laughter came from the closest attacker as she reached out with her spear and knocked his sword away.

His grip held, but his arm felt like it wasn't working how it was supposed to. "Impressive . . ."

The words seemed to swim in his ears.

Fight. Fight for Ava and the kingdom!

Taking a few deep labored breaths, Kaen tried to focus.

For families . . . fight for families . . .

His lifestone surged again, burning hotter inside him.

[Poison Resist Skill Increased x2]

He felt his head clearing as his body did something with the poison. His ears were still ringing, the noise not sounding right, but his arms and legs no longer felt like wet noodles, and obeyed his command.

Grunting, Kaen snapped his arm back, lowering his hips and moving his feet into a set position.

The woman with the spear furled her eyebrows and glared.

"How is this possible? You should be unconscious or dead by now."

His eyes kept blinking, fighting the numbness in his cheek as he focused his eyes as best he could on his attacker.

"I am Kaen. I am a Dragon Rider."

The words felt mumbled, but the moment he said the last two, he watched as the women pulled back a few steps.

Words began to fly between them in a different language, and a look of fear spread across their faces.

Kaen saw the hesitation to believe what he had said, his eyes finally adjusting better, shaking her head at those talking to her when Pammon's roar echoed across the treetops.

The one with the spear pointed to the trees, and the three women behind her took off running. As soon as they had started running, the woman tossed her spear to the side and laid down on the ground, her face in the dirt.

"Forgive me! We didn't know!"

Moments later, Pammon flew overhead, turning sharply and dropping to the ground in seconds with a massive thud, sending dirt and rocks out in all different directions.

The growl coming from his throat made the woman on the dirt shake.

Wait!

It took everything Kaen had to force that thought out.

No! They attacked you! Let me chase them down and eat them!

Pammon's snout came close to the woman, whose whole body was trembling as his breath and saliva dripped onto her.

She didn't know!

And so they had the right to kill someone else? Why should we wait?

Give me a moment to think. I need to clear my head from the poison they used.

The growling increased as Pammon reacted to the word *poison*.

Poison? You want me to let someone get away with poisoning you? What if you had died? I should not have left you!

It isn't your fault, so just wait. I need a moment.

Pammon began to move around the woman's other side, flanking her and keeping his eyes on her as she kept her face buried in the dirt.

"I'm sorry," she muttered over and over. "Forgive me!"

Putting his sword back in his scabbard, Kaen grabbed his pouch, sauntering as he stumbled sideways every few steps.

Digging into his pack, he pulled out a waterskin and took a few sips before pouring a little over his head and splashing some on his face.

After a few more sips, he made his way back to the woman, who never moved from her spot.

"You may rise," Kaen finally said, stretching his jaw afterward, noticing a weird taste in his mouth.

"Forgive me," she cried out again. "I am not worthy to rise. We did not know!"

"We both realize that. Now stand up, or my dragon may not listen to me when I tell him to hold off on taking his anger out on you."

The woman nodded and slowly inched her hips up until she was kneeling with her face on the ground and arms still outstretched.

"All the way, please," Kaen said, rolling his eyes at Pammon.

The woman nodded, slowly raising her head, glancing sideways to see Pammon's golden eyes glaring at her.

She was breathing rapidly but did her best to regain her composure as she sat on her heels, looking at Kaen.

He stood there, arms crossed and looked her over.

With the poison mostly out of his system, Kaen was surprised to see how fit the woman was. Her outfit was a collection of furs stitched together and only covered her chest and mid-thigh. Every inch of her body was toned, with tanned skin that conveyed a power waiting to coil out and strike. Living in this environment undoubtedly had turned her into the warrior Kaen knew she was.

"Let's try this again," Kaen said with a slight chuckle, "I'm Kaen, and this is Pammon, my dragon. Who might you be?"

48

An Unknown Land

"My name is Tioanoe."

Pammon had stopped growling and moved his head about four feet from the woman.

Kaen nodded and smiled. Tioanoe's voice had somehow not trembled at all when she spoke.

Kaen stood there, watching her as she kept her eyes on his feet.

"Why did you attack me?"

She winced at his question and seemed to glance toward her spear a few yards away.

"We meant to rob you and take your equipment. You are on our land and do not wear the colors that show you have paid the tax. That means you are free game to any who find you."

She slowly moved her hands and tapped an orange and red sash he had ignored around her belt.

"Most wear it around their arms or waist to ensure it can be seen."

You know she is stalling.

Yes. I watched as her hunting partners ran off. She was willing to sacrifice herself to let them get away.

Pammon's anger still flowed through their bond, and Kaen did his best to block it out. He couldn't be angry that the woman had attacked him because it might actually be their custom. It was more upsetting that they had snuck up on him and almost succeeded in taking him out. Without his previous encounter with poison, he probably wouldn't have even been able to contact Pammon.

Let's find out what we can about these people. We both know various tribes live in the harsh land out here. Elies and Tharnok also warned us to keep out of the desert because you aren't large enough to scare off everyone. Who knows what we might find here.

Besides another way to waste the precious time we have?

Chuckling at the truth of Pammon's comment, Kaen saw the woman lift her eyes to see why he was laughing.

"What is the usual fee to travel safely through this land?"

"It depends."

"On?"

Her eyes darted at Pammon, who was still glaring at her, and then back to Kaen.

"Who is paying the fee and how strong they are."

Pammon began thrumming, causing the woman to flinch a little.

"How much would the fee be for Pammon and me?"

Tioanoe studied Kaen's expression and how he was standing. She could sense he was relaxed and doing everything possible to not seem intimidating. Not counting the dragon sitting next to her.

"We would only require a promise to be peaceful unless attacked," she replied, her face wincing as she spoke those words. "Those who are obviously stronger than most hunting parties would not be provoked. A lesson I am learning first hand."

Pammon snorted, shaking his head for a moment.

I like her.

She is smart. I will give her that.

"What if I promise not to hurt anyone unless they attack Pammon or me? Would that be considered a fair trade?"

Tioanoe nodded, bringing her thumbs and pointer fingers together on both hands, making a triangle, and putting it on the ground before her, bowing to touch her head.

"I have heard the promise and am grateful to accept."

As she rose, she began to undo the sash around her waist. "This is for you, Dragon Rider Kaen. May you wear it so my people know you can travel our land."

Moving toward her, Kaen took the sash she offered, tying it around his arm. It took one hand and his teeth to get it to stay tight, but he managed it on his own.

"Now then. I guess this means I do not have to worry about you attacking me again?"

Bowing once more, Tioanoe smiled and replied, "I would be foolish to bring any more dishonor to my tribe."

"Good. Then come join me by the fire. I want to hear about your people and this land. I don't have long, but I won't waste this chance."

Slowly, Tioanoe rose to her feet, making her way to the fire. As she moved, she kept an eye on Pammon, who followed her every step.

There is another in the woods, about fifty yards behind some trees. She must have forgotten she is downwind.

Kaen sat down on the rock he had initially been on and motioned her to join him near the fire.

"Would you like to tell your friend she can join us, or would she prefer to hide in the woods?"

Tioanoe paused halfway between standing and sitting. Her mouth hung open as she glanced at Kaen, who was smiling, and then toward the trees. "How did you know?"

"Dragon Rider tricks," Kaen answered, giving her a wink before rummaging through his pack. "Tell them to join us, and they can share some of my food."

Standing back up, Tioanoe put her fingers in her mouth and gave a short series of whistles. A few seconds later, another set of whistles came from the trees, only to be answered again by Tioanoe.

Kaen could see movement, and a young woman with the same brown colored hair as Tioanoe with matching leather armor appeared from the trees. She hesitated until Tioanoe motioned her to come close.

When she drew near them, the young woman bowed before Kaen and scurried over to Tioanoe's side.

"This young one is Krudae. She is a hunter with me in the forest. She won't speak because you have survived her darts twice. You must be a ghost or a powerful shaman who could steal her soul for attacking you. As such, she must speak with our queen and hear from her mouth that she can talk with you."

Elies had told him about so many different tribes, countries, and other communities that all had different rules and rituals. Even having been prepared, he knew his face must have given away some of the shock he felt at such a punishment.

"I apologize then that I could not succumb to her darts. It pains me that you must remain silent."

The young girl snorted and grinned while Tioanoe rolled her eyes before motioning for her to sit on the ground.

Both women sat while Kaen pulled out some dried meat and offered it to them.

They glanced at it, hesitating to take it.

"It's not poisoned if that is what you are worried about. I'm not that mean of a Dragon Rider."

Both women grinned, and Krudae leaned forward, taking the meat and splitting it with Tioanoe.

"Now tell me about your people. I would like to know more about your tribe and how we might work together."

"Why would we need to work together?" Tioanoe asked. "No other nation has ever come to work with us. Some have traded, but most have only sought to enslave us."

Kaen took a small bite and nibbled while he considered what she said.

"I'm not like most people, and I don't need slaves or servants. I prefer to help those who need it and find ways to work together if possible. I will be honest. I know nothing about your people other than how strong you are to survive in this area. Tell me, do you have problems with orcs or goblins?"

Tioanoe spat on the ground and scowled. "We see the green ones rarely, but usually, we deal more with the scaled dogs. They attack our people in packs and then run off, leaving us unable to pursue and bring about retribution."

"Scaled dogs?" Kaen glanced at Pammon, who told him through their bond that he had no idea what she was talking about. "What do they look like?"

Biting her lip, Tioanoe stared toward the trees to the south and took a moment. A log in the fire popped and sparked, causing her attention to be drawn back to them, and she shrugged. "Brownish scales, not as large as your dragon's, but like a snake, yet stronger. They can run on two or four feet and have long snouts. Some wear armor and carry weapons, while others use their hands and teeth. They are not strong by themselves, but they can be very dangerous as a pack."

Nodding, Kaen bent down, found a twig, and did his best to sketch out what she had described in the dirt. Although he was not an artist, he was decently gifted and soon had completed what he thought she was describing.

"Exactly!" Tioanoe said. "How do you draw one so well?"

Tossing the stick in the fire, Kaen reached into his bag and pulled out a book.

"I have read many books, and what you described was in one of them. It had a picture of one like I drew. They are called Kobolds. Are there many of them here?"

Krudae poked Tioanoe's arm and made some movements with her finger. Tioanoe nodded and made more motions with her fingers in return.

They are using their hands to communicate. That is impressive.

It would appear they are more intelligent than one might have guessed at first glance.

I did not get a first glance. I was shot with a poisoned dart, remember?

Pammon's thrum caused the two women to pause their communication with their fingers momentarily.

Tioanoe turned her head back to Kaen and saw him smiling at her. "Sorry," she said, bowing her head. "I forget that it might be considered improper to talk like that before you."

Waving his hand at her comment, Kaen motioned to Pammon with his head.

"We have our own version of that. No worries here."

Both of their shoulders loosened up, and they were a bit more relaxed as their fingers began flickering in patterns and movements.

That is how we must appear to others when not paying attention to conversation around us.

At least we don't have to move our body parts. Imagine if you had to use your tongue or talons to talk.

After a few minutes, Tioanoe turned and ensured Kaen was watching her.

"These *kobolds,* as you call them, have been a nuisance for the last year. Krudae has been on more scouting runs than I have and has spoken with other villages. She says there have been rumors of thousands across the desert and larger attacks on some of the bigger towns. It's one of the reasons we have pushed north into the forest. The safety of our people, combined with less game, is moving us from the land we have lived on for generations."

Both women had scowls as Tioanoe spoke. Kaen could see Krudae tightening her hands into fists.

"Our way of fighting puts us at a disadvantage against large groups. Most of our targets are down in a few seconds with a well-placed shot. Even a bad shot takes less than ten heartbeats before they are on the ground." Tioanoe paused and a smirk appeared. "Watching you somehow resist not just one but two darts to your neck left us very concerned that our poison was no longer working. Only when I learned you were a Dragon Rider did I suspect how that was possible."

"But against a group of kobolds, you would struggle to fend back their numbers in a straight-up fight."

She nodded. "We have strong warriors but limited armor, which poses a problem against their claws and weapons. We could use better weapons, but we have little to offer other kingdoms, and most trade is for specific herbs or other rare compounds."

Kaen scratched his chin, feeling that his beard was getting thicker. He had forgotten it was still growing, and Ava had commented on how it looked good on him.

"Perhaps in the coming month, I might be able to help. I could speak with Ebonmount to see if we could send weapons and armor. I'm not sure what we might ask for in trade, but if I have learned anything in the last few years, we need to stand together."

Both women began speaking with their fingers again for a brief moment.

"Would you really offer us a treaty?" Tioanoe asked, rising to her feet. "A treaty with a Dragon Rider would carry much weight when I speak with the queen."

Kaen extended his hand, watching her look at him for a moment before she took it, squeezing his hand in return.

"I will ask the king of Ebonmount to assist you. That is what I pledge."

A bright smile appeared on both women's faces, and they hugged each other, seeming to forget the fear they had earlier in the evening.

"Then it's settled. You two will carry my message to your queen, and I will leave first thing in the morning and continue my mission. Once I return, I will inform King Aldric of my request."

Both of the women bowed low, tears streaming from their eyes.

49

Towns by the Sea

Both women had promised to keep watch over Kaen and Pammon, even though he had insisted it wasn't needed.

The matter of honor had to be proven, and when Kaen left in the morning, each gave him a small gift. Tioanoe gave Kaen a small blueish rock with sparks inside it. She had mentioned that it was often traded and thus was valuable. Krudae gave him the small vial of poison she had shot him with. It only had a few doses left, but it was her most prized possession, and she felt he was worthy of it.

Pammon had allowed each woman to touch his snout and scratch him, making them smile as he trilled before they ran into the woods.

You cannot help but run into trouble and always need me to help save you. Perhaps we should stop camping at night.

I would like to think I was perfectly fine on my own. After all, I did manage to hold them off till you arrived.

Snorting, Pammon shook his body, thrumming at the feeling he picked up from Kaen. He could tell that Kaen was a bit embarrassed that he had almost been robbed and stripped naked by a pack of women in the forest.

Perhaps we should not tell your new wife about all this?

Slapping the abused scale on Pammon's neck, Kaen laughed, imagining Ava's reaction to that encounter.

Moving on, I still think that worked out well. A potential new ally and some possible new reagents for crafting. At some point, Aldric will tell me to stop making decisions without his prior approval.

I believe he gave that to you the day he entrusted you with the defense of his kingdom. I may have been dozing, but he had promised to back anything you do.

Scratching the hair on his face, Kaen gazed out over the two landscapes beneath him.

After a distance, the northern side grew into a lush forest, moving into the part the elves claimed as their own. Underneath him, trees became sparse, and it was easy to see how little vegetation actually grew from up here. Like a wavy line, the landscape shifted from a sea of green to splotched colors of brown. Off to the south, the harsh desert came into view, with no greenery in sight.

It is incredible that they can survive so long in such a rugged land.

Kaen lost himself in the thought of what had been discussed last night.

Are you worried the kobolds are part of Stioks's plan? I can almost read your mind with how much you think about it.

Nodding even though Pammon couldn't see, Kaen couldn't shake the feeling.

Could Stioks have managed to reach this far and help the kobolds grow? The few things I read were that they often did not get along with orcs or goblins, but there had been one time they had rallied together before splitting again. How much evil can one man and one dragon really sow?

Pammon growled, and Kaen realized he was thinking about Stioks. The more time Pammon spent with that man on his mind, the more rage rose up.

If we have learned anything over the last few years, it is that he will do anything he desires, including capturing a dragon and killing those who stand against him. The rest of what we have seen is nothing compared to those actions.

His lifestone flickered for a moment, burning with conviction as Kaen knew there would come another day that they would face off. He would do his best to ensure that he and Pammon didn't run away next time, but end it once and for all, if they could.

Two more days of flying from sunup to sundown left them in a sour mood. Pammon had angled a little north, moving into the forest again, allowing them to find food to help limit the amount of dried meat Kaen had to eat. The trip across the ocean would be taxing enough.

Camped for the night, Kaen studied his map, moving his finger along the five-hundred-year-old copy from Herb. His map-making skills were getting better, but it was evident that the landscape had changed.

"We are two days out from the coast. That will put us in the kingdom of Golden Edge —"

Pammon snorted, interrupting Kaen as his gust of air almost blew the map from his hand.

Who comes up with these names? Are we expecting the entire landscape to be covered in gold along the edges of it?

Chuckling, Kaen fixed his map, carefully dabbing away a tiny bit of mucus that had landed on it.

"No, you overgrown eggling; it's because of the sea. Supposedly, they say the water turns golden as the sun sets on it." Flicking the mucus at Pammon that he had picked off the page, he pointed a finger at him. "Stop spraying all my stuff with your snot. I'm having a hard enough time staying clean without having to constantly remove your bodily fluids from my clothing."

Please, I didn't complain when you urinated on me.

Groaning, Kaen turned back to his map. "That was one time . . . I'm sorry I had to go after flying for six hours straight. It's not my fault either. At least I tried aiming away from you."

Opening his mouth, Pammon began to smack his lips together, glaring at Kaen, who ignored his dragon's moodiness.

"Forget it. We're both grumpy. You and I know what will happen once we reach the shore. Are you sure you don't want me to try and get you something to eat from the people there?"

No . . . the taste of dried food sickens me. It has no blood or flavor, even with the spices you offer. I will try to catch something in the sea if I must.

With a sigh, Kaen nodded and made a few marks on the map before rolling it up and tucking it into his pack.

He stood and moved closer to Pammon, running his hands along the base of the massive horns jutting from his head. A slight trill emerged as his fingers massaged the scales bunched around it.

"I'm sorry. I shouldn't have snapped at you. Just a lot on my mind, and I know the next part of this journey will not be easy."

Nuzzling Kaen with his snout, Pammon gave him a playful push.

It won't, and I forgive you for snapping at me and urinating on me.

Kaen turned and tackled Pammon's neck, moving it a little bit as he bore down with most of his strength until his dragon lifted his head into the air, taking Kaen with him.

"You win!"

Dropping to the ground, Kaen patted the scales along Pammon's side, moved to his usual spot, and sat down. Leaning against his friend, he closed his eyes.

"Get some sleep."

Pammon snorted, not spraying anything on Kaen as he grinned. Bringing his head close, he nudged Kaen until he opened his eyes.

We will manage because we do this together. Stop worrying. We are strong enough.

Raising a hand, Kaen scratched the top of Pammon's snout and smiled.

"I know you don't like this word, but I want you to know I love you."

Pammon held his gaze, staring at Kaen as he watched his rider and partner for a moment.

I love you as well. Now go to sleep. Some of us have a lot of flying to do.

Kaen laughed and closed his eyes again, quickly falling asleep to the rhythm of Pammon's beating heart.

That doesn't look like a good place to land. They have weapons that look like giant harpoons ready to fire into the air.

Well, how far do you think they can fire?

Pammon and Kaen circled the harbor town on the edge of the sea. There were still four hours of sunlight left, and a bell was ringing from inside a building at the center of town.

Kaen could barely make out the details of people running and what must be a militia of some kind moving to the massive siege-like weapons on each side of the town. Eight total were circled around the town, and it looked like one in the middle, on top of the bell tower.

I'm guessing they fear dragons.

That's the dumbest statement you have made in a while. It seems overkill against a man on a horse.

Ignoring the jab, Kaen took in the landscape as they made one more sweep around the town.

To the east is a road with a good bit of room between the town and where you could set down. It wouldn't be that far of a walk for me if you dropped me off there.

Do you actually want me to set you down? Are you not afraid of what they might do to you?

We don't have a choice. I must fill up all my waterskins and collect as much dried fish and meat as possible. I'm not walking in naked.

Pammon huffed and banked to the right, aiming for the spot Kaen had chosen.

You better take everything. No stupid risks because I don't want to have to come and try to save you.

Don't worry. I am going in fully geared.

Walking down the dirt road toward town, Kaen adjusted his shield again. Every piece of jewelry was on him, and with his sword on his hip, shield on his arm, and bow at his back, he doubted the town would be dumb enough to try anything.

Stop thinking that. People are stupid. You are stupid occasionally.

Smiling, Kaen nodded and ignored Pammon. It was true. People took risks if they thought they had a chance to come out ahead.

The group of ten men riding horses had been slowly approaching him since he had left Pammon's side, making his way toward the town. They had landed over a mile away, giving plenty of time for him to get ready and for the townspeople to decide what they wanted to do.

Kaen made his way down the road, sticking to the middle section, as it was free of muddy ruts. He could smell the saltwater in the air, and the sharp scent of fish. Lots of fish.

"Hello!" Kaen shouted as the squad of men and a few dwarves got within fifty yards of him. He had stopped and let them cross the last bit of distance. Their horses were not battle horses. They looked like ones used to haul carts, wagons, or plows. Each of the men seemed apprehensive by the way they glanced at him and over his shoulder at Pammon, who was sitting and watching them approach.

"I am looking to trade! No need to worry!"

He saw a dwarf spit off to the side when Kaen spoke but ignored it.

When they got within ten yards, all the horses stopped, forming a line across the road.

"A Dragon Rider?" an older dwarf with brown and grey hair and a very untamed beard snarled. "What brings you to our town? Dragons be bad business!"

The other men shifted in their saddles, some wincing from the tone in the dwarf's voice.

"I am Kaen. That dragon behind me is Pammon, my dragon, and yes, I am a Dragon Rider. Seeking to trade for some food and water. I'm not looking for a fight or to cause any problems. Just to fill my bags and head off."

The dwarf eyed him, picking his teeth with his tongue before reaching up with his pinky and digging out whatever bothered him.

"It doesn't matter who you are! We won't be bullied by you or your dragon! If you think—"

An elbow from a dwarf sitting next to him caught him in the rib, causing the dwarf to double over and start coughing.

"What's . . . the—"

"Shut yer trap, or I'll hit you harder next time, you blabberin' fool."

Kaen did his best not to smile but realized the dwarf who had hit him was a brown-haired female. The curves were there, but most importantly, her beard was in much better shape, and the scowl she was giving the dwarf she had just hit could have peeled paint off wood.

"Fergive that oaf. He wanted to be tough and strong, but he be nuffin but a wool-headed, fish-eatin' fool. My name's Nisrin, and I'm the owner of the main tavern in town. If you be needing food, I'll be the one ya talk to."

A few chuckles came from the others as the dwarf she had hit glared at her. She ignored his red face and eyes that were shooting her daggers, smiling as she watched Kaen.

Yanking off his pack, Kaen dug in it till he found the map Elies had given him. Rolling it out on the ground, he also pulled out the map he had copied from Herb.

When you are done, come look at this with me. I want to make sure we both know where we are going.

A thrum came from behind him, and soon Kaen felt the ground shaking as Pammon moved up behind him. The bronze snout appeared beside his face, and they studied the map.

Reaching up, Kaen scratched the underside of Pammon's jaw and looked out over the sea.

"If I'm reading this right, we need to go west but slightly north. That would take us straight to where the dragons supposedly live."

What about the islands further north at the halfway point? Do you want to try to find them and rest?

Using his tongue against his teeth, Kaen found a piece of dried fish between two of them and reached up with his finger to get it out.

"Seems risky. Fly too far north or not enough, and we miss them. The real question is, can you make it all the way to their land without resting and only eating fish if you can catch any?"

Doubt and frustration came through their bond, and Kaen kept silent. Pammon had to be the one to make this call.

We aim for the islands.

Nodding, Kaen began to roll up the maps, glancing at the town again.

What are you thinking? I know you are distracted.

After putting the maps away and grabbing his pack, Kaen pointed at the weapons still around the town.

"Why have those if dragons don't come to your land? What would require them to keep working weapons on their shores? Nisrin told me that the other towns to the south and north along the water had these, too."

Do you think they have actually seen or killed dragons in the last hundred years?

Scratching his beard, Kaen slowly shook his head from side to side.

"I'm not sure, but something doesn't feel right. If dragons don't want to come here, they would not need them. However—"

If dragons were coming and were killed after a long journey . . .

Pammon trailed off, sensing what Kaen was thinking.

"We need to go. Now, make sure you have a wide berth. I don't like it."

Pammon nudged Kaen with the side of his head.

If they attacked, you would have to fight alone.

Laughing, Kaen turned and moved to climb on.

"I doubt it would be much of a fight, but yes."

* * *

This water goes on forever. Even with my vision, there is no end that I can see.

Kaen felt a weird sensation in his stomach. It wasn't fear, but it was perhaps awe and concern. They had been flying for only a few hours, and Pammon was right. Nothing but water as far as the eye could see.

Seven days of flying over this. This much water could drown the entire world as we know it.

Pammon huffed, beating his wings in a steady rhythm, using the right angle to help fly against the wind.

Those clouds look nasty. I'm not sure if we should head north now or wait.

Our angle is the one we wanted to go. If you turn north now, we would have to try to adjust without any point of reference. Do you want to risk that?

Snorting, Pammon stayed on course.

No, but this may get rough and wet if I can't fly above it.

It's a good thing I'm not Ava or Selmah then.

Pammon laughed, and Kaen gave his usual spot a good pat.

A sliver of moon hung in the dark sky as Pammon did his best to stay above the clouds. Lightning and thunder took turns, one illuminating the dark mass below them, while the other did its best to deafen them.

There was little Pammon could do as he flew only about two hundred yards above the clouds, frozen mist occasionally sticking to him and Kaen.

Are you sure you can handle this?

Yes. Keep going.

Pammon ignored Kaen's labored breathing. The air was thin up here. The cold might not affect him, but the air was taking a toll on his rider, and he knew it.

Four hours had passed since the sun set, and the clouds rolled in beneath them. Great gusts of winds forced Pammon to fly higher. Kaen kept telling him to keep going, even when Pammon knew they were at the highest point he had ever flown.

Underneath him was a blanket of dark clouds stretching to the horizon. The winds blew in different directions, sending the clouds into a swirling mist below. The light from the moon and the lighting created a view that might be enchanting if it wasn't for the real danger that lurked everywhere.

I can get lower. We should be safe.

A few seconds passed, and Kaen finally answered.

No. We both felt the lighting that almost hit you. I don't think it is safe. Keep going. I am ok.

Trusting Kaen, Pammon stopped asking. He knew how his rider felt when injured. He had carried him through the effects of the poison. If he sensed that Kaen was going to be in serious trouble, he would know it, and then he would act.

Fine. Then try to sleep. I can tell you are tired.

Kaen drew closer to Pammon's neck, helping to reduce the air that seemed to catch on his body when he sat up. In just a minute, Pammon knew Kaen was asleep. He could feel Kaen's heart beating through their bond. It was slow and steady. Slower than usual, though.

Wake up, Kaen. You need to wake up.

Pammon shook his body, jostling Kaen enough to wake him from his sleep.

I'm tired. So tired.

Yes. Eat something. Drink some water. I will lower us some, but you need to eat and drink while I let you breathe a bit better.

Kaen glanced below them and saw the dark clouds were still all around. The sun was up on the eastern side, a bright light against a dark cloth. The air was warmer, but it was still thin.

There is still a storm, it is too dangerous.

No. Pammon said, his voice carrying far more authority than usual. **You are being an eggling and do not realize how much danger you are in. You need to breathe, and we need to go into the clouds for a bit. Now take a drink, and then I will go down there.**

Kaen considered arguing, but his head hurt. A massive headache pounded like dwarves on an anvil in his head. His throat was dry, and focusing on anything was difficult.

Fine.

He sat up, swaying a little and glad he was fastened in. Trying to get into the waterskin he had under his vest was hard. His fingers and arms didn't want to work right for some reason. It took a bit, and once the top was off, he got the opening into his mouth. Sucking slowly, he felt the cold water rushing down his parched throat. For being so cold up here, he couldn't believe how dry his throat was. After a few good sips, he fumbled till he got the cap back on and placed it under his vest again.

Why do I have my skin under my vest? Why is it not in my pack or on my hip?

A grunt came from Pammon, and Kaen felt them descending from the sky.

Elies told you to do that. Don't you remember?

He did?

Kaen wracked his brain, but it hurt, and memories were fuzzy.

Soon, the wet mist from the clouds below washed over them, awakening Kaen's skin as water droplets began to sting his face.

He took a deep breath and felt a little better.

Keep breathing deep. I need to go lower. And don't argue.

Kaen obeyed Pammon, doing his best to ignore the clouds off to their side when they turned white for a split second, almost blinding him from how bright they were before going dark again.

Holding his head, Kaen let out a small groan.

Oh, that was horrible. I am sorry.

Pammon said nothing, barely skirting the tops of the clouds for a few minutes before diving back into the sea of dark wetness.

I really was an eggling. My brain was not working. I couldn't think straight, and I felt tired and strange.

Elies warned you about that. He told you, but you didn't listen. I could tell you were not yourself. Now, finish eating and drink a little more.

Smacking his lips, water flowed into them as they flew, cold and refreshing. It tasted so clean. His fish was turning into a wet mush from the constant barrage of water that assaulted it, but he put another piece in his mouth, chewing it and swallowing it. He did feel better after eating and drinking.

Thank you. I owe you.

Pammon snorted, making sure to not hit Kaen with any potential bodily fluids.

We will add it to the growing list of things you owe me.

Taking another bite, he glanced at the mushy remains and tossed them into the wind, letting it be snatched by the god of the clouds.

Do I want to know how long that list is?

Not now, but one day, I will tell you. Then, I will be the wealthiest dragon in all the lands.

Kaen laughed, laying down against his friend's neck and rubbing his favorite scale.

Even if it is only seven copper.

For just a moment, Pammon's thrum was louder than the thunder that filled the sky.

51

Mirages in the Sea

Kaen could feel Pammon's body beginning to tire as the second full day of flying ended. The storm clouds had finally faded behind them, and blank skies, baking them in the sun over endless water, was all they had experienced for the last few hours.

This seems like a foolish question, but are you sure you don't want to try and get yourself some food?

Pammon's stomach growled, and Kaen knew he was hungry. He had flown nonstop and hadn't eaten anything since they left.

You realize that if I go down there and fail, I will have wasted enormous amounts of energy. It is far easier to stay up here, ignoring my pain and hunger. Besides, I would most likely end up getting everything on my back wet, and I don't want to ruin your food.

Getting wet had been expected, but Kaen hadn't considered the energy it would take for Pammon to fish and climb back up to how high they were right now. It had taken a while for Pammon to catch anything back in Roccnari.

How long can you keep going?

As long as I must. Stop worrying about me. Just keep talking about something other than food. The endless amount of nothingness out here is more challenging than I had imagined.

Laughing, Kaen understood completely. It was overwhelming seeing nothing but water. The storm clouds had been their own struggle, but the constant concern about being struck by lightning had served as a distraction.

Let me tell you about when Patrick, Cale, and I got caught stealing ale from the tavern in Minoosh.

Pammon thrummed before Kaen even began telling the story. He could only imagine how bad that must have gone.

* * *

The fourth day had quickly become the most challenging of the trip so far. They were scanning everywhere, trying to find land, all while talking, and Kaen had run out of life stories to share before falling asleep.

Pammon was noticeably weaker; his breathing seemed labored, and his body had shrunk. Kaen had to tighten a strap because Pammon had worked off the reserves he had built up from all his eating.

The islands should be out here somewhere if we are going to find them. It feels like my eyes play tricks on me; I must double-check what I am looking at.

Kaen felt it, too, and he had not pushed himself anywhere near as hard as Pammon had. Staring at the water for hours on end, he had imagined seeing land a few times already.

It is hard not to ask how much further, but at some point, we must decide to keep going north or focus more on heading west.

Pammon's frustration boiled across their connection. He was tired and moody, and Kaen felt desperation in his friend's heart.

I will not give up. If Tharnok and Elies said the islands are out here, we will find them.

Not risking another argument, Kaen leaned against his friend, scratching scales and hoping it provided enough comfort in this challenging moment.

The sun was on its way toward the western edge of the water, having passed over them hours ago, never once letting them get a break from its steady heat.

Kaen's lips were chapped. The limited water he was drinking and the heat and wind finally took a toll on him. He was trying not to keep licking his mouth; it only made things worse.

He felt the surge from Pammon first. A flicker of hope that was different from every other time Pammon thought he had spotted something. It went on for a few seconds and then extended to a dozen.

Unable to take it any longer and knowing Pammon didn't want to give false hope again, Kaen willed his lifestone into a flame, closing his eyes and letting his power flow into Pammon as he had a few other times that day.

He could see through those golden eyes. Across the water, brown and some green dots so far off against the blue waters that had seemingly swallowed everything else.

Pammon was beating a little faster now, and Kaen could feel his dragon closing his eyelids some, straining to see as far as he could.

The land didn't move or waiver as so many of the other false images had.

Minutes passed, and they both saw what they were focused on becoming larger as Pammon shifted direction.

Is it really land?

Pammon trilled, a bubble of joy flooding over him.

I believe it is. It has to be.

Kaen kept sending strength through their bond, feeling his life drain slowly but noticing the difference in Pammon.

I won't stop this for a while. You need this, and I owe at least this for now.

Pammon didn't argue as he had a few times before, accepting the renewed power that flowed through him. His labored breathing was gone, and his body moved faster as strength filled his tired muscles.

Each of them locked onto that patch of dirt, knowing there was a chance for rest if what they saw was really the promise of land.

Look, Pammon said after about thirty minutes. Kaen could see how large the island was, and there were other clumps of land stretching out from it. **There are multiple islands, and I believe I even see a ship.**

Kaen saw what Pammon was pointing out. Over a dozen small islands were spread out behind the one they had first seen. One or two appeared to be larger, sticking up higher from the sea, and there did appear to be a ship further back.

That can be good and bad. What should we do?

Pammon mulled over the information he had so far. He was tired and had done everything he could to keep how tired he was from Kaen. He doubted he could have kept going if his rider had not shared his strength. Rest was the most important thing he needed right now. Food could come later.

I cannot do much if a fight were to occur. I need rest, and the best choice right now is to land on that first island and allow me to do that. Tomorrow morning, I will be fine to explore the other lands and see what we might find to eat.

Sounds like a plan. Start heading down, and let's fly closer to the sea. It would be harder for that ship to spot you, as the land will hide us.

Pammon grunted as he angled toward the shore, allowing the descent to pull him down without the need to use his wings for anything but gliding.

The waves beneath him rolled as he flew thirty yards above the water, keeping his sight fixed on the land before him. The trees looked different than any they had back home, but Pammon didn't care. All he could think about was that he had done it. He had gotten them this far.

Fish! So many fish!

Glancing down, Pammon saw what Kaen was looking at. Large groups of silver-colored fish swam through the water beneath him.

There must be thousands upon thousands.

Kaen was laughing, and Pammon felt it through their bond.

You could catch at least one of them in a group like that, Kaen teased.

Pammon thrummed, allowing himself to appreciate the moment. He had hope, and that allowed him to laugh.

I could try now if you don't watch out.

Kaen's hand rubbed his favorite scale.

Somehow, I know that threat won't happen, but even if you did, I would be glad you are returning to your usual self. I missed my friend, who was steady as a rock and rarely worried.

Pammon snorted, letting some mucus fly back at Kaen.

It had been too long since he had allowed himself to smile.

Trees had cracked and popped as Pammon landed in a tiny clearing on one side of the island. These trees were covered in a weird bark and had hairy balls at the tops of them. Their leaves were so different from the leaves back home.

Collapsing on the dirt, Pammon sighed as he wiggled himself against the ground, ignoring the number of birds he had sent flying from the treetops near him.

Sorry for the noise. My ability to be stealthy is gone right now.

Don't worry about it. Go to sleep. I will get what I need and set about searching the island.

Pammon let out a slight thrum, his eyes already closed as he prepared to pick on Kaen.

Please don't let a pack of barely dressed women capture you tonight. I'm not sure I would even wake up if you called.

Kaen chuckled as he dug into the baskets, pulling out a few things before jumping to the ground. He moved to Pammon's head and scratched right above his friend's eyes, eliciting a soft trill as he sensed Pammon drifting off.

Sleep.

Kaen had his sword in hand and hacked at the brown hairy ball resting on the ground near one of the trees. It sliced open, milky white liquid pouring from where he had cracked it. Dipping his finger into it before putting it into his mouth, Kaen smiled as the sweet and savory liquid hit his tongue. Carefully, he took a small drink, and then poured it all into his mouth, amazed at how sweet it tasted. Juices ran down his chin, and he leaned forward to keep the liquid from running onto his clothes.

He spat out a few pieces of the brown hair that had come with the liquid and looked inside the broken ball in his hand. A white material was inside. Sheathing his sword, he cut a little piece off with his knife and chewed it, amazed at the texture and taste.

"Hess and Sulenda would probably love to try this," he said out loud as he cut off another piece and chewed on it.

Standing there, chewing on this wonderful piece of food, Kaen's stomach suddenly rolled, and he dropped the brown ball on the ground.

"Goblin shite," he muttered as he scanned the trees.

* * *

Standing in the water, Kaen cleaned himself off. The water was so clear he could see thirty yards away, watching little fish play along the shore's edge. He had heard of sand, and this place had white sand all along the water line. Soft on his feet as he stood there, buck naked, cleaning himself after the liquid he drank somehow activated the need to do something he hadn't done in days.

Diving under the water a few times, he felt refreshed and energized.

Looking out over the water and back at the island, Kaen couldn't help but feel a twinge of guilt. Everything felt so peaceful and serene. They had just overcome terrible odds and managed to find the first step in their journey to the land of the dragons. All he could think about was if Ava, Hess, Sulenda, and Callie were here, they could forget everyone else's problems and enjoy life.

With a sigh, Kaen flung his head back, running his hands along his hair and wrung it out. After that, he repeated a similar process with his facial hair and strode across the shore to get dressed.

There was an island to explore, and he wanted to see what was out here.

52

A Surprise Encounter

Walking along the sand had been more challenging than Kaen had initially expected. Even with his strength and dexterity, the constant way it sunk beneath his feet was new. It was sometimes like walking through mud that gripped at your feet.

That thought reminded him that his boots needed a good shaking out as the sand had begun rubbing all over his skin. It seemed to want to stick to every part of his wet body when he had gotten out of the water.

He had walked a few miles, making decent progress around the small part of the island, noticing the trees were a variety of different kinds. He found one with massive bunches of long yellow and green fruit. The green ones were so bitter and horrible to eat, but the yellow ones were soft and sweet. Eating two of them had been as big of a risk as he wanted to take after how that brown ball fruit had impacted his gut.

Different small animals had been spotted. One of the most interesting was the massive boar that had rushed him. The thing was larger than many of the ones back home, and its tusks were over eight inches long. He had killed it easily and afterward had gutted it before moving it to a rock for the trip home. It smelled gamey, but if there were more of these to be found, Pammon would be in a much better mood.

With the sun setting, he started the trip back, dragging the boar by its hind leg toward where Pammon was sleeping.

Kaen lay against his partner, listening to Pammon breathe as he gazed up at the stars in the clear sky. The fire was burning brighter than he had expected, the wood from the trees burning long and hot.

He had put the boar carcass near Pammon's snout and poked him a few times to wake him up. Pammon had grunted and complained but, upon smelling and eating his snack, simply trilled before falling back to sleep.

Sounds of birds and other animals called out near them, but none wanted to come close. The aura Pammon gave off just by being as big as he was left them safe.

Closing his eyes, Kaen rested better than he had in days.

A roar woke both of them up.

What was that?

A dragon!

Kaen was on his feet, scanning the area as Pammon stood up, stretching quickly as he raised his head and listened.

Another loud roar washed over the trees, and Pammon's head turned, facing the direction it came from.

It's not on this island. What do you want to do?

We came here to meet the dragons. Sounds like this one might need some help.

Pammon grunted, bending down as Kaen grabbed his gear and quickly stowed it in the packs.

I am fine now. That sleep was what I needed, and I owe you for that snack. I dreamed I had eaten something last night.

Strapping his sword on, Kaen hooked his bow back onto the loop on his saddle and buckled himself in.

I'm ready.

Pammon turned, facing the direction he had flown last night and took two giant strides before leaping into the air and flapping his wings.

The roar came again, back from one of the other islands. Pammon was gaining altitude as he scanned the land beneath him.

Two ships on that island with the large hill. I believe it is coming from there.

Kaen could see what Pammon saw as he used his lifestone to connect with his dragon. A few men were on the large ships anchored off the shore, while dozens of boats were on the beach. A small camp was set up on the beach, but no one was there that they could see.

Find the dragon.

Pammon had turned into an arrow, flying toward the sounds of battle in the trees. On the backside of the large hill was a group of over fifty people, holding chains, working together to keep a green dragon immobilized. It was doing its best to fight back, but they had pinned its wings and tail, leaving only its head and neck still moving.

Kaen felt the rage inside Pammon as it rose. That fire that occasionally sprang up was there, and he knew what was about to happen.

It is one of your own. I will fight beside you.

Pammon acknowledged his statement and dove down toward the trees, preparing for an attack that Kaen knew would change the course of this battle.

The second Pammon was past the tree line and into the clearing where the shouts of the men and the roar of the dragon collided, Kaen saw dozens of men dead, bitten in half, smashed beneath the body of the dragon, others wailing in pain. It was carnage, and yet the dragon was in no better shape as massive metal spears were driven into its body, looped through its wings, and attached to chains held by groups of men. Others were preparing to drive more into its body when Pammon unleashed the fire he had been building up.

A solid stream of fire ripped across the clearing, a single line of death consuming the men and women who were unprepared for his attack. Before a single shout could be raised, one side that had held the chains to the dragon's wing was gone, burnt to ashes.

Pammon whirled as he came up near the dragon's tail, where a few attackers had frozen. Pammon dove down and landed on them with his massive back claws.

Kaen leaped off his back, rolling the moment he hit the ground, unleashing death with arrows at those closest to him.

The green dragon didn't waste time, snapping at those within reach of its jaws that had paused when Pammon landed. The green dragon killed two men before others began to back up and shout.

Kaen took off toward the chains, still holding the right side of its body. Even without the men holding the chains, Kaen saw they had driven large spikes into the ground, pinning it.

We will save you. Give us just a moment!

Who is we?

My Dragon Rider and me.

Kaen saw the dragon's head spin in his direction. Its silver eyes were wide as it took in the sight of him grasping the chain in his bare hands. He had put on his jewelry and, with all his gear, had no doubts he could break it.

Grunting, he twisted the chain, protected by the wall of fire still burning to his right.

With a snap, the chain link burst open, and with a few more seconds of using his hands to push apart the open link, the chain fell loose, freeing the dragon from one of the two that held it.

You are a Dragon Rider?! How?!

Kaen heard the voice in his head. The tone was different.

You are a female dragon?!

They were momentarily shocked before Pammon's roar brought them back to the fight around them.

Protect me as Pammon protects you. I will break this last chain.

Kaen ran forward, pulling out his bow and sending a stream of arrows at the men and women approaching him with weapons drawn.

They fell, most dead, and only a few injured as he got to the last chain holding the female dragon and slipped his bow over his back.

The dragon was leaning her neck toward him, snapping at anyone willing to come in this direction, providing him the cover he needed as he repeated the process again.

Ten seconds later, the chain was broken, and Kaen was thankful that when she jerked her wing, none of the chain's pieces hit him.

I have these over here, Pammon announced as Kaen saw fire roar into the air on the other side of the female dragon. **Take care of the ones near her neck and head. Most are running.**

Already moving, Kaen drew his sword, deflecting an arrow that came toward him with his shield as he covered the ground like an arrow. His speed was unmatched, and these sailors were about to learn firsthand the legends of a Dragon Rider.

He was a blur, striking down one person and another before they could react. Their heads and bodies were cleaved in half before most realized they were dead.

Kaen could feel the eyes of the green dragon on him as he looked like a bolt of lightning, not holding back and ending every life he got near.

Don't kill them all! We need one!

Pammon's shout pulled him from the battle rage that was flooding him. He slowed down, sizing up the last three people he saw. A woman and two men, covered in tattoos and wearing armor, stood near each other, holding spears out as they backed toward the woods.

Dirt flew up from where Kaen's feet touched the ground as the force he created propelled him at his victims.

The man on the right, a bit heavier than the other two and looking to own a few more tattoos, lost his head before the other two realized what had happened.

Kaen appeared before them, shield up and sword out. His voice was stern and carried no doubt about what would happen next. "I'll give you one chance. Drop those spears and surrender or die like the rest."

They froze, glancing at their friend, who suddenly fell forward, his head rolling a few feet in the dirt.

Both flung their spears to the side and held up their hands as they dropped to their knees.

"We surrender!" they shouted in unison, a thick accent coming from both.

"You have seen me move," Kaen said, putting his sword in his scabbard. "Don't make me chase you; death won't be quick."

Turning, Kaen ran to where the other two chains were holding the female dragon and wasted no time freeing her.

I will kill them! She roared as she shook both wings.

Don't. We need to talk to interrogate them.

Pammon's voice was firm and strong. Stronger than Kaen had heard before. It felt like when Tharnok spoke to them.

The green dragon whirled around to see the dragon who gave the order, and she almost stumbled.

You are hurt. Rest. You can have your revenge later, but you need to rest.

Who do you think you are telling me what to do? I am Amaranth, and no one will command me.

Pammon growled and stood tall, puffing out his chest as he moved toward her. She was regaining her footing as the chains had tangled around her.

Kaen backed away, keeping an eye on the two still on their knees, watching the scene unfold before them.

Pammon was slightly larger than the female, but not by much. She had to be older than him, but Kaen still couldn't believe how large Pammon had gotten. The only two dragons he could ever compare him to were Juthom and Tharnok.

I am not commanding you; I am simply telling you that you are hurt. If you continue to thrash around, you will tear your wings more, making your recovery take longer. Do you wish to be stranded here, unable to fly?

The female huffed as she eyed Pammon. She took in his size and his color. Kaen saw her cock her head from side to side for a moment before she eventually laid down on the ground.

I have decided I will not argue with you. I have determined I shall choose to lay here for now. Tell me, what will your rider do with those two he has caused to wet themselves?

Pammon thrummed, and soon, the female dragon, Amaranth, thrummed momentarily as they each turned their head to Kaen.

It looks like you are up. Kaen, this is Amaranth. Amaranth, you are looking at the last Dragon Rider, Kaen Marshell.

Kaen gave a bow and a smile before turning back to the two prisoners.

"You two, come here now."

It was impressive how fast they moved, so remarkable that Kaen chuckled.

53

Amaranth

After carefully removing the spears and hooks that had held Amaranth down, Kaen turned his attention to the two prisoners.

He found out there was always a regular dragon hunting party stationed here. They never knew when a dragon might appear, but they kept a group present and, over the years, had slain dozens of dragons. They took the goods to the north, where they were from, using their organs and scales.

It had been hard for Kaen and Pammon to keep their rage in check as the prisoners blabbered responses to any questions he had. Once he had gained all the information he felt was necessary, Kaen turned to Pammon and Amaranth.

I want to go and deal with those ships. I need to send a message that things will change; to do that, we must sink one.

What do you want to do with these two?

Kaen glanced at the two people, watching them tremble as both dragons stared at them.

I would prefer not to kill them because they can be helpful getting my point across. Together, they have witnessed what we can do.

You would let them live after what they did to me?

Kaen saw the rage in those silver eyes. The way Amaranth's neck expanded, and her chest heaved from frustration.

I would prefer to use them to prevent more dragons from experiencing what you did. Look around you. Surely, you must have taken out enough rage on the ones who will not even be buried.

Amaranth glanced around the clearing and let out a growl.

Look at what they did to me! To my wings and my body! Do you have any idea what this will mean? I cannot make the trip I had planned!

Pammon grunted and cut her off as she turned her snout toward him. **Where were you going?**

She huffed and shook her head, almost as if she was displeased with Pammon interrupting her or asking a question. *I am going to the land to the east. Across the ocean, where dragons who are tired of the council and their rules go.*

Kaen looked at Pammon. He could feel the pain in his dragon's heart.

How many have left for that place?

Amaranth glanced at Pammon and then at Kaen and saw how they looked at each other.

You should know. Dragons have done that for over a hundred years. What is it you are not telling me?

Amaranth . . . there are only five dragons I know of in the land you are heading to. We are one of them. There was another, but Tharnok left to come to your land a while ago.

Yes! Those two came. It is sad that the man died. His dragon is the one that told me of this island.

Kaen turned, moved to the two prisoners, and bent down to look them in the eyes.

"Do not lie when I ask this next question, or I will turn you over to her," he growled, motioning to Amaranth with his thumb. "Why do dragons not reach the land I am from?"

The man shook his head and looked at the ground. The woman held Kaen's stare, and she smirked. "We are not the only ones who hunt dragons. The king of the Golden Edge pays handsomely for dragons' eyes."

Kaen saw the look in the woman's eyes. She was more than willing to share with him the details of how many dragons must have died over the years.

When we get back, the king of Golden Edge and I are going to have a talk.

Kaen stood up and grabbed the woman by the throat, lifting her off the ground. She punched and kicked at him, but her attacks were nothing more than what a two-year-old might do.

He carried her to Amaranth, and she sat watching Kaen.

"You can do whatever you like with this one. She will not pass the message along."

Amaranth thrummed as the woman tried to scramble to her feet. The lack of air from how Kaen had carried her prevented the woman from moving, and Kaen turned and made his way to the man who was hiding his eyes.

"Look at this," Kaen ordered. "Look at this and make sure everyone knows what is coming if they do not heed my command." The man glanced at Kaen and then at the dragon, who was beginning to do things to his companion he would never forget. "I will burn down the world if they continue to do this to dragons."

* * *

Kaen stood on the shore, watching the ship sinking into the harbor. Men and women were swimming toward the other vessel as the man he had set free rowed as fast as possible toward the one he had left alone.

They have no idea, do they?

Kaen shook his head. "This world may always find the need to battle and fight each other, but I will not allow the senseless slaughter of your kind. I may be the last Dragon Rider alive, but I will live by the code Elies taught me."

Pammon thrummed as Kaen put his bow back over his shoulder. Even he had been impressed with how far Kaen could shoot when he focused on something. The hole he had punched into the side of that ship was impressive.

Who are you? I mean . . . Amaranth paused as she watched Kaen and Pammon. They had walked to the shore as she could not fly. *How do you have this much power?*

Kaen turned and looked at the female dragon sitting behind Pammon on the beach.

Tapping his chest where his lifestone was, Kaen gave her a stern look.

"In here is what drives me. I will protect the innocent, and I will destroy those who seek to bring destruction for selfish gains. That is why I am headed to your land and must seek the council."

Amaranth looked at Kaen, threw her head into the sky, and broke into a loud thrum.

Oh, I cannot believe how fortunate I am, she said after laughing for a while. *I will join you and take you to my land. I cannot wait to see how the council deals with you.*

They spent two days resting on that island as Pammon and Kaen let Amaranth heal. During that time, it answered the question Kaen had been wondering.

A dragon that heals. That seems hard to believe.

Bah. I have been nothing more than a servant, ordered by the council to heal whoever got hurt during some fight. I could not do what I wanted because my power was deemed too critical. Imagine living your whole life under someone else's rule!

Kaen nodded and could sense the dragon's frustration.

And you are over fifty years old? I thought you would be larger by this age.

I might have thought someone would have taught you manners. As dragons, we do not discuss one's size. It is important; calling someone small is an excellent way to get eaten.

Pammon broke into laughter as he swallowed the boar he had been chewing.

Please do not eat him. He wouldn't taste good, and I would have to deal with his family back home.

Amaranth thrummed as she turned back to the boar Pammon had gotten her.

You will be looked upon with great interest for being as large as you are and not even four years old. It may strike fear into the hearts of some.

Chuckling, Kaen turned to his food and glanced at the map again.

The last thing we need is for him to get a big head.

The following day, they left, following Amaranth as she raced high into the sky, excited to return with her new friend and ally.

Kaen and Pammon talked about some of the things she had mentioned, and both were concerned with what they had learned.

I still cannot believe that dragons have been trying to come to our land for almost a hundred years. If what Amaranth said is true, then a hundred or more dragons have died, with less than a handful making it past the traps set for them.

We know the history of Dragon Riders. It makes sense that they would limit any chance for dragons to return, possibly have eggs, and allow what took place with us.

Rubbing his usual scale on Pammon, Kaen groaned as the wind swept over them. He saw Amaranth occasionally glancing back, but she seemed content to have Pammon behind her.

I wonder what the council will do when they hear about the people hunting them on the islands.

Neither knew if that would earn them points, but based on how Amaranth spoke of the council, they appeared to need as many as possible.

What do you think of her?

Of Amaranth?

Is there another her out here?

Kaen felt the frustration of that question oozing from Pammon and realized what he was asking.

Are you asking me if I think she is pretty or a possible mate?

What? No!

Kaen laughed, and Pammon snorted multiple times, trying to get something to land on his rider.

Your emotions betray you, my friend. You think she is a bit bossy and grumpy and likes to complain, but then again, I'm not sure how other dragons act.

Pammon bobbed his head as they flew, remaining silent for a bit.

It's weird to think that . . . I must blame you and Ava for what I may be feeling. These desires I have were not there until the two of you and your wedding night. Now I can tell Amaranth is intentionally waving her tail in front of me.

What? What do you mean?

Look at it. We have flown behind Tharnok many times, and you have

seen how I fly. One's tail would only do that if they were intentionally making it.

Looking ahead, Kaen studied how Amaranth was flying. Pammon was right. Her back, hips, and tail shift often, flicking around in circles and sometimes side to side.

You are right! She is flirting with you! Kaen announced, laughing at what was happening. It is like when a woman walks a certain way in front of you, knowing she will draw your eye by how she is walking. She is doing that to you!

Grunting, Pammon cleared his throat.

What should I do?

You are asking me for advice on how to talk to a female dragon? I could barely figure out how to speak with Ava, let alone any of the other countless women who shot me down.

Pammon thrummed a little and then stopped as he stared ahead.

Well, don't go blind from staring. I guess we will figure this all out in due time.

Pammon growled and gave a playful shake, causing Kaen to bang into his neck a little.

No jokes. Promise now, or I will find a way to make you pay.

I won't promise that, and you know it. If I can't make you suffer like you have made me suffer, how would that make life fair?

Bending his neck so he could look Kaen in the eye, Pammon glared at him.

I may need to nut rack you again.

Scratching Pammon's scales, Kaen chuckled and motioned ahead where Amaranth was staring back at the two of them.

I think she is looking and wondering why you aren't paying attention to her.

Pammon let out a sigh.

You are going to make me suffer, aren't you?

Just a little.

54

Land of the Dragons

As the western edge of the sea turned from water to a land mass stretching from north to south, Kaen let out a small sigh.

We made it. We actually made it.

Pammon grunted in agreement as he flew slightly ahead of Amaranth.

They had taken turns flying out ahead while the other drafted off to the side.

Tharnok had taught them this trick, and Amaranth informed them that most dragons only flew together if the council called a gathering.

I am still nervous as to how this might go. A land filled with dragons. I cannot imagine what this will be like.

Kaen scratched Pammon's neck, feeling his friend's hesitation through their bond. Imagining a land where there were almost no humans or other races. He fought back a shudder when Kaen considered how fights between dragons might ravage a land.

No matter what, I am here with you. You are not alone in this.

Pammon nodded, focusing on the land that was racing toward them.

Large mountains ran along the entire coastline, rising miles into the air and creating a barrier to those who might risk landing a ship here. The waves beat against stone cliffs, sending water into the air in a mist before falling back to the sea.

Trees dotted the land about a mile past the sea's edge and ran up the mountains, creating a lush green carpet that stretched as far as Kaen could see.

This place looks like something out of a dream.

As they approached the edge of the land, Amaranth moved up next to them.

You two need to follow me and keep your eyes open. There will be those who will come to greet us, but we must head to the council first. Your presence must be announced to them by you.

Pammon fell behind Amaranth, letting her move to the front as they slowly descended from the clouds.

No matter what happens, I will protect you.

Kaen felt the force behind that statement. There was a form of pressure that almost overwhelmed him as Pammon seemed to have changed somehow.

What is it? What is different?

A moment passed before Pammon finally spoke.

When I was small and weak, you and Hess protected me. You two shielded me from those who might seek to harm me. Even though I was foolish and felt I was able to overcome anything, both of you were willing to risk everything for me. Here, I realize you may be how I was. You may believe you are a Dragon Rider and, as such, stronger than you really are. Pammon paused, adjusting his direction as Amaranth shifted to south. **Keep all of your items and weapons on you.**

Kaen almost said something, but he held back. Pammon was right. In a land of dragons, he was weak compared to them.

After crossing over the mountains that bordered the sea, the land continued in a lush landscape with rivers and streams running along the base of the mountain before collecting in a large lake.

Kaen's lifestone was burning as he took in everything Pammon saw. Animals were scattered through the woods and grassy areas. Different kinds of deer, boars, horses, goats, and other creatures he had not seen before were abundant.

How are there so many animals? Don't you all eat a lot?

Amaranth thrummed as she glanced back at Kaen and Pammon.

We eat a lot, but there are no other predators here. We have removed those who might eat what we consume. The land is lush, and there is an abundance of rain from the sea. There have been years where the council has ordered us to eat even more because the animals have become so abundant. If our numbers were greater, then we might have to eat less, but that problem usually handles itself.

Pammon turned to look at Kaen before looking back at Amaranth.

Handles itself how?

Amaranth adjusted her speed to fly right next to Pammon, her silver eyes taking him in.

Dragons fight, and almost always, the loser dies. I have prevented a few of those deaths when I have been ordered to, but part of this land is claiming and holding it. Some factions here sometimes work together to push their boundary out, and when that happens, a dragon dies. The council only steps in when it must.

Kaen grumbled to himself. Amaranth had remained tight-lipped about the council and would not go into more details no matter how much he or Pammon had asked. She had stated that they would understand for themselves once they met them.

Twenty minutes into their flight, Pammon tensed up.

A yellow dragon is coming this way.

Kaen saw the dragon, its path set to converge with theirs.

Ignore that dragon. She is a pain.

She? You can tell that from here.

Amaranth started to thrum as she continued on the path she was leading them.

Yes. She is Glynnis, and this is where she typically hunts and waits for the one she mates with. Prepare yourself. She will ask more questions than you have bothered me with.

A snort came from Pammon, and Kaen gave him a gentle smack on the neck as he felt the amusement through their bond.

You do ask a lot of questions, and we both know it.

Yes, because you fail to ask any.

The yellow dragon came upon them, and right before she had reached them, Amaranth slowed down and hovered, waiting for what was coming.

A new dragon! And a rider as well! Welcome! Tell me who you are! I am Glynnis, and welcome to my home!

Pammon let out a soft thrum, and Kaen smiled, feeling the excitement and joy that washed over him as the female dragon came right up next to them, almost touching Pammon as she hovered near them. Her silver eyes drank in everything she saw.

I am Pammon, and this is my rider, Kaen. Thank you for welcoming us.

A Dragon Rider, how strange. We had one come just a few weeks or so ago. Did you know him? Did you know he was sick? It is a shame that he passed. His dragon, Tharnok, has not been one to trifle with since. Is that why you came? Do you—

Amaranth roared, cutting off the yellow dragon and causing her to slow down and fly back away from Pammon.

Enough Glynnis. We are headed to the council. There will be time for questions, but now is not that time. If you will excuse us.

Amaranth started shifting her weight and changing directions to begin flying again when Glynnis darted out before her. Kaen was amazed at how quickly the yellow dragon moved, who was basically the same size as Amaranth.

You don't know? Oh, that is funny indeed. You might want to reconsider going to the council. They are furious with you. They gave a decree. It was not a nice one. You should reconsider. I can take the new dragon, and you can go hide for a while.

Amaranth flew backward, turning her body and looking at Pammon and Kaen.

What do you mean? What decree?

Kaen and Pammon could sense the fear in her tone as she spoke.

Glynnis let out a thrum, which got louder and lasted a bit before she turned her silver eyes upon Amaranth.

I will not say, but choose. I can take them and you can hide, or you can fly to your own demise. I know what I—

Enough, Pammon interrupted. **She will lead us. We must go, but thank you again for the welcome.**

A snort came from the yellow dragon as she turned her snout toward Pammon and studied him momentarily.

With a huff, she stopped flapping her wings, plummeting toward the ground before twisting midair and suddenly darting off in the direction she had come.

That flying is impressive. She moves so fast and is very nimble.

I thought the same thing. I need to try and practice what she just did.

Both of them looked up and saw Amaranth watching the two of them.

Are you sure you want me to lead you? If they have made a decree, it could mean anything. I had not realized how upset they might be with me.

You brought us here. That should count for something.

Not replying, Amaranth continued to flap her wings as she hung in the air for another few seconds before turning.

Then we need to go. I need to make sure we arrive at the council on our own terms.

They had slowly climbed higher into the sky, hiding among the clouds as they flew in the direction Amaranth was leading them.

How much further?

One more day. We will move down to the forest later tonight, and we can hunt. Once we do, we should be fine to sleep until morning and reach the mountain the council resides in later in the evening.

Pammon shook his head as he considered how far in the council must be.

Another day. How large is this land?

It would take about seven days or more to fly from the top to the bottom, and it is at least four days across, depending on if one flew nonstop. There is a line of mountains near the middle that serves as the border for two of the factions. On the other side is another set of mountains stretching to the other end of our land. Two other factions reside over there. The fifth is far south and not bothered that often, as a large part of their land is covered in ice.

Does each of these factions fight that often?

Only when one intrudes on their land for more than a brief visit. Fights break out if they stay too long, laying claim to what is below. Other fights occur when male dragons seek to influence or steal a female from a faction. Sometimes . . .

Amaranth stopped talking for a moment as she scanned the land below them.

Sometimes, the council trades and offers male or female dragons to the other factions. Many do not like this but are unable to resist the power they have. The choice is to be bound to another clan or a mate or leave our land.

Kaen and Pammon both realized now why Amaranth must have left this place. To have the skill she possessed, as well as being female, meant she was probably being forced into a relationship or faction she did not want.

They remained silent that night as Kaen considered what kinds of dragons could wield that kind of power over a nation of dragons.

Pammon lay down on the green grass, his belly fuller than it had been in over a week. He had gorged himself on many different animals, sampling everything close. Amaranth had been a little pickier, tracking down her favorite deer and eating her fill before returning to where Kaen was.

You two are an interesting pair. How long have you two been together?

"Almost four years. Since the day he hatched," Kaen stated as he lay against Pammon's chest. "He was a handful but eventually stopped being an eggling."

Amaranth laughed at that statement and nodded. We have that same problem with new dragons. Learning to submit is a tricky thing. Tell me, how did you force Pammon to obey?

A thrum arose from Pammon, bouncing Kaen off the side of his body as both of them laughed.

"I never forced him to obey me. He is his own being, and we learned the hard way that we each make mistakes."

Some of us more than others.

Both laughed again as Amaranth's silver eyes sparkled in the light of the fire.

You two seem more . . . like you enjoy life. That you are not concerned with the things other dragons here are focused on. Why is that?

Because we are bonded. Dragons with a rider do not care about petty things like land, gold, or whatever else drives others. We care about our riders, and they care about us.

Reaching an arm so he could scratch Pammon's scales, Kaen nodded. "We do what is best for both of us and discuss how to handle things. Sometimes the moment doesn't allow that, but we trust the other and often know what the other is thinking."

Shaking her head, Amaranth laid it on the ground as she began to close her eyelids.

Tomorrow will be interesting. I have no idea how the council will treat me, but getting to see how they deal with the two of you might explain some things about the other dragon and his rider.

55

Enjoying the Fruits of the Land

Kaen sat up when Amaranth finished talking.

What? What are you talking about?

The green dragon shook her head.

It's late, and I am tired from flying for days. Tomorrow, I will share the little I know. For now, let me sleep.

Pammon started to stir, and Kaen could feel the frustration through their bond.

Let it go. I'm not sure why she said that, but I believe part of it is to rile us up. She enjoys it.

Yes, she does. I can feel her laughing inside. She will learn that I am not amused by these petty things.

Kaen couldn't help the laugh he let escape as Pammon settled back down.

Go to sleep. I know you are just as tired as she is. We will deal with what comes our way.

His dragon did what he always did, and turned his head and rested his snout against Kaen's side.

Kaen reached over and put his hand on his partner's nose and began to scratch it gently, smiling as a small trill sounded before it disappeared, lost to sleep that was long overdue.

Closing his eyes, Kaen thought about Elies and what he had said to him.

Tomorrow, he and Pammon would meet the Council of Dragons and hopefully find answers to their questions.

I have not seen a dragon eat as much as you have in a while.

Pammon grunted, ignoring the jab.

Stop wasting time and answer Kaen's question. What happened with the council and Tharnok?

Amaranth turned her head and watched the two fly next to her. Both Pammon and Kaen had their eyes fixed on her, and she knew they would not drop it.

The council was not happy to see them. I was there, having returned from being ordered to heal a male injured in one of the disputes. To say I was angry would be like saying the sky is blue. I was furious, having been forced into being nothing more than a tool they use to keep their power.

When I arrived, Tharnok stood before the five, and his presence was intimidating. When he spoke, the other five were not their usual selves, even as old and as powerful as they are. They were . . . restrained.

Amaranth thrummed loud enough that even Pammon and Kaen could hear her over the wind and distance.

His rider was basically gone. The man smelled of rot, and I know not how he had survived his trip. His voice was weak, and yet . . . She paused again for a moment. *It is like when you speak, Kaen. There is a power that comes across. Something inside me hates it and respects it at the same time. Yours is different than his, and part of that scares me even more. The first time you spoke, it panicked me. I knew that in my weakened state, I was no match for you.*

Were you worried I would attack you?

I was chained to the ground, and my body was being torn apart by their hooks and spears. At that moment, I was afraid even with my healing, I was going to die. Yet when you spoke, and I saw you move, I knew had you chosen to kill me, and I could not have prevented it. I doubt you know how that makes me feel as a dragon. To know that a human has that kind of power.

Pammon thrummed, his laughter filling the sky around them, and Amaranth looked at him angrily.

Do you think that is funny?

Shaking his head, Pammon gave a stern glare back at her.

Do not underestimate the dragon he sits on if you think he is dangerous.

Kaen noticed Amaranth altered her flying, moving slightly away from Pammon and Kaen. Her look of anger was gone, replaced with one of worry.

Please continue. We are no threat to those who do not seek to harm us and those we protect from harm.

Amaranth snorted and turned her gaze back toward the mountain she knew would come into view in a few hours.

Tharnok told them you two were coming, and they did not seem pleased. They argued for a bit about how a Dragon Rider could have happened. I couldn't hear some of it, but it appeared they were not prepared for it to take place ever again. As they fought amongst themselves, I saw Tharnok watching them, taking them in.

Finally, he spoke again, and for the first time ever, I saw the council afraid. They winced at what he said.

Kaen and Pammon waited for what felt like forever as Amaranth remained silent. After a minute, she snorted as she flew, and Kaen saw her chest shaking. She was laughing again.

He told them that you two were more dangerous than he was if they made you angry. He warned them not to treat you two as they do every other dragon when you come. He then swore that they were not to bother him. He would take his rider to his faction's land and bury him there.

Pammon turned his head, looking at Kaen with his golden eyes.

He could feel the confused sensation coming from his dragon's thoughts.

Does Tharnok really believe that about us?

Kaen took a deep breath, letting the cold air fill his lungs before blowing it out.

You and I both know Tharnok was a demanding teacher. He pushed us, yet after we resisted his command the first time, I noticed he was a little different. Once we freed Elies of his bond to Havannath, we proved just how strong we are.

Scratching his beard, Kaen stared ahead for a moment and continued.

We fought Juthom and Stioks and managed to hurt them and escape unharmed. It cost Tharnok his rider's life, and . . . Kaen paused, looking at the quiver on his side. *Seven arrows were all he had. Specifically made to fight against a dragon. If we had these when we fought Juthom . . . Perhaps I could have delivered a blow that would have won the war.*

Snorting, Pammon faced forward, disbelief coming across their bond.

I doubt seven arrows would have made a difference. We have not even had a chance to test them yet.

No, we haven't, but you saw what I did with regular arrows. These are different.

Kaen gave a gentle tap to the scale he always touched when flying. He knew Pammon was just as scared as he was about fighting a dragon head-on. They had gotten the jump on Juthom, which had allowed them to get away safely. Had the roles been reversed . . .

Kaen felt eyes on him and glanced at Amaranth, who was watching them.

Sorry. We were discussing things.

I could tell. You and the other Dragon Rider were alike. I offered my skill to Tharnok and tried to heal his rider of the sickness that plagued him. Ultimately, I could only add a few days to his life. Had I been there years ago, I could have done more, but there was little left of the man who rode on that dragon's back.

Amaranth smiled as she turned her gaze back to where she was flying.

Tharnok told the council he would require my aid to ensure that Elies could make the trip to his faction's land. They balked at first, but one of them said something, and they consented. Again, I saw them afraid. It's not something they have ever shown before.

How old are these dragons who sit on the council?

I do not know for sure, but every one of them is easily over four hundred years old. There have been rumors of one being over six hundred years old, but that is hard to imagine. They may not be strong like one thinks a dragon might be. It isn't some brute power behind them.

Kaen saw Amaranth shudder as she flew.

Over a hundred years ago, one of the council members, Valthor, had a member of her own faction try to rise up and take her position. The male dragon was well over two hundred years old and felt his time had come. Her breath melted the scales off him, it is told. Even as strong as the stories speak of him, he succumbed to her first fatal attack. Since then, no other council member has been challenged, and I doubt any will.

Kaen felt Pammon shifting under him as they flew.

How large is she compared to Tharnok?

She is at least a third bigger than Tharnok.

Kaen felt his heart skip a beat as he considered the size difference. Tharnok had been at least a third bigger than Pammon the last time they had seen him. If this Valthor was that much bigger than him . . .

So she is twice the size of us?

At least. And yet their size difference seemed to mean nothing to them when facing him. Even with all five present.

Kaen felt himself laugh. Even as terrifying as that sounded, he remembered the first time he and Pammon had met Tharnok face to face. The fear had been overwhelming.

And yet he told them we were stronger.

Amaranth's thrum of could be heard again over the wind. She laughed harder than she had last time.

I spoke with Tharnok after he traveled to his faction's land. They had given him a wide berth, and he picked a spot he deemed worthy of his rider's final resting place. I watched Elies, healing him as much as possible while Tharnok collected stones and used his talons to shape them. He dug a grave, and we waited.

For a full day, Tharnok had said nothing to me other than to ask me to stop healing Elies.

As the moments passed and his rider drifted off, Tharnok told me about the land he was from. He told me of the dream you and your dragon have. He told me of the battle that was to take place. In pity, I think he also told me the truth. That I would never be anything but a tool for the council, and if I desired to be something more than that, I must flee and make the trip many have tried, and I failed.

She turned silent again, and Kaen could sense something was different. Watching her closely, Kaen saw the wind sweep a few clear drops from her silver eyes.

Your friend showed me more kindness in the few days I knew him than my own faction had in my entire life. He told me to go when he knew Elies was taking his last breath. He told me what would happen once his rider actually died. The rage that would overcome him.

Pammon let out a deep sigh, and Kaen reached over and rubbed his favorite scale.

What is it?

We both know what happens when the rider dies. If Tharnok has been overtaken by grief and rage, do you really think we'll be able to reach him? He warned us about it.

Tsking his tongue against his teeth, Kaen tried to consider the truth of that question. If Tharnok was consumed by rage, could they hope to speak with him? Was there a chance he would still be sane?

I'm willing to try, at least if you are. There must be a part of him that hasn't given over to the grief.

Doubt swept through the bond, telling Kaen his dragon didn't feel so confident. Turning his attention back to Amaranth, Kaen knew what he needed to ask.

How long ago was all this?

A little over two weeks. I assume you know how bad he has become. The council is at a loss, and Aethux, the faction leader and council member of Tharnok's location, cannot do anything about it. Two younger male dragons were sent to try and deal with Tharnok, who has ravaged a wide area of land anytime someone comes near him.

Again, Kaen noticed the shudder she experienced even while flying.

How bad was it?

The rumor is neither male landed a hit before Tharnok killed them both. Since then, a large portion of Aethux's land has become a wasteland. No one will risk flying near it, and the other dragons in the faction have been forced to stay closer to each other, creating conflict within the faction. If something isn't done soon, there is no telling how many more might die.

Kaen's heart broke, and he felt Pammon reacting the same way.

You know what we must do.

I do. When the time comes, if we cannot reach him, we will find out just how strong we are.

56

The Council

The mountain range Amaranth had mentioned looked nothing like she had described. Neither Pammon nor Kaen could fault her. The size was even greater than the mountains surrounding Ebonmount.

Prominent black peaks rose so high into the sky that neither Pammon nor Kaen felt a dragon could fly that high. Ice covered the top of the mountain, and even with the sun hitting it directly, a glare could be seen the moment the mountains came into view.

Does that snow ever melt?

No. It has been like that for as long as anyone can remember. Ages ago, dragons used to compete to see who could fly the highest, but the councils of old made them stop, as it was told that none had ever reached the top, and so many had died from the attempt.

Kaen could feel Pammon gazing up at it, almost mesmerized by the possible feat, waiting for some dragon to accomplish what was deemed impossible.

Don't even think about it.

Too late, Pammon stated, thrumming a little as his eyes fought to break free from the challenge. There is a part of me that just seems called to try it, almost like when I see a new animal to eat, wondering if it will be better than any other I have had before.

Amaranth's thrum broke the moment. Kaen realized they had not broken the connection with her as they talked.

Dragons still attempt it, ignoring the council's decree, and all those who do not die in their attempt suffer at the talons of the faction leader when they return. Pammon is right, though. There is a longing in all dragons to fly beyond what seems impossible to reach. Sometimes, that desire takes over,

and a dragon that managed to return has said they never intended to try and yet found themselves soaring up the mountain.

Kaen felt Pammon agreeing with what Amaranth had just said. He could feel the pull.

Wanting to find something else to focus on, Kaen asked, *How much further?*

You have asked that question way too many times. I feel like a parent telling a youngling we will get there when we get there.

Pammon's thrum cleared the enchantment that had held him for the last few minutes.

Kaen does sound like an eggling on occasion. I deal with that same question more times than I care to admit.

Letting the wind sweep his laughter away, Kaen thumped Pammon on the neck.

Some of us like to know those things. Now, how far are we?

Two hours or less. The real problem is what you noticed an hour ago.

Kaen glanced behind them and saw that the entourage of dragons was still there. Four of them were flying a reasonable distance away, but one of them, perhaps a dragon named Glynnis, had flown ahead and told others they were coming.

I hope you two are ready for this. By the looks of it, there will be a host of dragons waiting to see you make your entrance.

Again, the description Amaranth had used by saying a *host* fell very short.

The black mountain was covered with dragons, some in the air and others clutching rocks and crags, all waiting to see who the new Dragon Rider was. Before them was every color of dragon imaginable. A group of green dragons sat near each other on one side while two pink dragons circled high in the sky. A gold and silver dragon appeared to be fighting over a spot on the mountain to claim as their own, and yet at least fifty or more dragons were all waiting near the giant mouth of the cave that would lead them inside the mountain.

I could not dream of so many of my kind. Pammon's usual tone in his head seemed in shock. **Had you told me this was real, I would have accused you of drinking again.**

Snorting, Kaen couldn't help but laugh. He couldn't believe it was real either. His whole life, he had known there were a couple dragons in the land where he grew up. Learning there were six, once he had Pammon, had rocked his mind.

Now, it felt surreal as the truth of what flew around him became real.

We will ignore them. They will not stop us. Just follow me and try not to hit the walls of the cave. You wouldn't want to make a bad entrance.

*   *   *

The cave entrance was well over two hundred feet tall and even wider. How one might consider hitting the walls seemed impossible until Kaen considered the size some dragons must reach. The cave was pitch black, with the only light coming from the entrance.

Kaen activated his lifestone, joining himself with Pammon and allowing him to see the world through his dragon's eyes.

The cave entrance came to life. No longer dark, he saw where the rock had been hewn from something, with scratches and marks in the stone walls. Even a mile from the opening, Pammon's sharp eyesight let him see farther into the tunnel, watching it go on for a while.

How deep is this cave?

Amaranth must have laughed, but it was hard to tell for sure as so much was going on around him.

We will be flying for a few minutes. There is a grand opening inside. Do not worry; there will be light in there for you, but I'll let that surprise have its own moment.

A few seconds later, Pammon entered the opening, the rushing of wind and sound coming over them as they followed Amaranth, who glided effortlessly along the stone walls. She had plenty of room, and Kaen realized that Pammon did, too. A few minor twists and turns came, but for the most part, the tunnel was a straight shot with no natural rise or decrease of elevation.

Pammon was anxious, and Kaen could feel it through their bond. He knew he felt the same and wondered if the two were causing each other to be worked up even more.

Taking a few deep breaths, he calmed himself, letting that flow through their connection and into Pammon.

Thank you. I needed that.

Scratching a scale, Kaen nodded, enthralled by the sights around him.

Suddenly, a glow appeared ahead, and blue lines ran along the edges of the cave. Kaen could see through Pammon's eyes what looked to be some kind of metal deposit that ran like a stream all over the sides and the bottom of the rock. It flowed toward the area they were headed, getting brighter as more and more cracks and fissures filled with the substance increased.

A turn came, and as they made it, flying to the right, both Pammon and Kaen felt their breath catch as they saw the massive entrance opening up into a cave that had to be a mile wide and tall.

Sounds of dragons grunting and roaring had echoed through the tunnel, but now there was silence.

Bursting through the opening, they saw up ahead, raised high on platforms, five massive dragons that dwarfed them.

The council watched the trio enter. A gold dragon sat in the middle, the one Amaranth had called Aethux, spilling over the stone pillar he sat on. To his right was an almost plum-colored dragon, Valthor. She was nearly as large as Aethux, and her gaze felt like someone boring into his mind. Next to her was a massive green dragon, only slightly smaller than Valthor, and with scales like emeralds. They appeared to not even be concerned with Kaen or Pammon, instead fixing their eyes entirely on Amaranth.

To the left of Aethux was a dragon that to call white would be an insult. Perhaps silver or pearl. Its scales gave off a glow from the blue and white light that the ore in the room was giving off, filling the entire cave with enough light to see with Kaen's vision.

The last dragon was a massive brown dragon, bigger than Aethux, and his scales looked jagged and sharp compared to many of the others, who had smooth scales.

"Hairy dwarf balls," Kaen muttered as he stared at them.

Amaranth led them on a path, which brought them to a massive platform that sat a few hundred yards beneath the five enormous stone pillars. She landed, leaving room for Kaen and Pammon to join her.

Be strong. I will protect you no matter what.

Kaen felt the same tone as the other day when Pammon made that promise. The fear and nervousness that had been there a moment ago was gone. It was replaced by the strong will of a dragon whose sole life's purpose was sitting on its back.

As they landed and Kaen began to unhook himself, he felt pressure coming at them from above.

[Charm Resisted]
[Fear Resisted]
[Intimidation Resisted]
[Glamor Resisted]
[Charm Resist Skill Increased x8]
[Charm Resist Skill Upgraded - Aura of Resistance gained]

Pammon started to thrum, and Kaen couldn't hold back either.

Their laughter filled the massive cavern as they gazed up at the five dragons who sat there, shocked looks filling their eyes.

You felt that, didn't you?

Pammon gave a slight nod before turning to face the dragons looking down on them.

Greetings, Council. My Dragon Rider and I appreciate the warm welcome.

The tone Pammon spoke in shocked Kaen as he slid off his dragon and moved to beside him.

Kaen glanced at Amaranth, who he realized was flattened against the stone floor, her head pressed so tightly against the ground that she couldn't move.

Looking up at the council, he saw them taking everything in.

Shaking his head, Kaen glanced at Pammon, who sensed what he was thinking and nodded.

The fire in his chest roared to life. He was angry.

Striding to Amaranth's side, Kaen noticed the green dragon was trembling slightly, her eyes closed. She couldn't see him as he came toward her.

Relax. I am here, and I told you I would protect you.

He put his hand on her head, scratching the scales along the ridge of her tightly clenched closed eye.

Watching her, he willed his might upon her. He wanted her to know he was there and would do as he promised. Slowly, her eyelid opened up. He saw her silver eye watching him, and she was still trembling.

"Resist it. Do not let that fear overwhelm you. Remember what Tharnok said and believe."

Her breathing, which had been small, short gasps of air, returned to normal.

Kaen felt Pammon behind him, smiling with a sense of pride rushing through their bond.

He continued to scratch her head and then gave it a few gentle pats.

"Stand and be the proud dragon that I know you are."

He took a few steps back and watched as the green dragon kept her eyes on him. Her head turned, fighting an invisible hand that seemed to want to keep her pressed down.

A wave struck Kaen again, but he felt it wash off him like water on a duck's back.

"Ignore it. Stand."

With a grunt, Amaranth turned her head completely toward Kaen and began to press with her legs. Slowly, at first, she began to rise, and suddenly, whatever had been holding her down seemed to be cut off, and she almost jumped off the ground.

Her eyes sparkled in a way Kaen had not seen before.

Shaking her neck and head, she sat on her back legs, puffing out her chest.

I submit my life to you and Pammon. You have done the impossible. You have freed me.

Behind them, a roar louder than any Kaen had ever heard echoed through the cave.

57

Who We Really Are

Who do you think you are?!

Kaen turned and saw Pammon staring at the green dragon that had roared.

He is Dragon Rider Kaen. And who are you?

When Pammon spoke, Kaen felt him projecting a boldness that surprised him. Facing down dragons well beyond their age, who contained immense power, and Pammon had not flinched. If anything, Pammon was standing taller and making himself seem larger.

A hiss echoed from the side of the cavern where the green dragon sat. It growled as it lowered its head toward them.

I am Elynudra, and that dragon who has broken the rules is one of mine!

Kaen stared at her as he reached out a hand to his left side, leaving it there momentarily, and felt Amaranth put her head against it a few seconds later.

"It would appear she has chosen differently."

The dragon's eyes went wide, her eyelids stretching completely open as hate poured from them.

Kaen saw the look directed at him and, after giving a slight pat to Amaranth's head, moved back toward Pammon with a walk that appeared he was out for a stroll.

You cannot do that! It is aga—

A growl from Aethux cut off the tirade, and the green dragon turned its attention to the golden dragon.

Enough, for now, Elynudra. You act like a mother protecting a dragon that has aged past its time. Do not insult yourself, or Amaranth, anymore.

Kaen saw the look Aethux had given the Elynudra, and she snorted, slinking back slightly onto her stone pillar.

The golden dragon turned its eyes back toward Kaen and Pammon and stared at them for a moment. No one was moving.

Tharnok warned us about you two. I wondered at first if he was lying, but it would appear he told some truth after all. Welcome to our lands, Dragon Rider Kaen and Pammon. Tell us why you have come.

Pammon eased up a little, and Kaen felt himself surprised by the sudden shift in the dragon's behavior.

"I assume Tharnok already told you why we were coming."

A few snorts came from the other dragons.

He mentioned that you would request our aid in a fight that doesn't affect us.

Pammon snorted, and every one of the dragon council members turned to see him shake his head.

Doesn't affect you? Why should the council worry about a man bent on ruling an entire nation and who is actively trying to bond with yet another dragon? Imagine what might happen if he succeeds and, in a century or two, he comes across the sea. Perhaps that might affect you then.

There were slight head movements from the purple and brown dragons, but Kaen heard nothing in response to Pammon's statement. He wondered if they were speaking to each other or simply keeping their thoughts to themselves.

Hundreds of years mean nothing to us. Perhaps you will begin to understand when you have lived for a hundred years.

The tone that dripped from Aethux's words showed disdain for Pammon's age.

A few seconds later, all of the dragons focused on Kaen. Their stares still exhibited force that he barely noticed, but it was evident they somehow were so powerful that even their gaze could impart it.

Tell me, Dragon Rider. What kind of man are you? Will you request our help and accept our answer, or will you be the kind of tyrant you claim to be fighting against?

Pammon snorted but said nothing, obviously bothered by the questions.

"I'm not sure what Tharnok has told you, so I will start from the beginning so you may know who I am and why I do what I must."

"That is why I am here. Because there is a world out there where not only dragons are being killed but humans and others as well. I will not stand by and watch such things take place if I can find a way to stop it."

When he was finished speaking, Kaen took a deep breath and let it out slowly. He watched the council to see how they might respond.

Some thrumming began. First from Elynudra and then the silver dragon. They looked at the others who had not joined in, and slowly, their laughing stopped.

The silver dragon lowered its head toward Kaen, and its black eyes locked on him.

I am called Rivenna, and my faction lives in the farthest land south. It is humorous to hear that you would defend dragons who cannot defeat those who attack or kill them. Are you offering to help my faction fight those who overwhelm and defeat us, who keep us isolated and cut off from the much more prosperous and bountiful lands?

A snarl came from the brown dragon next to Rivenna, but no movement was made by the silver dragon.

"I am not here to change how your kind has lived for longer than I can imagine. Each of you would possibly claim to be oppressed by the other. I can say that there are men, a race that I am very familiar with, cutting down your kind for the last hundred years as they attempt to find a new home across the sea. I already made my intentions clear to the men I let return home, promising that one day I would come back and put an end to how they treat dragons."

A few thrums came from Rivenna again, but she stopped after Aethux turned his eye to her.

"I know the pain of loss. Pammon knows the pain of loss. One man has been that reason for the two of us, and something that has not happened in hundreds of years took place, bringing our lives together. You ask about the kind of man that I am. I am a man who is committed to saving all those that I can by doing what I feel is right—"

Empty words, what you—

"I did not cut you off when you spoke," Kaen shouted, startling the silver dragon as its head rose. "I would ask the same respect I have given you."

Kaen waited a moment and continued. "I will make mistakes. I have made mistakes. Just ask my dragon. He will tell you I have acted like an eggling on occasion."

Thrums came from most of the dragons, and Kaen felt an approving sensation coming through their bond. He glanced and saw Pammon smiling and thrumming slightly.

"I will not be perfect, but I promise that everything I do is to protect all families. To give each human, dwarf, elf, and any other race that seeks peace a chance to enjoy life with their families. If violence and war is the only language they understand, then I will unleash something far greater than they can ever imagine."

Kaen knew his expression was probably not one they expected a human to give them. His eyes had narrowed as he spoke, and there was no smile on his face.

The dragons began looking at each other, heads moving slightly, cocking side to side as they spoke only to one another.

That was one of the best speeches I have ever heard you give. Hess would be very proud.

Resisting the urge to laugh, Kaen allowed his lips a slight smile.

I am lost about this council. Why would they even listen to us? What about us has prevented them from outright attacking us and removing us as a threat?

As the minutes stretched with the council not talking and Kaen and Pammon considering what might arise from what he said, Kaen almost jumped when Amaranth spoke.

Tell me, Kaen. Why did you do what you did? How did you break the hold my master had over me?

What hold are you talking about? I just knew they were using their powers to try and make Pammon and me submit. I knew I could give some of my strength to you, and I did it. There was no need for them to make you suffer.

Dragons are bound to their faction leader, all of whom are council members. At an early age, we declare our obedience to them. In time, one may gain enough strength to try and resist or break it. That usually leads to one of them dying. The bond may be passed to another when forced to join a different faction. It is renewed, often through force and threat of death. When you . . . when your hand touched my head, it was as if you were tearing open those chains the humans had bound me with. Slowly, one by one, they broke free. A moment came where only a few remained, and I knew that if I promised my life and being to you, I could be free from Elynudra and her power. The moment I did that, a . . . I'm not sure how to describe it. I could soar as high as I wished, not forced to stay close to the ground.

Kaen shifted, considering Amaranth's words.

Do you realize, I will not require you to make that same commitment to me?

A few seconds passed, and the only sound to be heard was the wind through the cavern.

I know that. That is why I willingly made that commitment. Someday, I may ask for you to release me from it, but at this moment, I know that if you were to do that, I would fall to the floor, crushed by their aura in a heartbeat.

Running his tongue over his teeth, Kaen considered what she was saying.

The aura . . .

She is correct, Pammon said, interrupting his thoughts. **Just like when Tharnok tried to force us to obey him the first time we met, you are the only reason I was able to resist that command. It tore at the very fabric of who I am as a dragon. A part of me wanted to submit, to follow him without hesitation. You kept me from giving in. My bond to you.**

When Pammon finished speaking, Kaen realized what the council was genuinely terrified of.

They are afraid I could free every dragon they control.

With his eyes open for the first time, Kaen realized what he had never known until this moment.

Focusing on his sole objective in life, he channeled his desire to protect others.

His lifestone roared within him, reaching a point where it almost hurt as he focused.

What are you doing?

Pammon's concern rushed through their bond, but Kaen ignored him and his question.

He let his memories flood through him. He was missing something, and he needed to figure out what it was. His meeting with Lady Hurem and Ava, where both of them had tried to bind him to their will. Each time, they had failed, unable to comprehend why. He had been unable to realize why.

Then, with Havannath. That bastard of an elf had tried to bind him and Pammon to a life of servanthood. A life obeying his every whim and desire. Life as a slave. No matter how the man had tried to lie about it, or the reason why, that's what it was.

Now, all around him were older dragons attempting to do the same to those they professed to care about. Questions flooded his mind about the things Amaranth had told him. How they culled the strong and kept the weak in check. They used their power and influence to keep the stone pillars they were sitting on.

His mind raced, his heart searched, and his lifestone pulsed. It thudded in his chest, telling him the answer he knew he was missing. It showed him what he needed. It provided the very thing he hated more than anything.

[Dragon Bind Skill Unlocked]
[Dragon Bind Skill Acquired]
[Dragon Bind Skill Increased x30]

His heart broke as he doubled over in pain, gasping for air and feeling like his mind was going to explode.

The knowledge that flooded through him. The power that he now felt inside of him.

It was too much. It was too dangerous.

That shock and hurt he was experiencing stopped as Kaen felt Pammon laughing.

Pammon's thrumming echoed through the chamber they were standing in.

Tharnok was right. I never believed him, but he was right.

5 8

A Threat Like No Other

Right about what?

Pammon continued to thrum as Kaen regained his composure and stood up, holding his chest still as his lifestone flooded him with its power.

The lifestone that was meant for a king.

A lifestone never meant for a Dragon Rider.

A Dragon Rider had broken the world the last time this had happened.

Kaen, you are who you were meant to be. Inside you is a power that threatens these beasts, and you have just awoken it. Look at them now.

As his eyes lifted from the stone platform he was standing on to the dragons high above him, he saw them backing away from him. If a dragon could have an expression that embodied fear and hate at the same time, every one of them wore it.

Elynudra darted her snout forward, her jaws beginning to open and green smoke rushing over her long teeth.

"Stop!" Kaen shouted, holding his palm out toward her.

As if someone had grabbed her throat in a gigantic fist, the dragon's mouth froze, unable to open or close, and Kaen could hear her gasping for air.

What have you done?!

He recognized her voice as she sat there, unable to move, tiny tendrils of green smoke coming out of her slightly agape jaw.

How? Please let me go!

Her eyes shook, clear liquid running from them as Kaen glared at her. His lifestone was an all-consuming fire, ready to snuff her life out at this moment for what she had intended to do.

Anger and rage flowed through him as waves of fury poured out of Pammon. He felt the fire inside Pammon begin to burn, and Kaen had to make a choice. He had to stop this path before there was no going back.

"Close your mouth and do not do that again, or it will be the last breath you take," he said, his voice like a file over metal, leaving no doubt in Elynudra's mind.

Her jaw snapped shut, and she moved as far back as she could on her pillar, risking falling off if she moved much further.

Turning his gaze to the other four, who were all trying to regain their composure, Kaen took a breath and let it out, feeling as if smoke were coming out his nostrils. The fire of his lifestone still raged inside him.

"Tharnok was right," Kaen declared as he spoke slowly and loudly. "We are far more dangerous than he is. I just now realized that. It would appear you five made a grievous error in allowing this conversation to go on longer than it should have. Now I know why you five fear me."

He took his time, letting his gaze fall on each of them one by one before settling it on Aethux.

"I was asked what kind of Dragon Rider I am. I will tell you once more, and do not make the same mistake in doubting what I say again. I am the last, but I will no longer stand by and let foolish men or dragons ignore me when I say I will protect anyone who needs my help. Do you understand?"

Aethux brought his head forward and then bowed it.

Forgive us, Dragon Rider. It has been a long time since one like you has commanded the power we sense inside you. What will you command us to do?

Kaen shook his head and grunted.

"I am not here to command unless I must. I will ask again. Will your kind help me? Will you allow me to ask the other dragons who might be willing to join me in a new place?"

The five dragons glanced at each other, and a moment later, the other four brought their heads toward him and lowered them as Aethux had.

You may make your request.

Kaen nodded and moved to where Pammon sat. His dragon's chest puffed out, and he had a smile that showed most of his teeth.

After climbing into his saddle and strapping himself in, Kaen looked again at the five dragons who had regained their composure. Each of them was silent, watching him, wondering what Kaen might make them do and if they would be powerless to resist as Elynudra had been.

"Pammon, Amaranth, and I will be leaving. I need to find Tharnok and see if I can find a way to stop his rampage. After that, I will return and expect to hear you have prepared for the request I will make."

Pammon spun around, not letting a moment pass, or the council members have a chance to reply. He launched himself into the air with a giant leap, flying toward the tunnel that had brought them into the mountain.

I doubt I have ever witnessed a dragon piss themselves, but if my nose was correct, I believe that Elynudra did just that.

Pammon began to thrum as he flew, his laughter echoing off the stone walls as they moved toward the tunnel. For well over a minute, he continued to laugh, letting himself enjoy the fact that each of the dragons who had considered themselves unstoppable had found their match in the boy sitting on his back.

Kaen sat there, letting himself smile as his lifestone finally released the torrent that had been burning inside his chest. It left him a bit tired, but there was no time to waste. Their next stop was going to be far worse.

Are you sure you want to stop here for the night? We could travel a bit further and have more privacy.

Kaen and Pammon both laughed. The green dragon looked around at the constant parade of dragons flying overhead for the last hour.

We will be fine. I doubt anyone will be foolish enough to risk bothering us, and I suspect the council will share the news of what transpired in their room.

Amaranth thrummed at Pammon's response, lifting her head and neck high into the sky. Her chest vibrated, sending the vibrations toward the two of them.

Never in my life have I seen a dragon more afraid. Not even the council members. How did you accomplish such a feat?

Kaen just smiled, poking a stick at the fire. His mind was still racing from everything that had transpired and what the long-term effects of it all meant.

Do you think that would work on Juthom?

He sensed Pammon's doubt and frustration.

I would not risk it. Something tells me it would not. That dragon is consumed by whatever Stioks has done to him. Perhaps if there is no other option left, you can try.

Kaen nodded, stirring the coals a little more before sighing and tossing the stick into the flames.

I don't want to be that person! I don't wish to . . . I can't be someone who breaks the wills of others just to accomplish what I want. If I do that, I am no better than the man I have vowed to stop.

Turning toward Pammon, he saw his friend's snout just a few feet away, those golden eyes staring into his.

You will never be that kind of man. I have no doubt about that.

Kaen nodded, reaching out with his arms and touching Pammon's snout.

Perhaps I should command you to do something stupid. That would be payback for all the times you have done something to me.

Pammon's tongue snaked out through a slight gap in his teeth, striking Kaen on the side of his face and leaving a trail of saliva dripping down his chest. A thrum began to rise as Pammon pulled his head back, and Kaen groaned, wiping the mess from his face.

That is not the kind of person you are. Do not forget that.

Through their bond, Kaen felt Pammon's joy and how his dragon was doing his best to break the funk he was in. It was true. Kaen could never do that to him.

"I guess I'll just have to find other ways to make you suffer," Kaen called out as he ran forward, leaping at Pammon's neck and beginning to wrestle with him.

Amaranth watched in amazement as the two acted like kids, laughing and playing as Pammon crushed plants and a few trees.

The following day, as they flew where Tharnok had last been seen, Kaen gave up counting the number of dragons who flew just close enough to be seen but not near enough to talk to.

I have no doubt that someone has learned what transpired by now. One of the council members has most likely shared some of your power and is warning the others to stay away.

It seems like they would then be breaking the agreement we had.

Turning her head as she flew, Amaranth looked at Kaen as he stared at her.

You will believe that, but they are not ready to admit defeat. If there is one thing those five have learned in their six hundred-plus years of life, it is that just because you lose a battle, you haven't lost the war. I have no doubt a few will try to bend your command.

She paused, and then Kaen saw her start to laugh.

However, I doubt that Elynudra will try that. I would assume she might not show up at all, if she has a choice.

Pammon thrummed in agreement.

Trying to ignore Kaen's frustration at that thought, Pammon turned his attention to the mountain they were flying toward. Tharnok had killed another dragon days ago, and something had to be done to stop him.

We both knew this might be a possibility. I can still feel you holding out that you can somehow talk him into being how he once was. Do not risk it. He is no longer the dragon who once trained us. He is lost. He is broken.

Pammon paused, and Kaen felt him thinking about something that hurt. A pain that he recognized before Pammon continued speaking.

He feels like you did when you thought Hess would die. All that rage and fear, except stronger. You were able to save Hess. He could not save Elies. Imagine for just a moment the person you might be had Hess died in your arms, or if we had been just a few seconds too late.

Rubbing his chest, Kaen winced as the air assaulted his face.

Pammon was right. That moment had almost broken him. Had Hess died, he would have become someone else. A person he doubted he would recognize at all.

So what should I do? Not even try? Just attack him when the moment comes? Ignore who he is and what he taught us?!

Pammon shook his head for a moment and bent his neck, looking to the side so that Kaen could see into his eyes. A few clear drops were swept from Pammon's scales that surrounded his golden eyes by the wind. Kaen could see how much this actually bothered his friend.

I remember everything he taught us. One of those things was to never allow yourself to let feelings make you do something stupid. Something you have ignored more times than both of us want to admit. I am almost sure I know what Tharnok would tell us to do if he could. You know as well.

Kaen nodded, reaching a hand up to his eye and realizing there was wetness.

He took a deep breath, letting the cold wind fill his lungs, and held it for a moment. He let it burn before he finally had to let it out and draw another breath.

Glancing down next to his leg, he saw what he knew would be used today.

Those seven arrows forged differently than every other arrow he had ever used in his life, with one purpose.

To take a dragon's life.

59

Hard Choices

Stay back, Amaranth. I don't want you to risk getting hurt or Tharnok being upset by your presence.

Without complaining, the green dragon turned to the right and circled back, staying at the same altitude.

Look at the land. I cannot believe Tharnok has done this.

Kaen nodded and felt a knot forming in his stomach. They had seen traces of the destruction half an hour ago when they got close.

Large swaths of the forest below had been burnt to ash. They could see the lines that Tharnok had formed by melting rocks and dirt and disintegrating the trees.

Very little wildlife was still around, having fled to other parts of the region they were in. The large trees that had stood for most likely three hundred or more years were gone.

Small sections of green still dotted the rolling landscape, but black ash was the new carpet of this land.

You must not risk your life. If he cannot be calm, do not hesitate to attack. Pammon paused for just a second as Kaen felt his mood go dark. **I will not hesitate.**

Gently scratching his dragon's neck, Kaen looked across the sky to where he saw the massive dragon coming toward them. Even as far away as Tharnok was from them, Kaen remembered the first time he had seen Tharnok and Elies years ago.

Has he grown?

Looking through Pammon's eyes, Kaen couldn't believe it, but it did look like Tharnok had gotten larger. His scales were now a dull grey color, reflecting no light. His eyes looked to have nothing but anger in them.

He has. I didn't even begin to think about what Amaranth said. She mentioned his size and how much bigger he was than us. She compared him to the council. But now I see what she meant.

His mind raced as Kaen tried to consider how it was possible.

Was it—

Yes, Pammon interrupted him, knowing what he was about to ask. **He has killed at least three dragons and consumed them. If he is not stopped, he will kill every dragon on this land.**

Grief and sorrow threatened to extinguish the burning of Kaen's lifestone for a moment. Knowing how badly Tharnok must be hurting with Elies gone overwhelmed him. The fear Kaen had hidden for so long was brought to the surface. If something like this happened to him, what would Pammon become?

Focus! Stop letting yourself get distracted by what may happen one day. If that was me, we both know I would need to be stopped. We are the only ones able to do that now. One way or another, his reign of destruction must end.

Closing his eyes, Kaen took a breath and focused.

He didn't want this path. It wasn't one he ever imagined. The weight of it all felt so heavy some days. Yet he wasn't alone. His friend and partner was carrying him right now. Back home, he had a family. He had a wife. Those reminders hardened him in this moment. Prepared him for whatever might come.

Both dragons flew straight toward each other. Kaen had his bow out, and an arrow already nocked.

When they were only a few miles away, Kaen felt the Tharnok's rage and hurt suddenly hit. It was as if someone had taken a club and smacked him in the chest. Even from this distance, they could now sense Tharnok like never before.

You must try to reach him now. If we get much closer, our only option will be to fight.

I do this for Elies.

That thought, that focus, turned his lifestone into a furnace again. The pain of being the one who had to carry this burden.

Tharnok stop! Stop right now! It is Kaen and Pammon, your friends!

Confusion flooded both of them, and they saw Tharnok's wings falter. His path for a moment wavered before he let out a massive roar, sending a wave of anger at them.

Ignoring the sensation coming from Pammon as concern rose in his friend's mind, Kaen focused his mind and his will.

Tharnok stop! Elies wouldn't want this! Fight the anger you feel!

Again, Tharnok let out a roar, but this time, he flared his wings out suddenly, coming to a quick stop in the air before beating them to stay where he was.

Pammon repeated the maneuver, and miles away, each dragon stared at the other as they felt the one they had called teacher and friend fighting with the beast that had consumed him.

You . . . must . . . kill me. I . . . can't fight this. You have become . . .

Kaen and Pammon waited as the wind blew over them, hearing the strain in Tharnok's voice in their heads.

Tharnok roared, shaking his head from side to side.

You have become a King of Dragons . . . What Elies, when Tharnok said that name, sorrow and pain swept across a bond Kaen had not realized they had, replacing the torrent of rage that had been leaking out every few breaths. ***He knew . . . knew you were. Kings make hard choices . . . Dragon Riders even more . . . end me. Send me to my friend.***

For a single heartbeat, Kaen's heart broke. When it did, his lifestone waivered.

Tharnok angled down and forward, coming at them again, his mind once more consumed by the rage.

Focus!

Kaen's head hurt from how loud Pammon had shouted, but he realized he had been lax. His feelings and concern had replaced the need to be unwavering.

Kaen's lifestone raged once more, burning so hot it flowed from him and into Pammon.

I command you to stop, Tharnok!

As if a mountain had appeared before him, Tharnok stopped, beating his wings again as he hovered and watched Kaen.

Do not wait . . . you are strong . . . but one mistake will be the end. Kill me. Set me free. Please . . .

Tears fell from Tharnok's black eyes . Kaen ignored the fact that they had not been black before. He was no longer the dragon who had trained him. He was a shell. A ghost living in the body of one he had once called friend.

I will set you free. Tell Elies thank you when you see him.

Those giant wings missed a beat, causing Tharnok to drop slightly in the air before recovering.

Pammon began closing the distance between them as he watched Tharnok's movements.

Kaen could feel Pammon's readiness to react if Tharnok did something aggressive.

Hurry . . . it hurts . . . I cannot hold on much longer . . .

Flying faster, Pammon flew straight for the dragon that had trained him for two long years. The dragon that had given him wisdom and advice. Told him secrets when it was just the two of them. The only other dragon who knew what having a rider meant. The pain and joy it brought. The closest thing Pammon had to a father.

As he flew at Tharnok, Pammon's heart was set. Tharnok had prepared him for this day. Told him that it would come. Explained what had to be done. Reminded him that if he failed, either he or Kaen would suffer.

Kaen felt the rock that was Pammon's will beneath him. As they drew close, Kaen pulled the arrow back. He felt the cold metal against his cheek. Power flowed into the arrow. It didn't just flow into the tip, as it had so often, but this time, the entire shaft and tip of the arrow was glowing. It burned. The silver metal turned red, and that red became blue, threatening to burn his face, yet it didn't. A few seconds later, the metal became white, glowing as it surged with so much power.

His lifestone told him it was time. Time to let go.

[Archery Skill Increased x1]

The air rushed against them as they fell from the sky. They flew behind Tharnok, watching his body flip repeatedly as it hurtled toward the ground.

The arrow had struck their friend right in his chest. Tharnok had not moved, doing everything he could to hold still. To be set free.

The arrow had blasted through his scales, torn through as if it was a scale on a youngling and directly to his heart.

The arrow erupted inside his body, snuffing out the life of their friend.

One second, Tharnok's wings had been flapping, and the next, he went limp and fell.

I can reach him before he hits. It will be close.

Kaen said nothing, trusting Pammon as he knew he had his own motives.

The ground was coming toward them quickly.

Pammon was yards away as he waited and watched the massive creature turn again in the air, his tail whipping around like a weapon.

When the threat had passed, he surged forward, beating his wings to dive faster, and used his massive back claws to latch onto Tharnok's body.

He then slowly adjusted his wings, adding resistance to the air rushing over them.

I need your strength. Give it to me.

Without a second's hesitation, Kaen poured the power of his lifestone and his own physical strength through their bond.

Pammon's wings began to beat, buffeting the wind that would have snapped them in half a year ago. He fought against the weight of the dragon he had a hold of, battling the wind and speed that wanted to bring him down.

What felt like minutes was only a dozen heartbeats before their descent slowed down to a point Pammon could control.

He angled their path, finding a section of the ground that would work.

Slowing down as much as he could, Pammon let go of Tharnok's corpse, watching it roll for hundreds of yards in the ash-filled ground.

I am good now. You can stop. Thank you.

Cutting the flow of his own strength, Kaen sagged for just a moment as the life force he had given began to return slowly. Taking a few deep breaths, he looked at Tharnok's body as it lay still on the ground, covered in black ash.

Pammon turned, coming around and preparing to land next to his mentor.

Kaen walked away. The trees were still a solid mile away, but he needed to keep walking.

He had said his peace. Put his hand on Tharnok's body and said a prayer.

Then Pammon had told him what he must do. It hadn't surprised him. Pammon had mentioned it before. Yet, at that moment, he couldn't watch.

Even having been well over a hundred yards away, he had heard the first crunch. The tearing of the flesh.

Pammon would eat every bit of Tharnok that he could. For days, he would sit there and consume his friend. Tharnok had told him that he must do it. To be as large as he could be. To grow to his full potential.

That first bite had been hard for Pammon. Kaen felt it through their bond. The moment he had started to walk away, he could feel Pammon trying to do what he said he needed to do and yet unable to.

Right now, both of them needed a moment.

Pammon turned, looking at Kaen, who was coming toward him. He could feel his presence as he began to return.

A slight thrum came for a moment as he swallowed the bite in his mouth.

His rider was dragging a log. No, not a log, but a tree through the ash-covered fields. It had to be at least thirty feet long, and yet there Kaen was, dragging it behind him with the rope he had walked away with.

Turning back, he took another bite and chewed. He saw Tharnok's head lying against the ground. His reservation was gone as each bite filled him with a power like nothing Tharnok had told him about. He would do this task not only for Kaen and himself, but also for Tharnok, and he'd always carry a piece of his family with him.

60

A Dangerous Past

Kaen spent the next two days watching his friend consume the dragon they had learned so much from.

While Pammon often ate in silence, driven by a task he knew he had to complete, Kaen also worked next to him, carefully cutting off and preparing sections of scales.

There had been a few moments where Kaen had to step back, letting a few tears escape as he took the scales from Tharnok's corpse.

Had it been a random dragon, neither would have thought anything about what they were doing. They had harvested many materials over the last two years, but this was different.

As flesh was stripped away and the scales were removed, bones began to show, the skeleton of their friend and mentor.

Amaranth had come and checked on both of them the day after they had struck down Tharnok but left quickly after seeing the pain they were in.

The four baskets Kaen had were sitting on the ground, bones already put inside that had been cut off and cleaned by fire.

"Call her and tell her to come. She also needs to grow, and you are at your limit."

Pammon snorted but knew Kaen was right. His body was bulging from the sheer amount of flesh he had consumed. His ability to eat had slowed down significantly, and even as he felt his body beginning to grow, there was no way he could finish off what was before him.

Pammon roared, his throat vibrating as he did, the sound warbling some, and soon, Amaranth came.

You need to come and eat.

Kaen watched as she looked at Pammon and then at the dragon's remains.

Are you sure? It is yours.

If you are going to come with us, you must get stronger and grow.

Amaranth stared at Pammon before turning her gaze to Kaen, who was looking at her.

He is right. You need this. What is coming will be challenging, and you will need every bit of strength this will provide you.

Amaranth moved toward the carcass without hesitation and began to tear off pieces, swallowing quickly, afraid they might change their minds.

It had taken five days for Pammon and Amaranth to consume Tharnok. Both of their bellies were distended, stuffed from the ordeal, yet Kaen could already begin to see a change in their bodies. It wouldn't be noticeable for most, but having spent almost every waking hour with Pammon for the last few years, he could see the subtle changes. The horns on his head were getting longer, the length of his wings had grown, and even his tail had gotten thicker.

His scales even took on a luster that made Pammon glisten in the light. His bronze scales almost became more metallic in color.

"You are already changing; can you tell?"

Pammon nodded his head slowly as Kaen lay against him. The stars were bright in the night sky, with only a sliver of the moon showing.

I can feel it, the power flowing through me. It will take a bit for me to absorb it all, but I realize now why dragons fear those who feast on their own. The power is absurd.

Kaen felt Pammon's gaze turning to Amaranth, lying on the ground near them. She had moved closer every night, almost touching Pammon as she lay beside him.

You can feel that coming from her, can't you?

Resisting the urge to thrum, Pammon instead let out a quick burst of air toward Kaen.

I do notice it. I am not ready to acknowledge it yet, but in time, I will. That will change things.

It should be expected. I'm not sure how this works for dragons, but I would assume you need to speak with her at some point. I would expect Ava to tell me.

Unable to hold back, Pammon began to thrum, noticing Amaranth shift some as he laughed.

Suddenly, the tip of her tail brushed his back, and all his laughter stopped, replaced by an eerie silence.

That was until Kaen began to laugh out loud, sensing the feelings flooding their bond.

Go to sleep and stop that before I do something to you.

Ignoring Pammon's threat, Kaen laughed until tears flowed down his face.

Then he felt Pammon's snout push him over onto his side. Still, Kaen continued to laugh, ignoring the frustration he felt coming from Pammon.

That night, they all slept well, the somber moment of the last five days having passed and knowing tomorrow would have enough problems of its own.

We are grateful and sorry for what was required of you to stop Tharnok.

Aethux had bowed lower than the others as all the council paid tribute to the fallen dragon.

He was a testament to the true strength a dragon gains from their rider. Just as you, Pammon, are already proving yourself to be on the path to a level none of us can hope to achieve.

Tell me, Aethux, why do you fear us?

A snort came from the golden dragon as he lifted his head and gazed at Kaen.

Fear? Do you think I fear you?

It is evident that you all do. We can sense it coming off you like water after being in the rain. Tharnok shared how you treated him and the others before. Why?

Each of the council members turned their heads to look at Aethux, staring hard for a moment before turning their gaze back to the two of them.

Do you know what you are? Rivenna asked as she bent her neck and brought it closer to them. *Do you really understand the threat you present?*

Pammon began to thrum as Kaen looked at his dragon, who was laughing, obviously enjoying how the council was acting.

We are no threat to anyone who means us or those we protect no harm. Why do you not believe us?

Because your very existence means we are not free! Ravenna said with a growl, ignoring the grunts coming from Aethux. *We are not free to do as we will because you can—*

Enough! Aethux cut her off, his aura and will dominating the other enough to stop her from talking. ***Rivenna is right. You two can force us to give up our freedom. Something that has yet to be done in more than a thousand years. Who and what we are can cease to exist as we know it. While our way may seem wrong, it has been this way since the first dragons. The strong rule. It is that we work together to maintain balance and cull the threat that seeks to bring disorder to our way.***

Unexpectedly, Aethux moved to the edge of his pillar and jumped off to the side, gliding down to the floor where Pammon and Kaen were, slowly moving closer to them.

The difference in size between Pammon and Aethux was on full display. The older dragon was easily twice Pammon's size. His wings looked to be able to stretch and touch the sides of the cave entrance. His mouth was so large, if he wanted to, a single bite would sever Pammon's head from his neck in one bite.

Do you think I have ever been afraid of one so small? Neither of you is anything compared to the five of us. We should be able to snuff out your lives with little effort, yet we cannot. What you are, Dragon Rider Kaen, has not existed for a long time, and we have worked tirelessly to prevent it from ever happening again. With a simple command from you, I would have to obey no matter how I felt. You saw that when you caused Elynudra to stop her attack. Imagine if you ordered the four of us to burn her down. Do you think we could disobey you?

Kaen saw the others shift in place. Each council member sneered. They all felt the same way.

Yet you treat the two of us like enemies, even though we have done nothing to earn your disfavor.

Pammon's tone felt like a snarl, anger coming across their connection, causing Aethux to slowly nod his head before he let out a snort.

Forgive us if we are leery. The last one, like your rider, almost wiped us out. His selfish actions, which he believed were right, cost us the lives of our council and hundreds of other dragons. We gave everything we had to help stop him. We only managed to do that by allowing our children to be bonded to men. Selfish creatures who desire power above all.

Kaen coughed, wanting to speak, but he knew there was a bit of truth in what Aethux had said.

And you would tell us that you and other dragons are not selfish, nor desire power above all?

Of course, we desire power so that we can keep order!

Pammon glanced up at Elynudra, who had interrupted the conversation; the fury she felt burned from her eyes.

That sounds like something those who desire to rule over others would say to keep that power.

Who do—

Aethux's growl cut her off, and he didn't spare a second to look back at her.

You are right. We desire power, but if we were genuinely self-seeking, we would consume each other and every other dragon. We would hunt down the strongest, using them as stepping stones to gain the power we each desire. Yet we do not. We hold each other accountable and have agreed not to hold back if one of us steps out of line, seeking power that would lead to such corruption.

Motioning with his head, Aethux turned and looked at the other four sitting on the pillars above him.

Every one of us knows the cost of what we do. We do not breed. We do not grow stronger. Our lives are confined to prevent a war from breaking out amongst our kind. Yes, we know about the men in the sea who hunt our kind. No, we will not stop them. Their actions serve as a way to cull those who cannot see the wisdom in the life we have carved out here. A life without the influence of dwarves, elves, or men.

Shifting his weight and taking a few steps to bring him closer to Kaen, Aethux ignored Pammon, who moved to block his way, and lay down on the stone floor, prostrating himself before Kaen.

We do not want to fight, and we cannot offer much in the war you are about to wage. One other dragon has offered to go with you and Amaranth. You have met her, and I doubt she will offer much in the way of pure combat power, but she is one of the best when it comes to flying and fighting in the air. She can teach you as well as support you. She was impressed with the two of you during your brief encounter.

Glynnis?

Snorts came from the top of the pillars as the council dragons thrummed a few seconds later.

Yes. The yellow dragon has answered the call. We can offer you one who is willing. As of right now, no other dragon desires to go. They fear what you are and what you can do. They all know how easily you defeated Tharnok.

Pammon grumbled. His frustration built up as Kaen moved forward and put his hand on his side.

I will not force anyone to join us. While you took the opportunity to spread the truth about us as you see it, we will not act in an unbecoming way. We will gladly accept Glynnis and prepare to leave this place. Just know this.

Kaen moved to stand beside Pammon's head, yards from the dragon that could have flicked out his tongue and snapped him in half. Kaen crossed his arms over his chest and looked Aethux in the eyes.

There will be a day that we return. When we do, do not think we will forget what happened here. I cannot stand bullying of any kind.

After speaking, Kaen climbed into his saddle. They felt all five dragons' eyes on them.

Farewell. As my rider has said, do not expect me to be so kind when we return. The older I get, the more I may find myself acting as Tharnok did.

Aethux thrummed, lifting himself from the ground, his chest reverberating from his laughter. When he stopped, he faced the younger dragon and smiled.

Pammon, I look forward to the day you return. I have no doubt things will be different.

Turning, Pammon said nothing and simply sprung off the floor, beating his wings as he aimed for the tunnel entrance.

61

A Friend and a Foe

Glynnis was darting around them as they flew east, headed toward the coast and the journey home.

I am so excited to see this new land and travel with you all! Things have been exciting since the two of you showed up.

Pammon grunted, doing his best to remain calm under the constant barrage of conversation Glynnis felt she needed to carry on.

She does talk a lot. Should I ask her to stop?

I already did. Remember? That bought us half an hour of silence before she started in again. I think Aethux sent her with us as a way of getting back at us for what we did.

Kaen laughed, having thought the same thing hours ago.

Amaranth had decided to fly behind Pammon, doing her best to ignore the yellow dragon's attempts at conversation.

You will have to deal with the two of them at some point. I'm unsure how that works as a dragon, but this is all you.

Snorting, Pammon glanced at the two females behind him and looked away when he saw them watching him.

Pammon grumbled, beating his wings a little faster as he looked at the landscape below them. They still had another day before they would reach the mountains that protected this land from the sea and any possible intruders.

I was actually hoping things would work out on their own. Are you sure we need both of them? Wouldn't one be enough?

I don't know, Kaen replied as he rubbed Pammon's scales. *We are facing four dragons, and while I would like to believe all it will take is me telling them to stop, I know it won't be that easy. Nothing about Stioks has been easy.*

What about your arrows? They were very effective against Tharnok.

But he allowed me to charge that shot and take it. We both know Juthom isn't going to do that.

Pammon's agreement came through their bond as they flew in silence for a while. Things were never that easy, and both of them knew they had other problems that would be awaiting them upon their return.

How dare you?!

Amaranth growled at Glynnis, baring her teeth as waves of anger and rage poured off her.

Stop this, both of you!

Both female dragons turned their eyes to Pammon, who had moved between the two of them.

Why are you this upset? I simply asked a question both of us were wondering. I can feel the desire you have every moment of the day. It is better to ask and resolve things than to fly around in this awkward state you have been in.

Another snarl came from the green dragon, as Kaen watched Pammon doing his best to keep the upset and embarrassed dragon from injuring the yellow one.

I said stop!

Pammon roared after speaking, causing the other two to take a few steps back and slightly lower themselves to the ground.

This is foolishness. I have not even begun to consider a mate, and neither of you should worry about that right now. We have a long journey ahead of us, and now is not the time to deal with this.

Actually, it is, Glynnis answered, keeping her head low, but her eyes locked on his. ***Do you really want to fly for weeks on end with a female who is all but throwing herself at you and not deal with that? Can you not see how she gets close to you? Can you not smell the scent she is giving off?***

Kaen could feel the frustration and embarrassment that Pammon was dealing with. He could sense all those things and had no idea how Pammon was supposed to deal with them. His dragon wasn't even five years old, yet neither of those female dragons thought it mattered. His size and presence told both of them that he was strong enough.

Be quiet! Amaranth shouted again, moving a little to the left to lock her eyes on Glynnis, who appeared to still not care how upset she was. ***I do not need you to tell him my intentions. I am quite capable of doing that on my own.***

A thrum began to come from Glynnis as she turned her eyes to Amaranth.

Then do it and end this foolishness. I came on this trip for many reasons; you know he is one of them.

Kaen couldn't help but cough when he swore Pammon's scales somehow turned a darker bronze color for a minute. His dragon had not considered a mate for a hundred years, and now he had two female dragons that appeared to want him.

A little help?

Kaen saw Pammon glance at him as he spoke. He knew that the message was just for him and that neither of the females had heard it.

Do you really want me to handle this? I doubt it will work out in the long run if I do. It reminds me of a lesson I had to learn the hard way. Tell them how you feel, even if you do not know. It is better they see that you are willing to discuss the potential.

Pammon's frustration melted away as Kaen felt him start to take control of his mixed emotions. There was a fire inside Pammon that desired Amaranth, but he wasn't sure how to handle that. Her *touches* brushed him as they slept; the scent she was giving off had driven him a bit crazy, but he had ignored them, focused on the task at hand.

Now Amaranth and Glynnis were giving off that same scent, letting him know they were interested in him and mating. It was making it impossible to stay focused.

Enough. I will settle this matter right now.

Both females turned their eyes to him, watching as Pammon swept his gaze between them.

I am still waiting to see how mating takes place or experience it for myself.

I would be—

Wait, Pammon said, cutting off Glynnis as she began to speak. **For the next two weeks, we need to focus on returning home. Your new home. The flight over the ocean will not be fun, and I do not need to distract myself with these things. The mental and physical strain is enough.**

He stared hard at Glynnis for a moment before shifting his gaze to Amaranth, who had raised her head and changed how she sat.

Once we return to Ebonmount and have completed the task at hand, I will discuss with the two of you how to handle your desires. I am unsure how most dragons treat their mates, but I will not consider a mate someone I just casually visit. If I have learned anything from my rider and his mate, there is a bond, and I will want that same thing.

His gold eyes watched both simultaneously, each side of his head taking the other in.

Is there a problem with that?

Neither replied. Kaen saw them shifting as they took in what Pammon had just said. He was surprised to hear how Pammon viewed a possible mate. The dragons on this island did not appear to have that same view on who they mated with.

I am intrigued and willing to wait and see how this works, Amaranth responded, her tone hinting at something Kaen and Pammon couldn't pick up.

I, too, am excited to hear more about what you want in a mate, Glynnis chimed in next, her perky tone present again.

Good. Pammon said as he let out a blast of air from his nose. **Then, if that is settled, we need to rest. Tomorrow will be a long day, and we must prepare for this journey's first leg.**

Lying down, Pammon curled up as usual, waiting for Kaen to come and join him.

After both of them were set, Kaen could hear the shifting of the other two as they drew closer to him. He felt Pammon almost cringing as he knew what would come later in the evening. They would find a way to let their tails brush against his scales at some point during the night.

Tell me I am not going crazy. Tell me this gets easier.

Kaen held back his laughter and reached up, scratching Pammon's side.

You remember how I acted. You know how I felt. Somehow, I don't doubt this will be twice as bad for you.

Pammon groaned, shifting on the ground.

Someone is punishing me for how I treated you.

Laughing, Kaen gently patted Pammon's side and closed his eyes.

Whoever it is, I owe them thanks.

The next day had been spent reaching the edge of the mountains, and each dragon had gone and eaten their fill, preparing for the flight to the islands. Another night passed, and no drama unfolded as both females seemed content to wait and see what would happen once they reached this *Ebonmount* that Pammon had mentioned.

Kaen had laughed when Pammon informed him that the smell both had been giving off was considerably less now. It was still there, but it was manageable.

The flight to the islands was uneventful. Gentle breezes came as they flew high in the sky, staying in a V formation that Glynnis had informed Pammon would help the three of them fly longer and with less work as they took turns, swapping out who flew in front every few hours. As the islands came into view, Pammon's mood went sour, and Kaen sensed the change.

Ships around the island where we found Amaranth. Half a dozen, in fact.

Kaen willed his lifestone into action, and using Pammon's eyes, he saw the ships spaced evenly apart, each larger than the two he had seen last time.

I'm guessing someone didn't like my message. Are those weapons on the beach?

Pammon's gaze shifted, focusing on where Kaen had spotted something.

There are five of those weapons we saw in the town of Golden Edge. They are loaded and appear to be able to turn. What do you want to do?

They still had four or five hours of sunlight left, and Kaen couldn't imagine how this would play out if they attacked right now.

The ships have those on them as well. It seems they have come prepared for whatever might return this way. You know what I am thinking.

Pammon snorted and then looked at the two dragons flying behind him. They had also noticed the ships, but neither said a word.

A night attack might work. There is no moon, and that will give us the advantage. Is this a fight you really want to have? We could land on one of the other islands at night and leave in the morning.

And what of your fellow dragons that might die in the meantime? Are we okay saying one thing and doing another?

Pammon weighed his rider's words. Who knew if other dragons might come this way in the coming weeks or months? How many might die if they did nothing?

Two roars erupted below, and Pammon's eyes tracked the sound.

Do you see that?! Tell me I am seeing things wrong!

Kaen shook his head in disbelief. It seemed impossible, and yet Kaen couldn't deny it at all.

Two dragons were coming out of the trees near the beach, each with someone on their backs.

62

A Threat Like No Other

Those aren't your friends, are they?

Kaen turned and looked at Glynnis and shook his head. He saw her silver eyes watching him.

They are not. I was not aware of any other dragons who had riders.

It appears they are allies of the men with the ships. That does not bode well for the three of us.

Amaranth was right, and Kaen knew it. Fighting the ships would be bad enough, even at night, but with those two dragons, sneaking up on them would be impossible.

That will make stopping for the night on another island unrealistic. Our options have become very limited now.

Pammon was right. Flying the rest of the trip without stopping was probably possible for him. The other two, he wasn't sure about. The formation had helped them fly faster, and Kaen could tell that Pammon was not nearly as tired as before, but he wasn't sure if that was due to eating Tharnok.

We could set down on that large hill and announce ourselves. That should be far enough away from the weapons and give us room to deal with the other two dragons without their support.

It's risky, but we don't have a lot of options. I agree that it is probably the best choice we can make.

Kaen turned and looked at the two female dragons and frowned.

We will land on the mountain. You two stay far enough back and away that if things go wrong, you can provide assistance from other directions. Be smart. I don't want to risk either of you.

He saw them nod, and then Kaen turned around, scratching a scale with his fingers.

Let's get this over with then. How about you deal with the dragons, and I'll deal with those riders.

Pammon thrummed. His enjoyment was obvious.

And here I thought you would just shoot the two down from the sky, and we would feast on them without saying a word.

Kaen groaned as Pammon began to angle toward the mountain.

You know I've never been the shoot-first-and-talk-later person.

Yes, and that is part of your problem.

When they were lower in the sky, Pammon roared, getting the attention of the two dragons on the beach, and Kaen could see through his dragon's vision the sandy area bustling with movement. Both of the dragons had begun flying higher into the sky. He and Pammon saw two people in a saddle on each dragon. The ships started raising their anchors and sails, preparing in case they needed to try and maneuver.

Nothing about that looks friendly at all.

There is still time to shoot them from the sky if you want. I am not against anything at this moment. My goal is to protect you and the two behind me.

Kaen grunted and watched as the dragons began to match their movements. Both of them were brown dragons, decently sized, and judging from the distance, close to Amaranth's size. It was hard to get a good feel for how big a dragon was while flying, but Kaen was getting better at it now, having had practice the last week.

The large hill provided enough room for Pammon to be closer to the flat area and for the other two dragons to come from the eastern side.

They are not responding to me when I try to talk.

Pammon grunted, having said the same a moment ago before he landed.

We are ready behind you. At the first sign of trouble, I will attack.

Kaen nodded, even though he wasn't looking at Glynnis. Knowing she had a lightning attack had given him an extra tool to use if it came time to fight.

Both riders sat on their dragons as they shifted from side to side.

Something is wrong. I cannot reach them at all. It is like the dragon doesn't respond to me.

I feel the same thing. It is as if nothing is there. It is different compared to how Tharnok was.

The rider on the left dragon, sitting in the back part of the saddle, held up a white piece of cloth tied to a spear.

It appears they want to talk.

Kaen nodded, keeping his bow over his shoulder and his sword on his hip. He attached his quiver and slowly slid four dragon arrows into it with a few normal ones.

I know you are a bit antsy, but I will see what they want. Do what you must if something happens.

I will burn them all alive if that need arises. Have no fear.

Chuckling, Kaen slid down from Pammon after unhooking his harness and began slowly walking toward the middle of the mountaintop, keeping his eyes on the person approaching with the spear and the two dragons who still had their riders on their backs.

When they were ten yards apart, the one with the spear stuck it into the ground and pulled off their helmet.

Long black hair tumbled over her shoulders as the helmet came off, and Kaen realized the rider was a woman. She had brown eyes that were taking in Pammon for a few seconds before turning her gaze back to him.

"You are the one who burned our ship and killed our men?" the woman asked, her voice thick with some accent that matched the man and woman he had questioned here last time.

"I am. You are the ones killing dragons?"

The woman chuckled and shrugged as if Kaen's comment meant nothing.

"We do not kill all dragons, but we do kill some. We tame them and bind them to us. They are our servants and obey our commands."

Kaen felt his eyebrows almost touching as he glared at the woman.

"You what? Enslave dragons? How?"

The woman ignored his question, tsking her tongue as she gazed at him.

"How much would you want for the two dragons with you? I can tell you won't give up the one you ride."

Kaen began to laugh, unsure if this woman was actually serious for a moment. He watched her face, saw how she appeared to disprove of his laughter, and realized she was completely serious.

"Do you know who I am? What I am?"

"I have been told but do not believe it matters. A Dragon Rider is a legend of old times. These are new times. Dragons are now nothing more than tools of war. The strong use them as they see fit."

Kaen could feel his lifestone beginning to burn. Everything this woman was saying angered him. Her lack of concern or care for anyone but herself was evident by her tone and how she stood.

"You have no idea who stands before you," she said as she glared at Kaen. "If you did, you would take me up on my offer and leave while you can."

"Tell me then. Who are you, and why should I fear you?"

The woman began to laugh, holding her stomach as she raised her face to the sky.

When she finally stopped, she wiped a tear from her eye and shook her head at Kaen.

"I am no one. I am but a weapon to be aimed at someone. I serve the king. King Vorlack the fifth. King of Hetaal, home of a hundred dragons and a binder of souls. He would give a lot to bend you to his will. He would make you a prince in his land if you willingly gave him the one you sit upon. A dragon like that would be considered a great gift, and he might even let you fly on it."

Kaen stared, doing his best to keep his mouth shut. Everything this woman was saying was ludicrous. A kingdom with a hundred dragons? A man capable of binding the souls of dragons.

Kaen, something is wrong. I can see no life in those dragon's eyes. I have heard everything that woman has said, and it seems impossible to believe, but I cannot help but wonder if it is true. There is no *soul*, as she mentioned, by the way they feel. It is different than the life I sense from Glynnis and Amaranth.

Kaen took a deep breath, trying to control the anger bubbling up inside him.

"And if I refuse to trade the two behind me or submit to King . . . Borlack?"

The woman's eyes narrowed, and she spat on the ground.

"His name is King Vorlack," she said, her tone sounding as if dragging a stone across a blade. "Provided you do not insult the king again and never return to this place, I will not stop you." She paused, a smirk forming on her lips. "Yet something about you tells me that is not going to happen. From what I was told, you do not appear to be the kind who will let this go."

"What if I gave you the same offer? Leave now and never return , and you can live. Choose to fight, and I will kill everyone but you and one ship. That way, you can return to your king and tell him I am not like anyone he has ever faced."

Kaen felt the fire inside Pammon beginning to grow. As he did, he saw the woman fix her eyes on Pammon, and her smile grew wider.

She crossed her arms, and Kaen saw her beginning to fondle a bracelet.

Fear crossed his mind. The way the woman was acting And how she had shifted, Kaen could sense she was prepared for something. He had faced down enough people and could tell that she wasn't afraid at all of Pammon. It actually appeared as if she was waiting. Baiting him somehow.

GO! Do not fight! You three need to leave now!

Panic struck Kaen as his lifestone began to piece it all together. He had seen one of those bracelets before but had not noticed it till now. It was on one of the sailors he had killed when he saved Amaranth.

She was baiting Pammon to attack. Wanting him to.

I won't leave you!

GO!

Kaen willed a power he had never imagined ever using on Pammon. It hurt like he had torn a part of himself, but there was no other choice. His dragon would not leave him, but he needed to. He had to.

A pain came across their bond as Pammon tried to fight everything he wanted to do. Felt like he had to do. His eyes were fixed on that woman. On her bracelet. It called to him. Told him to strike at her. To burn her with his breath.

Go Pammon! It's a trap! Amaranth and Glynnis fly! Do not engage them!

As he spoke one last warning, Kaen moved with purpose.

The woman was fast, but he was faster. She saw Kaen move, saw his body begin to shift, and she tried to draw a weapon from her sleeve, but before she had it halfway out, his fist hit her in the chest and he drove her back, knocking the wind from her and sending her tumbling end over end along the barren dirt of the hill.

He never hesitated, drawing his bow and activating Multishot, his lifestone roaring with power as he knew things were about to turn ugly.

Kaen unleashed regular arrows at the riders on the dragon to his right.

Their dragons tried to move, preparing to leap into the air, but Kaen was still running as he fired five arrows, each glowing red.

Two struck the dragon, one in its neck and another in its wing, sending scales and flesh flying from the explosion. The other three struck the two on the back, creating a red mist where only their legs remained in the saddle.

The dragon roared in pain from the attack and then stopped moving altogether, ignoring Kaen and the damage he had done.

Kaen saw the dragon on the left opening its mouth as it prepared to approach him. Its chest began to glow.

Kaen grabbed two arrows, one regular and one dragon arrow, activating Twinshot and empowering both arrows for a single heartbeat before letting go of the string.

The dragon arrow sped into the open mouth, traveling along its throat before exploding inside its neck, sending its head to the ground as its body pitched forward.

The second arrow hit its shoulder, creating a show of scales and flesh.

Somehow, the rider on its back rolled off and away as the dragon crashed to the ground. He was yelling some curses at Kaen as he pulled a dagger and sword.

The fifty yards between them were soon gone, and the rider swung both weapons in a barrage of attacks.

Kaen had slung his arrow over his back and pulled his sword while he waited for the rider to come to him.

All those hours of training, all that work he and Pammon had done for two years to get stronger and faster, paid off. The rider could not land a single blow.

It only took a slight shift of his step and a minor raise with his blade to deflect each attack and hold the rider at bay. Every strike felt like watching a new recruit at his academy try to attack him.

Kaen smiled as the attacker realized they could not do anything. Their blows went from calculated swings and technique to a wild salvo, hoping to land a hit.

Angry at all this death and destruction, Kaen shifted his feet, adjusting his hips, and with one swift move, deflected the sword, sending his blade through their neck and cutting the head off in one strike.

The body fell forward, off balance from the attack and the head fell to the ground behind it.

Flicking his blade clean of blood, Kaen slid it into his scabbard and turned. He locked his eyes on the woman he had knocked out.

63

Learning About the Threat

Come back now. Forgive me for what I did.

Pammon and the other two had been flying above him for the last few minutes as Kaen stripped the woman till she had nothing on, taking off the bracelet and examining it. He had cut strips of her armor and bound her hands and feet. She was still unconscious from the blow, but he had checked. She was alive.

Pammon was angry. He had every right to be, and Kaen knew it, but he had no choice. The rage poured through their bond, and when Pammon landed behind him, Kaen saw the glare in his eyes.

How dare you do that to me!

Lowering his snout till his face was just a foot from Kaen's, Pammon snorted at him.

"Because it was a trap, and you wouldn't listen. I told you to go, and you didn't. There was no time."

What was she going to do to me? She was nothing! I could have ended her life in one bite!

Kaen held up the bracelet and watched as Pammon's eyes gazed at the orange and red gem.

Pammon growled, anger rising inside him.

The same reaction came again as a fire began to churn inside Pammon.

"Tell me you don't feel that. A rage you can't control. Something telling you to unleash your breath, even upon me."

Pammon felt it. His mind struggled as it fought what was inside his heart and an overwhelming desire to burn something in his mind.

Kaen leaned over, putting his hand on Pammon's scale, and willed his skill.

Immediately, Pammon calmed down. The fire inside vanished, replaced with hurt and remorse.

Why? Why can't I resist it?

Kaen shrugged his shoulders and scratched his friend's snout.

"I don't know. I will try to find out, but something tells me this is how they trap dragons."

Putting the bracelet in his pouch, Kaen turned and pointed at the brown dragon. Blood seeped from its wounds, but it still had not moved or reacted. It was like a statue.

"Look at it. Whatever they did has left it a shell of itself."

Glynnis and Amaranth had moved closer, both able to sense that Pammon was no longer angry.

I saw that bracelet you held the day you rescued me. The woman had held it before my eyes multiple times, cursing each time nothing happened. Why is that?

Scratching his beard, Kaen considered the facts he had.

You don't have a breath attack. Every other dragon does, you said. There is no fire that burns inside you like the others. No way for you to even release it if you did. I think, somehow, this does something to dragons. Causes them to attack in a rage they can't control. When that happens . . .

Kaen turned and looked at the naked woman at his feet.

We will hopefully find out in a minute. Let me get some water and see if I can't wake her up.

The woman gasped as Kaen splashed more water from one of his skins in her face.

She snorted and snarled and cursed when she came to, seeing him and Pammon looming over her.

"How did . . . " her voice trailed off as she craned her neck and saw the carnage of the two dragons she had come in on. "Impossible . . . do you have any idea what you have done?"

"Released two dragons from bondage and rid the world of those who would do such a thing?"

She spat at Kaen, trying to hit his feet or legs, not getting close because of her position on the ground.

"You have made an enemy of the empire! We will hunt you down! We will enslave your dragon and make him eat you!"

Her eyes were wild with anger. A throbbing vein appeared in her tan forehead as she bucked and kicked against the bonds that held her.

Kaen heard them beginning to tear and moved forward, putting a hand around her throat.

"Stop. I'll tell you right now if I have to, I will use something stronger to bind you, but you won't like it."

She flinched as she felt his hand around her throat and saw the look in his eyes, which told her Kaen was not making an empty threat. Relaxing, he let go of her throat and she watched as he stood up over her.

Glynnis, you and Pammon move away. I will pull the bracelet out again and would prefer not to have to worry about you two getting affected by it.

How about if we scout from the air? I want to see if anyone is coming toward us.

Kaen nodded, and both dragons moved away, leaping off the ground and started to climb higher into the sky.

His eyes focused on the woman. Kaen pulled the bracelet out and held it before her face.

"I'm going to ask nicely, but if I don't get my way, I will do things that will make you want to tell me."

The woman began to laugh, her chest rising and her body shaking from how hard she was laughing.

"You think you can scare me? Do you think some threat of pain or suffering is going to break me? Do you have any idea what I have had to endure to get the position I have?"

He had already seen the scars all over her body. There were at least fifty. Some looked to be fresh, while others had to be years old.

"No, I don't think you fear pain. I think you might actually enjoy pain. The question I have is, how long can you endure constant pain? Pain that never ends? A pain that can stretch on for days, weeks, and months, without ever ending or having to worry about dying."

Kaen turned to Amaranth and motioned to her with his hand to come close.

Turning back to his captive, Kaen smiled.

"What is your name? I don't think you ever told me."

She glared at him and spat again.

"I don't have a name, just a number."

He took a deep breath and slowly let it out.

"Well, I am Kaen, as you already know. What is your number?"

She grunted but saw there was nothing else she could do, and giving it up wouldn't do Kaen any good.

"I am number three hundred and twelve."

Kaen frowned, and the woman smiled, seeing his look.

"There are hundreds of us waiting for a dragon of our own. The honor of having one is beyond anything else that can compare. The king—"

"You can stop," Kaen said as he pulled an arrow from the quiver. "I just wanted to know who I am about to do things to that I would prefer not to do."

He bent down, his eyes burning with anger.

"Know this. You can stop this at any moment. All you have to do is tell me what the bracelet does, and if I believe you are telling the truth, I will send you back on a ship."

He drove the arrow into her thigh, making sure the tip of it came to rest against her femur.

She screamed, beginning to shake her leg until she realized the pain from the arrowhead was scratching along her bone.

"Lie, and this will go on forever."

She was sweating all over, panting from the pain, and then frustrated at how amazed she felt for a moment before it began again.

You are darker than I imagined. To do this. It is brilliant, and yet . . .

Necessary. Imagine if Pammon or any other dragon suffers the fate of the one over there. It has been an hour, yet that dragon has not moved and barely breathed. Soon, it will die of the injuries if it doesn't do something.

Amaranth snorted, moving her head back from the woman.

Still, healing her like this with the arrows in her legs.

Kaen grunted, ignoring Amaranth's reservations.

Over and over in his head, he remembered what Pammon had told him. '*You will have to do hard things.*'

This was one of those things.

Kaen bent down, slowly twisting the shafts of the arrows, the tip tearing flesh inside the woman's leg and scratching against the femur.

She cried out in pain, able to resist moving her legs, as that only made it worse.

"I told you!" she screamed. "I told you what it does!"

Kaen stood up after letting go of the shafts and shook his head.

"You told me what I already know. You aren't telling me what I want to know. Who would be foolish enough to anger a dragon into using their greatest weapon on them unless they had some way to protect themselves from it? What does the gem do?"

She was already sweating again as blood trickled from the hole in each leg. Kaen had been right. She could resist pain, but after an hour of nonstop pain, which was healed before starting again, it was something else. Her mind wanted it to end. The cuts she had endured were nothing compared to this. They had been quick or slow, but they were wrapped up and left to heal.

She realized that Kaen was serious. He would do this for as long as it took, and she doubted he would let her die.

"Do you promise . . . " she said, gritting her teeth as an arrowhead scratched against her bone and moved. "Do you promise to send me back alive?"

Kaen looked at her. Saw the way her eyes were no longer trying to kill him by how she glared. Now, they wanted nothing more than the pain to end. He owed Elies more than he wanted to admit. The man had told him about things like this. The need arose sometimes. He had filled his mind with horrible things that seemed dishonorable yet had purpose. This was one of those moments that demanded such actions.

"I gave you my word. If you tell me what I want to know, I will heal you, take you to the last ship remaining, and send you home. However . . . " he paused, bending down and thumping the shaft with a finger, causing her to scream in pain. "Lie to me or hold back, and I will keep doing this."

She nodded as slowly as possible, trying to keep her legs from twitching more. Short, quick breaths were all she could take as she breathed through her nose. She ignored the snot that was dripping from her nostrils. She couldn't escape. Better to return home and plead to the king and hope she could one day earn her spot back and take revenge on this man.

She took a few more breaths and closed her eyes after letting one out slowly.

"When a dragon attacks you with it, a magical energy will absorb it. It will grant you control over the dragon. They will be unable to fight back. From there, we take them back to the kingdom and . . . "

Kaen waited as the seconds passed. She had stopped talking, opening her eyes again and looking at him.

"And what?"

"A ritual is done, and they become the dragons you defeated. Only a few know what they do, but no dragon has ever recovered. Anyone who wears the bracelet can control the dragon it is bound to."

She sniffed, wincing as the movement brought pain again.

"Did you destroy the bracelet for the other dragon?"

Kaen glanced at the dragon still standing there, blood dripping from its wounds.

"I did not."

He saw her wince as she closed her eyes again.

"Doing so will end its life. It would obey you if you wear it. You could command it to fly after you. The only way a dragon will eat is if you command it to, otherwise it will starve itself without permission."

Kaen didn't want that kind of power. Even though some might consider it a worthwhile weapon, it crossed a line.

Kaen bent down and grunted.

"You did your part. Now I will do mine."

Watching from up above, Pammon could almost imagine he heard the woman scream when Kaen pulled the arrows from her legs.

64

Giving Up Power

The sun was only an hour away from setting when Amaranth set the woman down on the beach, far enough away from the range of the weapons pointed in her direction.

She thrummed as the woman took off, running toward the camp, her naked body shimmering in the dying light from the sweat that still covered her.

Five ships were sinking in the waters, joining the one Kaen had sunk just a few weeks ago.

Two of them required a dragon arrow, leaving him with only three left. Their hulls had resisted his attacks, even charged as much as he could with a standard arrow.

The other three finally gave in to the barrage he sent down upon them.

Once that was done, Pammon and the other two moved back to the mountain, ending the life of the dragon still standing, consuming all the flesh they could.

Kaen dug through the remains as they ate, finding three more bracelets. His mind fought with the possibilities of these weapons.

You aren't going to use them, and we both know that.

Kaen nodded, knowing Pammon couldn't watch him; he could not risk seeing those bracelets again.

You are right. I see their potential and power, but at what cost? What would I become if I used something like this to enslave another being? I feel as if I would lose my own soul in doing that.

Put those away so I can join you. You need to come sit by me.

Taking one last look, Kaen put the bracelet he held in a pouch with the other three and tied it to his belt.

I'll join you. We need to talk.

As Glynnis and Amaranth worked on one dragon, Pammon continued eating the other.

Standing beside his friend, Kaen rubbed Pammon's haunches as he looked up at the stars.

"I'm sorry again for that. Having to do that to you felt like I had torn a piece of me away."

Pammon swallowed the piece in his mouth and turned to look at Kaen.

At the time, I felt the same thing. I know you did it only because I couldn't see the wisdom of your first attempt to warn me. I do not hold it against you. It does make me realize now how dangerous you are. The stories of the last rider like you, who did what he did, make sense.

Which is why I cannot use these abominations. Imagine if Stioks or someone else got their hands on one. Imagine our kingdom filled with these.

Turning slightly, Pammon moved till his nose barely tapped Kaen in the chest.

You carry a lot inside you. Do not forget you are not alone. I am here to help with that load that burdens you.

Kaen reached out with both hands and scratched the growing snout.

"If you keep growing, soon I may not be able to get both hands around your mouth.

Pammon thrummed, enjoying the scratches before returning to his meal.

Let me finish eating so we can rest. We will be back on land in four days, and we both know what is waiting for us.

Kaen nodded, even though no one was watching.

Too many things were waiting on that side, and none were good.

The following day, as they left, Kaen had commented that the only surviving ship was gone.

Still on the beach were the weapons they had set up, but Kaen imagined with a lot of survivors and limited ships, choices had to be made, and those were the least of their concern.

Are we poking a dragon we don't want to fight with everything we did?

Kaen sat there for a few minutes, letting the rising sun warm his face as they flew over the ocean.

I think they may ask themselves the same question once that woman returns. I cannot imagine a kingdom where a person has no name and just a number. What kind of horrors must take place there?

Pammon never answered that question, and when night came, Kaen took the pouch with four of those bracelets and tossed them behind Pammon.

A weight that he felt like he had been carrying was lifted as the pouch fell into the sea.

I doubt anyone will ever find those now.

That was the plan.

Four days of non-stop flying had each dragon, and even Kaen, in a less-than-pleasant mood. Each of the females had commented multiple times on how they were impressed with Pammon making this flight without another dragon to talk to.

Three hours after the sun rose, Glynnis called out in a cheerful tone that had been absent for a day.

Land! I see land!

Everyone fixed their eyes to the east as they saw the brown shape appear over the expanse of the water. Kaen felt relief flood through their bond.

You two have done well. I know this wasn't an easy trip, but soon we will be in a new land. I need to remind you both again to let me handle the people there.

Are they really as unpleasant as you say they are?

There will be some along the coast who are not happy to see us. As we get closer to our home, the people will be more accepting, but the presence of three dragons may cause some alarm. As you were all nervous about me, they will be the same. In time, I think we can prove ourselves worthy of their trust.

Glynnis seemed content with his answer as she turned back toward land, enjoying her turn at the front of the formation as it meant Pammon was getting a view of her.

Kaen could feel Pammon's fatigue when they landed on the shore, and they found a wide-open area near no towns. The three dragons were relieved to rest, choosing to hunt tomorrow as they bedded down in the forest away from shore.

Are you sure you are ok with keeping watch?

Kaen chuckled, giving Pammon another tap on his snout before moving to the fire.

You have carried me for a long time. Let me carry you right now.

The game in this forest was not nearly as abundant as Glynnis and Amaranth were used to. Each of them took over an hour to find enough food so that they felt ready to fly for another day.

Amaranth had complained only once, but a glance from Pammon had stopped her.

Kaen could tell the females were anxious about what might happen when they finally reached Ebonmount. Both had scooted so close to Pammon last night that Kaen almost couldn't keep back his laughter. It was like watching two predators moving toward the same unsuspecting animal from opposite directions.

They didn't fly south this time, as it didn't matter if anyone noticed them returning. The odds of that happening with how high they were flying were low, but it would be good if someone saw them and reported that three dragons were headed toward Ebonmount.

Are we going to stop by Roccnari and make our presence known?

I would prefer not to right now. I'm still unsure where Havannath's loyalties lie, and I do not want to tip our hand just yet. Rumors are one thing, but I do not want to give that man the ability to see us with his own eyes.

Are elves really as arrogant as the old stories say?

Glynnis, imagine a dragon's spirit but in an elf's body. They are pretty fond of themselves and consider others to be beneath them. Not all elves are like this, just as not all dragons are like this, but it often seems those in power exhibit this behavior more than others.

She replied that some dragons are like that, and Kaen saw her look up ahead at Amaranth, who was leading the formation.

Pammon thrummed, and Kaen couldn't help but feel the tension between the two females again.

Are they already making moves?

Yes!! Pammon exclaimed so loud it made Kaen wince. **They have begun to do whatever causes that scent again. It isn't as powerful as it was in their land, but it has been slowly getting stronger each day.**

Have you figured out what you are going to do about them yet? It seems that they may not take no for an answer.

Pammon snorted and shook his head.

Is it wrong that I would ask Hess and Ava for some advice? I figured perhaps the two of them might be able to help.

The mention of Ava sent a pain through Kaen's heart. He had purposely not thought about her for most of the trip. It was hard enough staying focused on everything they had dealt with, but when she took over his thoughts, he found himself distracted and missing her touch.

He closed his eyes, thinking about what he would do when he returned home. Her soft lips, her skin, her . . .

Pammon roared, causing him to open his eyes, and saw Glynnis and Amaranth swerve away from him.

STOP THAT! Pammon roared louder in his mind than he had just a moment ago. **You cannot do that right now!**

Kaen sat there and felt an urge coming from Pammon that matched his. Glancing at the two dragons in the air with him, Kaen realized they had also sensed it.

Pammon began to take big breaths, and then he saw Glynnis moving her tail rapidly in front of him.

Hairy dwarf balls, tell me this isn't happening, Pammon.

Pammon dove down suddenly, Kaen sensing the frustration in him.

[Flight Burst Activated]

Like an arrow released from a bow, Pammon surged forward, moving ahead of both of the female dragons as he flew as quick as he could.

Kaen could feel his friend's heart beating rapidly. His emotions were all over the place, yet what was coming through it more than anything was a yearning he knew all too well.

I'm sorry! I didn't know!

Pammon focused as he raced ahead.

Leaning forward, Kaen turned his head to glance behind and saw both females hot on their trail. It appeared they both had the same skill and activated it in turn.

Don't look behind you, but they are not giving up. They have used the exact skill you have.

A groan came from underneath him, and Pammon almost shook.

I cannot do this. Not with you here. If I did, you might get hurt or die.

Perplexed by the statement, Kaen tried to consider what Pammon was saying. His eyes went wide at the realization of what Pammon had meant.

What can I do to help? I don't want to ever be part of that moment.

A slight thrum came from Pammon as he sped forward, barely able to keep the lead on the two females tracking him.

Almost an hour had passed before both females had given up, falling miles behind Pammon.

[Flight Burst Expired]

Pammon took deep breaths as they slowed down. The speed at which they flew now seemed so slow, it was as if they were walking.

He turned his head back, seeing them still coming after him.

I am fine now. No matter what they do, I should be able to resist their attempts.

Are you sure? I need to know because I really don't want to ever come between you and one of them.

Pammon felt the joke through their bond and gave Kaen a massive snort, sending one of the largest sprays of mucus toward Kaen, who could do nothing but press flat against his neck.

That wasn't nice at all.

Pammon began to thrum, enjoying the moment.

I hope tonight, when I'm dreaming, I don't dream these same thoughts again.

The thrum stopped immediately, and Pammon turned his head back and looked at Kaen.

I may not kill you, but I will make sure to find a way for you to suffer. I may give into those desires while you are strapped to my back.

Kaen laughed as he pulled a waterskin out and began to pour it over his hair as best he could. Washing the mucus out of it as they flew across the sky.

Both of them wanting nothing more than to get home soon.

65

The Problem with Male and Female Dragons

Both females had expressed their frustration at Pammon and his running off. The aura he had put off when urges had run freely through him had only made their desires harder to hold back.

Each had managed to state they understood his fear of such a thing taking place with Kaen on his back. Of course, when Pammon had told them he wouldn't change his mind that night after Kaen had started setting up camp, they had grumbled for a while.

The good news is your little burst of speed cut off almost a day of traveling. How often do you think you can manage that?

Pammon shook his body as he considered how his body actually felt.

I could do it again for about as long as needed. It would drain my magic halfway, and I would only want to push it like that once in one day if I had to.

Kaen spun on his saddle and looked at Glynnis and Amaranth, who had voiced some displeasure at Pammon for not letting them take turns leading the formation today. Both appeared to be okay after yesterday's burst of speed.

I keep forgetting they are both over fifty years older than you. I'll ask them if they are willing to fly like that again.

A sensation of something new came across their bond as Kaen turned back around and tried to figure out what Pammon was feeling.

What am I missing? What is that emotion?

I'm not sure, but it comes from my bond with you. Talking about their age, knowing how young I am, and knowing it doesn't matter to them feels weird. I doubt I would even consider it had I not seen you fail so often with older women you flirted with.

The wind swept Kaen's laughter away as he scratched Pammon's neck.

I don't recall that many failed attempts.

Pammon's head turned, and he gazed back at Kaen, holding his stare for a few beats of his wings.

I think we both know that is not true.

Shrugging, Kaen ignored Pammon's stare and looked down at the map he had tied to his leg again.

I still can't wait to hear what Hess and Ava tell you. That my friend will be something I doubt I will ever forget.

Pammon started to snort but stopped, knowing that doing so would mess up Kaen's map, and he didn't want three individuals upset with him right now.

I should have never told you that.

And yet you did.

Ignoring Pammon's grumbling, Kaen ran his finger along the map as he glanced down below at the forest and landscape underneath them.

The map only helped a little as they were north above the path they had taken when they left Ebonmount, but it did provide something for him to do as he sketched the land below.

If I'm right and the three of you can manage a Flight Burst like yesterday, we might be home in two more days.

Ask them. I, for one, am more than excited at that prospect.

Sliding his pencil into its holder on his leg, Kaen rolled the map closed and tightened it against his thigh.

Glynnis, Amaranth, are you willing to repeat yesterday's Flight Burst? If we can do that today and tomorrow, we might arrive back home just before sunset.

Yes!

Absolutely!

The immediate response and enthusiasm caught Kaen off guard. He had expected the two to complain as they had most of the morning.

Uh . . . ok. Follow Pammon once he activates his.

Patting his dragon's neck, Kaen leaned in.

Ready when you are.

A quick snort came from Pammon, and then Kaen felt the wind begin to attack his body.

[Flight Burst Activated]

Leaning over a little, Kaen saw the land beneath them looking like water moving along a stream. The speed they were flying at now was slower than yesterday, but it was still fast enough to cut off large chunks of their trip.

As he lay there against Pammon's neck, with every stroke of those massive wings propelling them ahead, Kaen thought about how Glynnis and Amaranth had responded.

Then he understood why.

Are you laughing?

Pammon felt Kaen shaking against his neck. It was almost as if his rider was convulsing from how hard he shook.

Kaen, however, couldn't even respond. His chest hurt from how hard he laughed, and the cold air did not help his lungs recover. Tears were swept away by the wind the moment they appeared on his face.

Kaen . . . what is . . .

Pammon began to thrum. Kaen's laughter was intoxicating, and it was impossible to resist through their bond.

Streaking across the sky, a dragon and his rider laughed. The exhaustion and frustration from the weight of all the problems they felt began to fade away.

After a few minutes, the two of them finally regained their composure, no longer laughing and enjoying the flight together.

So are you going to tell me what made you laugh like that?

I would, but I need to wait till later. Tonight, when I can share it with everyone.

A sensation of the joke Kaen knew but still wasn't sharing itched in the back of Pammon's mind, but he gave up trying to pry it from Kaen.

I expect a good laugh then when you tell the other two.

Kaen began to laugh again, rubbing the scales along Pammon's neck.

Oh, I expect there will be lots of laughter.

Kaen sat on the log he had pulled close to the fire and turned the meat Pammon had brought back for him on the spit he had created.

The scent of the deer cooking made his stomach rumble. The thought of having to eat dried fish or meat anytime soon did not sound appealing at all.

As he cooked, he could feel Pammon's eyes on him. He had asked once what the joke was, and Kaen told him to wait, wanting to eat beforehand.

Glynnis and Amaranth had taken up their usual positions, lying right up against Pammon as they waited for what Pammon had told them would be a great joke.

He chose to ignore their actions. Nothing would change unless he snarled or snapped at them, and he didn't want to act like that.

Time seemed to stretch on as Pammon waited anxiously. Kaen was eating exceptionally slow, commenting multiple times on the meat's taste.

After consuming the last bite and tossing the spit and sticks used to cook in the fire, Kaen stood up and stretched.

Are you going to finally tell us what was so funny?

Kaen grinned, chuckling a little as he saw all three dragons with their eyes focused on him. Each pair shined with the light of the fire, and he couldn't help but stand in awe at the sheer mass the three of them took up in the clearing.

"Oh, I guess there is no better time than the present."

Looking at Glynnis and Amaranth, Kaen smiled and raised his eyebrows.

"You two remember when I asked if you both were willing to use your flying skills to cut down on our travel time?"

Though neither of the female dragons could see the other, they both lowered their eyelids some and slowly nodded their heads.

Yes . . . the way you ask that seems strange, Amaranth replied first.

I most definitely remember! I was more than happy to hear that news!

When Glynnis spoke, Pammon turned his head at the yellow dragon and saw she had shifted her gaze off Kaen and onto him.

Kaen couldn't hold back the smile he felt. Small chuckles escaped between his open lips.

"Why don't you tell me why you were so excited and happy to hear that news, Glynnis."

The yellow dragon turned her head to face Pammon, who had done the same, anxious to hear her reply so he could figure out the joke. Her lips curled into a smile as she stretched her neck toward Pammon.

That's easy. The sooner we get to your home, the quicker Pammon will have to keep his promise.

A snort came from Pammon as he pulled his head back, seeing Glynnis's silver eyes almost dancing with excitement.

Craning his neck the other way, he saw Amaranth looking at him the same way.

She is right. When we arrive at your home, we expect you to keep your promise to the two of us, especially after you teased us the other day.

Kaen began to wheeze. He had started laughing silently as the scene unfolded before his eyes. Part of him felt bad about it, yet in all his time with Pammon, he had never really managed to tease or give him a hard time about something like this. All these years, his dragon always had the upper hand, but tonight things were different.

Snapping his snout toward Kaen, Pammon glared, realizing what Kaen had done and why he was laughing so hard.

The only sound for a bit was Kaen trying to breathe between his laughter and the popping of the fire. Not once did Pammon turn his head from his rider, ignoring the gazes he felt coming from the two females on either side of him.

Finally, Pammon spoke, choosing not to keep it between Kaen and him but allowing the other two to hear.

I see. That is humorous.

Pammon's tone left no doubt that he did not find any of this funny, and the rage that bubbled and seethed through their bond couldn't be ignored as Kaen wiped away a few more tears and watched his dragon stare at him.

I must give Kaen a point for his well-executed plan tonight. He managed to do something he hasn't done in a while. For that, I will acknowledge the truth of what both of you said. I will keep my promise when we return to our home.

Glynnis and Amaranth shifted slightly, moving closer to Pammon, their bodies now almost against his as they each lay their tail against him.

Pammon didn't flinch as he stared at Kaen, a smile appearing along his mouth and his teeth reflecting the fire. He ensured the following words he heard were only for Kaen's ears.

You may have won this battle, but just know that when we get home, you may regret the action you took.

Smugness and bit of humor came through their bond as Kaen considered Pammon's words.

What are you going to do?

More teeth appeared as Pammon's smile grew bigger.

Like your joke today, waiting and showing you when we get home will be best.

Another wave of satisfaction and excitement struck Kaen as Pammon laid his head down on the grass of the clearing.

Don't stay up too late. We need to fly fast tomorrow.

Cocking his head to the side, Kaen tried to read his dragon, who had closed his eyes, appearing to not have a care in the world.

Scratching his chin through his beard, Kaen considered what Pammon might be thinking or planning. Nothing came to mind. He wasn't sure if this was a bluff to mess with him in the coming days, but something inside him told him it wasn't. If Pammon was good at one thing, it was ensuring he always won their little games. He would need to be on guard for whatever his dragon might do.

66

Home

Kaen sat there in amazement as all three dragons had yet to let Flight Burst expire.

Pammon had been cheerful that morning as they took off, acting as if nothing was wrong, but the hair on the back of Kaen's neck stood straight up, making him worry about Pammon's promise.

Are you sure the three of you don't need to stop? I don't want you to push yourselves too hard.

A slight thrum came from Pammon as he continued to streak across the sky.

We are all fine, and you are right. Getting home sooner rather than later is important. Glynnis and Amaranth both told me that they could match me in stamina.

Kaen coughed, trying not to see the humor in that last part of Pammon's statement.

Hours had passed, and finally, Pammon slowed down.

[Flight Burst Expired]

Glancing behind him, Kaen saw Glynnis and Amaranth had dropped out the same time Pammon had. The looks on their faces seemed different. Kaen realized what it was.

Anticipation.

Keeping the groan he wanted to express to himself, Kaen looked at the landscape below them and realized where they were.

You three made fantastic time! We should be home well before sunset.

Kaen could feel Pammon breathing deeply, trying to regain strength after that prolonged stretch of flight burst. They had never used it for that long before, yet it seemed so much easier on Pammon's body now. He had noticeably grown in size since eating Tharnok. The dragon he had consumed on the island had also helped him to grow and sustained Pammon as they flew across the ocean.

I hadn't realized it till just now just how much you have grown. I know it has been a while, but have you checked your stats lately?

Pammon grumbled, and Kaen saw him shake his head.

I have not, but it is not time. I can still feel the power I gained from Tharnok and the others in me. After they are fully absorbed, I will let you know.

Kaen nodded, feeling Pammon's frustration at his question.

Why does that bother you so much when I ask about your stats? I know you joked about how Hess and I always teased about who was bigger, yet there must be something about why you dislike it so much.

Let me ask you a question, and then I will respond. Why do my numbers matter?

That's an easy one. It helps me to track how you are growing.

Does my size not do that for you? After today, is there any doubt how much I have grown and how much stronger I must be to have maintained my skill for so long?

Kaen realized what Pammon was saying and felt a twinge of guilt in his chest.

Do you feel I am insulting you when I ask that question?

Pammon thrummed for a moment and then stopped.

How would you feel if I asked you what your stats or skills were every time we finished a fight? Would you eventually begin to wonder if I thought you were weak or unskilled? Perhaps you might doubt that I trusted you to be up to the task before us.

Pammon . . . I'm sorry. I never realized—

Kaen cut himself off, only now understanding why every time he has asked that question, Pammon groaned and gave in. Something was different about him now, and Kaen could feel it through their connection.

You never have to tell me your stats again, and I have never doubted that you were strong enough. I am alive only because of you and your strength, and I hope you know how grateful I am for that.

Pammon said nothing. The only sound was the wind rushing against them as Pammon beat his wings steadily.

You are fine, Pammon finally replied, a hint of embarrassment coming through as he spoke. **For a moment, I was frustrated with that question. I know why you asked it, but it bothered me enough to finally voice it. After all that we just went through and overcame, and as much as I have grown, the part of me who is still less than five years old felt perhaps I still wasn't good enough.**

Pammon, I—

Wait. Let me finish. The day we risked everything and attacked Stioks and Juthom, you did not ask me for my stats. You trusted me to be strong enough. Just like I trusted you to be strong enough to attack him. Trust me now when I say this.

Pammon turned his head and looked back at Kaen, his golden eyes locked on to Kaen's brown eyes.

Soon, no dragon will be stronger than me one-on-one. The power coming through you is as powerful as the strength I grant you. I have felt it since you came to claim whatever skill you gained when you faced down the council. I know you are probably considering checking your own stats, but I would tell you to wait. Stop relying on numbers to measure your value and worth. See the things you have accomplished and the power you possess.

You took on two dragons by yourself, simultaneously killing those who enslaved them. When was that a possibility? You could not have done this two years ago, but now you can.

You have given everything to gain this power. You were willing to sacrifice your love for Ava. The only thing you would not offer is me, and I know that. That truth is the greatest strength I have held onto since the day you made that commitment before we left with Elies.

Stop letting the measure of the rest of the world define you. You are a Dragon Rider and, if Tharnok and Elies were correct, a King. Aldric does not let those beneath him define who he is. He rules by the values he holds dear. You must do the same.

Pammon paused momentarily, shifting his neck slightly before focusing on Kaen again.

You are the only man I know who has willingly thrown away power and admitted the difficulty of that decision. We both know what those bracelets were worth. I know what men would have done to own just one, let alone four.

That is why I felt you the day you came close to my egg. The first day your presence came near me, I could feel a soul that desired one thing. Hope. In the midst of kingdoms that fight over petty things, you choose to hope for peace and for families to be allowed to grow old together. That has not been tainted by the lure of power. More power than has ever been given to a man in over a thousand years.

So when I say this, believe me, that it is true.

Pammon stretched his neck as far as possible to get his head closer to Kaen, ignoring how it affected his ability to fly.

I will always be strong enough for whatever you need me to do.

Kaen reached out with his hand, stretching his body as he put his fingers against the tip of Pammon's snout.

Forgive me, my friend. I will never doubt your strength. Thank you for putting up with me and my eggling questions.

Pammon snorted, sending a small shower of mucus at Kaen, who just closed his eyes and let it cover him.

I'm sorry, Pammon apologized as he pulled his head back some. **I had not meant to do that.**

Kaen laughed, wiping the mucus from his face with his hand.

Don't worry. I deserved it, for many things.

Pammon thrummed, turning his head forward and focused on the task at hand.

We should be home soon. I wonder how the three of us showing up will be received.

Ava! We are almost home.

Mrs. Marshell yelped and jumped in surprise as Pammon's voice filled her head.

She dropped the cup sitting on her knee as she watched Sulenda read a story to Callie. The young girl enjoyed the picture book Hess had made for her with a dragon that was supposed to be Pammon.

Every page turn had brought out the same two words, 'Pammon! Kaen!' as Sulenda nodded and smiled.

"You ok?" Hess asked, seeing the drink spilled on the floor and the flushed color on her cheeks.

Pammon? Is that you?

Unless there is another dragon you have the ability to speak with, then yes, it must be me. We are just outside the mountains to the west. We should be home in no more than an hour.

Her hands began to tremble as she lifted them to her open mouth.

"They're home . . . Kaen and Pammon are home."

Tears began to run down her face as Hess bolted from his chair, and Sulenda sat Callie on the couch with her book.

"They're in town?" Hess asked, moving close to Ava, who was struggling to react.

She shook her head and took a deep breath, calming herself.

For so many weeks, the fears had been overwhelming. It had been one thing when Kaen was in Roccnari, but knowing he and Pammon were attempting to fly across the ocean was hard to comprehend.

Now, with Pammon in her head, telling her they were home, all of her fears were gone, and she was bursting with excitement.

"They are on the other side of the mountains," she whispered. "They should be here in an hour, Pammon said."

Hess grunted, and his face contorted. Excited that Kaen and Pammon had returned and yet bothered that he could not hear Pammon speak.

"Where are they going to go? Surely not in town?" Sulenda asked as she started to smooth off her outfit, sending small crumbs from Callie's snack onto the floor.

"Let me ask!"

Pammon. Where are you going to land?

She felt laughter coming through their bond. It was weird and yet comforting. The closer he got, the stronger it became.

We will land at our house. Do we need to come pick you up, or should I expect Hess and the rest to join you?

Ava giggled and then, realizing what she had done, coughed to clear her throat and stopped.

You can tell where Hess and I are?

I can. Tell me what you want me to do, but I must warn you that we have company, and they cannot land in town with me.

Why can't they . . . Dragons! There are more dragons?!

Hess and Sulenda watched as Ava's mouth fell open.

"This is what it was like watching Kaen and Pammon when I had no clue what was going on," Sulenda whispered as she elbowed Hess in his side. "You best not know what is being said."

Hess waved his one hand and gave a shrug.

"Pammon is too far away for me to hear."

Ava was oblivious to the other two as she focused on Pammon and his words.

Two females are flying with us. They would prefer to not come to town. Tell me what to do so I can tell Kaen and the others the plan.

Ava felt a sense of awe coming over her. Knowing that Pammon and Kaen were home was one thing, but hearing that two more dragons were with them filled her with a hope she had not had in a while.

Give me a second. Let me talk to Ava and Hess!

As she prepared to talk to people staring down at her, Pammon added one last thing.

Tell Callie I'm coming, too.

Oh, that is just mean, Ava replied. You know what that would do to Hess and Sulenda after all this time.

Exactly.

Ava chuckled and shook her head.

Focusing her attention, she looked up at Sulenda and Hess, who were looking at her, waiting for more information.

Glancing at Callie, who was still looking at her book and saying 'Pammon' repeatedly, she chuckled and motioned for the two adults to come closer.

"Pammon has two dragons with him," she whispered, ensuring Callie had not heard her speak. "Pammon said he will come and pick me up but that they want to head to our home. The other two won't land in town for obvious reasons."

She saw Sulenda and Hess look at each other, their faces stretching as their mouth and eyes went wide.

"Two drag—"

Sulenda elbowed Hess as he started to shout, silencing him as he rubbed where she had hit him.

"Two?"

Ava nodded, shrugging her shoulders and then looking at Callie.

"He wanted me to tell her he was back, but we all know what will happen if I do that."

Sulenda growled, frowning at that comment as she nodded. "Let's say you did and not. I want to sleep sometime tonight."

Hess, on the other hand, began to move.

"Hess Brumlin, where do you think you are going?"

Grinning, he turned around, pausing at the handle on the door he had been reaching for. "Why, my love, Ava cannot walk to Bren's place by herself. She will need someone to keep her safe."

Sulenda rolled her eyes and shook her head. "You are going to owe me big for this."

Winking at his wife, he opened the door and motioned with his head to the room outside it. "Coming Ava? I'm sure you might want to tell a certain someone where we will meet them."

Laughing, Ava leaned over and gave Sulenda a hug.

"Sorry," she whispered as she squeezed and then took off to join Hess.

Sulenda sighed and just smiled. She knew what it was like when the love of your life returned from a mission you were not confident they would return from. She couldn't fault the girl at all.

67

Passion Unbound

Cheers could be heard rising over the city as Pammon swept low, his bronze scales absorbing the last of the sunlight soon hidden by the mountains. Above, the two females stayed higher in the sky, circling to keep from causing panic or alarm since word of them had not spread yet.

"He has grown," Hess muttered as they watched Pammon begin to land inside the courtyard of Bren's place. Bren had cleared the building, allowing no one but Hess and Ava to stand there with him while they awaited the return of Pammon and Kaen.

"By a lot."

Ava looked at the two men, both shaking their heads in disbelief. She could also see the change, but she was more focused on the man sitting behind that massive bronze neck.

Clenching her hands together, Ava fought the shakes she knew would come if she didn't focus on fighting it.

It had been almost five weeks since Kaen had left, and she felt sadder every day they were apart.

Pammon swooped down, his wings going wide as dust buffeted the walls and the three of them as he landed in the courtyard.

The moment he had started to descend, Ava was running toward them, seeing Kaen hit the ground and run to her the moment Pammon's claws touched down.

They ran to each other, Kaen grabbing her in his arms and swinging her around a few times before kissing and holding her close.

She smelled amazing. That flower scent from her hair.

They pulled back from their embrace, looking at each other and smiling before coming together again and spending a little more time with their lips against each other.

Please stop that, you two. Kaen, please tell her why.

Kaen started to laugh as he pulled back, seeing the questioning look on his wife's face.

"Those two dragons are females, and when we do what we do, it makes it harder for Pammon to resist certain urges."

Ava turned and looked at Pammon, who had moved close to the two of them, and lowered his head.

She laughed and nodded, reaching out a hand and waiting for Pammon, who moved his snout over and let her touch him.

"Thank you for coming home safe. I owe you a lot of cows."

Pammon thrummed and smiled as he let Ava scratch his snout.

"Did you two eat everything on the other side of the world?!"

Kaen turned his head and saw Hess standing a good distance away, not wanting to intrude on the moment he and Ava had been enjoying.

"Go," Ava said as she let Kaen free of her embrace and watched him move to Hess. "Those two are something. Don't you agree, Pammon?"

You have no idea how hard it was dealing with them.

Ava laughed, scratching Pammon's head as she leaned against him.

"Thank you for bringing him home," she said, pausing a second before adding, "and thank you for sharing him with me."

Pammon let out a trill as her fingers worked his scales, and he started to thrum.

Don't forget your statement about owing me. I am going to earn that in a different way.

Ava cocked her head for a moment as she stared into Pammon's gold eye as he continued to thrum. Shaking her head, she chuckled, wondering what in the world Pammon was talking about.

Flying over the city as they came close to their home, Kaen was fighting the desires that he felt as he wrapped his arms around Ava.

She gasped when she saw the two females flying toward them.

How is this going to work? Are they here to help us fight against Stioks?

That is a much larger question that we can deal with tomorrow. For now, you should focus on getting to enjoy being home with Kaen. He has mentioned multiple times on this trip how much he has missed you.

Ava felt her cheeks turn red as Pammon spoke to her. She turned and saw Kaen looking at her, and he gave her a wink. Raising her eyebrows playfully, she leaned back and kissed him quickly before turning back around.

Kaen is going to owe you, Pammon, for those words.

Pammon began to thrum and didn't respond. They were minutes away from their home.

* * *

Ava helped Kaen as he undid all the baskets and set them on the ground.

She watched as the two female dragons sat down across the field, keeping an eye on her and Kaen, but neither approached.

Pammon was intent on getting the baskets off as he had been forced to endure them for so long. The ropes were lucky to have survived from the looks of it as she coiled them around her arm. His scales had rubbed against them in so many spots.

Ava went inside and started getting things put together, checking to make sure nothing needed adjustment. She had come out here twice a week, ensuring things were in order for when Kaen and Pammon would return.

She sat on the edge of the bed that overlooked the massive open area, watching Kaen as he carried in the second basket filled with the scales they had collected from Tharnok. Neither Pammon nor Kaen had wanted to talk about that yet, but she didn't seem to mind.

As Kaen set the basket down across the room, a loud roar echoed through the house from outside.

Two more roars responded, and she felt something coming through her bond. Glad to be sitting on the edge of the bed. It almost would have knocked her down. It was so powerful. So primal.

She saw Kaen on his knees, struggling to stand as he turned and looked at her.

His face was different, and she saw him stand.

Forgive me, you two, but I cannot help what will come next.

A surge of desire flooded Kaen, and he groaned. He realized it wasn't a groan but instead a moan.

He could feel what Pammon felt, and he knew, even though he couldn't see what was happening outside in the night sky.

His body yearned for Ava, and all the feelings and longings he had held back and suppressed this past month broke the damn that he had built. With Pammon's surge of desire and his own mixing together, he turned and saw his wife sitting on the bed looking at him.

Kaen fought the desire he felt from Pammon and forced his own desire to overcome it.

Rising to his feet, he ran toward her, stopping just a foot from the bed, where her eyes were open wide and she was panting.

Pammon's words rang in his head.

Kaen could see that Ava, too, was partially affected by Pammon's temperament. He saw Ava smile, and then both were ripping the other's clothes off, grateful that Kaen's strength made doing so no issue at all.

* * *

Amaranth will be first. Then it will be your turn, Glynnis.

He eyed both of them, no longer containing what he felt, as they had increased the scent they had given off tenfold since landing on the field earlier.

He roared, unable to hold it back, letting his desire consume him.

Kaen and Ava were both about to give in to their desires, and he felt it boiling inside of Kaen. How his rider had locked it away for so long was amazing, but now they were both a torrent of passion, each fighting for what they wanted.

Fine, but you will regret it if you do not keep that promise.

Glynnis roared once, backing up as Amaranth moved forward.

Her silver eyes glowed, and she let out a roar that almost matched Pammon's.

Let us begin this.

Amaranth leaped into the sky, her wings beating faster and faster as she rose quickly into the night sky.

Pammon leaped after her, his body driving him to catch her and overtake her.

She had gotten a head start and would not make this easy. It couldn't be easy. She fought his attempts to block her path as he came up from behind, darting to the side and continuing the straight path toward the stars. She could feel Pammon's hot breath on her scales, and his desire filled her lungs.

Catch me!

She took off like an arrow shot from a bow.

Pammon realized what she had done and responded quickly.

[Flight Burst Activated]

They flew like two arrows, aiming for those balls of fire that were present every night. As the miles passed and the air began to grow thin, Pammon saw Amaranth suddenly slow down, her skill stopping, and he had barely deactivated his before he nearly slammed into her.

She tried to turn, but he leaned over, his wings covering hers as his other wing wrapped around hers.

A throaty growl came from her as their bodies intertwined and began to plummet to the ground below.

Kaen fought what he was experiencing through Pammon.

The love he had for Ava and the longing he felt while gone all came together in a moment of unbridled desire.

He was able to smell her more than usual somehow and wanted to touch every inch of her skin.

She watched him, smiling before pulling his head close and moaning as he kissed her neck.

*   *   *

The following day, Ava and Kaen woke up to a roar.

Both snapped up, slower than usual but wondering what was happening to cause that noise.

Pammon?

Laughter came through their bond, and Kaen let out the breath he had been holding, wondering if he was about to run outside and fight while entirely naked.

Good morning, you two. Sorry, I just felt the need to do that.

The massive doors to their home were open, and where Pammon usually slept showed no signs of him coming in at all last night.

Scratching his head, Kaen tried to recall some of the memories that had flooded through his brain but realized he did not want to after a moment.

How long . . .

"All night," Ava replied, chuckling as she laid back against her pillow and pulled the sheet over herself. "All night long."

Kaen started to laugh a little as he saw the smile she had on her face.

He leaned over, and she shook her head.

"I need a break. It was nice, but yeah . . . give me a day."

He nodded and slid out of bed.

"Are you ok then if I cook something for breakfast? For some reason, I'm starving."

She laughed and threw a pillow at him.

"That is fine, but put some clothes on. I'm sure Hess and the others will come by at some point, and we don't need to scare Callie like that."

Bending down, Kaen picked up his pants and gave them a sideways glance. "Did I?"

Each leg was ripped in half on the backside, and there was a tear that ran through the crotch.

Unable to hold back, Ava roared with laughter at the sight of Kaen's cheeks turning red as he held up his pants.

"It was a little . . . different. You have other pants in the dresser. Those will probably need to be burned."

He laughed, picking up all the clothes that needed to be burned to hide the evidence.

How are you this morning? I can feel that you are . . . satisfied?

Pammon's thrum came from outside the house, and he started to move to the doors and stopped.

Kaen saw him standing outside them and began to laugh.

"Hairy dwarf balls," Kaen said as he saw Pammon towering over the entrance of the massive doors by at least ten feet.

We are going to need a bigger place, something for me, Glynnis, and Amaranth as well.

Having forgotten about them for a moment, Kaen darted to the door, ignoring the laughter he heard from Ava as he ran buck naked to Pammon.

Outside in the field, he saw the two of them lying beside each other. Neither were moving, but their eyes opened briefly and then closed again.

"Should I ask?"

Only if you want me to bite off that worm that has taken hold of your crotch.

Placing one hand protectively over the area Pammon was referring to, Kaen moved back, heading toward the dresser.

I don't want to know . . . keep that to yourself.

Have no worries. I am not planning on sharing any of that with you. Just like I don't want to see you with Ava.

Kaen smiled as he pulled a drawer out and took out a pair of pants.

Nobody needs to talk about this anymore.

Agreed.

68

A Lot Changes in a Month

Ava had been right that they would have guests, but who they turned out to be had ruined the day.

You need to come and meet them. Bring the table and the chairs.

Who is it?

Aldric, Herb, and Hess.

Kaen felt a twinge of angst at that announcement. Two of the men had been on his agenda to visit tomorrow, but for them to ride out here . . .

How do they look?

Their faces tell me there won't be good news.

The three men arrived on their horses, each of the beasts covered in sweat from the speed at which they had been forced to move. The men accompanying the three stayed across the fields, watching all three dragons and murmuring.

Kaen had walked across the field to greet them and knew Pammon had been right when he saw their expressions for himself.

"I would make some joke, but it appears there is nothing to laugh about."

Herb and Aldric tried to smile, but it was forced.

"Words cannot describe how excited I was to hear that you had arrived last night," Aldric said, moving forward to shake Kaen's hand. "When news arrived late last night that you had brought two more dragons with you . . ." The king stopped, looking across the field and taking in the sight he no doubt couldn't have begun to imagine. "How is it possible that Pammon is that large now?"

Herb stood by Aldric, acknowledging Kaen a nod before noticing what Aldric had pointed out.

"Hess, you failed to tell us about his size."

"That is a lie, Herb, and you know it," Hess stated, moving past the men who had stopped to gawk. "I told you he had grown. A lot."

Rolling his eyes, Herb began to follow Hess toward Kaen's house.

Aldric moved next to Kaen and put a hand on his shoulder.

"I cannot tell you how much I feared for your safety," he whispered as he motioned with his head toward the other two men. "There is much to share, and I need to hear how you will respond to what I say."

The four of them walked in silence for a while.

"Havannath and Huethea are dead?"

The news shocked Kaen to a degree, but simultaneously, he knew the two choices.

"Most of the people in their castle were wiped out. They welcomed Stioks and Juthom, and no one knows what happened afterward except that soon the entire castle was on fire." Aldric paused, looking at Herb, who was rubbing his thumb along the lip of his cup and not looking up. "You have been there. The tree that it was built into is gone. My reports say a smoldering stump is all that remains. When it fell, it crushed a large part of the city."

"Who rules the land?" Kaen asked as he felt Ava squeeze his hand gently.

"No one. It's been four weeks, and the threat Stioks made has the nation gripped in fear."

Tapping the table with a finger, Kaen considered the news and how this would impact so much in the coming months and years.

"Does anyone really believe he is serious? How can he maintain both kingdoms? It would require him to travel, which puts him at risk."

Looking at Kaen, Aldric put his cup back on the table and crossed his arms as he leaned against his chair. "If he leaves a dragon there as it is rumored he might, then what? As far as the people in that land know, you are gone. No one has seen you in over a month. The last report came from a town in Golden Edge, saying a Dragon Rider went across the sea. It reached us two weeks ago. That means Stioks must surely have heard the same news by now."

Kaen looked at Pammon, who was lying near the group of men and Ava. His eyes were barely open, but Kaen knew he saw everything.

What are you thinking? Do we go and make our presence known?

A fight is always coming. I know you want to help the elves, but they have yet to earn that from you. Right now, we need to deal with what we can here. Too many things are in motion, and we still need to figure out how Glynnis and Amaranth can best help our plans.

Kaen turned and saw everyone waiting silently, knowing what he was doing.

"Ignoring that problem, what about the cave?"

Herb grunted and slid a piece of paper over to Kaen. "We risked it and opened up the cave you spoke of from our side. Days after you left, a massive group of adventurers and troops moved to the area and cleared the rubble. Inside, one of our scouts reported the same thing you had. No goblins or orcs were present when they got to the swirling wall, as she described it.

"We weren't sure if they heard us clearing the debris from the cave entrance, but we couldn't risk it. We blew four massive cave-ins inside that tunnel. If anything will try and come out at us, they will need to move a lot more stone to do so."

Looking at the paper Herb had given him, Kaen scanned the report and grunted as he handed it back to him.

"Is that Wall of Concealment spell really that powerful?"

Herb nodded, bringing a groan from Kaen as he looked at Ava.

"Can you cast the spell?"

Ava chuckled and shook her head. "Most in our kingdom couldn't. I'm unsure if Selmah could have cast this even in her prime. That spell requires a certain focus, and none of us here would spend our time on such an endeavor. It would take a year, most likely, to be able to cast it if someone knew how. Someone of at least a gold rank."

"Which means . . . "

"That Stioks has higher-level casters working with him and the orcs to accomplish things none of us have prepared for," Herb interrupted as he flipped through the pages he had pulled out after sitting down. "Based on what you told us and the data we have on hand, we need to keep working on our defenses and make sure our scouting stations to the south are ready to relay any threat as quickly as possible."

Kaen turned and looked at Hess and then at Ava.

"Well, at least there is nothing bad in your world."

Both of them shook their heads no and gave him a smile.

"At least that's something," Kaen replied as he looked at Pammon for a moment.

All is not lost. Tell them of your agreement with the tribe that tried to rob you.

Kaen coughed and then smiled as he looked at the four watching him.

"I did manage to make a new ally, and I made an offer in your name," Kaen informed Aldric as he pointed at him. "I have the paperwork and more in my bag, but I must dig it out. It's at the bottom of some stuff I'll need to give you and the dwarves."

"What kind of stuff?"

Frowning, Kaen shared the news about Tharnok and what had happened on his journey to the dragon homeland and back.

"You threw them away. Why would you do that?"

Kaen leaned across the table, putting his hands together as he held Aldric's gaze momentarily.

"I don't believe in enslaving anyone or anything like that. What I saw, what I learned. Those things shouldn't be done to a dragon or anyone. If you allowed that, or if you used that, where does the line get drawn? Is it okay then to use something like that on dwarves? What about elves? Or maybe people from another kingdom? How many people need to be enslaved and have no soul before we decide that we have done too much?"

Aldric lost the battle of glares as Kaen's words and aura struck a chord.

"Still—"

"No," Kaen said, interrupting the king. "There is no other choice. Either we become worse than Stioks or stay on the path we fight for. I, for one, will never use that kind of power. I will not stoop to that kind of abuse."

A sigh came from Aldric as he hung his head for a moment. "Forgive me. You are right. As I just demonstrated, the temptation is too great, and the risk of losing ourselves is too easy."

"I know how you feel. Trust me, I do. Only after I threw them into the sea and knew they would be gone forever did I finally feel released from their power over my mind."

"And this other kingdom? Hetaal? Do we know anything about it?" Hess asked.

Herb and Aldric exchanged glances, and both men shook their heads.

"We would have to inquire of the nation of Golden Edge, but I doubt they would be willing to share that news if what Kaen says about their fortifications is true. Do we really need to worry about them right now?"

Kaen shrugged and leaned back, clasping Ava's hand in his and gently squeezing it. "I don't think we need to focus on them for now. There will come a time when they either come at us or I travel to them. I don't believe that time is soon, though."

Pammon began to thrum, and everyone turned to watch him.

I doubt they want to risk losing more dragons and ships after how you defeated them.

"Pammon agrees that they will most likely wait a while before wanting to cross paths with me again."

Aldric stood up and started to stretch.

"Forgive me, but sitting here for this long has worn me out. Is it possible for me to meet the other two dragons and welcome them to our kingdom?"

Kaen and Pammon stood up, and a small smile appeared on Kaen's lips.

Do not say it. I can feel you already thinking those words.

Fine, but soon enough, it will be known, and then what?

That will come in its own time. For now, let it be.

Kaen moved to Pammon and scratched his neck, and motioned toward the yellow and green female dragons sitting not far from Pammon.

"Come meet Glynnis and Amaranth."

Tell the king I appreciate him coming to see me and welcoming me personally to his land. I will do what I can to avoid problems, provided no one attempts to bother me or Pammon.

A snort sounded behind everyone gathered, and each turned to see Pammon huffing.

"Amaranth wants to thank you for personally coming to see her, and she will do her best to be no trouble, provided trouble does not come to her or the other dragons."

Aldric gave a slight bow and smiled.

"I will do everything I can to ensure that does not happen."

Kaen motioned back toward the horses and led the men away.

"Behave, Ava," Kaen said as he winked.

"Please, I'm just going to answer some questions Pammon says he has for me."

Kaen began to laugh and then stopped when he felt Pammon getting upset through their bond. He knew what the dragon would ask and could only imagine what kind of advice Ava could give a male dragon about two female dragons.

Herb and Aldric walked ahead of Kaen and Hess, giving them a moment to talk privately.

"Those arrows, how many do you have left?"

"Three, why?"

Hess grumbled something under his breath and then motioned at Herb.

"I have a quest for the items that we need to make more, but no one has reported finding any of that metal since I have put it in. In fact, the mines believed to have some are picked clean."

Kaen stopped moving and grabbed Hess's arm, halting his movement. "What do you mean picked clean?"

"Imagine a quarry like the one we worked. For months, there has been plenty of rock to work. An order comes in for a certain type of rock, and nothing remains when you go back to harvest what you know should be there. The groups that went into the mines said every metal in there was gone."

Kaen instinctively reached up and scratched his chin. "But that would mean . . ."

Hess nodded, holding his hand up. "Someone is paying attention in the guild house again."

Kaen groaned and turned to look at Herb, who was still walking with Aldric, not paying attention to either of them. "Does Herb know?"

Hess nodded, beginning to walk toward the horses again. "He does, but nothing he has done has turned up a suspect. Using the guild crystal to question every adventurer isn't going to happen again either."

"Goblin shite," Kaen cursed as he bent down, picked up a rock, and threw it so far it disappeared from sight. "Tell me something good. Something that isn't going wrong."

Hess put an arm around Kaen's shoulder and pulled him toward the others. "You're home. You and Pammon have brought allies. Ava is back to her joyful self, and a kingdom still needs you. There are lots of good things. Just look around, and you can find them."

Filling his lungs with all the air they could hold, Kaen let it out slowly, finding himself smiling and letting Hess pull him along.

"You're right. I guess there are some good things after all."

69

A Chance to Live

Three weeks later, the moment Kaen knew would come arrived.

Word had reached him that Stioks had found out about Glynnis and Amaranth, and a separate message had just arrived by horseback.

He glanced at those gathered in the courtyard of the adventurers' guild training grounds and saw the looks on everyone's faces.

Ava gently scratched Pammon's snout while Aldric, Herb, and Hess looked at Kaen, waiting for him to open the letter. They all had waited for the mage from the hall to verify that there were no spells or traps hidden in the letter.

"Open it," Hess grumbled, scratching his stump without realizing it.

Breaking the black wax seal, Kaen slowly unfolded the paper and began to read it.

Kaen Marshell,

No doubt you expected this letter to come at some point.

It would appear I had misjudged you, and that mistake has brought about an impasse.

I must also congratulate you on your successful ambush against Juthom. It took weeks for me to calm him down as he demanded blood. I doubt you understand a dragon's fury yet, but they are not easily quenched.

Not being one to waste words, I will offer a truce until the inevitable happens. We both know the cost of battle, and Roccnari serves as that example. That fool elf thought himself stronger than he was. Know that his actions brought the destruction I rained down upon his people. To think he could bind me to him . . .

I will no longer unleash my wrath upon that kingdom if they do not provoke me.

Tell Aldric I will cut ties with the orc horde, but I cannot guarantee they will stop their assault. Their king has waited long for the day he feels is close.

As long as you do not intrude upon my domain, I will leave the kingdom of Ebonmount to its own devices.

—S

Kaen read it twice to himself and then once to Pammon before handing it to the three men, who almost fought over it like dogs.

Confused at the letter, Kaen considered why Stioks had written it.

Could he be that afraid of us and the other two?

Maybe, but something feels off about the letter.

Pammon felt the same way.

It seems that Havannath got what he deserved. Sadly, his actions cost so many of his people their lives.

Kaen nodded after hearing Pammon's thoughts and watched as the men took turns handing the letter to each other, even though they had read it over each other's shoulders.

"This sounds too good to be true," Aldric said. "Not to downplay the potential victory this brings for a while, but why would that man suddenly stop everything he has done?"

"He won't," Herb muttered as he moved to hand the letter to Ava, who was patiently waiting. "He might not publicly show himself taking steps, but he will always be doing something in the shadows."

Hess nodded in agreement and stood silently, scratching his chin as he frowned.

Kaen crossed his arms and watched the three men he believed could provide him with the best advice on how to respond.

"It is a dangerous choice for both of us," Kaen said when Ava handed the letter to him. "The longer we wait, the greater the chance for Stioks to acquire a dragon egg. If that happens . . . "

"But the more time we have," Herb cut in after Kaen paused, "the better we can defend ourselves against the orcs and whatever else comes."

"Do you really believe he will not attack us in the middle of the night after sending this?" Kaen smiled as Ava spoke and moved beside him, sliding his arm around her shoulder. "Do we believe this monster will do anything that he promises?"

"What choice do we have? Launch a war against him? Would your new dragons risk their lives like that?" Hess asked, throwing his one hand in the air in frustration. "We are still in the same spot we have been for years. Unsure if we will be attacked on both sides. The only difference now is we have a little more help with the air problem."

Pammon snorted, and everyone turned to see him looking at them.

Glynnis and Amaranth are not going to be able to stop Juthom. That would fall to you and me. Perhaps Glynnis could be of some help against the other females, but from what I have learned, they will most likely stay out of the fight, waiting to see who the victor is and then choose to follow him.

Kaen relayed what Pammon had said and saw the frustrated looks on Aldric's and Herb's faces.

"So we are barely in any better of a position . . . "

Hess elbowed Herb after he spoke, glaring at his friend and silently chiding his gloomy outlook.

Rubbing his face and eyes with his right hand, Kaen tried to figure out the best option. He felt Ava squeeze his waist with her arm and looked down, seeing her smiling at him.

Bending his neck, he kissed her on the forehead and knew what needed to be done.

"Draft a letter," Kaen said, his voice taking on an authority that had been common since he had returned. "I want to read two or three possible responses to his letter. They all need to say that I will stay out of this as long as he does not act aggressively against any kingdom."

Aldric and Herb looked at Kaen, and each then looked at each other.

"That's it?" Aldric asked.

Kaen nodded, holding the letter in the air before him and giving it a shake. "Anything else could provide too much information or make us look weak. I won't say I think his actions were right against the kingdom of Roccnari, but Havannath brought that disaster upon himself. His pride and arrogance would have made that kingdom suffer far worse in due time. Acknowledging the horde shows our weakness against them."

Kaen paused to toss the paper onto the table as if it was trash.

"There is no doubt they know we are aware of their actions in the tunnel. How that impacts their relationship with Stioks is anyone's guess. He may be trying to create distance because of a conflict with them right now. He might be trying to buy them time. We don't know."

He turned and looked at Ava. She was smiling and he mouthed the words, *I love you.*

"This woman standing before me reminds me that there must be more to life than war and hate. I will not focus my days on that alone when I know there are more important things."

Turning back to the group of men, he saw Hess nodding and Aldric starting to smile.

"We have spent the last years focused on surviving. We now have a chance at possibly living for a while. Let us ensure we do not miss this chance, or everything we have done will be for naught."

The sound of a set of hands clapping caught him off guard, and Kaen realized that it was Aldric.

Herb joined a few seconds later, and Hess slapped his thigh a few times.

"You have grown, Kaen. Faster and greater than I could have imagined was possible," Aldric stated. "Herb and I will take charge of that draft and have something for you to look at in the next day or two. For now, go and do what you do best. Inspire others and live. We can take care of the rest."

He is right. You have grown. Do not forget what Tharnok and Elies taught us.

Kaen smiled as he nodded and led Ava to Pammon, who shifted so they could climb on.

"You better stop by Bren's place sometime soon, Pammon, or that girl of mine may forget your name!"

Pammon snorted, a smile appearing on his snout.

We both know that isn't true.

Hess roared with laughter and nodded, waving goodbye as the three of them prepared to leave.

"Who is that man that just talked to us like we are all below him," Herb asked, watching as Pammon disappeared over the city.

"He's just like his damn father," Hess replied, unable to keep from smiling.

"You both are wrong," Aldric answered, watching both men look at him. "He is something far greater than his father or any of us will ever be. He spoke to us as he should. He spoke as a Dragon Rider must."

Epilogue

This plan is foolish, and you are a fool to not listen to me!

Juthom whipped his tail into the stone wall of the throne room, sending pieces of stone flying and stirring up a dust cloud.

Whatever game you are playing will not bring us the victory you promised me!

Stioks turned and glared at the dragon whose black eye seethed with anger and rage.

"You seem to forget why we have made this move. There are countless pieces in play on this board, and right now, we need to reposition if we want to win it all. Do not forget what your anger already cost you."

Juthom unleashed a massive snort, sending vast amounts of air through his nostrils and making the cloud of dust swirl around the room.

That was your fault! If you had let me—

"Quiet!" Stioks shouted, his voice booming through the room as Juthom actually flinched and stopped communicating. "I am not the one who did not expect an attack from above. I am not the one that allowed them to sneak up on us. It was not me who wanted to keep chasing that boy who was taking off your scales with every shot. We could not catch them, and had we continued to chase, we both would most likely be dead."

Blood began to seep out of the black skin on Stioks's face as it cracked. His entire face was scrunched in anger as he shouted, ignoring the pain as he unleashed his torrent upon Juthom.

"You," he continued, pointing a finger at the black dragon, "killed one of your females, who we spent years working so hard to acquire. It was your rage and inability to allow it to go that had you tearing her neck out. So do not blame me for the actions we must now take. He has two more dragons, which would make this an equal fight, yet I know it must not be. His skill with a bow is known around every part of the lands we have traveled. You experienced it firsthand."

Stioks took a deep breath and held it as he gently massaged the eye on his face that was now leaking blood over his finger. As he pulled his hand away from his face, he opened both eyelids and again glared at Juthom.

"Tell me, what is a few years to win a war? How old are you? Is it not just a brief moment in time?"

After a few seconds, Juthom's rage and anger were gone, and he spoke.

They are but like months to you.

"Then count them as months or a few seasons. Let us move on and secure the future we know will allow us to win. Trust that I know what they will do, and that will bring us victory."

Juthom laid back down on the black stone floor and said nothing else.

"Good. Now, I will return in a few. Do not destroy the room in my absence. This will be the last time I fix it."

Stioks couldn't help but wonder what emotion he felt right now.

Giddy? Am I actually feeling like some child?

He chuckled, and a smile that represented joy cracked his blackened face for the first time in years.

"You will be well rewarded, Upsi. Know that I will never forget this."

Upsi bowed her head low and smiled, white teeth showing the entire length of both sides of her mouth as she let out a trill.

Stioks walked around the egg she had encircled, running his hand over its hard shell.

He stopped, bending down till his lips were almost against the grey shell, and whispered, "Grow strong, little one. Soon, you and I will be kings of this world, and you will get a front-row seat for all of it."

Though nothing happened as he spoke, Stioks believed he could feel the dragon inside the egg shake with excitement.

About the Author

Shawn Wilson is the author of the Last Dragon Rider series, originally released on Royal Road. Movies, shows, books, and more provide inspiration for his stories. Wilson is a father of six and enjoys spending time with his wife and kids.

DISCOVER
STORIES UNBOUND

PodiumAudio.com